I0598256

Book Cover by Todd Van Linda

Illustrations by Todd Van Linda

First Edition 2025

TABLE OF CONTENTS

ACKNOWLEDGEMENTS

First, a grateful thank-you to God—for the imagination that sparked this story, for the quiet nudge to keep going when I wanted to quit, for helping me sort fact from fiction in the ancient past, for healing me from childhood cancer, and for blessing me with parents who loved both God and books.

To my wife, Beth—you're the reason this book exists. Your daily "stories matter" pep talks worked. To my parents, Lowell and Sarah, though you're not here to see it, your love of reading shaped me. To my sister, Wendy, if I hadn't moved you across the country, this whole idea might never have happened.

To my furry co-workers—Perry (2018), Tucker (2018), Riley (2020), Zeb, and Mac—thank you for keeping my feet warm and my heart full.

To my editor, Elias Kollias —thanks for asking the right questions, and the gentle reminders about tense, and the not-so-gentle ban on the word *would*.

To my illustrator and cover designer, Todd Van Linda—you took my wild ideas and made them beautiful.

And to my friends and social media crew who've been waiting ten years for this, thank you for sticking around. You're proof that patience really is a virtue.

"Usually I compose only with great difficulty and endless rewriting." - J.R.R. Tolkien

With all my love, Jonathan

CHAPTER 1

The phone rang in the office. I was preparing iced tea to share with my girlfriend, Rachel, who was waiting for me on the deck. This was odd. The phone rarely rang since he passed; weeks or months would go by with no sounds coming from that room.

I pushed open the French doors and grabbed the receiver. "Hello?"

"RJ, this is Jacob. Sorry to disturb your morning." Jacob was the police chief for the sleepy little Colorado town I called home.

"Not disturbing anything, just Rachel and I enjoying the deck. What can I do for you?"

"Well, now I will be disturbing you. Have you gotten any communications from Apex?"

Apex Mining Company. At the mention of the name, I felt my blood pressure rise. "Yes, I received a letter from them last week. I haven't opened it despite the 'urgent' stamped in bright red ink on the front."

"You had better open it! Call me back when you have read it." There were a few moments of silence. "RJ, you hear me? Call me when you get done reading whatever they sent you."

"Copy that, Chief." As I slid the receiver back on its cradle, I stared at the packet I had tossed on Dad's desk. The giant red urgent stamp glared at me. I glared back. I turned to head back to the kitchen to finish making the iced tea.

There in the doorway stood Rachel. "What was that about?"

"Just the chief."

"Robert John Armstrong! Don't you dare 'just the chief' me!"

I met Rachel shortly after my retirement. If I had to blame anyone for my current situation, besides myself, of course, it would be Jim and Becky, who had set us up on a double date. Rachel and I had been dating for several years, so I knew when she wouldn't let something go with that simple answer. I had been good at my job, but the military seldom teaches the skills one requires to navigate the fairer sex. My dad often told me I was a major dating the general's daughter. While her father had not been a general, it was Dad's way of saying I was dating someone beyond my reach.

Don't get me wrong, it wasn't that I was an average Joe. In my line of work, if you weren't a fine physical specimen, you might not make it as a career. No dad bod here. My six-foot-tall frame could easily cuddle her five-foot-six frame. At 32, she was perfect for keeping my 48-year-old self in check. She was loyal and feisty. If she were a gold digger, she found the right guy. I had four mines on my property. A ball gown or camo, she looked great in any outfit.

I prepared myself.

"Does it have anything to do with that letter from Apex that you refuse to open?" she asked.

"Yes. I don't want to deal with their nonsense right now."

"I was standing right here and heard Jacob tell you to call him back."

At that point, the game was up. There was no way around the situation. No matter what rank a man may have held, a woman changes that. Outranked, outgunned, and often outvoted. It was usually a better course of action to raise the white flag of surrender and then regroup from a place of strength. Rather than pursue a course of action that most assuredly would land me in the dog house. I snatched the packet off the desk and waved her toward the kitchen. At the table, I sat staring at the envelope for a moment.

When I looked up, Rachel was there, sipping her glass, wearing that cute red T-shirt with the US flag and the writing that said "my happy place."

She raised her eyebrows. "Are you going to open it, or am I?"

I recognized that mischievous look and decided it would save much grief if I got this out of the way, so we could return to enjoying the sun on the deck. I neatly opened the envelope with my pocket knife and slowly folded back the letter. It started with the usual salutations and legal mumbo jumbo.

A line in the second paragraph caught my eye. "Happy to accept your offer under certain conditions to be discussed in person."

Rachel instantly recognized the change in my demeanor. "RJ, what is it?"

"They've accepted my offer to buy the old mine."

The mine. Trying to acquire the land had been a thorn in my father's flesh for many years. A preacher from Georgia had purchased the two hundred acres sight unseen. It's understandable when enticed by an impressive photograph of Mount Princeton; a million-dollar view.

There was one issue: there was no access to the acreage. Nearly twenty-five hundred acres of my property surrounded the preacher's land on three sides. The terrain on the fourth side was treacherous land owned by the Bureau of Land Management. The owner had received a yearly letter from my father with a standard offer to purchase at the going market rate. The pastor ignored the message more often than he answered.

After Dad passed six months ago, I attempted the same purchase offer. However, the preacher had recently passed away, and this time, a letter from the man's estate responded to my query with a counteroffer. It proposed a sale at three times the value of the land, payable to the estate and, in turn, to the man's son. I certainly had that kind of money. Nevertheless, I am not a fool, and I had the advantage.

"Well? Are you going to accept the offer?" Rachel brought me back to the question at hand.

"It says, I must meet with the attorney while he's still in town."

"How long is he in town?"

"Till tomorrow."

"It appears that Jacob called just in time."

I was intrigued by the offer, but what were the terms or conditions the attorney was proposing?

"Are you going to sit there? Or are you calling Jacob back?"

I reached for the cordless and dialed the Buena Vista police station. Jacob agreed to set up an appointment for the next day. I hoped for a nearly painless solution, one that would only require me to sign a few pages and tear out a check. An end to this decade-long debacle may be in sight.

The following day, I threw my pack into my truck and headed for the main road. I passed by Rachel's cabin and waved. I had never gotten around to proposing, what with Dad's illness, but I did have a plan. Pulling onto the highway, I made my way toward the small town.

It was a summer destination for white water rafting and a winter stopover for skiers. The rest of the year, it returned to the sleepy, two-stoplight town it had always been. There were no fancy franchise restaurants, although a good burger and prime rib were easy to find if you knew where to look. I had an excellent military pension, which meant I could live anywhere I wished.

People often asked me why I remained here after Dad's death. There was no short answer to that question. Drawn to the land, staying seemed more natural than figuring out a different strategy. I parked the truck and walked into the police department's small lobby. The desk sergeant, Jimmy, looked up from his computer.

"Chief will be right with you, RJ." Jimmy looked busy with paperwork, but how much paperwork could this small town conjure up? I listened for repetitive keyboard clicking but only heard the tapping of an index finger on the mouse.

"Hey, Sarge, are you winning?" He talked under his breath as he finished his card game and began working on the stack of paperwork in his inbox.

A moment later, Jacob stuck his head out of his office. "Hey, RJ! Be with you in a jiffy."

I have always had a connection with Jacob. We were similar in age. He had left for college while I joined the military. I became a decorated military officer, rising to the rank of major. He became a decorated police officer like his father, whose office he now occupied. I had also returned and filled the void left in the community by my father's passing. Both of us had suffered losses, drawing us back to our roots. Hoping time would indeed heal all wounds?

Jacob exited his office, and we headed to the parking lot. "Let's take my car. I have to gas up. Do you want a coffee or a soda?"

While he filled the gas tank, I entered the local convenience store. I grabbed two colas from the line of coolers offering what seemed to be every beverage known to man. We had a shorter distance to go in the squad car than expected. He pulled into the nearby mini-storage facility and drove until we turned a corner to face the final row of units. Parking, we walked to the end group, where a sign posted on each unit stated, "Apex Mining Co. No Trespassing."

In the doorway of the last unit stood a man in a suit, both hands on his hips. "Did you wait until the last day to repay me for all these years?"

Before I could respond, Jacob answered. "Your letter must have gotten lost in the mail, friend. When you called me, I called RJ"

It was a simple story, told by a humble man, not based on fact, but entirely plausible. It calmed the lawyer down. Placing his briefcase on a wooden desk that had seen better days, he continued.

"Here are the papers to sign for the land sale."

"Before I go any further, I need to know why. After all these years, why are we finally coming to terms with this?"

"RJ, in the last letter I sent you, the one not received, I annotated the required stipulations to satisfy our contract."

"Okay. What does your client want from me?"

"Since you didn't get to read the latest proposal, I will give you the shorter version. Find out what happened to our employees. In exchange, we will accept your last offer to purchase the land owned by my client."

"Your employees?"

"Yes. We commissioned some men to help us with the mine."

"And they are now missing?"

"Yes. They haven't cashed a single payroll check in the last couple of months."

"Are you sure they didn't just steal your gold and leave the country?"

A questioning expression was on the lawyer's face. "We had a written contract which..."

I cut him off. "You know plenty of men out there would disregard your written contract if they found a substantial amount of gold or silver ore. Right?"

I had three ancient gold mines on my land. Few friends knew they existed. Even fewer knew their exact location.

"I know scoundrels may take advantage of some people, but these men worked for Amex for many years before they were hand-picked for this assignment. They worked the site for nearly a year when we stopped getting their shipments and monthly reports."

"A year?"

" I can show you their reports and our payroll records."

Then it hit me, "How did these men access the mine? Better yet, how did they report their monthly findings?"

Jacob raised an eyebrow. "Were your men trespassing on the major's property?"

The lawyer squirmed. "I am not privy to how they entered the property. I assumed there was a way in, or perhaps they asked your father's permission."

"They certainly did not ask my father or me, nor would we have granted access!" Now, I would never have hit a man in a suit, wearing glasses, who would not weigh more than a buck fifty when soaking wet, but Jacob could not be sure, so he stepped between us.

"Let's be reasonable. What are you asking RJ to do?" he asked.

A nervous step backward to the pile of paperwork made it clear that the lawyer wanted to get right to the point.

"Our new counteroffer is half the amount you last proposed. In return, we ask that you access the property, investigate, and record what happened to our employees."

Jacob looked at me, "Sounds reasonable to me, RJ What do you think?"

"That is all you want? I look around the mine and bring those idiots down off my mountain? Then you will sign over the land deed?"

"Yes. That is all we are asking."

I took out my wallet and peeled off several hundred-dollar bills. "Here, book a couple more days at the hotel on me. I can round these men up or tell you where they've gone."

The lawyer nodded his thanks. Jacob and I made our way back to his patrol vehicle. I slid into my seat and looked at my friend. "Those dirty rats have been crossing my property all this time?"

He shrugged. "RJ, they're probably long gone. Look on the bright side. You find out for sure, make a report, pay the man, and the land your dad has tried to acquire for all those years is finally yours."

"Copy that, Chief!"

CHAPTER 2

Returning home, I found Rachel sitting in what we called the great hall, with the couch and television at one end. We didn't have plans for this evening. If I recall correctly, she was the one supposed to be going out with friends.

"I thought you had plans?"

"A little bird told me I should be here for support," she smiled at me her face looking like an amusement mirror in the bottom of the wine glass.

"I guess I will wait for John's hourly billing since he couldn't trust me to tell the whole story."

She had opted for a support role rather than a night at the local pub, eating pizza or wings, and having a glass of wine with her girlfriends.

"What happened?" she asked.

"What do you know?"

"I asked first!"

"So... nothing? Just be here to make sure I don't do anything unbecoming of an officer?"

She just smiled. My lawyer was a close friend of the family, and he had simply done his duty by providing a heads-up to Rachel, but nothing more.

I felt obliged to retell the events of the morning, regardless.

"Request a QRF. There is no straightforward way to enter that property. I don't want any of the horses injured."

"Call Andy, copy that," I responded.

I loved that this woman got me. A QRF is a Quick Reaction Force, a team on standby used in emergencies or as reinforcements. While she said this in jest, it was an easy call to make.

Of course, she was correct about Andy and the inaccessibility of the land in question. Andy was my best friend. We met early in our military careers. I was just a young white boy named Robert, and he was a young black man named Andy. We were barely out of flight school. Andy had saved my life more times than I could count, but somehow, he knew the number. He was the five-year-younger version of me, just a different rank and color, from a different momma.

I nodded, pulling out my cell phone as I sat beside her on the couch. She curled up to me with her head on my chest as I dialed. At the third ring, a familiar voice answered.

"RJ, my main man. How goes it?"

I chuckled, "I am doing well. You?"

"Never better, my brother! What is going on? We talked just a couple of days ago. You in trouble with the lady again?"

"What? No. Why would you say that? I need you and Betty for a mission."

"Plausible deniability, Okay. What are we doing? More photography?"

"Yes and no. We can put on those new lenses I bought, but another matter needs immediate attention. The window is short on this. Are you available?"

"I could tell you I have other pressing matters, but you would never believe me." In the background, Rachel snorted out loud. "Hey, Rachel, girl! I hear you there."

"Hi, Andy!"

"So, you need Betty and me ASAP; it sounds like."

"Tomorrow, if you can manage it, my friend."

"I'll pack a bag and head out at first light."

"Copy that! I will throw some steak on the grill. Rachel will make some of that sweet tea we all love. We'll make it worth your while."

"Aw, getting to see my two favorite humans is payment enough. See you on the flip side!"

The following morning, Rachel and I drove into town to pick up food for the next few days. We returned to the main lodge to await the arrival of Andy and Betty. The dogs heard Andy before we did, and they came barking up the road in anticipation of their friend.

I waited a few moments and then stuck my hand out to help Andy with some bags. "Wow, Betty. Why would you choose to stick around with this joker?"

"Because I treat her right, that's why!" Andy proudly puffed out his chest.

I was often amazed at the relationship Andy and Betty had developed over the many years I had known them. "Come on. Rachel is waiting along with those steaks!"

We reached the deck steps and saw Rachel in the clearing below. She looked up to acknowledge our arrival, pulled back the bowstring to her ear, and released it. As she came up the stairs, she hugged Andy but seemed slightly disappointed with her target practice.

"How is your chopper?" she asked.

"Hey, that is not some normal helicopter. That is a piece of beauty…"

"A piece of art?" Rachel and I finished his sentence together.

Betty, the helicopter had become integral to the family, even if she wasn't flesh and blood.

Serving the steaks and all the fixings, we sat with the ever-vigilant dogs nearby. "What is the real reason you called me?" Andy asked around a mouthful.

Rachel chimed in. "We need a reason?"

Andy laughed. "I can honestly say that there's never a dull moment with the two of you."

It was time to get into the issue. I started to fill Andy in on yesterday's meeting with the lawyer from Apex Mining Company.

"These guys have been moving goods across your property line without permission? Considering the photos we took from Betty, showing the harsh terrain, it seems highly unlikely that they could do anything but trespass."

"I agree. The deal is the land for half of what I offered after Dad passed. But first, a full recon to find out what happened to the men working on the mine."

"Wait, the men working the mine are now missing?"

"They haven't bothered to cash their paychecks for the last few months."

Andy smirked. "Can you say I have your gold, so I don't need your paychecks?"

"The lawyer says these were hand-picked men. He's sure something has happened to them rather than they ran off with whatever they found." My face registered my skepticism.

"Well, you've got my attention now. There is a spot I could land Betty, although it seems pretty far from where you thought the mine was located."

"I seem to recall that as well. Do you want to take Betty for a spin?"

Rachel interjected. "Would you give the man a break? Work on this tomorrow."

Andy was always up for an adventure. "Never fear, mi-lady. We shall return before the dinner bell sounds."

"I am not cooking tonight!" Rachel stood with arms crossed.

"Dang woman!" He laughed, "We'll swing down and bring back Chinese take-out. Is that good with you?" Andy added.

There was the happy bobbing of her red hair as she began to take dishes into the kitchen. "Okay. You guys get started now, and get back before dark!" After a few mock salutes, we headed to the clearing built especially for Betty.

Andy took Betty to a suitable altitude. We moved north in the direction of the mine. "This is like old times! How many search and rescue missions have we been through?"

"More than I care to remember," I replied.

"It would have been nice if the lawyer man had given you a little more intel on the matter."

"You're preaching to the choir, friend."

"Ironical, considering the former owner was a preacher." Andy was the self-proclaimed Emperor of Puns and the King of Sarcasm. "You did bring some heat with you, right?"

"Man, have you ever known me not to have some combustibles along for the ride?" I asked.

"Just checking." Andy looked away from the cockpit gauges and held my gaze, "Are you expecting trouble? It sure would be nice to know in advance of the L.Z."

"I am not sure. You know my motto."

"Which one? Blow stuff up and ask for forgiveness later. Or shoot first and ask questions later?"

"You know I don't show favoritism with my mottos." I chuckled.

"Tru Dat."

"There's a wide variety of 9mm and .45s, and your choice of a tactical shotgun. Or, if you prefer, something in 7.62 caliber is also available."

"You are always a tactical delight."

"You know my motto."

"Oh, always be over-prepared! Or if it can be shot, fired, or launched, bring it?"

"You know me too well, my friend. Remember the time in Mogadishu…."

"Really? I was thinking more about that time in Kandahar."

"Ah, we will go with your gut feeling on this."

I looked out as he pointed out our destination. "L.Z. straight ahead, Major."

"Copy that. Steady as she goes."

CHAPTER 3

The area we descended to was greener than either of us remembered. Surrounding us was rough terrain, but this green patch rose slightly and had a stream at the far end. Perched atop the hill was a command-style tent made of canvas. Andy landed, and we exited the bird once we had geared up.

"I'll take the lead," I stated.

"No, you most certainly will not! Do you know the trouble I'd be in if I arrived back with Chinese food and didn't have you along? No, sir, RJ, you're welcome to commence court-martial proceedings after we return in one piece. I am taking the lead."

I shrugged. "You always have some excuse to hog all the glory."

"It's what pilots were born to do! Hog the glory!"

Using hand signals, we began to work our way toward the tent. The terrain forced a landing closer to the camp than expected. All secrecy had been lost; if you missed the Blackhawk landing, you might need your eyes and hearing checked.

Brushing aside the tent flap with the shotgun, Andy gave the 'all clear' sign. A stench that we were all too familiar with hit us like a boxing glove.

I proceeded through the entrance into the structure's large main room, followed by Andy. In the corner, a cot was lying on its side. There was a rotten stench in the air. When Andy approached it, he snapped his fist shut, signaling for me to stop, then pointed his hand, with fingers and thumb outstretched, towards the overturned cot.

Someone was hiding behind the cot.

I approached from a different angle than Andy. There would have been very little resistance from a person caught between us. "You are trespassing on private property; interlace your fingers behind your head. I will only warn you once. I suggest you comply."

Not a sound.

Andy reached forward. I knew that the moment he pulled the cot out of the way, I had to be ready to do whatever was necessary.

The cot tipped over. The only thing that identified this mess as a body was the tattered remains of his clothing. His skin was a deep red color, and his teeth had fallen from his skull. Portions of the skeleton were already bursting through the decomposing bloat.

"Oh, God help us, RJ!" Andy moved his shirt up to cover his mouth and nose. I followed suit.

The body looked like it had several gashes across the torso, but that was just a guess at best. The coroner would have to reveal the true story.

"We're too late. No wild animal did this," Andy whispered.

The last seconds of this poor man's life showed in his face: horror and pain.

I handed Andy a blanket from the floor, and we covered the body.

"What we've just stumbled into makes no sense. How long has he been here?"

"Two, maybe three weeks?"

I nodded in agreement, "Back to Betty."

In a different place and time, I would certainly not be calling any of the local authorities. There would have been exact military protocol regarding the course of action. Now, I was a civilian with limited options.

"Get us in the air. I'll call Reggie once we get back to the lodge."

At home, I brushed past Rachel in the kitchen and headed for the sanctuary of the office.

"What's up with him?" she asked.

"We found a dead guy on the property," Andy said grimly.

"Wait! Really?" She stumbled and took a seat at the table, visibly shaken.

Andy shook his head. "Yep. And he was right messed up. No animal that I know of could do that."

"You two have to find out what happened to him. What sort of injuries are we talking about?" Rachel asked.

"Precise strikes. Equal distances between cuts and depth in the wound. He looked like he had seen a monster right before he died."

"His face?"

"Contorted. Horror. Pain. He was terrified in those final moments."

"Oh, Andy. How horrible and so close to our home."

"Don't you worry, none, Miss Rachel, the major and I will figure this out."

"If it wasn't an animal, have we discounted the two-legged variety?"

"Not altogether, but no gun-related injuries."

"What's RJ doing now?"

"I think he is trying to get in touch with Reggie."

"That makes sense. We are out in the county, which is out of Jacob's jurisdiction."

Rachel started fixing a light supper. With RJ distracted, she knew that Chinese take-out would wait.

Andy watched her hand tremble as she tried to slice the tomatoes for the sandwiches. He took the knife from her, "I got this, you go sit down."

Sheriff Reggie answered on the third ring. "Hey, Major, I haven't seen you at the diner in a few weeks."

"I have been a little busy. Andy is visiting. We'll stop in for some of those pancakes."

"You bet. You know Martha loves seeing you guys. What's going on?"

"I don't know how to say this."

"Spit it out. We won't know until you do."

"Reggie, a dead man is on my soon-to-be new property!"

"Did you shoot him?"

"No, sir."

"Are you sure? No blackout or flashback?"

"No, this was an unarmed man. I would have winged him and called you."

"Well, I'll be a monkey's uncle. Long time since we had a murder! Do I need to send Bobby tonight, or is the first thing in the morning all right?"

"The first thing would be great. Tell Bobby biscuits and gravy at seven-thirty sharp."

"Sounds good. Enjoy the rest of your evening, Major."

"You as well."

CHAPTER 4

I hung up the phone and headed for the kitchen, toward the enticing smell of toasted bread. Grilled cheese and tomato soup! Comfort food was just what we needed. I was a little chagrinned that I had forgotten the Chinese food in my haste to report the murder.

"Cheating on me again, are you?" I bellowed as I jumped out of the doorway, ah-ha style.

While waiting for dinner, Rachel and Andy sat at the table, sharing a tub of ice cream. "Cheating?

Everybody in this town, maybe even the whole county, knows you are a chocolate peanut butter guy."

"True. Speaking of that, are we out?"

"RJ, put a ring on that finger because two new cartons of your favorite flavor are in the freezer.", Andy teased.

It wasn't a reluctance issue but a timing issue. When I first met Rachel, I was still married to the U.S. Army. Then Dad's tests came back positive for cancer. I took my retirement. Rachel moved into the cabin at the junction of my land and the county road. She helped me care for Dad until he passed six months ago.

"You know that when Rachel leaves the room, I am going to smack you so hard that no search engine will be able to find you."

Andy laughed. "You know Jacob can't tell a joke properly. Why do you bother to repeat them?"

Rachel laughed. "I thought it bordered on funny!"

"Funny? I would build a wall to keep out jokers who think that was funny."

"Okay, everyone knows I'm far better at sarcasm than jokes," I said.

"Well, at least we agree on that."

"What did Reggie say?" Rachel asked as I diverted Andy's attention so she could get the last spoonful of ice cream from the carton.

"I put in a code 30. He is sending Bobby out first thing. I told him we would have a hearty breakfast of biscuits and gravy."

"Code 30. Officer needs assistance. Seems appropriate for finding a dead body. Haven't seen Bobby around lately?"

"Reggie sent him to a special boot camp for training a few months back. Tomorrow, we'll find out what soaked in and what leaked out."

I have profound admiration for the law that keeps us safe. As with any organization or workforce, there are varying degrees of competency at every level of law enforcement. For example, Jacob grew up with a father who was a police chief, attended college, went to the academy, and worked his way up to the rank of captain. When his dad's position became available, Jacob applied.

Another good example would be Reggie, who has no formal education. Before being elected sheriff, he had spent twenty years as a deputy. The guys on the other end of the professional spectrum cause banjo music to play in the background when they open their mouths; enough said.

We turned in for the night. Rachel showed Andy to one of the guest rooms before curling up on the couch, surrounded by dogs, to fall asleep while watching television.

In the morning, I could smell more than just biscuits and gravy. Bacon! I threw on a T-shirt and a pair of jogging pants and let my nose do the walking. There were far better cooks in our circle of friends than Andy. Nevertheless, his most exceptional skill beyond romancing Betty was crispy bacon.

There was fresh fruit, coffee, biscuits, and gravy. And Rachel.

"Morning, my dear." I greeted her with a quick hug and a peck on the forehead.

"I think your friend ruined a piece of my French cookware."

I laughed and almost spilled the creamer. "Andy?"

"Okay, so sue me, Rachel. Better yet, put a set of that snobby, overpriced cookware on your wedding registry."

"Oh, snap," I declared. "Just keep digging that hole!"

Andy either chose to notice Rachel's disappearance from the kitchen table or failed to notice until she attacked him with a sofa pillow from the other side of the room. This battle might have continued, leading to tickling. I would have had to mount a rescue attempt, but the sound of the doorbell and barking dogs stopped the current conflict.

We had all forgotten about Bobby. While Rachel answered the door, I hurriedly set another place at the table.

"Morning, Bobby. Or should I say, Deputy Bobby?"

"No, Miss Rachel, just Bobby."

"Bobby, just call me Rachel."

"Yes, Miss Rachel."

Once started, that conversation could have continued indefinitely. I interrupted and announced breakfast was ready. "Let's sit down and eat."

After I said grace, we all dug in. Bobby arm-wrestled Andy for the last strip of bacon at the end of the meal, not realizing that Rachel slipped in and took the bacon prize as they huffed and puffed for victory. With the dishes washed, we men headed for the lower field where Betty waited.

"Have you ever had a ride in one of these, Bobby?"

"One time during boot camp. We had to jump out of one with ropes."

"You rappelled out of a moving helicopter?" Andy asked, impressed. "That is no small feat."

"No, it was sitting on the top of a wall to simulate, or something."

"So, not from a moving helicopter. More or less, you just scaled down a wall."

"Yes, I guess so."

"Well, Betty is a smooth ride. I see you brought your weapon. 9mm is a good choice, unless someone is wearing body plates."

"Yes, I have my 9mm and crime scene kit."

"Good. We need to figure out what happened."

"I was at the top of my class in crime scene investigation," said Bobby with a note of pride.

"How did you do on the weapons course?" Andy inquired.

"I think Bobby will be just fine. You want to take the lead when we get there?" I asked.

"Sure, it is my case, after all," Bobby proudly stated.

"Indeed, it is."

Once more, Andy set Betty down in the field not far from the tent. Andy and I were gearing up when I saw Bobby casually walking toward the tent. His firearm remained holstered. To compound the risk, he was lugging the rather bulky-looking red crime scene case over his shoulder.

"Gee whiz. What training has Bobby received?" I asked.

"Well, in his defense, the guy is dead."

"What about whoever or whatever killed the guy? That should make him pause and not waltz in and announce himself."

"It's a little late to call him back. Let's catch up."

Duck and run was the game; make yourself a small and hard target to follow. Andy and I had caught Bobby just before he entered the tent. I was relieved when he carefully placed the case beside the tent wall and drew his gun.

"Deputy, take us in."

Nothing had changed in the tent. Bobby went out and returned with his crime scene case, which was pretty cool. It contained everything from a decent camera to what appeared to be a fingerprinting kit.

At first sight of the bloated body, Bobby dashed to the rear tent door flap. We could hear breakfast being heaved up. Red-faced, Bobby promptly returned.

"Bobby, you going to be okay?"

"Sorry about that. My first dead body."

"Seriously? You haven't seen any other dead bodies?" Andy asked.

"I have, but those have been barely dead," Bobby stated.

"Okay. What can we do to help, Bobby?"

"Take some of these yellow number plaques. If you notice anything unusual, place a number beside it. I will get some photos, too."

"Just like on the TV, Bobby?"

I looked at Andy and mouthed the words, "Knock it off."

"Yes, Sir Mr. Andy. That's how it's done. You can learn a lot watching those CSI and murder shows." Bobby knelt to place a numbered placard and take a photo.

"Copy that." Andy and I headed outside to look around. We hadn't dropped our guard, as we had only encountered one of the three men working at this site. Who knew what else we might be facing?

"Sarge, let's locate those other two men."

"Copy that," Andy replied.

We began a mini-grid search and shortly found a second body.

"Wow, this one looks like his entire center mass was carved out," Andy observed.

The two of us had experienced so much horror and bloodshed in our years of service that we were not overly disturbed. Things that went bump in the night feared us, not the other way around.

"Mountain lion?"

"Even a starving lion would likely leave two or three grown men alone," I replied.

"No wolves in these parts," Andy stated.

"No. Further north, maybe, but I haven't heard of wolves being this far south."

"Too clean for a bear."

"I agree. A wild animal would have left nothing but bone."

There was the snap of a twig. We froze back-to-back; instinct kicked us into survival mode. Bobby appeared carrying his case.

"Dang nabbit, son, you almost became the third victim at your own crime scene," I said, disgusted.

"Sorry. There's another body?"

I pointed out the location, and he got right to work. "Do you have something we can rig up to take the bodies back with us?"

"Andy?"

"Yes. Betty has two collapsible spine boards that we can use. I'll grab them."

"Well, Bobby, what's your current hypothesis?" I asked.

"One guy looks like someone took an ax to him, while the other looks like a mountain lion got him. What do you think?"

"I think you're half right. It looks like a crude-bladed weapon on the first victim, but any wild animal capable of doing this should have eaten him. Why waste a perfect dinner?"

"True. Maybe you scared it off yesterday with the chopper," Bobby said.

"Maybe, but as soon as it realized Betty was taking off, it would have returned at night to finish its meal. And these aren't recent wounds."

Andy arrived back with the two body boards and the necessary body bags." "I don't want the bag back, but the boards I do."

"I promise to return them."

"While you are doing your crime scene, we will load the first body and look around the meadow."

Andy and I moved down the slight rise and found the remains of a stone fire ring with large logs for seating. Behind one of the

31

stumps, we discovered the third man. Well, his body. His head was twenty yards further on, possibly severed with one blow.

"He was a big man. You can see from the wounds on his body that he went down fighting. No wild animal did this. See this precision cut?"

"Please tell me you're not about to say a sword?" Andy asked.

"Of course not. However, it fits."

"How so?"

"A machete, sword, or ax would be quiet," I said.

"Except for the screams of bloody murder."

"Yes, but the sound of a scream would not travel across two and a half thousand acres. The discharge of a firearm might."

"Major, I see where you are going. The perp used the bladed weapon to kill them and steal the gold or silver. Still doesn't explain the guy missing his vocal cords."

"Anomaly?" I asked.

"Listen, you don't blame everything you can't explain on Anomaly! She will get a complex."

"What happened here?" I wondered aloud.

"I fear we may never have the answers. What are you going to do with the mine and land?"

"It can sit here and rot for the rest of eternity."

"How about we arm wrestle for it?" Andy asked.

"You have plans for it now? You know Rachel would kill me if I let you have it."

"Yep, the way I see it, I could be at your house for every meal, living this close." Andy teased.

"Not going to happen." I laughed.

"I always counted you as my smartest friend, RJ. Happy wife, happy life... oh wait!"

"Knock it off with that."

"Okay. Okay, you know I want you to get this right for once in your life," he pressed.

"I have the rock, you know."

"Wait, you have a ring? What are you waiting for, man?"

"The perfect moment?" I sheepishly replied.

"You can't wait for the perfect moment, RJ You have to make the perfect moment."

Then, our beautiful moment was interrupted by Bobby. "Is that another body? Dear God! Is he missing his head?"

"Yes, and yes."

"Do we have another board and a body bag?"

"No more boards, but there are plenty of body bags. They come twenty to a box."

"That was a bit of exceptionally useless information, Andy. Thanks," Bobby added.

"Once we get them to the bird, we have to tie two bodies to one board."

"Good idea. Let me take some more pictures. I don't want to be up here when it gets dark."

For once, I agreed with Bobby. The score was three for the things that 'go bump in the night' and zero for the good guys.

CHAPTER 5

We loaded the bodies. Bobby called Reggie and the county coroner to meet us with transportation at the regional airport across the valley. When we arrived, Joseph, the Coroner, and Reggie looked at Bobby's photos first.

"You have got to be kidding me! Who or what did this? Better yet, why?" Reggie asked.

Joseph was nearly speechless, shaking his head. Finally, he took me aside. "RJ, you know I am half Ute on my mother's side."

"I knew you were Native American. I was unsure of what tribe."

"Turn around and look at the side of the valley you came from."

"You mean the mountain where my land sits?"

"Yes. What do you see?" Joseph asked.

Then it hit me, a conversation I had with my dad when I was very young, "You're talking about the Sleeping Indian?"

"Yes. You see it, don't you?"

"Yes, of course." I pointed out the head, arms, knees, and upright foot positions across the mountain range. "How does that concern my land?"

"Did your dad tell you any stories regarding the mountain?"

"Yes, but that's a bunch of old wives' tales. Isn't it?"

"Old, yes, but an Indian tale, not something made up to put fear into white children to get them to sleep." Joseph grabbed my arm, "Be careful and leave nothing to chance. There are reasons we have oral traditions and stories passed down through the generations to keep us safe. Have you ever wondered why Native Americans don't live on Sleeping Indian Mountain? There are old and horrible things that live in the dark places of the Earth."

After his final warning, I watched Reggie's patrol vehicle, lights and sirens for maximum effect, lead Joseph's county coroner's truck with the bodies off the airport property.

Andy walked over. "What was that all about?"

"Just catching up is all. I haven't seen Joseph since Dad's funeral."

"While we still have some daylight, do you want to find the lawyer for Apex?" Andy asked.

"Yes, but first, I will get a hold of my attorney, John, and see if he wouldn't mind joining us. How about you get a rental from the airport, put it on my account, and let them know it is only for the afternoon."

I called John and then Reggie. Both said they would join Andy and me at the local steakhouse for lunch.

"Are you paying?" Reggie asked.

"I am paying."

"I can't pass that up," he said.

"Bring a copy of Bobby's report, please," I requested.

"You bet!"

When we arrived at the steakhouse, we were ushered to a back room where we saw John, Reggie, and the Judge. It really didn't matter what day of the week it was; this is where the Judge could be found outside of regular courtroom hours.

John had many questions. He studied Bobby's report from the county and the aerial photos we took with the new equipment. "Judge, now mind you, we don't have anything official from Joseph yet for any autopsies. Looking at these photos, I don't see how anyone could have reached the mine without crossing your property."

"There is no way. It is not feasible by vehicle or horse. By foot with any amount of gear would be treacherous."

"Okay. RJ, what are your thoughts? Do you want a lawsuit, or compensation?" John asked.

"The major shouldn't have to pay for that land. I can draw up an invoice for the chopper time alone that will be more than what that land is worth." Andy chimed in.

"We should work on something like that, which I can have served on the other party's attorney. Bobby's report and the photos would have any judge on our side in this." He pressed an elbow lightly into the Judge's side, and they both chuckled.

"John, do you think so?" I asked.

"Only one way to find out." John cleared his throat and waved down our waitress. "Shelly, when can you bring us each a slice of your mile-high meringue pie?"

A few moments later, Shelly returned with a piece of mile-high lemon meringue pie and a cup of coffee for each of us.

John relayed the entire story to the judge, showing him Bobby's initial report and crime scene photos, the aerial photos, and the sworn testimony of Andy and me taken by Bobby at the scene.

After a lengthy discussion, the judge informed us that we had a sufficient case for his court. The Apex lawyer should be waving a white flag shortly after the trespassing fines are paid and a petition for costs incurred in locating the men is filed.

I was relieved and thanked the judge.

"What is the next step?" Reggie asked.

"I will return to my office and draw up a counteroffer. Let's meet there around three. Give me enough time to get the facts and figures in order." My attorney replied.

"Sounds good. Thanks, John."

How do you waste two hours in a small town? First, you hit the hardware store and buy items you probably don't need. This little, locally owned store existed, so I wouldn't have to drive 30 minutes to buy the same things in Salida. Then Andy and I crossed the road to the Chinese restaurant to place our order and collect it later that afternoon.

We stopped at the famous local hamburger joint on the highway through town and bought soft-serve ice cream cones. Large vanilla and chocolate twist cones that would take some time to eat.

Finally, we headed over to John's office. John called the hotel and had the front desk connect him to the Apex lawyer's room. After a quick conversation, we waited for the other lawyer to arrive at John's office. The lawyer hurried to open his briefcase and pull out the papers he wanted me to sign.

John had other plans. "Put those away. RJ, why don't you tell him what you and Andy found on the property?"

I nodded. "I regret to inform you that your three employees are deceased."

The Apex lawyer now had a dazed and confused look on his face. "How? Why?"

"We don't have any definitive cause of death." I showed him several of Bobby's crime scene photos.

The Apex lawyer turned his head away. It appeared he might lose his lunch in the same fashion as Bobby had, but he regained his composure. "I agree, this is a terrible turn of events. Why was I called here?"

"We have papers for you to sign, instead," John stated, handing the file to the other attorney, who began shuffling through the legal documents.

"You can't be serious? You want the land without cost and to be compensated for your lawyer fees?"

John nodded his head yes.

"I can tell you that you have wasted my time and yours. Good day, gentlemen!"

Reggie stepped out of John's office into the conference room. "Are you the official representative of the Apex Mining Company?"

"Yes, Sheriff. Why?" The attorney was now clearly confused at the presence of a law officer.

"As the company's representative, I am informing you of your rights."

"My rights?"

Reggie dangled his silver handcuffs at the Apex lawyer, "You can re-read those papers and sign on the dotted line, or I can read you your rights. We can head down to the courthouse if you prefer. Although I am not sure the judge will be in session this late, you may have to spend the night in jail."

"You can't do that!"

Reggie now smiled as his palm rested firmly on his .45 Colt. "I can't?"

There was a great deal of blustering while the color drained from the lawyer's rosy complexion. "You can't arrest me over this!"

"I won't have to arrest you if you rethink your position on the property."

"This is blackmail!"

I didn't want this to escalate, so I calmly stated my offer. "If you pay me the cost of recovering the three bodies and the trespassing fines, we don't need to involve the judge. I am not an unreasonable man. Please look over the paperwork again. Explain to your boss that this was the best course of action for all parties. If you want to spend a couple of days in jail waiting for the official findings of both the Sheriff's and Coroner's offices, you are welcome to do that."

It took only a few moments for the lawyer to realize he had little choice. He quickly cut an Apex check. I reminded him that I had access to a helicopter. If the check bounced, I would personally visit him. He promptly reassured me that the account had sufficient funds.

"We need a notary to make signing over the land official."

"That's easy," John called Carol from her office, and she brought in her stamp. "Major, you are now the proud owner of two hundred acres of wilderness." John declared.

The Apex attorney couldn't get out of the offices quickly enough. I am sure he was on the first charter flight to Denver that he could arrange. Somewhere up in heaven, Dad was dancing a jig! Or was he? I am sure Dad would want us to find out who had murdered those men and get justice for them.

Later, I attempted to write a check to John for the legal services rendered.

"Are you kidding? Your father would haunt me if I accepted that. I wish he could have seen this day and tasted the sweet success," John declared.

I thanked John and Reggie for their time. Andy and I headed out to grab the Chinese takeout and head home.

CHAPTER 6

Rachel was out back practicing her archery again. She came up to the deck to help set the table. "So, how did that go?"

I recounted the day with some dramatic help from Andy. "Bold move with Reggie stating the judge would put the lawyer in jail! Wow! What's the plan now?"

Andy raised his hand and waved it enthusiastically, followed by, "Oh, oh, I know!"

"Yes, Andy?" Rachel laughed.

"I say it's time to get the band back together!"

"Cool idea." I agreed. Andy affectionately referred to "the band", a small group of friends with various specialized talents.

Rachel was on her tablet, looking at something, when I asked, "Rachel, can you start calling everyone and see if they're free?"

"Calling all your friends?"

"Hey, they are our friends." I laughed and saw the light bulb turn on inside her head. "How much will this cost me?"

She passed the tablet to Andy, who declared, "Oh, Rach, this is an awesome bow!"

Then the tablet came to me. "Wow! That is a cool bow!" Then I looked at the price. "Wow! Who would pay that much for a bow?"

Andy laughed and pointed at me.

Rachel giggled and nodded her head as well.

"Really? I'm paying for this bow because you're making the phone calls?"

Andy and Rachel both nodded yes.

"Dang nabbit!" I exclaimed.

I was a U.S. Army major. I had shown courage in the most extreme circumstances, under conditions that would make most men beg for death to take them. I had the medals to prove it! However, I flew the white flag of surrender more often than I cared to admit when it came to a certain redhead. I got out my credit card and handed it to her as she began tapping the tablet screen to finalize the purchase.

Rachel left the room, smiling. We could hear her on her cell phone, first talking to Gretchen, then to Becky.

A little while later, the phone rang. It sounded like she was speaking to Bill. "All the calls have been made. Bill will be here in three days, and the rest will show up over the weekend." She hugged me and gave me a peck on the cheek. "I love my new bow!"

Andy made a sound like a whip cracking and laughed.

"I am glad you like it. I am sure it's needed."

"Oh, I know it's needed, so I had them overnight it."

"Dang nabbit! What did that cost me?"

Andy was miming a swipe across his throat, behind Rachel.

"Never mind. I'm keen to see what you can do with it."

While I was not the most romantic man, it was easy to see that I had charm and appeal. I was a complex individual. Sometimes, I just needed to let go and live a little. We spent that evening watching a couple of movies. One mushy one picked by Rachel and a classic shoot-'em-up action film, which Andy and I voted on.

Andy and I spent the next two days gathering supplies from town and ferrying some of the black cases to the miners' vacated tent. My friends were coming to help me explore the newly acquired two hundred acres.

I was excited about an adventure!

Bill was the closest thing we all had to a shared dad. We met him on an exploration in Montana a few years back. He brought transportation to the table. The dogs announced his arrival. We watched from the great room window as the ranch truck, with dual wheels and pulling a large horse trailer, arrived.

Our dogs welcomed Bill's German Shepherd. The barking pack raced off to explore the countryside. We helped Bill get all the horses and mules into the lower meadow for much-needed food, water, and stretching. Later, we took them to the horse stalls for the evening. Once we had a light supper and had sat down to relax, Bill seemed to want to get right to the point of this excursion.

"What do we need the horses for, this time?"

"Bill, do you remember that property my place has got hemmed in that's north of us?"

"You mean that tract of land with the mine your dad kept trying to buy?"

"The same."

"What about it?"

"Well, it is now my land and my gold mine. Thanks to a misstep by the mining company and the support of my friends, the standoff is over."

I received a solid slap on the shoulder from Bill. "Congratulations!"

"Thank you! There's no access road. We need the horses to cross my land. We will check out the area and see if we can reach the mine. We need to investigate what the three Apex individuals were doing that led to their deaths. Everyone else is arriving some time over the weekend."

"What? Killed? So, how did they die?" Bill asked with sudden concern.

"I don't think it was wild animals that attacked them. I am usually on the other end of that conversation. I will leave it up to the experts to determine the cause of death. With Bobby's help, Andy and I got the bodies delivered to the coroner, took pictures, and filed reports."

"Sounds like you've had an interesting time recently."

"Well, as always, we appreciate that you brought the horses, so our trip makes us saddle-weary rather than having foot blisters."

Bill smiled. He wouldn't have it any other way. "If it had just been you, I might have declined, but Rachel is such a sweet talker."

We all knew Bill loved our little group adventures. He always insisted on being in charge of the horses, mules, and the 'chuck wagon'. While we didn't use an actual wagon, but packed mules, he was the chuck wagon equivalent to the historical much-loved 'Cookie'.

Then he asked a serious question. "Did you catch whoever killed those men?"

"No, sir. That's a mystery." I pulled out the laptop to show Bill and Rachel the photos we had taken from the air for the deputy's reports.

"I can't say I know of an animal that could take out three grown men. Were they armed?" asked Bill.

"We didn't see any weapons in the area," Andy confirmed.

Bill scratched his beard. "I remember a few years back, maybe twenty-ten or eleven, a fellow here in Colorado taking down a seven-hundred-pound black bear. Popping a guy's head clean off is not an easy thing to do. I doubt even that bear could have done this kind of damage. Which leads us to the question, what could have done this?"

"Well, it wasn't pretty. After seeing this, I don't think I like the idea of Rachel living alone at the cottage." I replied.

Andy shook his head in agreement. "Poor saps, never knew what hit them."

"Not that Rachel can't take care of herself, with that bow, but that takes distance," Andy pointed out. "If something is stalking you and gets close, the bow is not your weapon of choice."

Rachel poked her head in from the hallway. "You would be surprised what I can do in close quarters with the bow I am getting."

She sat down next to Bill with her laptop, brought up the bow manufacturer's website, and pointed out the model to Bill.

"Impressive, darlin'. If we come to a dark alley, I will let you go first," he said.

Andy nodded his agreement. "Always beauty before age in those situations."

I didn't look at the bow's statistical information. It was the price that first caught my eye. One thing was sure: if whatever had taken out the three miners came stalking us, the outcome would be drastically different.

Andy and Bill had arrived. That just left the appearance of the four remaining adventurers.

Allen and Gretchen were flying in from California, where Allen was part of some think tank. He had developed algorithms that led to some brilliant discoveries. His genius work led to some nice financial gain for the computer whiz. Gretchen worked as a surgical nurse for a private clinic.

Jim and Becky were catching a plane from Baltimore International. Jim had just retired from his second career teaching at the Army War College for the past ten years. In his first career, he held the rank of Chief (C5) and commanded a SEAL team. Becky's career had been spent in public service, teaching where she could, depending on Jim's assignments.

The two couples would spend Friday night at a hotel Rachel had picked out in Denver. I almost said something sarcastic about the price, but saw Andy stick his tongue out at me. Without a word, I handed over my credit card.

"That looks like a charming hotel. I hope they like it." I presented my best light-hearted smile.

Rachel smiled in return. "I hope so, too! Did you figure out how to get them from Denver to here?"

"Let's go to the car rental websites that service DIA and get them something that will fit all their luggage but still be comfortable," I suggested.

Early Saturday afternoon, we got the call that our guests had arrived at the Regional Airport to drop off the DIA rental car. We headed down in two vehicles to pick them up. I suggested that we grab a late lunch in town. We found ourselves in the back room of my favorite pizza joint, talking, laughing, and enjoying our food.

Allen had his laptop out. When wasn't he on the computer? He was always working on something. The pizza on Allen's plate was getting cold. I interrupted his thought pattern. "What are you doing?"

"Checking stock values." He responded, not even making eye contact.

"Apple?" I asked, trying to catch him off guard.

"Up by thirty cents from yesterday. I just made another three grand. You?"

"I took your advice last week."

"Then you made a couple of grand as well. Are you buying lunch?" That was about all the humor and sarcasm you could expect from Allen.

Andy chuckled. "The plane tickets, hotel, and rental car weren't enough for you?"

You could see Gretchen making hand motions, but it was too late.

"Andy, I was just trying to make up for the trip to California that Allen and Gretchen hosted," I stated.

Andy played along. "Oh, right. Remember the tour Allen gave of his think-tank warehouse, clinic thingy?"

I couldn't help myself. "I couldn't believe all the child labor at that place."

Allen, who had reached critical mass, exclaimed, "Hey, I thought you guys would like Disneyland!"

The whole table erupted with uneasy laughter. I had other friends, but these were the ones who consistently showed up. How we had remained so close, for so many years, remained a delightful mystery.

Later that evening, we gathered at the table in the great room. Bill had prepared a light meal. After we ate, we mulled over the aerial photos and those of the crime scene.

Gretchen pored over the medical report's details, which the coroner had kindly copied for me. "This was no wild animal. Allen, find me a list of late bronze or early iron age weapons that could have removed a man's head with one sweep."

"You're suggesting a sword?"

"The coroner found metal traces in the severed vertebra at the back of the neck. This cut is not clean."

"What does that mean?"

"It was a forged weapon, but not one forged by a highly skilled blacksmith. Both the fifth and sixth cervical vertebrae are completely missing. The blade severed the longitudinal ligament, stern hyoid, and platysma muscles."

"What sort of weapon are we talking about?"

"I would have to say a large sword, or more likely, a battle-ax."

Looking over Allen's shoulder, Andy mused, "Well, are we talking hellebarde, sparth, or perhaps a bardiche?"

"No way to know for sure, without a sample," Allen replied.

"Who uses a medieval ax to kill people on my property?" I asked with a frown.

"Without more data, I can't be of much more assistance," Allen replied.

Jim had been silent. "Deception."

"What do you mean, Jim?"

There were a few moments of pause, which brought all of us to focus on him. "If I wanted to throw a wrench in the works, I would use a hard-to-trace weapon."

Rachel was the first to say, "For instance?"

"Like using a Dragunov sniper rifle here in the United States. Who would be a suspect?"

Andy raised his hand. "Besides, you dummkopf!"

"Hey, you asked," Jim said.

"Right, but use a weapon that is virtually untraceable?"

Allen looked over the laptop. "I can trace this if I had a sample of the metal pieces left behind. However, that would take weeks, maybe even months, with no guarantee of a match. This weapon could be ancient and stolen from a collection. If a new weapon, it may have been hastily fashioned, solely for this purpose."

Bill set his cup of coffee down rather loudly. "Why?" That had our attention. "Why would someone go to the trouble of making a bladed weapon? Why not use a pistol or a rifle? The sound, of course, so why not use…"

"A bow," Rachel interrupted excitedly.

Bill smiled and nodded. "Exactly!"

Gretchen reinserted herself into the conversation. "How tall would the attacker have to be to decapitate a man six and a half feet tall with one stroke, in the middle of a field?"

After some brief scribbles on his notepad, Allen announced, "The assailant would be about twelve to fourteen feet tall."

The room fell silent.

Bill shook his head, "Allen, you need to rework those numbers. Unless RJ has a neighbor with a polar bear for a pet, that is impossible."

"My numbers are never wrong; you're welcome to give or take a few inches, but they are spot on."

"What if the person was standing on something?" Rachel asked.

Allen crushed that idea. "No. There is no furniture or tree stump out here that would provide the proper height. The items here that could be stood on are not supportive of the weight required to swing with that kind of force."

"Whatever or whoever this is, we must take them out if they're still on the property. I would propose that for the safety of our party, we shoot first and ask questions later," Jim added.

We all agreed.

Bill and Andy checked on the horses and mules before we prepared to bunk down. Anyone who thought messing with my home was a good idea would find out the folly of their ways the hard way.

CHAPTER 7

The early breakfast was grab-and-go. Afterward, we quickly cleaned the lodge before moving our packs to the barn. Now I am not talking about a big red building with dairy cows and a grain silo to one side. The barn is about a quarter mile from the lodge. The barn addressed our need to house some horses and put a roof over a few expensive toys I had acquired over the years, along with the four-wheelers, a couple of snowmobiles, and the hatch. The hatch is the addition I built to protect Andy's love, Betty, from the weather. Push a button, and the roof and walls fold away to reveal Betty, aka Andy's Blackhawk helicopter.

Below, locked ammunition and weapons storage lay under the hatch. I assure you that this is not where I keep the heirloom shotgun. No, that priceless gun is where it should be: in the house, over the mantle. This storage is for the more unconventional weapons that beg for proper storage.

Oats for the horses and mules, camping gear, tents, camp chairs, sleeping bags, the stove, and food were all loaded onto the helicopter. Additionally, there were the cases marked 'fragile' that Allen always insisted on taking.

Most of our group will be traveling on horseback with their backpacks. Bill hand-picked and prepared the most suitable mounts for each rider's skill level. Andy and I will fly the chopper to the meadow, unload, and get the camp ready for our friends to arrive on horseback. The dogs will be accompanying the riders, but they seemed to have their own agenda, running off ahead of everyone.

Upon arrival at the miners' abandoned campsite, Andy landed the chopper in nearly the exact spot we had been several days earlier. We wasted no time in setting up two tents for the couples and a shelter for Bill near two trees, where we could tie up the horses and mules for the night.

Andy and I planned to use the miners' tent as our own sleeping quarters. No one else would want to sleep there after the events that had taken place. We set up Rachel's tent a few feet away from it. There was already a large ring of rocks for a campfire. We gathered wood to keep it fueled long into the night. Cooking would not be an issue this evening as Bill had packed a full evening meal in ice and sent it ahead with us, in Betty.

About six hours later, we could hear the dogs nearby. An hour after that, the riders began arriving in the meadow. Andy and I helped Bill with the horses, while Rachel handed out cold drinks and snacks to both human and canine friends. Everyone moved into their respective tents until the dinner bell sounded. The menu included pulled pork sandwiches, several cold salads, macaroni and cheese, and cookies. We all settled into our chairs around the campfire.

Bill passed around mugs filled with his incredible cowboy coffee as the evening meal ended. Not that oil-like, thick coffee you imagine cowboys drinking. It was a mouthful of pure joy created with a French press, which Bill called 'liquid gold'.

The smooth, hot coffee tasted good, as the Colorado evening rapidly cooled. From where we sat, in the fading golden hues of sunset, you could see the lights of the towns of Salida to the south and Leadville to the north. Directly in front of us was majestic

Mount Princeton. It was 180 degrees, with a spectacular view covering just under 60 miles.

Scrub oaks took hold wherever they could, with the landscape occasionally dominated by massive Juniper trees. I certainly could not lay claim to this impressive scenery as mine. It was God's country. There was no doubt about that.

I thought about the men who had died, and why they had lost their lives.

The horseback trip along the rugged trail had been exciting and tiring. Minimal grazing land lay between the lodge and this spot, prompting several breaks to feed and water the horses. The dogs had taken the trip with one goal: the lush grass beside the roaring fire and the hope that someone had remembered to pack treats.

The scenery was breathtaking from here, and everyone was taking pictures to capture the trip's many wonders.

Becky, a little saddle-weary, asked Andy if they could get a ride back in the helicopter next time. This remark sparked a heated but comical argument between Bill and Andy. Bill argued that horses were essential to such a trip. But he finished by stating that he would not stand in her way if she insisted on riding with the Madman of Tikrit.

Bill grunted something about checking on the horses. As he moved away, Andy stuck his tongue out at Bill, which brought laughs from us and a considerable chuckle from Bill. It wasn't that Bill didn't like Andy. Bill always said that if he had to leave the ground, it would only be onto a horse or into his truck, relatively safe rides.

Today's helicopter journey had been uneventful, but that's only sometimes the case. Everyone had heard Andy's and my stories of daring night raids and extractions under fire. Due to my experiences, I knew that while not everything in war is harrowing, most of it is.

"RJ, this would have made a beautiful spot for a cabin," Rachel commented.

"Living this far out? Not me," Becky responded.

"Me either. Three people were murdered here," Gretchen stated.

"We should try to get some shut-eye. Let's not forget that whoever or whatever killed those men, may still be nearby. Are we drawing straws for the first watch, or do we have volunteers?" Andy asked.

Jim put his finger up. "I got it." He moved towards the case that held his favorite weapon.

I woke near midnight to relieve Jim, who sat with a pair of night-vision goggles, his back to the campfire, and his coveted sniper rifle across his knees. You might think such a weapon is overkill on this trip, but Jim would disagree.

I could hear him saying, "It's only excessive if you can't afford the cost of four dollars per shell to fire it."

He was a quiet man. You didn't have to say a lot when you could reach out and touch a hostile at over three-quarters of a mile with your rifle. If you didn't want the enemy getting too close, this was the containment or interference required to keep a platoon of good men alive, or the bears out of the coolers.

I had to chuckle as I approached the nicely roaring fire. "Any movement out there?" I asked.

"Some rustling at the outer perimeter, but nothing more than a pair of red eyes in the night," Jim replied.

"Maybe a mule deer or mountain lion," I suggested.

"There was something else, too, but you wouldn't believe me if I told you," he responded as he began to unzip his tent.

"Oh? Why not?" I asked. The two of us had encountered many strange and dangerous situations.

"No. I'm sure I heard a wolf."

I saw that look on his face. "Really? They haven't been seen in this area in over a hundred years."

"Well, that's what I think I heard. There was something out there. Big. I couldn't get a clear view of it in the dark. Maybe a bear. Keep alert. I don't want anything getting into the food. Bill would never let that go," he said, tossing me the night vision goggles.

I nodded in agreement and began the short hike to the horses and Bill's tent. Bill was out like a light; the deep snoring from the shelter was evidence of it. I had to chuckle. The dogs were all lying around Bill's fire.

As I approached, they gathered around me briefly. A slight breeze picked up at the end of the valley, carrying a strange odor to the group of canines. An unspoken alert passed between them. I saw some of the dogs' hackles standing on end. There was something out there. A bear or a mountain lion would never risk its life with a pack of dogs this size unless on the brink of starvation. Because it was late spring, there were plenty of signs of wildlife. The starvation theory was abandoned. Someone or something was watching us; I was certain of that.

Wolves had made a remarkable comeback in the north of Wyoming, Idaho, and Montana. We had spent several weeks in Yellowstone, and the wolves there were plentiful. No wolves had made it this far south that I was aware of, at least not into the mountains of central Colorado. The last thing Jim mentioned was the feeling that something substantial and bear-like was moving in the night just beyond our vision.

These thoughts gave me flashbacks to my dad's stories about a creature he called The Midland Monster. Starting in the late 1800s, the Colorado Midland Railway once graced my property's southern border, where the county road now runs. Paired with the word monster, you can imagine the fear it instilled in me at a young age. I'm not a man who fears much, but the hair on my neck took notice and stood at attention. Are the stories Dad told true?

I thought back to the warning that the coroner had given. Joseph was part Ute, a tribe that lived in the 'Great Basin' area. Like other Native American tribes, the Utes are the keepers of ancient knowledge and secrets. Joseph was sincere in his belief.

My motto. You can never have enough dogs or guns, came to mind. I let out a nervous chuckle. I had fought in twenty countries. When you ran out of bullets, you pulled your standard-issue blade. After that weapon was gone, you fought bare-knuckled or, as Jim would have said, 'It's Marcus of Queensbury' time.

Some folks fear things that go bump in the night. This fear has them hiding under the covers. For men like Jim, Andy, and me, we were the things that go bump in the night. Getting my hair to stand up on the back of my neck is a whole different level of fear.

I returned to the central campfire and set aside my agitation about whatever local wildlife had placed the dogs on alert. Before finding three murdered men here, I might have envisioned a nice cabin here overlooking the meadow. I was unsure what to do with it at this point.

Rachel popped her head out of her tent, and I motioned for her to join me for a while. Around three a.m., we kissed and Rachel returned to her dreams. After thinking for a moment, I returned to the command tent. I woke Andy for his turn at guard duty. Exhausted, I sank into my cot for a well-earned rest.

At the sound of the first shot, I sat bolt upright!

My tiredness slipped like a blanket from my shoulders as adrenaline coursed through my veins. Thirty seconds later, I was out of the tent with my .45 in my right hand and carbine slung over my shoulder. I saw Bill running up the meadow towards us, clutching his shotgun. Did he sleep in those boots?

"What in the blue blazes is going on?" Bill shouted, slightly out of breath.

"Trouble, Bill." Andy nodded at Jim as he emerged from his tent. "Jim, do a perimeter sweep with RJ, while Bill and I ensure the horses are alright."

Another of Andy's shots pierced the night.

I placed a hand to my throat and asked over the comms, "Jim, how many hostiles?" For a moment, my mind flashed to the past, and a firefight on the edges of Fallujah.

I moved between the tents, then heard Jim squeeze off a round.

"Perimeter breaches at your ten and twelve o'clock," using his hands to signal. He had already dropped to one knee without missing a beat and acquired a new target. "Number of hostiles unknown, but there are more than three." Typical SEAL humor. "Friendly on your six."

Rachel had appeared with Gretchen and Becky in tow. "What's happening?"

"Could you be a sweetheart and shed some light on the subject?" I asked.

Rachel headed for one of the black cases with her initials on it.

I returned to Jim and told him he might want to remove the night vision goggles. "How many hostiles are we dealing with?" I asked again.

"Unknown. Do you want me to count the hostiles, or shoot them?" Jim responded again.

Usually, sarcasm was an accepted form of communication within the group, but my brain switched gears in the heat of the battle. I touched his shoulder and motioned him forward.

"Copy that, chief. Greenlight for enemy target acquisition. Fire at will. Anything that moves gets burnt!"

Andy had grabbed a flare gun from the open helicopter. The burst spread its eerie light over the meadow with a great whoosh.

The flash revealed a pack of several dozen wolves in the field at the far end, with additional wolves scattered around the outskirts approaching our camp. The instant the light showed the wolves, the dogs went wild, ringing the horses and mules in a protective formation with Bill at their center. I was sure Bill would die before he let one of his horses fall prey to the pack before him. Weapon fire from our group ceased as the flare's light died, but Andy sent another immediately after.

The massive booms of Bill's shotgun echoed in the night above the distinct sounds of the rifles. Bill got that shotgun for Christmas last year. He didn't like the modified weapon then, claiming he wanted his old standby, the double-barreled one. However, right now, six shots at a time seemed far better than two and reload!

Rachel was at one of her cases using a flashlight. She was a skilled archer, but it was far too dark to be accurate. She sat on a nearby log with her bow across her lap and pulled out a small case with the red danger logo. Removing her standard arrow tip, Rachel opened this new case to reveal a dozen oddly shaped, red-tipped broad heads. She carefully screwed one of the heads to a shaft and stood up.

"It won't be dark for long, babe. Enjoy the fireworks!" she said, grinning as she drew the bowstring back to her ear. I heard the distinct sound of the arrow's release, followed by Rachel roaring, "Gentlemen! Fire in the hole. Three, two, one!"

I had been drawn to Rachel for many reasons. For one, she was an actual redhead, a must for a Scottish-Irish lad like myself. Another attraction was her love of archery.

What happens when you combine a world-class archery competitor, a SEAL chief, and a mechanical engineer with too much time on his hands? I am glad you asked - explosive-tipped broadheads. Yes, you heard me: arrows that fly further and faster and explode on impact.

A moment later, at the far end of the meadow, the trees erupted in flames. I was still determining how we would extinguish the fire if it spread beyond the first few trees. No one in town would be able to see any fire with the saddle hills blocking the view. Because it was dark, no one would notice the smoke for several more hours. However, if detected, a plausible explanation for any smoke seen from my land could be a controlled burn. A quick phone call to the county sheriff's office would quell any questions from any townsfolk.

The whistle of another one of Rachel's red-tipped arrows added to the flare's light. It exploded in the middle of the large pack of wolves, several hundred yards from where Bill and the dogs protected the frightened livestock.

In that instant, chaos erupted within the wolf pack. They began to retreat to the relative safety of the trees. Few would make it as Jim, Andy, and I continued to reduce their numbers as they ran.

The crack of small arms fire sent another flash over the camp.

The unlikely couple of Allen and Gretchen faced a group of wolves attempting to infiltrate the field from the eastern edge. Allen produced his set of matching 1911 Kimber .45s. He may be the nerd of the group, but he could handle a weapon. He and Gretchen had gone around the back of the tent compound to cut off a smaller group of wolves who had worked their way in a bit too close for comfort.

When the wolves seemed ready to charge, Jim and I answered with a salvo of gunshots, calmly picking off the nearest targets while the rest turned tail and ran.

We looked to the far side of the meadow where the remaining wolves were withdrawing. I could see large, clearly defined red eyes in the deeper foliage. The eyes were above average height, between ten and twelve feet off the ground! I must be looking at something that had climbed into the trees. The other possibility was just too frightening to consider at the moment.

I shouldered my rifle again, put my green dot reticle firmly between a set of those eyes, and slowly began to squeeze the trigger. The target in my sights exploded, as Jim or Andy had sighted on the same goal. I found another grouping of red eyes and began to lay down fire.

It was then that I heard Rachel shout another warning.

After her shot, the mass of wolves and red eyes lit up the night; it was like adding gasoline to a bonfire. The dogs had remained with Bill, instinctively protecting each other and the livestock. Although several of the dogs would require some medical attention, they managed to keep predators at bay from the horses, mules, and Bill.

"I have never seen a wolf this size," the old cowboy mumbled.

It was true. While taking wildlife photos and traveling to different places, I had to agree that even the largest wolves I had seen didn't measure up to these monsters.

"Where in the world did these brutes come from?" Bill muttered.

Where in the world, indeed?

"Canis dirus guildayi!" Allen suggested putting a new magazine into each of the Kimber's.

Turning towards Allen, Andy said, "In English, please. My Latin is a little rusty."

"Dire wolves," Allen stated.

"What do you mean, dire wolves?" Andy asked. "Those things have been extinct for ten thousand years."

"How much do you think these things weigh? Two hundred to two-hundred-fifty?" Allen asked.

"Yes, sir, easily," Bill responded.

"Well, that's the size of the dire wolves that called North America their home."

"What do we have here, someone playing with DNA like in the movies? Alternatively, could this be some hybrid that got away from a breeder?" Jim asked.

"Too many for a breeder. A small group of men couldn't hope to control this many," Rachel added.

"Secret government program!" Bill declared as he pointed at Andy. We all had to chuckle at that. Bill was right. Andy was the closest thing our group had to a conspiracy theorist.

"I would have heard a rumor or run into an old colleague if this involved the government or a special program this close to my home," I responded. "Whatever they're doing here, they're trespassing."

"If they were part of a PSD, you would think we would find some human remains, but there are none," Jim replied. Seeing the questioning look on Allen's face, he continued. "Personal Security Detail or private government contractors. Where are the humans controlling the hybrid animals and this experiment? If Rachel hit a group of these things, then shouldn't we find some human bodies too?"

"Reset the perimeter. Since I own the land, it's well-marked. Let's make them regret a second incursion onto my property." I had to wonder. Everyone in the area knew who I was and what my capabilities were. Why take such a risk, operating on my land?

CHAPTER 8

The dawn crept in, pushing the night's blackness into the west. The wolves that had survived the battle had fled, leaving the dead in the meadow. Allen, Gretchen, and Becky took a closer look at the large, wolf-like corpses.

The sun advanced higher in the sky as Bill, Jim, Andy, and I headed to the meadow's far end. Crossing the stream, we found the dead remains of something much larger than the wolves. Thanks to Rachel's devastating shots, there wasn't much left but burnt fur and the body's charred trunk. We found no other survivors or bodies.

Now is an excellent time to answer thoughts bouncing around in your brain. Why all the firepower? First, we are on my property, rather than public land. No one was around to worry about the noise or what we did for recreation with that much land. Second, there is the military viewpoint. Always be prepared for anything!

In the military, this is the difference between survival and death. That difference usually goes to the one with the most guns and ammunition. Everything we had acquired came to us as payment for services rendered, as gifts from government leaders, or as purchases made legally. And sometimes, we disarmed the bad guys and kept their toys.

Let's return to the significant, stinky, charred remains before me. There was no longer a head or appendages, but the body's trunk alone could have weighed five hundred pounds. It appeared to be wearing a leather outfit, but it had been burnt beyond recognition.

Not what I expected.

If someone from my past were out to get me, they were doing a poor job. A commotion from the group pulled me from my train of thought. Jim had found a trail. The trail led away from the meadow along the stream. Large bodies had been dragged into the forest. Along this path were paw prints of a dozen or more wolves. The attackers moved the injured and carried away as many dead bodies as possible. The unrecognizable chunks of flesh left behind would not be enough to identify the responsible parties, but it was still possible to obtain DNA evidence.

We heard a commotion from where the horses were tethered, as we headed back across the stream. My male Great Pyrenees, Perry, and Rachel's Irish wolfhound, Athla, emerged, dragging a large black wolf from the brush. The other dogs quickly surrounded the two and their captive wolf. Bill was right there with them. Upon seeing that the wolf was still alive, he adjusted his shotgun. The wolf was severely wounded and made no effort to attack or escape.

Bill shouted towards us. "It's making some noise. I think it is trying to tell us something."

"Nonsense, animals can't talk! They mimic and learn, but certainly not speak," Allen retorted.

One of my dogs was an Alaskan husky named Tucker. His 'talking' often sounded almost like speech. He could say 'mama,' which delighted Rachel. I approached the wolf without fear, as the dogs would rip it to shreds if it attempted any harm. Several of our larger dogs weighed in at close to but no more than one hundred sixty pounds, but this beast had at least fifty to sixty pounds more than the largest of them.

I will not say I believed what I heard. Yet, I am sure it said something to me.

Bill turned to me. "What did it say?"

I regarded Bill. This old cowboy was great at telling tall tales that would raise the hair on the back of your neck. At this moment, he looked intense in the early light of day.

I returned that look with a stare of my own. "Bill, I think he told me to go back, or stay away."

A moment later, the wolf's body, racked with wounds, rattled off its last breath. Realizing it was no longer a threat, the dogs sniffed it and ran off to where Becky handed out treats while she examined each dog for signs of injury.

The scene seemed like something out of a Hollywood nightmare movie.

"Hey, I 'm still alive!" Andy quickly pointed out. After a moment or two, there was some nervous laughter. "You know the brother always dies first, then the pretty ladies!" He was right. More often than not, that is precisely how those movies began.

"Let's get some grub and figure out where we go from here," Bill concluded.

"Who wants to return to the lodge and pretend the last four hours didn't happen?" Allen responded with his right hand high in the air.

At breakfast, I asked for a show of hands. "I need a vote on going forward or going back." I knew no one wanted to go back and sit on the deck, forgetting that this night had happened. As a group, I couldn't remember ever giving up, let alone turning tail and running.

"The size of these wolves makes me worry about the welfare of local or out-of-state hunters, ranchers, and local wildlife. One of these could bring down an elk or horse. Think of what a pack could do to the town?" Gretchen stated.

"A pack this size could quickly destroy entire cattle herds, not to mention residents," Bill replied.

"We need to resolve this issue before such a nightmare moves from RJ's land to the town or local ranches, that is for sure," Jim agreed.

"Okay, Allen, Jim, and Bill stay at camp with the horses. The rest of us are going back for a few more items. I will make a few well-placed phone calls to try to get to the bottom of this," I said.

I still had some clout. Someone up to no good will regret their decision to operate so close to my home. What exactly had we gotten ourselves into this time?

Andy helped the three ladies into the helicopter. At the same time, I conferred with Bill and Jim about the additional items they expected us to need. After compiling a shortlist, I joined Andy in Betty's cockpit. He took us up and pointed us toward home.

As soon as we landed, I told Becky to find a couple of field first aid packs. Gretchen went to pack any additional things that she and Allen might want. Everyone packed extra clothing, food, ammunition, and small arms, and I saw Andy loading a few select black cases, nodding in agreement.

It's better to be safe than sorry.

Walking into my dad's office, I saw the many photos hanging on the walls. Some were from his family, but many more were from our time in the military. I stepped behind the ornate desk, moved the large painting above it to the side, and punched the code into the wall safe. I quickly found my black book. There were names — sometimes code words — and phone numbers of people who might help me uncover the truth behind this mystery.

I began with page one and dialed my first number. No luck.

A little later, as my frustration grew, so did the tone of my voice, accompanied by wild gestures. I saw Rachel walk by on her way to my room. This office was soundproof, yet I wondered what she thought. Irrational man with crazy gestures?

The further I progressed through the book, the less each person knew about what I was saying. My level of annoyance increased. Some people I called gave the typical "no unusual activity in your area" answer.

At the same time, they said they would look into it. A few claimed they would have to call me back, which implied they were doing something wrong, but I doubted they were stupid enough to pull this little stunt in my area.

One call was to an old friend, more of a father figure. I will only call him 'the Colonel.' He warned that there were already people talking about my phone calls. Some people even asked the government to revoke my clearance. One even requested that I have a complete psychiatric evaluation. I knew the Colonel could squash most of their requests, as I had just forwarded a picture of the one wolf beside my dogs. He assured me he knew of nothing 'going down' near my land, or even remotely close to what I had just reported. He asked me not to put my reputation at risk.

I assured the Colonel that I was just a little heated, as this looked like the work of a military or para-military research group.

Hanging up the phone, I sat in that comfy leather chair that Dad loved. My mind went to the beast with the red eyes that I briefly had in my sight. Had the tales Dad told me of the Midland Monster been more than just some story used to keep children in bed at night? I'm not saying that I am void of fear. I give it no place to take root.

Last night, I experienced emotions I hadn't felt for a long time. My mind drifted as I sank further into that chair: Somalia, Iraq,

Afghanistan, and some less-savory places than those rushed forward in my memories.

Occasionally, I had night sweats. I would wake from a realistic dream where I smelled gunpowder and saw the muzzle flashes. Those dreams may have been the one thing keeping me from moving forward in my relationship with Rachel.

I'm sure she has heard my screams from time to time in the dark of the night, and those nights usually ended up the same. If she were at the main lodge, we would end up watching some chick flick or a comedy in front of the television. If alone, I would sit with a rifle across my lap in front of the fireplace, surrounded by the dogs.

Yes, I had been to plenty of doctors whose cures ranged from 'take a vacation' to 'go over to the pharmacy and get this filled.' I enjoyed the vacations, but lived in a house as exceptional as any resort. Why leave all the comforts of home searching for peace? Mostly, I spent my time with people whom I loved. The days filled with joy and laughter far outweighed the occasional moments of loneliness.

I must have napped and woken as Rachel entered the room. I jumped to replace the picture and put it over the wall safe.

"Did you know, I knew that safe was there?" She giggled.

"Really? Since when?"

"I caught your dad sleeping like you with the thing wide open."

"What did Dad say?"

"He waved me to the desk and pulled a little box out. That same one right there," Rachel said, pointing.

I knew instantly what my dad had shown her: my mother's engagement ring. He had not buried it with Mom.

I asked Rachel to help Becky move the remaining items to where Andy waited. When she had left, I pushed the chair back under the desk. I removed the ring box from the safe and put it into my vest pocket. I securely closed the wall safe, sliding the painting back into place to conceal its existence. I glanced over the office and walked out, closing the French doors.

When I arrived, Andy loaded the last additional bags and cases into the helicopter. Included were boxes of MREs ('meals ready to eat,' add hot or cold water), ammo and weapons containers, a silver crate that looked like something Allen had requested, and packs with extra clothing and bedding.

Arriving at camp, I noticed that the guys had built large stacks of wood further into the field. These piles would be set on fire tonight, allowing us to view more of the meadow in the dead of night. Jim had jury-rigged some flares beyond the campfires that would launch if a tripwire was released.

Andy took the opportunity to place a warning at the trailhead where the path entered the woods by the creek. It was the wolf's skin and head that the dogs had captured. If anything came creeping out of the woods tonight, the impaled body of the wolf would be the first thing to greet them.

I appreciated the gesture. It was tribal.

CHAPTER 9

That evening, the campfire discussion centered on our next move: tracking these beasts down and eliminating any immediate threat. We knew how to follow them. The question was whether to split up to cover more terrain or stay together.

"Should Andy take the chopper up for a better idea of the surrounding area?" Rachel asked.

Andy turned towards her. "I don't need to do that. From yesterday, I can tell you that the stream disappears into this forest and continues for several miles until the tree canopy makes it nearly impossible to track from the air. I can say with certainty that it heads toward that rugged outcropping you can see poking up through the canopy. I am guessing that's where the mine itself is located."

Bill nodded, "Perhaps they're using the mine as an underground facility?"

Jim had been silently cleaning one of his guns and looked up. "Surely they would have known that messing with land near RJ would be a mistake. Let alone right next door?"

I had to agree with Jim. Many people knew where I lived, whether they had attended my Christmas or New Year's parties or had been invited out for some much-needed rest by my father.

"A bad choice indeed on their part. Now, how do we guarantee they pay for this intrusion?"

Allen looked up from his laptop; his fingers continued to work the keys. "Not a good idea to split up. The current numbers based on our firepower and their lack of firepower show that splitting up would help us cover more ground, however..."

Bill placed a hand on Allen's shoulder, then interrupted. "Allen, we all agree your brain is far too valuable to be eaten by dire wolves. We stick together since we do not know what the next wave of these things might have for weapons."

"I agree with Allen. We need to stick together, all the firepower in one place," Jim said, nodding.

"Andy, what about the chopper? Should we attempt to return it to the lodge for safekeeping?" I asked.

"Not going to worry about it. We can put a tarp over Betty before we leave. How long could we be gone?" Andy stated.

"Guess you're right. We won't be gone more than a couple of days," I replied.

After a quick breakfast, everyone helped Andy cover Betty to keep her out of the weather. With Jim and Becky taking point while Bill and Allen brought up the rear with the mules, we set out to locate the mine.

"Lock and load. We could be riding right into an ambush." Jim yelled back once we were all mounted and moving. "Keep your eyes peeled for anything unusual."

We urged our horses forward. I was side by side with Rachel while Andy brought up the rear, beside Gretchen. "I am taking a look ahead with the dogs. Set your comms to channel three," Jim stated.

The meadow narrowed as we entered the wooded area. The location was lush and green, unlike the scrub oaks and pinon pines that covered most of my land. The water was clear, with little deep pools. The forest trail began to disappear, pushing us to follow in the stream. It was then that I noticed the bottom of the stream.

"Are either of you seeing this?" I asked Rachel and Andy.

"What exactly should we be seeing?" Rachel asked.

"He's talking about the water," Andy stated with more than a hint of sarcasm. "It does seem wetter here than a little further back."

"Sarge, you know full well that is not what I am pointing out," I said. Two could play this game.

"What then?" Rachel asked.

"The streambed has been unnaturally smooth since we started," Andy countered.

"Oh, like an ancient roadway now covered in water?" Rachel added.

All I could do was shake my head and mutter a few things. I chuckled out loud for their sake. The streambed appeared paved as if someone had taken great care to lay out this ancient roadway. Had I watched too much of the National Geographic channel or one of those alien shows?

Turning to catch Andy's eye, I gave him the 'keep the game going' look. I remarked, "Very Roman in appearance!"

Allen glared at me and gave me his 'nice try, genius' look. It was all Andy and Rachel could do not to laugh out loud. "Not very Roman at all, in my humble opinion." Allen launched into the start of a long-winded lecture. There was seldom anything humble about his opinion.

"Oh?" Andy had to add for good measure.

"Yes, I would think much older than Roman times," Allen continued.

"Made by whom and to what purpose?" Andy asked. I was curious if Allen was playing the game or a pawn. It was hard to say until the last person had the final word.

"My guess would be Aztec or Mayan." Allen had begun the sentence in a normal tone but blasted the last part. "Because this spot right here is at least four thousand four hundred miles to the nearest Roman outpost!" He was flustered, pawn indeed.

Gretchen gestured at Andy, giving him the 'I'm watching you' look.

Andy realized he had to fix this, as it may have gone too far. "Allen, is there any proof that either of those civilizations made it this far north, or could it have been something else entirely?" He asked sincerely.

"You had better mark it on your calendars. I don't like to admit that I do not know who may have done this or why. Perhaps the Anasazi or Hohokam people, or maybe something much older, are responsible for the road? Right now, there are more riddles than answers," Allen responded, looking at me over his glasses.

"Okay, folks, let's stick to the task. Let's try to catch up with Jim. We haven't seen or heard him or the dogs for a while now." Bill, as always, was the voice of reason.

I rode on, glancing at the well-worn path and the waters that flowed over those ancient stones. The Native Americans didn't have the tools or knowledge to accomplish this work without an outside force.

Occasionally, we would see the broken body of one of the wolves tossed up onto the stream's banks. They were those wounded enough to be carried off the battlefield but had not survived the journey.

I recall the tingle going down my spine when I had those red eyes in my crosshairs - the eyes of a monster. I frequently dealt with wickedness. It was a mandate to stamp it out wherever it was. Many in our group had sworn oaths against any evil, foreign or domestic. It was in our job description and expected.

The darkness we felt when a man used a child or a woman as a shield against us. And when we saw an enemy leader in the heat of battle, we knew that killing him might save hundreds or thousands of lives.

This malice was the kind that sent chills down your spine and made the hair on the back of your neck stand up. This kind of wickedness casts doubt on all your training and vast knowledge. This evil made grown men clutch the cross around their necks or pray to God in their greatest despair. This malice caused men with my years of training to think back and wonder, "Did I pack enough ammo?"

Much of the Colorado terrain was harsh and arid. People fought over life-giving water. Running water meant a chance for green and the possibility of more than the usual number of trees. In this case, the stream bordered the green meadow and the many trees that lined its banks. It was an oasis in the dry, rugged wasteland.

The creek continued to narrow. Or perhaps the forest pressed in on us from above and on either side?

The trees were thick with shrubs and undergrowth. The further we progressed, the more concerned I became. In the case of an ambush, getting out of the stream and into the forest was becoming more complex. The current was slight, allowing four horses to walk abreast if needed. The flow seemed to lie in a mostly straight line, with an occasional bend in the road, as it were. The forest canopy was so entangled and twisted onto itself that it nearly blocked the afternoon sun. In the Colorado heat, the shade was a blessing.

We rode on in silent vigilance. At any moment, Jim and the dogs could come thundering back with the enemy in hot pursuit. It was getting late. We had just eaten our lunches in the saddle when we heard the dogs in the distance. We saw Jim and the dogs moving back upstream toward us several minutes later.

Although not being followed, he was excited about something. "Ahead of us, where the tree cover opens up a bit, there is a mine entrance where the streambed forms a small island."

CHAPTER 10

"Can we camp on the island?" Bill asked.

"Yes. The island is not large, but it is easily defended, with a small grove of trees in the center. The end closest to us has a small sandy beach," Jim stated.

"Let's get there and set up a camp before we lose daylight," I added, urging my horse forward.

Rachel and I went to the island's side to see the mine entrance. Someone had built a crude wooden storage building on the left of the opening. The mouth here was nearly twenty-five feet high by roughly fifty feet across. The storage shed was decent and held many relatively new tools. A modern-looking sluice was on the banks of the stream. On the right were some narrow-gauge railway tracks. It looked like they had expected a substantial amount of ore would come out of the mine.

We headed back to the island when we caught the scent of what Bill was cooking. The mules and horses had been unloaded and fed. Now, it was our turn. Looking at the weather on his laptop, Allen had concluded that there was no chance of rain. Since the small island would not allow the erection of a whole camp, 'under the stars' would be the best course of action for this evening.

Bill, as always, was ready with plenty of food. A hearty stew, sourdough bread, hot coffee, and goodies were on the menu.

"RJ, Andy, and I have a perimeter established, but I haven't seen any recent signs of those red-eyed beasts or the wolves." Jim started after most of us had finished our meals.

"Thank you. It feels peaceful here. If those creatures have moved on, we should get a good night's sleep. If not, we are in a good defensive spot. We can fall back into the mine should things go badly to defend from the point of strength," I added.

"Any signs of where they went?" Rachel asked.

"The area here has been pretty trampled. We will know better in the morning light," Andy answered.

We drew straws in pairs for watch duty. The rest of them crawled into their sleeping bags while Rachel and I took positions at the island's north and south ends. Thankfully, the night was uneventful.

We woke up refreshed to the tempting smells that wafted through the camp. Bill's breakfasts were not for the faint of heart. The calorie content was extreme, but it was worth it as long as you were active. I thanked Bill as he added more bacon pieces to my plate.

"You have to keep your energy levels up!" Bill nodded as he moved around the fire, refilling coffee cups and plates before eating his own meal.

"I appreciate your concern," I replied, slapping Andy's hand from procuring any of my bacon.

Everyone had a good laugh as we finished our meals. Gretchen and Allen grabbed everyone's dirty dishes and headed to the water to clean them. Bill was a stickler for sanitation. After being rinsed off in the stream, the dishes were submerged in a pot of boiling water to complete the cleaning.

We began the morning by setting up a series of search grids to determine which direction the enemy had fled.

"Listen up. We will split up into teams of two with search grids. You know what to do if you see signs of the enemy. Rendezvous back here in two hours." I said a quick group prayer for safety before we moved out.

Rachel and I began with the grid closest to the mine opening. It was a moderately steep slope. Once we reached the top of this low-lying ridge, we realized no one would have chosen this direction to move wounded troops. We climbed a couple of trees from this spot and could see the meadow and the several miles of the forest we had crossed in the far distance. We climbed back down and decided to enter the mine.

Bill was tending to the horses and mules when we stopped by the camp to refill our canteens. He remarked that the comms had been extremely quiet, so I told him I would check in on everyone.

"This is Sapper One, calling all prospectors. Any gold found? Over."

Rachel smiled, suppressing a laugh. She loved how we never seemed to make sense to anyone but ourselves. The response was a resounding "no joy" from every comm.

"RTB, over," I finished, calling the group to return to base.

Since they were all on foot and would take about an hour to return, Bill said he would join us for our second look at the mine.

"Looks to me like they had everything they needed to get started," Bill called out from the pile of narrow-gauge rails.

The three of us grabbed lanterns from the mine's storage shed and began to explore.

Rachel called from inside the mine, "They started to lay track. There are several new mine carts still in crates here."

"How far do the tracks go?" I yelled out to her as I walked towards her light, with Bill following.

"It narrows some further on, but it seems to keep going quite a ways," Rachel responded as we approached.

It was then that we found carcasses of several more wolves.

"These wolves didn't die from the fight with us," Rachel said, pulling an arrow out of one.

"Those are arrows, yes? You did fire a few the other night." Bill stated, trying to shine more light on the area.

"Bill, these are wooden arrows with bronze tips. I haven't used a wooden arrow since I was a girl." Rachel answered, showing Bill and I the crude projectile.

"Wonder what happened here?" I asked, staring down into the darkness.

We were jolted out of our contemplation by the sound of barking dogs.

"The others must be back. Let's get a bite to eat. Then we will come back here with a few more eyes." I suggested.

We all welcomed the chance to eat. Bill had been busy fishing while the rest of us were searching. He was building up the coals. The smell of fresh corn on the cob and grilled trout filled the campsite.

"Bill, you never let us down with your meals. We might starve without you on these adventures." Andy toasted Bill with his coffee cup.

"Yes, thank you, Bill. If left to Andy's cooking, the question wouldn't be if we starved, but when we would starve," Allen added.

"I admit that everyone would get tired of canned baked beans and hot dog pieces pretty quickly," Andy said with a laugh.

"Okay, when we have everything cleaned up from lunch, we will take what remains of the day and rest or explore as you feel. We found a couple of dead wolves inside the mine and some railroad tracks they had laid. If anyone wants to join us," I announced.

Allen and Gretchen went with Bill to catch more freshwater trout so they could watch the nearby livestock. The rest of us grabbed lanterns and walked back to the area in the cave where we had found the dead wolves.

"Certainly not the work of Red over here. These are not composite arrows," Jim stated. Red was what they sometimes called Rachel because of her hair color.

"Nope. Not me, that's for sure," Rachel agreed.

We continued moving farther back into the narrowing mine shaft. We were several hundred yards into the tunnel, following the track as we went.

"This is more like a cave system than a mine tunnel," Becky announced. She and Jim were the resident spelunkers. I was sure she was right about that.

Jim nodded his agreement. "The cave must have first been discovered, explored, and then mined later."

A bit further on, we found a large natural cavern with wall paintings. What story did they tell? Rachel took some pictures. In one corner, there was a vertical shaft carved out of the dense rock. An imposing iron pike protruded from the stone; the remains of an attached rope dangled into the dark void below.

"I think they did this to allow the stale air from the mine to escape," Andy proudly stated.

He had been paying attention when my father had taken us into one of the mines on our property. It was nearly ten years ago that I last stood in an ore mine.

"Glad you were paying attention." I said, "What was the rope for?"

"I suppose to climb back out?" Andy replied.

"Maybe, but I don't recall reading about or seeing a rope in an air shaft," I stated. I had no answer for the rope.

"Any volunteers to go down the rope to see where it goes?" Becky asked.

"I'm game," Jim said.

"Ah, I wouldn't worry about that. If this hole is simply a shaft for fresh air, we'll see the end somewhere ahead once we start our descent into the mine," I said.

"No bracing timbers needed here. This cave is all naturally occurring," Becky observed..

CHAPTER 11

The passageway narrowed, continued for maybe fifty feet, and opened into another cavern. This time, there came a gasp from Jim, who had taken the lead. Jim was not easily surprised, so the question was, what was ahead?

Gasps also came from Rachel. "RJ, you need to see this!"

A massive lion's head appeared carved in the stone of the cavern's far wall. It stood thirty feet high. On its forehead was a triangle with some odd markings. My first thought was, "What the heck?"

Andy voiced what I thought as he walked up to stand beside me.

"What in the world! RJ, is this a joke you're playing on us?" Jim asked, to which I heard some agreement from the rest of the group.

Now, I am the practical joker. It is true.

"Oh, come on, guys. Really? You see this, and the first thought that comes to mind is that I have created some elaborate murder mystery for all of us to participate in?" I pointed at the carving in the solid stone, "On top of that, I somehow managed three real human corpses and a bunch of live dire wolves?"

Rachel was looking at me. I shook my head, "Hey guys, I don't think RJ had anything to do with this."

I nodded, "I would love to have thought this up, folks! In my defense, don't you think I would have insisted that all of us be here for this astounding revelation? There is also the matter of the dire wolves." How strange that Jim's first thought would be that I was playing a joke. Perhaps because any other explanation would have been even more bizarre?

"There are carved figures on the stone?" Becky asked.

"Of course, there is. Allen is outside, and we need an expert here. I have no idea why this is here or what it means. You rest while I grab everyone else." I had to be the one to tell Allen.

"I'll come with you." Jim turned and started back the way we had come.

I quickly caught up to him when he stopped, just out of view and hearing of the group. Placing his hand on my shoulder, he looked me eye to eye and laughed. "This has to be the best stunt you have ever pulled on us!"

With my hand on his shoulder, I stared right back at him. "This, my friend, is not some gag. I have never been to this place or even the meadow until just a few days ago. I did not carve that massive stone image in that cavern, or ask anyone else to put it there. Let's go! We need Allen and the rest of the team."

Jim watched me with a doubtful expression, as if waiting for a punch line.

"I'm sorry, my friend, but I am not the one who put this here. This is a major feat of engineering, and I don't even have vehicle access to this location. And explain the strange creatures and the dire wolves! Even I don't have those kinds of resources," I insisted.

I pulled my pocket-sized New Testament from one of the many compartments in my cargo pants and held it out to him.

"I swear on this book and my father's grave that I have nothing to do with this."

Seeing the seriousness in my eyes, he merely nodded. We moved at double time in the direction of the mine entrance.

Arriving at the entrance, we saw Bill, Gretchen, and Allen leading the pack of mules and horses toward us.

"Don't look so surprised. Rachel told us over comms what was going on." Bill responded with a wave. "Luckily, we've caught plenty of fish for tonight's meal. I had already started loading the supplies when we got the call."

Allen passed me and pulled Jim aside. There was a brief conversation about whether I had brought them on some great practical joke. Then Allen started running for the cavern entrance, throwing his laptop bag over his left shoulder.

We lead the horses and pack animals into the mine. "Bill, are you sure we should bring the animals in here?" I asked.

The old cowboy just smiled and nodded, "They'll be fine. Yes, I think we will need them with us."

That was all I needed to hear. I took the lead horse and urged it into the mine.

"Wow!" was about all anyone could muster.

Finally, Bill spoke. "Looks like writing on the lion's forehead."

"You are correct, my bearded friend," Allen replied. "That is a Tetragrammaton."

Andy, of course, said what we were all thinking. "A what?"

Allen was never tired of sharing his great wisdom. "A Tetragrammaton is a word consisting of four letters."

"Thank you, professor, but what does it say?" Rachel remarked.

"Well, let me see. The first letter in English would be Y, then H, followed by W, with another H."

"That spells YHWH in Hebrew," Gretchen added.

"Do the symbols on the forehead spell the ancient Hebrew word for 'God'?"

"Yes."

The powerful beam of my tactical flashlight now illuminated a doorway chiseled into the mouth of the lion. The carved teeth of the great cat's mouth were realistic and sharp from the look of pain on Andy's face. Along the door frame were eight inscribed lines, each enclosed in a decorative carved outline.

Allen pushed his way to the front. "More illumination! Less talking!"

The lion's mouth now clutched Allen and his equipment. Allen gave each girl a drawing on a sheet of paper. They headed back to the mine mouth to do an internet search.

Becky arrived and passed Allen her cell phone with another character on it. Allen jumped up and headed back toward us. The light from Bill's lantern revealed the first carved words.

Allen's eyes grew wide with excitement, which was far from his usual demeanor, especially for a guy who claimed to know 'everything'.

Allen smacked me on the back and quietly said, "I know it is not you playing a joke. You should have found smarter people to help you with this puzzle. You also would have had to start this joke 20 years ago, to carve all this."

He winked at me and pulled Bill's lantern closer to illuminate the next row of words. "Tell the girls I need pictures of each of the runes in this line."

Jim waved me over to the entrance of the cavern. "I told him this was not a joke, but he wouldn't believe me. He thinks that the faster he gets the answer to this riddle, the faster we return to the lodge."

I knew that these adventures were different from Allen's favorite pastimes. To continue believing this was a practical joke after Jim told him I had nothing to do with it was par for Allen's immediate reaction.

"We'll leave him to his task. Maybe he'll figure out something from all this," I reassured Jim.

Around four hours later, Allen completed a three-dimensional rendering of the cavern, the lion, the doorway, and its carved writings. He jumped up and announced, "I don't have a signal here. I need to run back to the surface."

"What are hieroglyphics telling you?"

"Runes," Allen said. "I need to access my database. Did it get packed, or is it still at the lodge?"

"You mean the mini-RES server?" Gretchen asked, "I packed that for you. Third mule, top black container, marked 'fragile,' the second compartment."

Allen seemed shocked. "You packed it for a horse ride?"

Gretchen smiled and nodded. "Yes, I did. I knew you would get bored or something."

Like a kid in a candy store, Allen pulled the small protective container from the pack with Bill's help. The algorithm sorted through both symbols and pictorial archives. When the computer matched a file to information on the server, the symbol's depiction would turn neon green. Looking up from his notebook, he smiled at Gretchen. "Thanks for bringing this. What made you think of packing it?"

She smiled. "I just knew you might need something off it. I didn't want you pouting the whole trip."

"Thank you, my love," Allen replied. Once more, he gazed into the laptop screen.

Gretchen arrived to look at the arches as more items began to match between the identifier software and the pictures we had taken. I had to ask, "Every bit of knowledge in the world is on that one piece of equipment?"

She laughed and shook her head. "No, RJ, that would take many more servers than we have."

"How many of those would it take?" I asked.

Bill showed no interest in her answer.

"Well, at his office, he has six twenty TB servers," Gretchen replied. She lived in Allen's world, while I did not.

Bill had already wandered off.

"Okay. I have one TB of memory on my laptop. It says I still have almost ninety-nine percent capacity. What in the world is Allen doing that needs one hundred twenty TB?" I asked.

Gretchen smiled at me, "That is classified, RJ!"

I laughed. Everyone looked at me for a moment to see what was so funny. I just waved for the girls to keep working on the project. I was usually the one pulling the 'sorry, that is classified' card.

I had to ask. "Does Allen have one of those compact servers he keeps with him when he travels?"

"One?" Gretchen laughed into her hand so as not to draw attention again. "No, he has three for travel."

"But you only packed this one?" I already knew the answer. However, I must press on, having started down that road.

"No, I staggered them among the mules. Never keep them on the same side or all on the same mule in case something tragic occurs," Gretchen stated.

"How did you know which mule had what server?" I asked.

"Inventory. The inventory list is photocopied and stored in waterproof and fireproof cylinders. Finally, we hide the cylinders in fewer than eight locations during any given trip."

She had that glimmer in her eyes that said I was about to be stunned by what she said next. "You know that little silver canister Allen gave you with strike-anywhere matches?"

I knew the item she was talking about and pulled it from my pack. She unscrewed the lid of the container. Inside, there was a bundle of matches. She fished for an item at the bottom of the canister, pulling out a micro-SD card.

"He must have put that in there the first night in the meadow. Remember when he asked you for a match? You tossed this to him," she explained. "Thank you for being his friend. Most people don't understand him. Fewer even attempt it."

Instantly, I felt ashamed. I had raised my voice not long ago when I found that Rachel had invited this couple to another Christmas party. Rachel had told me I could at least stand him for one weekend a year, so she could see her friend.

 It had taken several years for my attitude to change and for me to involve him in more of the adventures the guys were having. Our relationship had evolved. I knew that if anyone in the group could answer the question of what we had just found, it was Allen, his computer, or a combination of the two.

We were all startled when the laptop made a musical sound. Allen jumped up again, shouting, "Eureka!"

What did Allen's algorithm have to say?

Rachel was the first of us to regain our composure. "What have you discovered?"

CHAPTER 12

Allen took a deep breath and began. "I have found ancient symbols and glyphs from the Hallstatt, Scandia, Kemet, and Indus peoples. The oldest I've seen are those from Mesopotamia. Our friend, RJ, did not create a hoax. The research required to pull this off would have been astounding. We are examining a five-thousand-year-old, or possibly a six-thousand-year-old, carving. Maybe even older."

"As I suspected, the writings seem to name specific locations and warnings. I can't ascertain whether the warnings are original or newer additions. Some appear to be much less timeworn than others."

Before anyone could ask a question, he gulped air and continued. "This is a list of locations; none are here on Earth." He mentally stumbled to regain his train of thought and began again. "Not on Earth, this Earth."

"Wait. So, nothing in any of these writings coordinates with any location on Earth?" Gretchen asked.

Then Jim asked what we were all thinking. "If it doesn't state any Earthly locations, then where do these locations exist?"

Allen buried his head in his laptop again, raising his hand in a gesture for silence. "Give me a moment, please!"

We all stared at each other in grim silence for several minutes. Allen moved back inside the lion's mouth. Kneeling, he reached out to steady himself while his other hand held his laptop. At first, it seemed like he was muttering under his breath. But then we realized he was brushing away sandy dirt from the base of the mouth, revealing another series of larger, tablet-like stones.

"This one looks like Sumerian. I am certain this one is Egyptian. I don't know either one. Is this one in Sanskrit? This one is Greek. This one, I am certain, is Chinese. We have already identified this one as ancient Hebrew."

Becky leaned in since her hobby was languages. "Oh, wow! This one is Akkadian. I believe the rarest one yet, is Tamil."

"Okay, that gives us eight languages. Now we have to figure out what it says." Allen paused. "Do they all say the same thing? Maybe it's a warning!"

Bill said, "Wait, I didn't graduate from college with some fancy degree, but I am pretty sure that none of those cultural groups ended up in Colorado."

Becky nodded. "Bill, you are right, but we are talking about thousands of years. If you consider the Tower of Babel, when there was no longer a 'common tongue'. We just haven't found records of it. May not predate Noah, but it comes close to it."

"You just have to figure out what they say?" Jim asked. He should have known Becky already had the answer to that question.

"Looks like 'stay.' No, 'walk'! *Walk in the paths or ways of the Maker*. Since it says that in at least three of them, I can only assume without checking that it means the same thing in each language."

Everyone here believed in God, but what were these symbols trying to tell us?

"Do we continue or turn this over to the government? I, for one, don't relish the military digging up my mountain or using whatever we have found for some evil purpose." I was saying what everyone had been thinking.

"If we're going to move forward, how would we?" Bill asked.

"I could try this algorithm. It takes each symbol, pulls facts about it, and then the voice synthesizer produces an audio for each line. I should test on the words we know."

Allen looked at Becky. "What language do we know the best? I need pronunciation for the algorithm to work."

"Hebrew, without a doubt. That is what I would try first. What are we expecting to happen?" Becky asked.

"Want to know what I think this is?" Allen scratched his head.

I thought, "Here we go again," but Andy was already ahead of me. "Are we going to get sucked into a black hole and taken somewhere else?"

"No, Andy!" Allen was shaking his head. "Once again, let me tell you that a black hole kills you. A wormhole transports you to another place in the universe."

"I thought a wormhole was what you found in a nice red apple?" Andy said, trying to keep up the banter.

Allen had had enough, ignoring Andy. He was busy putting the Hebrew runes into the computer for the first of the eight lines. "This is the ancient Hebrew word for God. YHWH."

As the speakers on the laptop began to "audible" each character, a bluish glow spread across the rune borders on the carving.

Suddenly, snow poured through the opening where the doorway's solid stone lion's mouth had been!

Chill filled the cavern.

Gretchen yelled, "Shut it, Allen!"

There must have been a timing device within the doorway. When no one entered it, the gateway closed.

"I didn't pack for a visit to an ice planet," Bill exclaimed.

"None of us has," Jim added sarcastically. "Find us one with sun and palm trees!"

"I can try a different line," Allen replied.

"Will there be sand and palm trees?" Andy asked.

Gretchen glared at Andy. "You know that we have no idea where these places are."

"Doesn't it tell you the name of the location? Shouldn't there be something to identify the place in the words?"

"Let me run some of the words and see what I can find," Allen offered.

A few moments later, he and Becky agreed that one of the lines contained the word 'plains'. They looked at me.

I shrugged my shoulders. "Give it a try!"

Allen carefully typed in the line of runes. We waited for the laptop to be audible. Once more, the runes began to glow. When the last rune was blue, the doorway opened. We could see the blue sky beyond the dense green vegetation. No one went through, so the door closed once more.

"That one doesn't seem so bad. It says something about an old house hidden from the plain."

"No, not a house. I think that is a city," Becky suggested.

"Folks, it's time to make a decision. Do we go through the portal, or go home?" I asked the group.

"Can Allen guarantee we can return here once we go through?" Bill asked.

Allen looked pretty confident. "Ninety-nine percent sure. I will take snapshots of all the locations, and below the last line is what appears to be our location. Adamah."

Allen was the first to raise his hand. What did he have to fear with the rest of us gun-toting teammates? Rachel's hand just narrowly beat out Andy's. Only mine remained at my side.

"Okay, you have a go."

Allen looked at me until Andy said, "That is military for, let's do this!"

"Oh, of course." Allen began retyping the last address back into the computer.

I took a piece of paper from my backpack and wrote a few words, including our chosen location. I then signed my name and included the party's names, should we fail to return. I felt a twinge of adrenaline course through my body. I could never live with myself if anything were to happen to anyone, especially Rachel.

I had been in love with Rachel since Jim and Becky had intervened. It had taken a long time to acknowledge my love for Rachel to anyone else and a bit longer to say it to her. The first time wasn't the way it should have happened. I blurted it out one night over dinner, surprising my dad, Rachel, and myself.

Never awkward around the fairer sex, I thought I was protecting them from my world. Another factor that kept me from taking a woman seriously was my commitment to my country and the military. I was married to the Army for many years. From my viewpoint, a military career may not be ideal for marriage. Not only did you face the danger of a spouse returning wounded physically or mentally, but the possibility was there that they might not return at all.

Some found themselves committing adultery or filing for divorce. On the other hand, some faced struggles hand in hand, holding tight to what they knew would carry them past every hurdle. Love.

Today was not the first adventure that had led us into grave danger, nor would it be the last. It was, however, the most interesting of all so far.

The next second, I heard myself saying, "Let's see where this takes us. If it's too dangerous, Allen can get us back to this point."

I began waving each group member forward through the door, leading their horses, followed by the dogs, Bill, and the mules. Only Betty was left behind.

The last one was Allen. When he approached the doorway, he turned and snapped a picture of the rune above the tunnel opening.

"I nearly failed to take a photo of the only symbol that will get us back home." His laugh was nervous as I turned to allow him through.

The doorway pulsed and closed behind us.

CHAPTER 13

The forest we saw as we entered the doorway disappeared on the other side. We entered a very similar cavern to the one we had just left. Turning around, we found the familiar large image of a carved lion with lines of runes.

"All these lines of runes are different except the one that says Adamah. Also, there is another word here. If we don't like what we see ahead, we return here and say we want to get to Adamah. I assume it will take us back from whence we came," Allen explained.

"What do you think the word behind Adamah means?" Jim asked.

Becky answered this question. "If there are other locations on Earth or Adamah, the second word might pinpoint the location on Earth."

"That makes sense," Allen added.

"Is everyone okay?" I asked as we all moved into the new cavern.

"I hope there is a sun beyond this doorway because I desperately need to recharge my laptop and server," Allen replied, heading for the doorway.

Andy stopped him in mid-stride. "Jim and I are going to take a look. If there are hostiles in the area, this may be the safest spot for everyone."

I nodded my agreement. We all sat down to wait. Rachel began passing out some beef jerky to the humans, which excited the dogs. Bill found his puppy treats bag, and they soon joined him, sitting patiently as each got their good-behavior reward.

It wasn't long before we heard Jim and Andy returning.

"Well?" I asked.

"There are human tracks and horse hoof prints in the dust: no giant paw prints or anything out of the ordinary. No sign of the beasts we're tracking. No one has been through here in a very long time," Jim answered.

"No sign of wolves, just footprints?"

"The wolves and their handlers must have taken one of the other doorways, is my guess," Jim pointed out.

"By the slant of the sun, I think we've got about two hours until sunset. The air is cool; there is a brook-fed pool to water the horses and a lush blanket of grass to sleep on," Andy added.

We began to move toward the sunlight. We could see further down the passage. Allen immediately had to find his small portable solar panels, hook up his laptop, and set up his server.

When we emerged from the cavern, Andy helped Bill water and feed the horses and mules. We decided it wasn't worth the effort to unpack the tents. Another night under the stars was acceptable as no rain clouds were in sight. Rachel and I found the black cases holding Bill's cooking gear. We gathered enough firewood to start supper.

While the others continued to prepare the camp and supper, Rachel and I explored the surrounding area. We discovered a small path leading out to what appeared to be an overlook at the tree line. The main trail split off and wound down the mountainside, while the other trail led to a crude stone stairway out to the overlook. Once there, the view was incredible. Below, a valley stretched to a mountain range that made the one we stood on look like a small hill.

Almost immediately, I heard the dinner call over the comm. It hadn't seemed that long since we began our walk. Holding Rachel, looking out upon this new place, I stole a quick kiss. We headed back to camp.

Sitting down to enjoy the grilled fish and the last corn on the cob, everyone had some theory about what was happening to us.

Allen disputed the 'journey to the center of the Earth' theory. The multitude of stars shimmered overhead. "If we are somewhere on Earth, one of us would recognize the constellations above, yes?"

Shockingly, his calculations showed we were no longer on the third planet in the solar system.

Jim took one last swing at a theory. "Did we go forward or backward in time? Is time here slower or faster than on Earth?"

"I don't know the answer to that question," Allen said, squeezing Gretchen's hand. This was an admission we seldom heard from Allen. "But I can walk back into that cave and press one button. Then we can walk through the lion door back to Earth and Colorado, of that I am certain."

"You will need to map the new Lion's Gate. I suggest we leave a traceable marker that Allen can find with the laptop should we get lost and need to return here promptly," I cautioned.

"Copy that." Jim went to his pack, pulled out a watch, fiddled with it for a moment, and then started up the tallest tree in the grove.

"What's he doing now?" Allen asked.

"He's attaching a Garmin watch at the highest point on this hill. Jim will then feed you some information. You can use the

'TracBack' software to create a map and up to 1,000 waypoints. It won't provide a chart, but it will bring you back to each point with pinpoint accuracy. Allen, I know you can make a detailed map on the laptop. The software allows us to coordinate where we use the stars despite the foreign land and sky."

I had great confidence in Allen's computer skills.

"How many of these watches do we have?" Rachel asked, knowing that the fewer watches we had, the smaller the exploration radius.

"I own three. I am sure that was not Jim's only watch. We have enough to build a good-sized MGRS. Remember, the most important watch is in the tree above us," Andy answered.

"I'll need most of the night to work the stars into the equation. Tomorrow, I can add the geographic features. I can find this spot wherever we are by downloading the software from one of the watches," Allen said with confidence.

"I suggest that we set up sentry duty and get some sleep." I had no idea what creatures roamed the nights here.

Thank you, God. Our first night was peaceful.

The following day was mostly uneventful as we primarily rested and talked. We gathered more firewood and took walks in the forest. A pleasant discovery was a wild berry bush with edible fruit. All the while, the solar panels sustained the map that Allen was building. All the research from the previous night was analyzed and incorporated.

Around noon, he showed the finished product to those of us who were in camp. "If these stars are in the night sky, I can get us back to this point." Allen had been hard at work. "Now, I could use someone who knows some old-school navigation to help me with the land map."

With a grin, Andy raised his hand. "I know I may not like this, but I'll help if possible."

"Great, now let me think for a moment. I can take a picture with the laptop, giving me the focal length and the object's distance. I know I need to figure out some angles. How does the law of tangents figure into this?"

"No idea what you just said, but if I use my rangefinder to give us a distance with whatever object you need, would that help?" Andy asked.

There was a pause in the muttering.

"Who has a Ph.D. in geodetic data?" I asked with a chuckle.

Allen glanced up, stuck his tongue out at me, and replied, "Yes, a rangefinder will help greatly with this."

Andy proceeded to his pack and pulled out his G7 rangefinder. "We need a static spot to take all the distances and for your photos, right?"

Allen nodded, "Somewhere easy to get to and a flat spot where I can set up my equipment."

"I suggest using the overlook below us, where the main path splits. There are a few steps, but the rest of the area is comfortable and flat. You can see for miles," Rachel offered.

"I agree with Rachel that this would be an ideal spot for this. We can set up a tarp to keep you and the computer out of the direct sun." If this worked, we might have a working map of the general area in hours or, at most, days, rather than months and years.

Andy looked at Rachel, then back at me. "And it's comfortable there too!" Andy's teasing comment had the desired effect, making Rachel blush. The blush continued, and Rachel punched Andy in the arm. When I laughed, I got hit, too.

"What was that for?" I asked, rubbing my bicep. Rachel didn't usually hit that hard. It certainly felt like a bruise would develop this time.

Rachel frowned at me. It wasn't the "I will never talk to you again" glare, but was more likely the "I am not mad, but stand up for me" glare.

"Andy, all she and I did was kiss there last night, nothing more. Apologize, or I may shoot you and leave you for dead in an alien world."

He knew I was joking, but this time, he had crossed the line. "Apologize!"

Allen was deep in thought. Everyone else seemed to have disappeared from view.

"Sorry, RJ, I still didn't think you guys were that sensitive. I will make this right." Andy mock-saluted me and headed in the direction where Rachel had stormed off.

"Make this right, Sarge!" I yelled after him.

Rachel could never stay mad at Andy for long. He returned shortly, with Rachel following soon after. I couldn't tell from either of their faces how the reconciliation had concluded. I made the motions to help Andy and Allen prepare for testing.

"So, what did you tell her?" I whispered.

"Oh, the usual. That I am an insensitive idiot, I'm jealous of your relationship, I'm an insensitive idiot. I mentioned that one already. Don't worry. Rachel has standards and doesn't want anyone to think any differently," Andy replied, partially under his breath.

"Standards?" I pressed.

"Yes. You know. Standards. When are you going to ask that poor girl to marry you?" Andy looked at me. "I'm retired as a wingman. You have the girl."

While not the first conversation of its kind, it was the first time his tone had been severe.

"I'm waiting for the right moment. I don't want to rush things."

"Rush things!" Andy's voice was now a mix of frustration and anger. It took him an effort to lower his tone again. "Rush things? You have had three years to ask the question! Above and beyond the normal time frame that polite society allows. What time do you have to stand around with your hands in your pockets, stealing kisses?"

I was worried that Rachel seemed to have shared some of her frustration with my best friend. "Thank you for the advice."

I gave Rachel breathing room and continued helping Allen and Andy with the map project. Allen set up to take pictures of the mountain range that loomed over the plain below. Meanwhile, Jim and Andy went down the main path to the valley floor to determine the distance to the plain.

Andy stayed on our side of the valley using the comms while Jim began to walk out onto the prairie. It wasn't long before Jim ran as if his old instructor were hot on his tail at basics. Andy used the rangefinder to help Jim cover a mile and a half, which was the maximum distance for the G7 to calculate. Then Jim used his rangefinder binoculars to confirm that it was another three-quarters of a mile to the tree line from his position.

Andy relayed the information on the comms.

Then Allen took a picture of the vast plain, using Andy and Jim's locations to begin his MGRS grid. Allen called over the comms, asking if Jim could aim at the mountain's peak from his position or from a nearby spot to provide an angle comparison and the distance from the valley base to the summit.

Allen and Jim went back and forth for several minutes, discussing numbers and recalculations, until Allen was satisfied. Andy and Jim began their journey to our position again.

Allen was delighted with the work he had accomplished. "You know what I am doing in several hours would have taken you guys a lifetime to figure out."

I could have argued with him, but I merely stretched out my hands to tip my hat and bow to him.

He smiled while I headed up to see Bill, who was working on supper. Rachel was helping him. I asked her to help me refill some water bottles from the pool.

"I'm sorry for not shooting Andy when he insulted your virtue." I had to start somewhere. Usually, if I begin with the worst-case scenario, it would be downgraded if I were lucky.

"I would certainly not want you to shoot your friend and mine. He didn't insult my virtue. It was more teasing than insulting," she responded. I saw the beginning of a smile.

I often relied on my wit and humor to get me out of worse situations than this one. "So, I don't need to shoot him? "I asked, then in a more serious tone, "I want you to know that everyone is aware that we kiss. They are also aware that we have standards. We've made promises to each other regarding said standards," I replied. Rachel and I had agreed that if she needed to wait until marriage for physical intimacy, then I would abide by those standards.

"I know. I'm glad you are a man who stands by his promises." Rachel replied by taking my hand. We headed back to where Bill was almost through with his supper preparations.

"I'll go see if Andy and Jim are back. Everyone will be eager to know it's almost time to eat." I winked at Rachel and headed back down the hill.

As always, the food was incredible. While most of the fresh food we brought was gone, you would never have known that from the feast Bill placed before us. A salad made of greens had a slightly bitter taste, but the REM dressing was sweet, making it edible. The main course was lasagna with smoked sausage, and the side was iron skillet-baked cornbread. To our surprise, a berry compote, promptly named "Campfire Cobbler," was for dessert.

I wasn't sure how Bill had managed to pull off such culinary delights. Coffee was the go-to beverage for most meals, but Bill told us it would be reserved for breakfast only, as he didn't know when we could restock our bean supply. He made lemonade from flavor sticks using fresh spring water from the nearby pool. Refreshing but not caffeinated.

"Can I have everyone's attention, please? I have a question that I need to ask," I said.

A few murmured around the campfire, "Yes." The rest just stopped what they were doing to look at me.

"I have waited far too long to ask this. I think that while the place may not be optimal, the company, however, is perfect."

Without missing a beat, I turned and dropped to one knee in front of Rachel, causing some playfully traded punches from the gentlemen and a series of gasps and giggles from the ladies.

"Rachel Stratmoor, I am the most blessed of men. I would be even more blessed if you would agree to be my wife?"

There was a yell of joy. She managed to say yes somewhere in the middle of the jumping and hugging.

As I placed the engagement ring on Rachel's hand, I felt my parents' blessing deep in my soul. My dad had placed this ring on my mom's finger many years before. A second, perhaps two seconds of silence, and then a full-blown party broke out by a pool, on a hill, in an unknown land, on an alien world.

CHAPTER 14

Rachel and I talked long into the night, making plans for when we returned to Colorado. Who would make up the wedding party? Who to invite? We lingered over the meaningful conversation that immediately followed the most glorious moment in our lives to that point, next to our anticipated wedding day. Where to honeymoon?

Finally, Andy showed up on the overlook for his watch and shooed us back to our sleeping bags. It was challenging to slow my racing mind enough to allow sleep.

I had barely closed my eyes when Bill shook me. He and Andy were waking everyone, but cautioning them to be silent.

Andy gestured for us to follow him. The trail would have been hard to navigate in the dead of night if not for the light of the full moon hovering over the far mountain range. When we reached the lookout, Andy again made the signs to keep low and move fast.

Andy's hands were outstretched, then pushed up and down, and his fingers pointed in the direction he needed us to go. Once in position, Andy pointed to the northeast and handed us his binoculars. There, we could see the rather large glow of a village on fire, about five klicks out.

We missed this settlement's existence in the daylight, but the dark of night readily revealed the flames despite the distance.

"Should we take a closer look?" Andy asked.

"Too far away for us to be of any help tonight. Let's get back to sleep, and we can check it out in the morning," I stated.

With dawn came an alarming sight. From the eastern edge of the plain, a small army of humans led by a company of cavalry moved across the plain. A small group of what appeared to be scouts was sent off to look at the smoldering remains of the town, from the night before.

Suddenly, a commotion to the rear of the army prompted the Cavalry to peel off and form a defensive V, forcing the infantry to march faster. Panning my binoculars back to where the plain met the forest, I could see wolves and creatures much larger than the humans, trying to catch the human army in front of them.

"There!" I pointed, as everyone had gathered at the overlook with Andy and me.

The human army was on a forced march to try and gain the advantage of a small hill, just south of where Jim had crossed the plain earlier for his GPS reading. A group of human cavalry and infantry was retreating towards this rise. In pursuit were fantastic beasts at least ten to twelve feet tall, hairy, fur-covered beings with blood-red eyes and horns, like some cross between a Texan steer and a Sasquatch. They were wearing leather armor. With them were packs of the giant wolves we had encountered.

The cavalry charged in a V pattern and, before breaking off to the right or the left, reforming in the center again as the furry monsters re-formed ranks. The Cavalry just needed to let the infantry take the hill, so they wouldn't get overrun.

The human cavalry was armed with spears, bows, and swords. They wore metal armor and had a distinct advantage over their beastly enemy.

The creatures outnumbered the humans below, and the creatures they fought towered over them. In most cases, the combined height of the horse and human rider could put them eye to eye.

Finally, the cavalry reached a point where their commanders called a retreat. They moved off in smaller cohorts to harass the adversary from the rear and flanks.

The two main forces of infantry now faced each other. The humans created a circle using the small hill to their advantage, with the archers and their commanders at the highest point, with spears and swords forming shielded barriers below.

"RJ, we have to do something. It was those beasts alongside the wolves that attacked us on your land," Andy said.

Allen looked at him. "If we are voting, I disagree. Any interference on our part could change the course of history here, the timeline, and even the space continuum."

"Okay, 'Mister Prime Directive.' We can't just sit back and watch a complete slaughter occur when these are the same brutes that attacked us." Andy reacted with his usual, not-so-subtle sarcasm.

"RJ, I agree with Andy. We have to do something!" Jim interjected. He already had his sniper rifle with him.

"Can we hit them from here, or must we endanger our position to give help?" Rachel asked. "I vote to help."

"As long as they aren't more than twenty-five hundred yards or so, yes, I can hit them from here," Jim added. With a suppressor on his rifle, they literally wouldn't know what hit them, or from where.

Andy and Jim returned to camp to grab additional munitions while Rachel took me aside. "You know those two can only make a limited impact at the rate of one bullet, one kill! We have to do better than that."

"What do you want me to do? Ride down there with six guns blazing?" I asked.

"Yes! You're the lawnmower and I'm the flame thrower!" The look in her eyes said, 'Either you're with me, or I am going alone.'

"No. We don't have any tactical advantage in broad daylight," I stated.

"Then what, just leave them to be slaughtered?" she asked.

"No, I guess we can't do that either." It was about as far from ideal as you could be. "Okay, I'll have Bill watch the trail. Should this go badly, we will be ready to retreat into the cavern." I did not mind interfering from a distance. I was skilled at fighting, but riding right into the fray was far from wise.

We raced back to our camp. While I gathered two horses and informed Bill of what was happening, Rachel grabbed her bow and replaced the standard tips with the bright red points.

I slung my Mossberg 500 with tactical grips over one shoulder. An M4A1 with an M203A2 grenade launcher attached was over the other. These beasts were about to learn what 'go all medieval on someone' meant. I threw Rachel a shotgun and noticed she had a pair of 9mm pistols for backup.

We rode out of camp with Bill's warning ringing in my ears. "If you lose a horse, you get to ride a mule for the remainder of the trip."

Riding down the mountainside trail, Rachel and I quickly discussed our approach. Rachel was to proceed along the forested side closest to Andy and Jim on the lookout. If the enemy charged, she could retreat and count on friendly fire to allow for her escape back up the mountain. I would travel the long way around and attempt to engage the enemy from the far side of the encircled human infantry.

Suppressors would keep the noise down and reduce the chance of the beasts breaking away and coming to look for our us.

On the comm, I asked Andy how things were going. "Madman to Crow's Nest. Have you scrambled any eggs? Over."

"Madman, this is Crow's Nest. We are cracking Royal Terns. Over." 'Royal Tern' means that Andy and Jim would attempt to cause the maximum amount of chaos by killing what we suspected were enemy officers.

I flipped my headset to the rangefinder and moved to about 300 yards from the enemy's left rear flank. Pulling a high-explosive grenade out, I loaded it into the launcher and aimed. I would attempt to time my attack with one of Rachel's to make it less likely that anyone could pinpoint my attack position.

"Three, Two, One. Go!" I heard Rachel call out of the comms. On the one mark, I was already squeezing the trigger. The M406 grenade dropped about two hundred feet into the enemy creatures' ranks, followed by bodies and body parts flying. From Rachel's side, a similar explosion echoed mine. I reloaded and waited.

Again, Rachel counted down. I unleashed my growing anger upon an unsuspecting enemy. By the third series of blasts, the creatures on the outer ranks began to retreat. As they turned to run, they faced the fury of the M4. Leather and fur were no match for lead propelled at two thousand nine hundred feet per second. I emptied three clips into the nearest group and galloped east away from the human position on the hill. Moving further to the east and south, I repeated the tactic until I ran out of grenades. "Crow's Nest, this is Madman. Out of bugs. Heading for the nest. Over."

"Copy that, Madman. Over," sounded the reply from the comms.

Rachel was waiting for me at the bottom of the trail. I was eager to see whether our dual-pronged attack influenced the ensuing battle.

Making our way back to the overlook, Bill handed me one of the scoped rifles.

I took a position on the ground next to Jim. "How did that look from here?"

"I think the seven grenades and the half a dozen arrows from Rachel did significant damage to those beasts," Jim said as he squeezed off another round.

Andy nodded. "I agree. Your ordinance did not injure any defenders, which is a plus."

We watched the battle where the human cavalry continued to harass what remained of the enemy army's outer ranks. Having evened the score in favor of the humans, we concentrated on picking off the enemy from a safe distance.

About fifteen minutes after arriving back at the overlook, we heard horns. Shortly after, a large group of human cavalry swept in from the west. Seeing a large company of fresh horsemen, the enemy creatures began a retreat back into the east. They pursued but veered off when the creatures started to enter the forest and its protection.

CHAPTER 15

Late in the afternoon, I got a call from Andy on the comms. "Looks like we will have company shortly. A small cadre of horsemen is heading for the trailhead."

"Copy that. I'm on my way to the trail junction." We were going to make new friends, or it was time to leave this place.

I rode my horse down to where the trail forked to the overlook or down the mountainside. Andy and Jim joined me there. "Be prepared. Not aggressive, just prepared." I cautioned the rest of the team who gathered behind us. "Allen, how are we going to communicate?"

It didn't take long for a dozen people on horseback to arrive. Although battle-weary, they displayed impressive courage, with banners waving in the breeze.

These troops were slight in build and had a distinctly Asian appearance. The largest stood under six feet tall, and spears were held high in a non-threatening posture. An older group member dismounted and pushed his way through the horses to the front. He had a sash across his left shoulder tied at his waist, displaying some impressive medals. He appeared to be in charge.

I dismounted and waited for him to speak, not wanting to breach some protocol. I wished we had thought to have Allen with his laptop, and some translation software.

However, amazingly, I knew what he said as soon as he began to speak. It was bizarre.

It's like watching one of those ninja movies where the lips don't match the dialogue while the English subtitles scroll at the bottom of the screen. I understood the words, but he was speaking another language! Eventually, our brains caught up, and we just knew what they were saying, and their lips matched our 'English' brain waves.

The older gentleman with all the medals put his hands together, palms facing up, then brought them to his face and back to his sides. Possibly some form of thank you or greeting, and then he spoke.

"Greetings in the name of the Maker, who sent you to us in our most desperate hour."

In that moment, I wished I had paid better attention to the TV. After teasing Allen about the 'Prime Directive,' it was now I who was lacking the proper words. But before I could bring my thoughts and tongue together, he began to speak again, only to be interrupted by one of the standard bearers standing just behind him.

"I present to you, General SunGru, Grand Marshal of the First Imperial Order, Duke of Hu'ang Se City, Protector of the Throne and Defender of the Seas, friend to the great Emp..."

The older gentleman hushed his bannerman. "I am but a humble servant of the people. You may call me SunGru."

"Nice to meet you, SunGru. I am RJ." I pointed out and named each member of our party.

"We wish to thank you for your assistance in the battle..."

The bannerman interrupted again. "Sorcery!"

I could now understand the bannerman. Our modern weapons could lead someone using medieval weaponry to think that we were using magic.

Bill now whispered in my ear, "I don't think it's a bad thing to allow them to think we hold the upper hand."

I agreed. "SunGru…"

I was now interrupted by the bannerman. "Grand Marshal!"

This time, the bannerman was hushed and dismissed to the rear of the group.

I started again. "General SunGru. It was our honor to assist."

SunGru had a look of concern on his face. "You helped us. Do you not fear the Fallen? They will most assuredly attack your lands when they find out about this battle."

I explained that we had already been attacked on our land. Our purpose here was to identify those responsible and gather information about their activities.

We were thanked for our part in turning the battle in favor of the Q.

The Q, known as the Quaylin and several other races, were gripped in an age-old struggle between the giant creatures known as the Skaldi, and their wolf allies. We learned that the man I spoke with was an essential member of some Imperial family and the Quaylin military.

The Q army had begun to set up camp on the valley's west side nearest the road to the mountain. We accepted the invitation to join them for a celebration feast.

As General SunGru departed, he and the other military leaders bowed deeply to us, mounted their horses, and began to move back down the mountain.

I heard the word, "Shen."

Back at camp, I asked Allen if he would search his database for references to the name. Allen ran the word through his system.

"Well, well, well. They think we are some hybrids between a mythical hero and a deity, which also explains their thinking that we used magic to help them defeat the Skaldi."

I said what we were all thinking. "That's not good. How are we to address this? We are just like them. We bleed, and die in battle." We didn't think about this complex issue when using modern firepower. How do we solve this misconception?

We broke camp and moved down into the valley. The Q had left an open space near the general's tents to set up our tents. Anyone who wanted to attack us would have to go through the entire Q army to reach us.

Besides our weapons, our tents were now a thing of awe. How could a tent only take a few moments to set up? We were full of surprises.

Later that day, we sat with SunGru and his captains to share a simple meal. While we waited for the food, I explained that we were not hero gods and that our weapons were relatively conventional in our world. SunGru was sure I must be a great military leader.

I explained that in my country's military, I was still at least three ranks below his own. He replied that the army I was a part of must have been significant if I had not reached the rank of general, or perhaps politicians had gotten in the way. I wasn't the only one who laughed. Politicians interfering in the military must be a common problem, regardless of which world you call home.

I explained that my country's army contained more than a million men, with a reserve of half that number. I was not sure SunGru understood the amount, but he seemed impressed. He said he realized now why I was not a general.

Word passed that the meal was ready to be served. SunGru stood and said what appeared to be a blessing over the food. "Thanks to the Maker. He provides all things in his time."

The men across the camp repeated, "Thanks to the Maker." While interesting, thanking a deity for providing them with food was not new to our group.

CHAPTER 16

The platters began to arrive, containing bread and stew prepared to the head cook's satisfaction. Our end of the make-shift table was served first as honored guests. I watched Bill dip his spoon into his meal. He raised the spoon toward his mouth but paused to sniff at the concoction. I saw the utter disgust on his face as he chewed and swallowed. I almost said something as Bill stood up and inspected the enormous pot of stew before the head cook.

The kitchen hands continued to dish onto large serving platters. The head cook placed a generous heap of stew on SunGru's plate and personally served it. The cook awaited the general's command to feed the troops. I watched SunGru's face turn sour upon his sample bite. His eyes revealed his aversion to the food, yet he waved his hand. The chow lines opened for the rest of the army.

Bill could no longer remain silent. "General, I mean no disrespect, but how can you consume that?"

SunGru replied without missing a step. "In the field, we must eat and sustain ourselves. No matter how distasteful, I eat no better meals than my men."

I saw a twinkle in Bill's eyes as he removed the general's plate from him. "General, captains, honored guests. While the other members of my party claim they have used no magic in battle, I make no such claim regarding food."

With that, he took a small box from one of the many pockets on his hunting jacket. Once opened, several vials containing various powders were found. Setting the box on the table, Bill carefully sprinkled different colored spices onto the general's food. After several attempts and tasting small portions from the general's plate, Bill finally approved the results and set the newly enhanced platter of stew before the general. The general summoned the head cook to stand beside him.

SunGru insisted the head cook taste the food in case of poison, much to the cook's dismay. I truly believed the poor man would pass out. Mustering courage, he managed to take a taste of the stew. Many eyes were on the cook as he chewed and swallowed.

He ate another mouthful. A look of delight passed across the man's face. If the general had not snatched his plate from the cook, he might have stood there and eaten it all. To the amazement of his captains, the general finished his stew and promptly asked for another serving. Bill had to quickly enhance each plate with his limited spices so, everyone could stomach the meal.

The camp's head cook threw himself at Bill's feet and pleaded for help improving the remaining meals.

Bill grabbed the head cook by the shoulder. "Begging the general's leave. I want to show this man how I work my magic."

SunGru had no issue with this and quickly granted his blessing.

Bill said as the two men walked away, "How could you serve something so foul? Who taught you how to cook? It doesn't take that many spices to take the worst-tasting food and make you think you were sitting at the king's table. Do you know what salt is? Unbelievable! How did you get this job?"

Anyone could throw a variety of items into a pot of boiling water and call it 'stew', but not just anyone could make those same ingredients taste great, let alone be edible.

Bill had the privilege of watching the Earth's best cooks on cooking channels, and committed many recipes to memory. Allen had a section on one of the servers devoted to Bill. No matter what world you find yourself in, food should taste good with the right ingredients.

Bill's spices were superior, but I doubted his small quantity would last long in these conditions. Bill was already rooting through the herbs that the cook had on his wagon. He tasted them one by one. Spices were added to the basket the head cook carried, if they met Bill's approval. On several occasions, he tossed the spice container into a nearby fire. The one good thing Bill had found was a large amount of salt, which is a spice that could make almost anything taste better. Soon, the two of them were sprinkling spices and taste-testing the stew.

Once satisfied, Bill allowed the men to be served, and sent off smaller stew pots to the tents filled with the Q army's wounded. Salt, I had often taken those tiny grains for granted.

Patrols were sent out, and the night watch was posted around the camp.

Our second night under the stars of a new place began.

After a light breakfast, I noticed Bill, the head cook, scouts, archers, strong laborers, and two wagons heading into the woods. Someone was about to learn what to bring back to camp and what to leave undisturbed.

Our team spent the next several hours getting to know our new friends and, more importantly, their enemies. We soon learned about their most deadly adversary, the Fallen Ones. When described, they reminded us of angels. What they were doing, however, sounded totally out of character for the servants of the Creator.

It was then that Jim reminded me, "You know what else was out of character for angels?"

I shook my head. I was sure I didn't know what he was talking about.

"Before Noah, at the time of the Patriarch Jared."

"Oh, right. RJ, Jim is talking about The Watchers and Mt. Hermon," Rachel exclaimed.

Allen nudged my arm as he looked at pictures on his laptop. He then turned the computer screen towards the general and his staff; their reaction was immediate. Chairs pushed back or knocked over, and drawn swords flashed. There were oaths that I shall not translate here. All because of a picture!

"We meant no harm, General. Is this in some way resembling those you call the Fallen Ones?" I asked, motioning for everyone to return to the table.

"How have you captured one of them and now hold it inside your magic box?" pointing at Allen's laptop, SunGru asked.

How could I explain the computer image?

Allen saved me by speaking first. "General, this is simply a drawing or rendering of your fear. Like a map drawn on animal skin, this box can produce a picture of almost anything you ask of it, such as a horse." After a few keyboard clicks, a great warhorse appeared on the screen, bringing a cheer of approval from those gathered around the table.

One of the lords dropped a large bag of coins in front of Allen. He stated, "I will buy that horse!" and pointed to the picture of the warhorse on the screen. Allen shook his head. Again, how do we explain?

It was late in the afternoon when Bill and the foraging company returned to the camp. There were numerous baskets filled with roots, herbs, and berries. A wagon arrived loaded with several deer, and it also contained several larger, goose-sized birds.

Behind the wagons were a set of men carrying a wild boar on a pole. The second small wagon was filled with baskets of what appeared to be a large apple-like fruit. While it wasn't enough for a grand banquet, it would feed us.

A few hours later, the smells from the cook tents were almost overwhelming, so SunGru had to place guards to keep wandering soldiers out of the area.

Bill gathered some large shields from a pile of supplies and dipped them into boiling water, at a loss for proper serving platters. He then covered them in large green leaves, followed by a large helping of each meat with vegetables. The shield platters arrived on the field, steaming hot. Bill first served the general and the captains.

They were pleasantly surprised by the venison, game birds, vegetables, and wild mushrooms. Great baskets of freshly baked bread in the style of the open-fire flatbread, passed through the ranks. We were well aware that bread would easily fill an empty stomach.

I suddenly realized that most of these men had never had such a "good meal". The majority of the army was of men of low birth. The fact that Bill could take something as simple as food to lift the spirits of an entire army was humbling to me. I do not think Bill had been hugged so many times in one day, perhaps in all his days.

There was music, and stories of the great deeds of yesterday's battles, including stirring renditions recounting Rachel and my explosive attacks on the Skaldi.

Standing, SunGru raised his glass in a blessing. "Thank the Maker for bringing new friends. My honored guests have not seen such a meal since we left the capital. Our vanguard duty was to draw the enemy away from the capital city, our friends, and our families. We lost many men, but our efforts allowed plenty of time for our Quaylin brethren to evade their pursuers. This valley was where we hoped to be reunited, but I fear they have moved on or succumbed to the enemy. Maker, help us find our families!"

While eating our meal, I learned more about the Quaylin history from SunGru.

He told us the Q were great seafaring traders. Their lands are located to the east across the sea. About two years before, two angels had visited the court of the Q Emperor. The angels had a large force of Skaldi hidden in a valley; some distance from the capital.

Whispers of the executions of several allied leaders had made their way to the court of the Q emperor. If the Q didn't try to stop the Fallen and their minions, they would overrun every civilized point until they ruled the other realms.

The angels used the Skaldi and Ator races to instill fear and panic in human populations. It had taken them decades to build enough forces to attack the Q Empire. The imperial army and the Fallen's army of Skaldi and Ator broke upon each other like the ocean waves upon the beach. Was the army that SunGru now led the last remnant of the Q Imperial army?

The emperor wined and dined the two angels until finally their actual intent was revealed. The emperor could turn the city over to them, or he could face their army in battle. The angels returned to their army, and the emperor prepared for battle. The imperial Glav bodyguards, along with the Q military leaders, prepared to defend the city and the harbor. Civilians were instructed to gather any available food and supplies, and proceed to the ships for evacuation.

The people of Hu'ang Se City, or the "yellow city", didn't panic; they had been secretly preparing for this from the moment the two angels had arrived. They boarded the ships they had been assigned, and boats of every size headed across the ocean.

When the boats were full, the remaining households of the military leaders and the imperial court set out on horseback and in wagons, heading north to the land bridge that connected the eastern and western lands. SunGru and his military divisions were tasked with holding a vanguard position to protect the refugees' rear flank.

When the plains before the city were lost, the retreat was sounded, and the city and harbor were defended. SunGru split his forces, and at the narrowest point on the land bridge, those troops fortified and waited for the enemy forces. SunGru took his remaining troops and followed the refugees.

This brings us to the present moment. The refugees had either passed through this point and continued west, or they had fled north.

SunGru said, "We can't be sure in which direction they passed."

SunGru told how the greatest minds in the imperial court had been searching through the ancient records for any objective evidence of an ally that could stand against the fallen angels and their armies. Deep in the archives, information had been discovered that at least provided a clue to the location of such a place – an ancient kingdom or stronghold far to the west, beyond a place known as Midia.

SunGu said that the Kingdom of Midia had not been a trade partner in his lifetime, but that it could be found on some ancient maps. Midia was on the very edge of those maps. The Q did not know the lands beyond that, or of any ancient strongholds that might exist.

It was late when we settled into our tents. "What is everyone thinking? Should we stay long enough to help them find the people they are searching for?" I asked.

"I don't have anywhere to be. This trip is just starting to turn into a real adventure. I vote to stick around for a bit longer and learn more about our new friends," Andy replied.

Rachel raised her hand. "The girls are up for it if the men are."

I wondered when the girls had snuck off and held their meeting. I nodded my head in thanks.

"I've just started showing these guys that you can still have a great-tasting meal regardless of your place in life. I am sticking around to see them through their first culinary battlefield cookery course," Bill replied, shaking his head. Everyone laughed and agreed with him.

"It makes sense to stay on for a while longer. We got justice against those who attacked us in our world and lent a hand against those same beasts in this world. Because of us, many more men will be reunited with their wives and children.

"SunGru mentioned an ancient city, rumored to be located in this region, away to the west. Maybe that is where the people have taken refuge?" Jim said.

"The portal we used said something about an ancient house or city. It sounds fascinating. Do we all agree? Allen, you seem unusually quiet?"

"This isn't what any of you expected to hear from me, but I vote to go on as well," Allen replied, glancing up from his mug of coffee. He then mumbled something about missing his king bed and hypoallergenic pillows.

Like every other team member, I had that 'doubtful but surprised' expression.

"Ancient city! Do you think I would vote against seeing an ancient metropolis on an alien world?" Allen looked at all of us. "I would walk through a pit full of rattlesnakes to see that." As he finished, most of us had tears streaming down our cheeks from laughing so hard.

As everyone regained their composure, Bill added, "You owe me a dollar for using my quote."

Allen laughed. It always took him two or three days to lighten up enough to make it seem like he was having fun. Sometimes, he returned from the trip the same way he had when he left, with his emotions bottled up.

Bill laughed and added, "Allen, passing on the opportunity to see an ancient city on an alien planet would be like passing up a rifle with a ten-dollar tag at a yard sale."

There was a confused look in Allen's eyes.

Then Andy added, "Wouldn't happen. Ever!"

Laughter overtook us again. We agreed to join the Q army in their search to find their people.

In the morning, I spoke to SunGru. He was unsure how many Skaldi were still in the area, but he estimated their numbers were significantly reduced by the battle that had just taken place.

Long-range Q scouts had reached a position where the plains intersected with another mountain range and had found a pass with a rough dirt road. Unwilling to continue, the scouts returned with the news and a possible direction in which the lost Quaylin civilians may have retreated.

No proof of a large group of refugees traveling on the dirt road existed. The Quaylin army would take several days to reach the location where they believed the ancient city existed. The wounded would slow us down. Our team offered to go with an advanced Q-scout team.

Bill decided to stay behind with the cooking crew. We were given a wagon for our boxes, bags, and gear. A sturdy driver was appointed to handle the oxen team. Bill's mules seemed happy to be free of their burdens for the first time in days. They were tethered to the cart, walking behind it.

"All right, Bill, you have your comm. If there is trouble, we'll warn you," Andy said over the comms.

Bill acknowledged over the comms with a hearty, "Okie Dokey."

I said, "I don't have time to explain the comms to SunGru. Please don't tell him about them, yet."

Bill laughed and nodded, as we rode off to the front of the army column with the ten scouts SunGru had ordered to follow us.

CHAPTER 17

With no intelligence on enemy movement, we were scouting blind. The only benefit was that the Skaldi we had battled retreated in the opposite direction from which we now traveled. If they were the main fighting force, their numbers in the area have been diminished.

However, the other possibility was that these Skaldi were just a token force. They could go back to report their losses to a much larger company. Then, they might return and stomp us into a mud puddle. The military unit I had been part of left nothing to chance. I could not be responsible for leading this remnant of the Quaylin civilization into such an obvious trap.

We pressed forward toward the pass. We were prepared to lend a hand if the enemy forces were to discover this lost city that SunGru spoke of.

As if reading my mind, Jim said, "Don't look so worried. We have taken ancient cities with far fewer men."

He was referring to the places where we had seen action, such as Iraq and Afghanistan. He had the same mental picture I did – one that mixed the ancient and the modern. Did the Skaldi hold the city as their base of operations? If so, our best option would be to move along rather than attempt to dislodge them from their ancient stronghold.

We moved towards the mountain that formed the left side of the pass. About a quarter of a mile from the canyon entrance, I called a halt and spoke briefly with Jim, Andy, and the ladies. I didn't relish any of us being a decoy on the pass road. I explained to the Quaylin scouts that we had a distinct advantage over the Skaldi, with our long-range weapons.

Agreeing to our plan, the scouts split into two groups. They moved off into the underbrush with one cadre on either side of the pass, leaving their horses with us.

I had sent the ladies with the scouting party to the left. Rachel aimed to find the highest point on the ridge and attach one of the GPS watches. Allen would then have our exact location and offer a fixed position for his mapping software.

Allen and Bill had remained with SunGru and the Q army. Allen could begin mapping as soon as he received the GPS information. As Allen got closer, he used helmet-mounted cameras to provide a 3D imaging overlay of the geographical data. The results would enable us to develop a mobile application that lets us access the map and view the general locations of other team members. Each watch, equipped with its tiny solar panel, could transmit the necessary data.

Jim, Andy, and I moved to the pass entrance and began working ahead, as the units on the upper slopes. I found it odd that there were no defenses guarding the pass entrance. Where was a wall, tower, or even an attempted shield, such as a raised earthen defense?

Were we on the slow road to a well-laid trap, or was this the worst defensive effort I had ever seen? We still needed to learn how far we might have to travel to reach the end of the road or the dangers we might encounter along the way.

I knew Jim, Andy, and I could quickly cross ground, even in an unfamiliar region with an unknown number of hostiles, and still arrive safely at ground zero.

As a precaution, our units remained separated, eating and sleeping wherever we chose to end the day. I called to make camp as we began to lose light on the first day. Over the comm, I cautioned the ladies that even a single torch or flashlight beam might give away our position. I allowed no fires. We ate the bread and dried meat that Bill had sent with us.

On the first day, we covered a respectable eight miles. By the end of the second day, another ten miles. Although there was no sign of the enemy, there were signs of a diverse array of wildlife. On the evening of the second day, we had a short conversation with Allen, as the army's main body had set up camp at the mouth of the pass.

I assured SunGru that we had not encountered a single enemy outpost or scout. SunGru insisted that he and a small contingent of heavy cavalry, each carrying an archer, could ride forward and join us if we met resistance at the end of the gorge. I reluctantly agreed after he granted us at least one more day on foot to survey more of the corridor.

If there was a trap waiting for us, it might be around the next bend in the road.

I called the two teams from the ridges down to join us. We camped together that third night and, in the morning, broke into two units again, one to each side of the gorge. We could see each other through the binoculars. I hoped that neither group would run into trouble.

The canyon's height seemed to reach its apex on the second day's march, then slowly tapered off. We all agreed that this likely meant that the pass would end shortly. At the campsite, on the fourth night, we could see what appeared to be the end of the passage, perhaps a half mile ahead. We set out, leaving a scout at the campsite to meet SunGru's advance group upon their arrival.

The sun lowered as we approached the end of the pass. I expected to see a medieval castle encircled by a wall, with a small, quaint village surrounding it, also enclosed by a low stone wall.

I have witnessed many ancient cities, but they all paled in comparison to what I now beheld!

Most ancient cities I had toured or fought in, were crumbling into dust, their builders and rulers lost and long forgotten to the sands of time. This sprawling metropolis seemed intact, but it was hard to say for sure, from this distance. It gleamed at us! Not like some legendary marble castle in some fairytale children's book, but like a city out of the future trapped in the dark ages.

The sun's fading light left us wanting more of this incredible sight. I was eager for Allen to arrive and archive this astonishing find. We returned a little up the valley and made camp, with the plan to leave most of our gear behind to travel more lighter, now that our objective was in sight.

The next day, in small groups, we took turns watching the towers and bridges across the chasm for signs of the enemy.

As the darkness of the evening crept in, we could see torches marching along the walls. One glance through a rifle scope at the giant shadows, and Jim declared, "Yep. Those are Skaldi! Depending on their numbers, this may be a nearly unattainable goal."

What happened here? Had the Fallen angels sent an army that overthrew this great stronghold city? Where are the signs of a great battle? Why are there Skaldi walking the walls?

A few hours into the morning, SunGru and Allen, with almost fifty riders, arrived to make camp on one side of the pass, where a group of trees jutted out to form a slight sound and sight barrier. I sent Andy to find Allen and get the two working on the city's documentation and defenses. Meanwhile, Jim and I worked on a plan to get a closer look at the city than we currently had.

There was very little ground from the narrow end of the pass facing the city. The distance between the passage and the metropolis was so great that no attacking army could bring siege weapons to bear against the city's walls. Between the metropolis and the pass lay a series of towers stretching across the chasm with drawbridges. The city was an island itself. We seemed unlikely to take possession at first glimpse, even if the enemy were but a handful.

The first tower seemed abandoned. None of the Skaldi wanted to be exposed and trapped. The next tower had pulled up its drawbridge. There were several upper windows where we had seen lights and the occasional sentry carrying a torch the night before. Further, additional towers led to a rather impressive fortification in the distance, the last defensive line before the city gates and walls.

At the second tower, we noticed a gap. It was the only one with a raised drawbridge. If we couldn't bypass it, we would be at an impasse. Only a few guards defended the second tower. If we could gain access, we would quickly overtake it. The tricky part was the sixty-foot gap between the roads that extended beyond the first tower to the retracted portion.

"Well, this is an interesting problem. How do we span sixty feet? Do we wait for someone to lower the drawbridge and attempt to storm the second tower before they can raise it on us?" I asked.

Jim nodded. "Interesting, indeed. I have a new toy we could try out that Becky and I bought for rock climbing."

"Oh, do tell." I loved new toys.

"This new apparatus I had built to my specifications. I haven't used it for this exact purpose, but I think it could hold one of our smaller scout friends. It's a gun that fires a rock-climbing bolt into solid rock. We can then send a man over from there with a higher gauge rope attached. Once there, we assault the tower under the cover of darkness to lower the bridge. We gather more of our forces in that tower while we wait for the night to attack the castle. Finally, we breach the city gates." Jim ended by opening up his pack to reveal the bolt-firing device.

"A good plan," I replied. "Secure all the towers and hope we meet with little to no resistance." I glanced at SunGru and his men, who appeared confused.

"Allen?"

"Already working on it, RJ" Allen was typing at a furious rate. A few moments later, Allen announced that he was ready. Gathering SunGru and his men around the laptop, Allen played a crude slide show depicting Jim and one of the scouts firing the bolt gun. Then, hand over fist, shimmying sixty feet across the first cord to attach the thicker climbing rope while trying not to look down into the abyss below. Despite the crude movie, SunGru and his men vaguely understood the goal.

"Shall I find a volunteer?" Jim was ready to take the targeted tower tonight.

"Find a volunteer about the size of a jockey. He must be without fear but with a firm grip." I was ready for some action, too.

"Copy that," Jim replied as he headed for where the scouts had set up camp beyond sight from the towers. He returned quickly, with several men who looked determined as he explained the plan.

Jim and several team members planned to take up positions in the first tower. When Jim fired the bolt gun with the thin metal line, the smallest man could travel across the void, hand over fist, until he was at the tower. This first scout needed to fasten the second line, which he carried to the second tower, allowing more attackers to take positions. We could then assault the second tower. Once the second tower was under our control, we could lower the drawbridge, allowing more troops to cross.

I heard a pop from the bolt gun, and it echoed for a tense moment. Skaldi stirred in the second tower. Torches appeared. The line was far too thin for anyone to see in the darkness. Clouds kept the moon at bay on our behalf. The cord had also been powder-coated for a dull tone, so it didn't gleam or reflect when the torchlight passed over it.

Then began the long wait. We had to be sure that the Skaldi had gone back to sleep.

Jim finally gave the 'all clear' call over the comms two hours later; it was time to get to work!

He was not going to leave anything to chance. He attached a climbing harness to the line and pulled a pair of sleek climbing gloves out of his pack for the volunteer to use. Once the scout was ready, he began the painstaking journey across the void. The more significant line would then be strung from a third-story window in the first tower to a second-story window in the second tower.

The zip line provided a faster way to transport more troops into the fortification for an assault. Five scouts, Andy, Jim, and I, entered the building in less than an hour.

Prepared to start our assault, I saw the light of a torch moving down the stairwell toward us. I noticed a sizeable Skaldi warrior raise his flaming torch and peer out the window. I heard a resounding thud as Rachel embedded an arrow in him from her position atop the first tower.

I initially feared that the warrior she had just killed would come crashing down the steps and awaken the rest of his hairy friends.

Thankfully, that was not the case since his arms and upper torso had fallen partly out the window. He was stuck halfway in the tower and halfway out.

Rachel's voice was calm as it came over the comms. "One in the window and one standing watch on top; both eliminated."

"Copy that," Jim responded.

Moving out, Jim and the five scouts quietly descended the stairs while Andy and I pushed through the second floor to find the drawbridge mechanism. We removed any threats there and progressed to the first floor. There were no sentries at the lowest level. The two stationed at the drawbridge only knew pain for a brief moment.

On either side of the drawbridge were giant metal braziers. I lit them for heat and guidance for the rest of our party. Jim arrived a few moments later. He had stationed the scouts with torches to indicate that everything was still routine to the Skaldi manning the massive fortification before the city gates.

The drawbridge mechanism was not like any I had seen before. The end pressed against the tower was too short to cover the necessary distance. However, once it reached its lowest point, the metal door's exterior extended to cover the gap. The mechanism itself was swift, given the magnitude of what it accomplished. The device was also quiet, not without sound, but surprisingly fluid in its movement. I thought it would make such a ruckus to awaken the entire city. It would be dawn shortly. I realized that we must warn SunGru and the rest of the camp to take cover until darkness allowed us to continue our work.

At dusk, I received word over the comms that SunGru and a select group of warriors were coming to our position. It was not an easy trip, as we could not afford to have people walking across the bridge carrying torches. They had to be very careful and follow a line of sight to the enormous burning braziers in the second tower.

SunGru, Andy, Jim, and I climbed to the top of the second tower. If we could not develop a plan before dawn to take the final fortification, we risked losing another day waiting for the cover of darkness. There were too many uncertainties. We moved back into the tower as dawn arrived. Our plan did not come with the rising sun.

From the top floor of this tower, we could better estimate the forces we had to face. When SunGru surveyed the city, nothing in his expression gave me any reason to suspect he had ever seen such a city.

I asked, "SunGru, is this city like your capital?"

"No, not the same design. This city looks like the Old Ones built it, whereas we built the Quaylin capital. It is an ocean port and quite large in size," he answered.

I pulled a pair of field binoculars from my pack. "Take a look through these."

He took them while I began to rummage around for a second set. He stood holding the binoculars with a puzzled look.

Rachel pushed the optics up to his face. There was an immediate change in SunGru's demeanor as he looked through the glasses and then quickly lowered them. The general looked from side to side and then back through the lenses. A murmur of awe slipped from his lips. He looked again toward the city. He then tried to return the glasses, but I told him they were a gift from one military commander to another.

I watched as he showed each of his captains, who returned the same look of awe, followed by reactions as if they had never seen this technology before.

Andy suggested we wait for the sun to set and see if infrared photography might reveal enemy troop numbers. During the daylight hours, there were virtually no patrols. At least certainly none that ventured this far from the castle.

I call it a castle because of its size and its defensive importance. Due to its strategic significance, there were more Skaldi in the castle. As for the city and its massive walls and towers, we never saw any torches or movement, which just added more questions. Andy estimated that there was an eighth of a mile between the towers.

SunGru and his captains seemed ready to build siege ladders. When we realized they planned to sound the charge at first light, in a full-scale attack against an unknown number of Skaldi, we had to convince them that stealth and sniper tactics were a far better strategy.

Jim tapped me on the shoulder, winked, and showed me two tin cans.

I knew where this was going, but I wasn't sure I liked it.

Andy took the can targets with a canteen and headed to the first tower. When he got there, he signaled. Jim had SunGru use the binoculars to watch Andy, who filled the cans with water and placed them in the window. For added effect, Andy also propped a dead Skaldi between the two targets. "First the right can, then the left can, then the headshot," Jim heard Andy over the comms.

Jim explained to SunGru what he was about to do. He nodded in understanding and watched the window in the first tower.

Jim pulled out his suppressor and threaded it to the end of his rifle. He shouldered the weapon and then announced that he had acquired his primary target. SunGru looked at the window again as Jim fired, followed by a slight cracking sound. You cannot silence a weapon. You might almost completely block the noise from a .22, but no chance with a subsonic sniper rifle.

A hole appeared. Water poured out of the first can and was repeated on the second can.

Finally, Jim put one right between the eyes of the dead Skaldi. We then explained to SunGru that we could do this repeatedly over long distances to eliminate the threat in the castle. SunGru agreed that we had a far better chance of taking the defensive castle in front of us with this method, than by brute force, given the limited time available to build siege weapons.

Jim and Andy planned to set up a sniper nest in the tower closest to the castle. The plan was for me to also be there with a rangefinder to help them make the best shot possible. The scouts would defend any retreat necessary. Andy rigged some C4 on the tower's drawbridge in case the enemy overran us. It was time to put our skills to the test.

I gave Jim the first target: location, range, and wind factor.

I then did the same for Andy.

The cracks co-occurred in the human ear. Two more Skaldi warriors ceased to draw breath.

Then we waited. There was some clamor within the castle as the remaining enemies discovered the dead bodies. Imagine the reaction of those who found the bodies! For them, there was no feasible explanation. There was no intruder to point the finger at and no sign of an arrow to explain the deaths.

I felt a slight tinge of remorse. It was hardly a fair fight, but then I reminded myself of the battle I had seen earlier. Recalling the ferocity of the Skaldi attack, I quickly overcame my regret. The drawbridge remained across the chasm from us, but two guards arrived to stand on either side of the gates. We could get through the gates if we had to, but if the enemy raised any drawbridges, it might spell game over for us.

An hour went by.

I had SunGru gather a cadre of elite warriors and their captains. When Jim and Andy took down the Skaldi at the gate, this team needed to move as swiftly as possible to take positions inside the gates. If anyone tried to raise the bridge, we had troops to stop them. The assault group readied itself.

They moved forward with all haste when they saw the Skaldi fall backward and tumble over the side of the bridge, into the chasm. With this small unit inside the gatehouse, Jim and Andy began to take out sentries they spotted at will. We sent five soldiers across the bridge each time this happened to bolster those inside the gatehouse.

The second squad that crossed included two of SunGru's battle engineers. They had their group carry across some interesting metal pieces they had found. If the portcullis dropped, the wedges would stop the metal gates about four feet off the floor. The weight of the iron itself would prevent the devices from moving. If the Skaldi attempted to follow, they would be crawling on their bellies, making them vulnerable to attack.

At the same time, it kept access open to us, which is the key to gaining control of the drawbridge and portcullis mechanisms. What if they shut and barred the large wooden doors inside the gatehouse? Would we have to start a fire to reach the courtyard?

Jim and Andy had each passed their eighth kill shot. We had easily eliminated sixteen of the Skaldi warriors without losing any of our own, which impressed SunGru. Jim and Andy were to remain in the tower to eliminate threats while SunGru and I moved a few more men across. We joined the men already gathered inside the gatehouse.

"Overwatch, this is Thor. Time to end this," I said over the comms, getting the men ready to move on my mark.

"Copy that," Jim replied.

CHAPTER 18

We split into two groups and prepared to work through the gatehouse towers, then along the outer wall to the next building, clearing away any resistance. Meeting at the gatehouse and towers on the opposite side, closest to the city, the two groups planned to join forces and work our way across the open courtyard to the main building. The main building was a substantial fortress.

We met little resistance in the outer rooms of the first level. The main gates to the first level were open when we arrived. At first, I thought this might be a trap. Had they been so sure that no one could cross the gap in the bridges that their security had been virtually nonexistent?

On the third level, we found a doorway that most likely led to a great hall. These doors were closed and lightly guarded. After a brief skirmish, we posted men at the main staircase entrances on either side of the room.

We continued up to the fourth floor of the complex. Here, we discovered four doors leading to a series of balconies overlooking the great room. In the darkness, we surrounded those in the gallery below. Unbeknownst to us, every Skaldi who still drew breath within the compound was now in our crosshairs.

SunGru was about to order his archers to fire upon the Skaldi. I held up my hand and pointed to the doorway.

SunGru had an expression between slightly annoyed and confused. I owed him an explanation.

"I have been listening to their discussion. They are fighting among themselves over whether or not to remain enslaved to the Fallen Ones. They think this city is the key to their freedom from the Fallen Ones' oppressive rule. The smaller group wants the larger group to join them, which is not going well."

If SunGru decided that everyone in that room was to die, I surely could not stop him.

"RJ, they are animals. Why are you defending them?" SunGru responded. He was not a rash man.

"Yes, they act like animals, but one leader among them opposes the Fallen Ones. What if there are lots of Skaldi who feel the same way? Wouldn't they make a better ally, than an enemy?" I asked.

"Why make any Skaldi our allies? It's one thing to kill our warriors, but slaughtering innocent farmers, their wives, and children? I don't think they can be civilized enough to work with us side by side," SunGru replied.

I might not win this fight. "If no one has tried to speak with the Skaldi, how do we know their hearts? My friend, if you command that all of those below us must perish this day, I will be the first to raise my weapon and take lives. However, there is an ancient saying in my world. 'The enemy of my enemy is my friend.' Does that make sense?"

I had to allow at least the thought process to begin. "Imagine how the tide of war would change for us if even a small number of Skaldi committed to our cause. If a small number here opposes the Fallen Ones, surely there are more Skaldi weary of years of senseless death and destruction?"

"What would you have me do?" SunGru asked. At least he was open to a new idea from someone he barely knew.

"Have your bowmen fire on the opposition to the smaller group's leader. That will certainly give him something to ponder. If it goes badly, we also kill the smaller group," I answered.

The plan was passed among the Q. Some of the younger officers were visibly upset by the commands.

On the other hand, the older officers had been with the general for many years. They trusted that he had a reason for his decisions.

Below us, the two Skaldi groups moved from arguing to yelling threats and brandishing weapons. It was clear that the leader of the larger group intended to order the death of the opposing group's leader as a traitor.

A hail of well-aimed arrows flew from the four darkened sides of the balconies, quickly finding their marks. Members of the smaller opposition group then cut down those not instantly killed. They had no real idea of what was happening, but seized the moment. SunGru and I showed ourselves above the great hall when the brief fight ended. The small group of remaining Skaldi warriors saw our archers, and surrounded their young Skaldi leader.

We unbarred the doors to the gallery below. At the same time, the archers remained overlooking the hall from above. SunGru, several guards, and I entered the room to trade words with the remaining Skaldi leader.

Before SunGru or I could begin, the leader of the surviving Skaldi raised his hands and spoke.

"I am Kraq, son of Krund, of the Blue Clan. I see those who oppose me now lie dead at my feet, but not by my hand. While I am still happy to draw breath, I wonder why I am here to witness this. Why do I still live? There is no silver in my beard yet, but what day has come when a Quaylin archer has a mighty Skaldi prince in sight and hesitates to release his bowstring? Is there a truce? I do not know.

Our masters insist that the Q have no honor. The Q would say the same about us. Our masters have taught us to hate and find pleasure in killing the innocent! I will ask again: why do I still draw breath? Can we break free of the oppression of the Fallen Ones? Before I stand before the Maker in judgment, I will ask one last time. Can Skaldi and Quaylin unite against the Powers of the Air? They are foes who wish the lands we love destroyed rather than Skaldi and Quaylin count each other as allies."

When Kraq mentioned the Maker, many of the Quaylin shouted blasphemy.

Kraq continued. "Does the greatest general in the Quaylin people's history believe such a thing is possible? Can honor be regained? Can forgiveness be granted for unforgivable sins? Come, SunGru, did you not think I knew who stood before me? You could control when I would breathe my last breath with a simple word. Do you truly seek peace?"

A stunned silence filled the room. I had heard some speeches in my time, some to give courage amid overwhelming odds in the face of certain death. This eloquent guy might even get Andy to follow him into battle.

I turned to SunGru. "Now is the time. Embrace change by making the enemy of your enemy your friend. The other choice is to command the archers to finish this horrible deed."

It was now the general's choice. While I was inspired, I witnessed SunGru's face turn red, then pale, from insult and pain. The outcome of this encounter could change everything.

SunGru placed his sword back in its sheath. "Lower your weapons. I would speak with Kraq, son of Krund, Prince of the Blue Clan."

I walked over to a table at the center of the room and suggested it as a meeting place.

"Who are you?" Kraq asked me. "You are not Q. You don't even have a proper military uniform."

I hadn't considered that this might unfold differently from what I had planned.

"What rank do you hold? How many men fall under your command?" Kraq demanded.

I may have overstepped my authority. I had no flashy medals on a silk sash. I began to plan a hasty return to the comfort of the dark corners of the hall.

SunGru stopped my retreat with a hand on my shoulder. He had already decided to save me the trouble.

"This is my aide-de-camp, Major Armstrong. If I were to die tomorrow in battle, he alone would continue to lead the remnants of my army to whatever end he deems necessary."

I was stunned, but no such expression was on the faces of the Quaylin captains and their men. They were steadfast, and the general spoke law into their lives. They would live and die by SunGru's words.

Kraq nodded and waved me towards one of the empty chairs. "I will accept the words of SunGru, even though I see no spear, sword, or symbol of office," Kraq stated.

SunGru, of course, responded in fashion. "Major Armstrong is a warrior of great renown in his lands. None in this realm can match his weapons. Both fire and death come from his hands. Show him the power of Grenda!"

Grenda? What was SunGru suggesting?

Seeing my confused look, Andy, who had arrived with Jim, pointed at my belt and pressed the comm. "Grenade, RJ!" Andy had been explaining the different weapons of our world earlier. He must have mentioned the grenade.

I took SunGru aside. "I don't think this is a good idea."

SunGru shook his head. "You must show them your magic, something that convinces them of your power. You must do this!"

SunGru was insistent, so I turned back to the table.

"Kraq, while it is true that I don't wear a traditional military uniform or carry a sword, I do have weapons that do far more harm."

If this was the easiest way to prove my worth, so be it. "If I can ask everyone on the balcony to come down to this level. Everyone to this side of the hall."

This proximity put some comfort levels at odds as Quaylin and Skaldi came together to watch my demonstration. With several Skaldi volunteers' help, we piled the dead bodies of some of Kraq's most recent opposition like sandbags in the corner. I pulled a grenade from my belt and prepared to lob it into the far corner when everything was ready.

Andy had estimated that the rock wall was four, maybe five feet thick and very solid, able to withstand the concussion the grenade would produce. It was an easy target. I wondered if I should build on my reputation by shouting something mystical before pulling the pin.

Andy beat me to it with a loud "Fire in the hole."

I sent the canister flying into the space between the piled bodies and the stone wall. My team must have warned the crowd of men, as most of them had taken a knee and covered their ears. They had not moved when I looked at SunGru and Kraq standing to either side of me. I quickly pulled at their coats. After a moment of resistance, they joined me, kneeling.

A moment later, the explosion rocked the hall. Bodies were blown halfway across the room while a mist of blood covered the wall behind. Many of the stones were blackened and chipped.

When the air cleared of some of the smoke, Kraq pulled me up, roaring he embraced me, and spoke. "Wizard, you have formidable weapons indeed! Brothers of the Blue and Red Clans, if I should fall in battle, you must follow the human wizard and this Quaylin general in the battle to whatever great end awaits you. We will restore our honor!"

It took nearly three days to convince Kraq to stop calling me, "Wizard Armstrong." Call me RJ or Major!

It would be lying to tell you that I made a thousand years of distrust disappear, or that everyone began to work together from that moment. A significant step toward peace had happened for the first time in a thousand years. Quaylin and Skaldi spoke without having to brandish weapons.

The deceased Red Clan members were tossed over the walls and into the chasm. We could not see the bottom of the abyss. We seemed almost to be floating on clouds. The few dead Blue Clan members we buried in honor near the southern pass. The Q cavalry remained outside until they found a place of pasture. The castle had a well for clean water, and units were dispatched to gather firewood and food.

We sent scouts to bring the army in to secure the city's outer defenses. I sat there, listening to the two leaders. Occasionally, I gave my opinion. Finally, I could no longer suppress my curiosity.

"Kraq, my only question is why you were not living inside the city?"

Kraq took a moment, almost as if he was ashamed of the reason. "It was not for lack of trying. Perhaps Wizard Armstrong would care to try to open the gates for us?"

Several days later, a party of scouts unattached to SunGru's army arrived, having seen smoke from one of the watchfires at the pass entrance. These were advance scouts for a group from the Q capital city. They informed us that the bulk of the group was still several days' march from the pass. The new problem would be housing and feeding these Quaylin civilians, who are living in the same compound with their former Skaldi enemies.

I had to get those city gates open! There was no other choice.

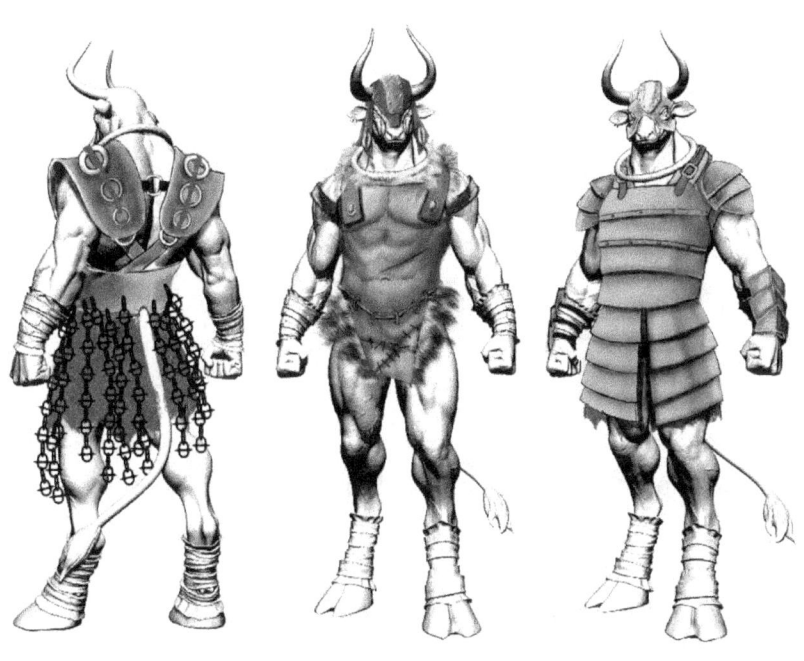

CHAPTER 19

Very soon, an enormous group of Q survivors of an unknown quantity would show up on our doorstep. We had nowhere to house them or feed them.

While the South Gate Castle was large, it was a fortification not intended for a large civilian population. Quaylin leaders, Skaldi clan members, and my team met at the point where the castle drawbridge met the city gates to address this issue. The space between the city and the castle gates allowed only a small number of men to stand.

Kraq recounted the various attempts to scale or breach the barriers. He called forward one of his captains, an immense Skaldi who stood a head above the rest of his men. This nearly twelve-footer carried a giant war hammer. He stood solidly before the gates, and I didn't doubt that doors might whimper and open themselves.

With a great battle cry, the Skaldi soldier raised his weapon and braced himself for what would happen, almost as if someone had asked him to do this once before. The Warhammer hit the gates with tremendous power. The massive display of raw strength and the weapon's sheer size would have splintered any standard wooden door. The gates and the wall to either side absorbed the blow and pushed it back with force, sending the Skaldi staggering back into the crowd.

Standing beside me, Allen said, "Wow! I have to patent that!"

The gates showed no visible damage, not even a scratch or a dent. What substance could withstand such a blow?

Allen took a piece of his notebook paper and attempted to slide it between the two sides of the great doorway.

"You can't even slide a thin paper between these doors? C4 is of no use to us here," Andy stated.

Another Skaldi took out a grappling hook and lobbed it over the wall. It slid back to the ground because there was nothing to hook into on the other side.

SunGru seemed tired of the Skaldi attempts and called for a ladder. When the top rung hit the edge of the wall, the ladder snapped back violently. The only thing that saved the man attached to the ladder was a couple of larger Skaldi, who managed to catch the ladder and the man.

"What magic do you have that will open these gates?" Kraq asked, turning back to me.

If we didn't get into the city, we risked being trapped and starved by any assailing force.

As I approached the gates, I felt a sense of awe. How long had this city stood abandoned? What secrets did it hold? I laid my hands on the gates, one on either side of the center of the gates. At the spot where my right hand touched, a small panel appeared with several intricate inlaid symbols.

As I felt the gates, I heard Andy through the comms say the word "Mellon".

My earbud echoed with laughter. Once again, I found myself the butt of another wizard joke. Nothing happened, of course! As if I had superhuman strength, these gates would quiver and open in my presence! However, it was worth a try.

When I turned to walk away, I heard a snap. Not like a twig in the forest as your boot lifts away, but more of a great hinge that time had nearly welded fast against its doorway. I was now facing everyone. The crowd was moving back in the direction of the castle — a puff of rusty dust followed by the release of stale air after a thousand years of captivity.

An odd sensation tingled through every part of my body in those same fleeting seconds after touching the gates.

Rachel ran towards me. "Are you okay, RJ? What happened to your forehead?"

The next few heartbeats are a blur to me. One minute, I hugged Rachel, and then she screamed in my ear that something was behind me. Andy and Jim pulled her from my embrace back into the protection of a ring of Skaldi and Quaylin steel as their warriors reacted. My neck hair stood on end.

I could hear the crowd yelling for me to run, urging me to join their protective shield.

My usual reaction to the fight-or-flight impulse was an overwhelming urge to fight. I would not run from whatever had appeared behind me in the gaping void where the gates once stood. It wasn't just my training or some morbid death wish. It was part of my DNA.

I turned to face whatever doom had emerged from the city. As I did, the great shadow of a giant Skaldi covered me. It was the one who had initially delivered a tremendous blow to the gates. He dashed past me to swing at the being in front of us. All my money would be on the giant, hairy warrior, and his massive war hammer under normal circumstances. But today was not a typical day. With a wave of its hand, the creature behind me sent the Skaldi warrior flying through the air. His hairy body came to rest before the circle of weapons that guarded the only way out of the city.

I heard the voice of SunGru above the crowd, calling to me in a calm but urgent tone. "RJ, it's one of the Fallen Ones. Fall back to us!"

The Fallen One was as fierce-looking as described in the stories recounted to me by both the Quaylin and Skaldi. Angelic, with incredibly ornate wings, the tell-tale sword with red flames running along the blade's edges greeted my eyes.

Other beings also rushed through the city gate, but they were only a blur to me.

Now I faced an angel. It was then that the creature spoke, not the typical "I bring to you tidings of great joy which shall be to all people." But something much darker came from its lips.

"Bow, Son of Adam, before your true master. I will have blood for my imprisonment! Five thousand years! Did they not think that was enough for my crimes against the Maker? No, it was not enough for them. They killed my firstborn in front of me. When I fled, they hunted me. Even as I fled the Earth, they gave chase. It was here on the nearby plains that they caught me. I killed many of them before I was overwhelmed and imprisoned inside the bowels of this accursed place.

"I waited; a hundred years was nothing compared to what I had already suffered. Those who guarded me grew lax in their diligence. I broke free once more from the deep dungeon, killing my guards. Only to realize that my prison cell included this whole profane city."

Time stood still around me and the Fallen One. Slowly, unsure where it came from, my courage began to push down my fear.

At first, everyone there, including me, saw a vision of God's brilliant messenger, portrayed as the angel wished. However, the image everyone else was seeing began to fade before my eyes. The stereotypical bearer of glad tidings and great joy, the very warrior of heaven, disappeared in the light.

In its place, a being of pure evil replaced the former being of glory.

"I will not bow, you who are cursed and fallen!" I shouted.

The look on the being's face shifted from anger to raw hatred in an instant. I reached for the .45 at my hip and felt metal caress my palm. The Fallen One lunged forward, its sword heating the air as it narrowly missed me. The .45 felt odd. When I glanced down, it was not in my hand but still at my side. In its place, the metal I felt was a sword to match the one my enemy was now swinging in my direction.

I had some basic knowledge of swordplay, at least enough to know that I should counter-move as the two blades sparked, glancing off each other. Everything was happening in slow motion.

Later, everyone I asked claimed I had, by the grace of the Maker, single-handedly defeated the rogue angel. But I knew better. I dodged and pushed my assailant back into the city itself. To my horror, the gates closed silently behind me, isolating me from my comrades. It was then that I saw three figures. I could not tell if they had materialized or had come from within the city. The three warriors overwhelmed the enemy before me. The middle one grabbed the fallen angel by the hair, causing his head to snap back. The two on either side restrained his arms.

The middle angel began to speak. "The day of reckoning is upon you, Batariel! For crimes committed against the Creator and creation, your sentence is death. Your sword and your titles are forfeit. Your end is at hand."

The same angel said to me, "Son of Adam, come now! Pierce his body. For this is the Maker's will."

An unseen hand pushed me forward and my sword pierced the fallen being's chest. There was a burst of light, a gasp as the last air left the being's lungs. A burning sensation raced through my body, ending as a terrible pain in my temple.

Just inside the main gates, the blackened imprint of the fallen angel's body appeared on the city street's pavement.

Later, I would learn this was called a 'Soul Burn', a stain to endure as a reminder that all have come short of the Glory of God. Allen's research enlightened me regarding this fallen angel, once known as Batariel. He was a chief among the two hundred Watchers. His name meant 'Valley' or 'Rain of God.' Captured and imprisoned, he escaped when the lesser angels assigned to watch him had been deceived and killed.

The middle angel then spoke to me again. "We will take the body of our fallen brother to his final resting place. It has been nearly an age since Adam's son received the 'Mark of the Maker.' The mark on your forehead will make you a leader among men. God willing, you will rule this place with courage and wisdom. May your reign benefit those assembled in this hour of greatest need. We that serve the Maker salute you now, Àrd-Rìgh."

No idea what he was saying. What is an Àrd-Rìgh?

The three angels revealed their true identities – an elite team that hunted and eliminated the Fallen. The angels to either side were Jophile and Zadkiel, who stood as the standard-bearers of Michael the Archangel himself during battle. The center angel was Metatron, a prince among the Ophanim.

As the angels left the city, the gates rolled open again, leaving only me and the image of the Soul Burn, at the entrance to the city.

The next moment, I was being pulled almost off my feet in the grip of the Skaldi leader, Kraq. "Àrd-Rìgh, your face! Are you injured?"

155

I could hear Rachel screaming for Gretchen to help me.

As my companions gathered around me, I wondered why Kraq had called me Àrd-Rìgh. What does it mean? Most words are translated into a semblance of English for us. This word did not.

Gretchen pushed everyone else aside and began to examine my eyes. "RJ, are you ok? Show me where you are hurt." Her small flashlight crossed my line of sight, first left to right and then up and down on each eye.

"I assure you, I can see just fine. Why?"

"There is an odd blue membrane on your forehead, although it seems to be fading."

They all seemed much more concerned about my health than that I had just killed some supernatural being. When it ceased to exist, it had left the outline of a large, winged angel-like being, inside the gates.

"He is unharmed in the traditional sense," one of SunGru's advisors stated. He was the oldest Q that I had encountered. I did not recall ever seeing him in the camp before. "He has killed one of the Fallen Ones in single-handed combat. All hail the Àrd-Rìgh!"

I looked down. As I walked back into the gatehouse, the sword was no longer in my hand. The elder Quaylin was following me. At first, his mutterings made no sense. "Àrd-Rìgh, are you all right?"

"I appear to have misplaced my sword," I said.

"Sire, your sword comes when you call for it," the elder Q explained.

"What?"

"Your sword. It is a thing of power. You do not carry it in a sheath like a physical sword. Think about it in your mind. The sword will appear."

I tried, and nothing happened.

"Close your eyes. Imagine that you once more are facing down that evil being."

My eyes closed and opened. Standing in front of the Soul Burn, I saw it once again.

"There it is!"

I looked at my right hand. There was the sword wreathed in blue flames.

"It is more of an instinct, while adrenaline doesn't hurt either," he explained.

"How are you so well informed about this? Why is everyone suddenly calling me that name?" I felt confused.

"My years are many. I served the Quaylin Emperor. This fallen angel is not the first Fallen One I have seen killed. As for everyone calling you Àrd-Rìgh, the origin is ancient, and the meaning is High King."

"Why wouldn't they use the word for High King in Quaylin or Skaldi?"

"You are from Earth; your heritage is Celtic, correct?"

"Yes."

"It is something in the air, Àrd-Rìgh. If you haven't noticed, I can understand you even though my language is a variation of the Chinese spoken in your world."

"Yes, now that you mention it. Very handy to understand everyone."

"It can be annoying. To keep a secret, write in your language, as writing that remains untranslated is secret. Sire, I suggest you have guards set about the gate until you deal with the Ator."

"The Ator?" The older man pointed behind us at the battle that had ensued while I was inside the gatehouse, dealing with the Fallen Angel. "SunGru and Kraq, my friends, I need counsel. Set a guard about the gates, and no one enters the city until granted permission." The only ones who were looking strangely at me were my friends. "I will explain in a moment," I reassured them. When I turned back around to thank the elderly Q man, he was gone.

When the danger began, my friends naturally ran to safety within the ring of steel provided by the Skaldi and Quaylin warriors, who immediately engaged the handful of beings that had emerged from the gate as it closed.

These were the Ator, a race of reptilian giants sworn to the service of the Fallen Ones. Thus far, in our adventure, we had not encountered these creatures. Usually, they are not immediately unleashed. They tend to poison their spears and weapons. The sight of Skaldi and Quaylin warriors working together had caught the Ator off guard, giving our side the advantage of dispatching this new foe quickly.

"I need to know what you saw. Please, in your own words, what happened?" I queried SunGru and Kraq.

"Àrd-Rìgh, I saw your forehead glow blue before you walked into the gatehouse. As the gates closed, I saw you brandishing a flaming blue sword," SunGru replied.

"That is what I saw, as well. When the gates opened again, you had destroyed the Fallen One. His Soul Burn was marked upon the stone," Kraq added.

"Why is everyone calling me Àrd-Rìgh?"

I wanted to know their interpretation to compare it to what the old Quaylin had told me. My training in 'trust but verify' has served me well. There was no reason to lose my habit of logical thinking during unlikely circumstances.

SunGru was the first to respond after a thoughtful pause. "Àrd-Rìgh translates as High King. While a foreign word to the Quaylin, it would compare in stature to our Emperor. Maybe for Kraq and the Skaldi, it would compare to their highest tribal leader?"

"You killed one of the Fallen Ones in single combat," Kraq said, kneeling. "You are the Àrd-Rìgh. I hold no other allegiance but to Clan."

SunGru also knelt. "In the absence of my Emperor, I swear no other allegiance whatever becomes of us. Àrd-Rìgh, this city is now firmly in your hands. Blessings and wisdom of the Maker to you," SunGru proclaimed.

"Please, my friends, when we are alone, try to call me RJ or Major. This high king nonsense makes me uncomfortable." There were nods of agreement. Show off your otherworldly fighting skills, make a truce for the first time in thousands of years, kill a lesser deity, and suddenly they make you king. It was a nightmare of my own making.

SunGru waved his hands and struggled not to repeat the word 'Àrd-Rìgh,' as it seemed to be causing me discomfort.

"RJ, try not to worry about titles right now. We have much to discuss. The city is now open, thanks to your prowess and masterful touch."

I had one last question, "Why do you claim that I killed the Fallen One?"

Kraq was quick to answer. "I have only ever seen such a mark on the ground once, long ago, when my great-grandfather took me to a place of meaning for the Skaldi. Holy ground, if you like. The story is of one of my ancestors. Far back in the memory of time, a Fallen One challenged him for the Blue Clan rule. The challenge is to succeed without weapons, relying only on raw strength. When the Fallen One agreed, they began to wrestle. One of the chief's bodyguards, not wanting to see his leader fail, put a spear between the Fallen One's shoulder blades. It left a mark in that spot, not unlike this one."

"What happened after that?"

"The Blue Clan was hunted like dogs until only a handful remained, and then the persecution stopped. It was ages before anyone saw another Fallen One in the Other Realms."

From this point forward, everyone tiptoed around me. Àrd-Rìgh this and Àrd-Rìgh that. I ignored the awkward situation and began to direct our team and the Skaldi and Quaylin leadership.

CHAPTER 20

Over the next several days, we began moving the Q refugees into the city. There was much rejoicing among some of the men as they were reunited with family or friends, but at some point, a split emerged within the group over which direction to take, with a choice between going west or north.

Unfortunately, SunGru's family was not among this group of Q refugees. Naturally, the poor fellow was distraught upon discovering this.

Scouts were placed at various intervals from where the plains met the pass through the defile, right up to the first set of bridge-towers. If we got hemmed in by a Skaldi army, we would want advanced warning.

Companies of scouts took to the walls to set up guard posts. These men were tasked with watching for any enemy still within the city, and sounding the alarm.

"Gather anyone with architectural and engineering knowledge, military or otherwise. Allen, please do your thing. We need to map the city carefully. Or is that a waste of time? I know we will only have one map."

Allen seemed to be a little off, considering what he had just witnessed. "Once we build the map, I can send an application to each phone. Everyone can follow the map using POIs. As exploration continues, I can track where the phone is on the larger map."

"POI?" I asked.

"Points of interest. We can tag outstanding buildings, intersections, artwork, and monuments," Allen stated. "Then over the comms, I could say, 'Meet RJ at POI number five.' Anyone with a phone can see it on the map. Eventually, everyone would know where that location is and what makes it a point of interest."

"The only problem with our phones is power. Mine is dead." I had forgotten to turn it off to conserve energy.

"Maybe Andy and Jim will help me set up? I need a secure location from which to coordinate." Allen began, "Shelter is necessary. Once we get set up, everything must remain in place for days, perhaps weeks. The location needs to be higher, have a good line of sight, and be covered."

Shortly after the broadcast request, Andy spoke over the comms. "Allen, I need you to come to my location. I believe I have the perfect spot, directly above you."

To either side of the city's gates were high twin towers that stretched an imposing eight stories into the sky. The gatehouse was a six-story building that housed the gate mechanism.

The gates did not swing on hinges but glided over nearly invisible tracks. Gates, yes, plural; there were two sets. The fallen angel had opened the first pair. Behind each gate, there was also a portcullis. The gates were thirty feet in height, four feet thick, and the opening was sixty feet across. Above the gates were another three stories containing barracks.

There was also an old armory and weapons storage room, which looked unused; the blades were still sharp after a thousand years.

The rooftop of the gatehouse was the perfect spot for Allen to set up the command center. SunGru had taken up residence in the South Gate Castle. He graciously gifted his spacious tent for use on the gatehouse rooftop, providing shade and allowing unparalleled city views. Several Skaldi arrived with high wooden tables and chairs to place under the tent canopy. Allen quickly began work. For the moment, all Allen had was his laptop. However, Bill and our wagon load of cases crossed the bridge system. While we waited, we completed a survey of the nearest buildings.

The walls and buildings appeared white, but not a harsh white or reflective to hurt one's eyes. Five stories in height and sixty feet thick, the walls stretched as far along the city's outer side as the eye could see.

The exterior wall was impact-resistant from the ground to at least twelve feet high, the height of the Skaldi warrior who earlier bounced back upon hammer impact at the gates. This characteristic would serve as an excellent defense against battering rams or explosives. I made a mental note to investigate this fantastic material when time allowed.

We were impressed by the care given in the design and usage of the wall space. Inside this thick outer wall were inner chambers at least forty feet deep. Rachel estimated the rooms on the first level of the wall to be twenty feet tall from floor to ceiling. "These rooms remind me of retail and warehouse spaces. Very high ceilings."

Gretchen continued the thought. "The second and third levels remind me of the townhouse that I lived in, at college."

"How convenient that the shop owner and family can live above their retail area," Becky observed.

The fourth and final level, situated just beneath the wall's parapet, was a continuous room that appeared to span the entire length of the wall. The interior, or city side, of the room housed barracks and armory storage. Upon further exploration, we found that every fourth wall section contained a kitchen. There was also what appeared to be a command position with a panel of instruments that no one was to touch until Allen examined it.

Next to each command center, there was a break in the wall containing a tower. These were at five-hundred-foot intervals. This plan was ingenious. It allowed large numbers of troops to access different areas of the wall undetected by the enemy outside.

In the late afternoon, Allen's voice came over the comms, interrupting my thoughts and copious note-taking efforts.

"RJ, do you think we could get someone to ride around that main avenue along the outer side of the city to give me some idea of what we are dealing with here? If SunGru could loan a runner?"

"What would he be doing?" I asked.

"I would attach one of the watches to him, and the watch's accelerometer application would calculate how far he ran to give us the city's perimeter in yards or miles."

"I don't think it's safe for someone to be out there in the city alone."

"You could send several runners and some horsemen. If a runner got tired, he could take a break on the horse while the man who was on the horse took a turn running? It wouldn't be as precise, but I guess the total would only be slightly off from the actual distance," Allen stated.

Allen gave me a moment to catch up with him on the top of the wall. He pointed out across the expanse of the large city. "I can average out the times. It will roughly give me an idea of the total possible circumference, based on calculated shorter distance times."

I saw where he was going with this, although explaining the science in simple terms seemed to have exhausted him. I nodded in agreement.

Allen continued, "This will certainly take longer than expected. We should wait until tomorrow to begin. The upsetting thing is that this will not be an exact measurement. I expect that my final report will be off by several feet. I hope no one will hold me accountable due to the lack of appropriate equipment."

Allen seemed upset that there was no better way to secure the information. I bit my lip to stop myself from laughing. I donned a look that I hoped showed concern and sympathy instead.

He continued, barely noticing. "The crudeness of the method bothers me a bit. Yet what are a few feet when measuring a wall of perhaps twenty-five miles?"

I was bounced momentarily from my thoughts. "Wait, Allen, are you saying the wall is twenty-five miles long?"

"Yes, I can't be precise, of course. I thought I already explained that part to you?"

"Well, I'm just trying to fathom the size of this city itself."

I wanted to wrap my mind around the possibility that we may have found a permanent home for the Q and any allies. Imagine a city large enough to support a growing population and its military needs. Allen was already several yards ahead. I raced to catch up, hoping I had caught everything significant that he said.

"There were some nice-sized walls built on Earth. Perhaps you recall the Great Wall of China?" Allen grinned almost awkwardly. His attempts at humor seldom happened, so you needed the grin to be sure. "For instance, Avila in Spain has nine gates and eighty-eight watchtowers. In China, Pingyao has six gatehouses and seventy-two towers. The ancient city of Babylon was over fifty miles around and was nearly three hundred feet high in some places."

"I understand, Allen, but what are the odds of finding this city in our moment of need?"

Allen's facial expression shifted from one of explanation to that of a computer genuinely attempting to quantify the actual odds of this event happening down to the decimal point and the numbers that followed.

I gave him a gentle push. His eyes followed my pointing finger across the horizon, jolting him out of computer mode and back to reality. "Wow, this place is amazing. So could you rig something up, like a camera, so we can see what they see, while they ride or run?"

Allen nodded again. He had been multitasking on several ideas as we walked and talked. "I'll make a helmet for Andy with a camera facing forward, you will get a 180-degree line of sight. Then I can combine the footage to make a movie about the city."

"Brilliant idea!" I praised Allen's skill.

The movie will show the city and any damaged areas. We might find distinct buildings worth exploring.

The next day, we started early as the ride would take the entire day. Allen fitted Andy with the helmet and checked the cameras and the connection to his laptop. As soon as Andy was ready, he went to stand over the city gatehouse.

"Hey, the other riders and runners are waiting down there for you." I pointed at the riders below us on the city street.

Andy chuckled, "I will be taking the high road. If I ride down there, you won't see anything on your movie but walls."

"How are you going to get a horse up here? Have a Skaldi carry it up for you?"

Another chuckle came from Andy as he opened a door on the side of a gatehouse tower.

Inside the wall, a ramp ran from the top on the left side and ended at the bottom tower door on the far side. If adventurous, you could ride a horse up the ramp. Or, if you were cautious, you could lead one. This critical and ingenious device allowed heavy cavalry to defend the city.

Messengers could ride along the top of the wall without disrupting the civilian population below.

"Whoever designed this place thought of everything, didn't they?" Andy seemed genuinely impressed. He had also told the volunteer riders they would receive a double portion of wine. They were invited to sit at SunGru's table during a feast in their honor, celebrating our good fortune and the Maker's blessings.

I still had to inform SunGru of that little addition and hoped that the movie 'magic' this evening would more than make up for the extra arrangements.

Andy moved out with the first set, but it was not a race for him. It aimed to get a 'big picture' look at the city and the surrounding topography across the chasm.

Meanwhile, not far from the tent Allen was using, SunGru and Kraq continued to make progress in figuring out the communication lines. They formed a fast friendship. Seeing the two of them talking on the battlements was nearly comic. While Kraq sat at ground level on the wall's walking portion, SunGru sat on the parapet's merlon.

I knew these terms. I had been quickly schooled on parts of a castle by the general the day before. Merlons are the high points of the parapets you take cover behind, while the crenels are the dips through which you dispense your spears and arrows. I had always loved the idea of the castle. I was beginning to understand the building's aesthetics and the reasons behind each part of the defensive structure.

Using my binoculars, I scanned the city's grandeur. A pang of hunger made me cast my eyes over the side of the wall down to where they were unloading the kitchen wagons into a sizeable warehouse structure. Bill and Cook were directing and helping set up the large open area in front. This evening, a feast and celebration will include Allen and Andy's film efforts. This wall was the perfect spot to project the movie.

I could still see a long train of wagons continuing across the bridges. Then Jim pointed out an odd grouping of carts halfway across that carried sixty-foot-tall trees stripped of their branches. "What do you suppose those are for?"

I shook my head. "I'm guessing the three Fs. Firewood, Furniture, and Field Artillery."

Jim shrugged and laughed. "Better guess than mine."

I laughed, "Field artillery? Really?"

Late in the afternoon, the sets of riders began to appear so Allen could calculate their times and distances. Andy arrived about two hours after the last group. I could tell he had enjoyed his ride. As soon as he was off the horse, he tried to recount all the details. It was all Allen could do to secure the camera helmet from Andy.

I calmed Andy down and told him we would all see the incredible things he found on his journey as soon as the celebration ended.

I had the three F's conversation with Kraq and SunGru as we ate. They reassured me that the trees were for firewood and furniture.

We already had adequate defenses, and field artillery would be useless here.

Allen had a 'Eureka' moment and announced his calculations based on the riders' travel times and speeds. "I estimate that the city is sitting on a seven-mile-wide plateau. The outer perimeter of the city wall completes a perfect circle and covers twenty-two miles. Additionally, as items of special interest, there are identical bridges across the chasm, just like this one, located directly north, south, and east. The one we occupy now faces south."

I thought that was a bit odd, "What about the West?"

"No pass exists to the west. It appears to me that there is a castle and there are bridges, but they face a large body of water. I will say no more, or I will ruin movie night," Allen finished.

"Twenty-two miles in circumference and seven miles in diameter. Bridge systems and fortifications every five and a half miles! Impossible to pull off without advanced knowledge and technology", Andy began as the movie played.

Allen had guaranteed a show at nightfall, but everyone seemed a little upset about having to wait. So I asked Rachel to go for a walk. We chose to walk the grand hallway below to enjoy the cooler air provided by the battlements. We craved shade from the sun and a sense of privacy. We discussed the journey thus far and the encounter with the Fallen One at the gates. I attempted to explain my experiences in those moments.

My forehead no longer glowed, suggesting that it only changed in conjunction with the sword, possibly anger related. I told her about seeing the angels. It was a harsh pill to swallow, considering I was the only one who had seen them.

The wall's hollow interior at street level had twenty-foot interiors and grand arches that opened to the street side. The second and third levels above seemed ideally suited for a living area and only connected to the 'warehouse' or 'storage' area below. The fourth level, located under the wall, contained long hallways where men could move unseen—these housed barracks and armories. Every five hundred feet, steps led to the parapets.

We walked through the upper level and up a tower onto the westward open wall section. On the main road below us, a group of Skaldi was cutting firewood for the kitchen and for heating. Rachel and I waved to them, and they waved back, some pointing excitedly and shouting "Àrd-Rìgh" at us.

What was the next topic of discussion? "Allen and Becky have confirmed that Àrd-Rìgh in the old Celtic language means 'high king.' Metatron called me right before the angels left the city. The name has been impressed on everyone's mind, and now I am being called Àrd-Rìgh. I find it uncomfortable!"

I told her I would openly discourage being called 'high king'.

Rachel disagreed, "If an angel has pushed it into everyone's precognitive mind, there was a reason."

We turned and began to walk back when Allen's voice came over the comms. "RJ, I have a few more calculations to show you."

I knew what was coming next when I heard Andy's voice. "That would be 'Àrd-Rìgh' to you, peasant."

I understood the fastest way to cool off this conversation was with a promotion.

"Allen, I grant you both title and land. You will forever be known as the Count of Abacus." There were chuckles all around on the comms. Even Allen had a good laugh.

Then I waited for it. "Does the great Àrd-Rìgh' have a title and land for me?" asked Andy.

He was finally warming up. "Lord of the Air, I should think. Commander of His Majesty's Royal Air Force? Oh, wait, I forgot you're indefinitely grounded."

More laughter over the comms. Andy mumbled something about deserving that and missing Betty. Left sitting in a Colorado field, his helicopter weighed heavily on his mind.

CHAPTER 21

Bill announced that the 'pre-show snack shop' was now open for business, interrupting Allen and Andy's teasing. I had to wonder what Bill had in mind. Oddly enough, it was an excellent pudding-like dessert, a jellied pastry, and a cup of what tasted something like warm mulled cider.

Everyone settled onto the benches or leaned against the walls to watch the movie Allen had made. We explained again that this was not magic. However, the technology that surpassed all others in this realm was challenging to interpret. I returned to Rachel and our friends, who were seated on a balcony immediately below Allen and his laptop with the movie projector.

Some shouting, oohs, and aahs came from the crowd below, but as the calming music began, everyone settled in to watch. Allen pulled a chair beside me and passed me some notes and a flashlight. Like most cities, the city consisted of blocks with streets and cross streets.

As Andy moved along, I noticed that the city's second-level gateway came halfway between the South Gate Pass and the East Gate Pass. Another entrance was half the distance between the East and North Gate Pass. This pattern continued.

There were two marketplaces between each gatehouse, similar to the one we overlooked now, and an arena in the center of each city quadrant. The person who designed and built the city had taken great care in its planning. We also saw a small, hospital-like building in each quadrant, along with what remained of these once beautiful gardens.

The movie was a huge success. Everyone insisted that we watch the video again the next night. Bill guessed it was just an excuse to eat his goodies and went to plan an even better snack for the following night's showing.

SunGru introduced me to an older Quaylin couple who had lost everything in one of the larger villages burnt and ransacked by the Skaldi army. The man had held the position of Guild Master and had been a tailor by trade. He now offered his services to manage the marketplace. The gentleman and his wife wanted to establish their tailor shop and be responsible for finding suitable shop fronts based on the artisan's or craftsman's needs. It was necessary to begin this process as word had arrived that the Quaylin refugees were only a day outside the city. The Guild Master and his assigned men will register the arriving families and assign them homes based on their talents and skills.

My team went into a mode similar to that of famine and disaster relief aid. No one would be cold or hungry if we could help it.

The Quaylin refugees were now arriving through the South Gate Castle.

We made progress in devising a system to secure housing and workshops for skilled merchants and artisans. The other groups, such as farmers, were another story altogether. The accommodation of refugees was the least of my worries. Food was a commodity that might become scarce if we didn't come up with a solution shortly. Some families brought wagons pulled by oxen filled with food and household items. At the same time, many had only a few ragged clothes, worn-out shoes, and little else. A few had livestock, some cattle, sheep, and pigs that they had saved, but those were far too few to feed our numbers.

I suggested, "We should check out the western quadrant of the city for food sources. Notice how the mountains surround us to all sides except to the west of the city walls. There, the land drops away. Andy, your movie shows that a fortress identical to this one sits to the west. The difference is that it opens to a large meadow that slopes to a large body of water."

The bridge at the western castle crossed over the gorge. Then, the series of defensive towers led down a narrow stretch of land to the lake. A large body of water of unknown size stretched as far as the eye could see. Lush grasslands covered either side of the body of water, and to the west, far-off mountains completed the ring in the background. A series of waterfalls flowed from the lake over the edge into the canyon below.

We used the bridge system from the castle to cross the gorge and reach the lake. SunGru enlisted a group of his men who had been fishermen. We had no boats, nets, or fishing gear, but these men were our best hope for securing another source of food.

"We should take a few Skaldi warriors with us as well, just in case we run into trouble," Andy suggested.

While I agreed that the protection would be invaluable, we now must get Kraq to consent. His men might be in harm's way for the benefit of the Quaylin refugees. How deep had Skaldi's friendship with the Q become?

We saw a sizeable stone structure built beside the lake as we approached. Ancient was the word that sprang to mind, upon seeing the timber-and-slate roof in ruins. A stone fishing pier reached out over a hundred feet into the lake. Inside the building, a series of small boats and canoes were stored upside down. Most looked solid enough to float, although someone might get wet to test that theory.

The next room held several workbenches. There were carved wooden buoys and various metal hooks, but all netting or lines had rotted over time. The final rooms were a prep area for fresh fish and a smoking area for the catch. I had to call Bill on the comms and tell him what we found. We needed to make nets and fishing lines, but other than that, we would have another source of food shortly.

Andy pointed out, "This is all great if there are still fish in the lake. And if they are the edible kind."

The men were already shouting and pointing to ripples on the smooth surface. An occasional fish jumped out to snap up a flying insect. We were fortunate; there were plenty of fish. The palatability and nutrition of the fish would have to be determined by Bill and Cook.

The far end of the building was in deplorable shape. However, an exciting find was several metal wagon wheels hanging on the end wall among the rubble. The group of Skaldi that Kraq had agreed to send along boasted of their wainwright skill. They promised a wagon to transport fish by the time the Quaylin could catch enough to carry. For a moment, I feared the Q might be insulted.

The oldest and most experienced of the Quaylin fishermen grasped the hand of the Skaldi, who had started this boast. "You have a bet."

The big Skaldi laughed. "Hurry, my Q friends. My breakfast was long ago! A meal of fresh fish would be a tasty reward for our morning labors."

Then, everyone laughed as the fishermen began testing the boats for buoyancy. The Skaldi, with their great battle axes, marched off to the closest trees to start work on some wagon or cart parts to go with the wheels.

I called Bill on the comm. "We are at the lake, and you will be relieved that we found fish. I hope they meet your culinary standards. While the Q fish, the Skaldi, are building transportation."

Bill replied, "Wonderful news. Jim and I are on our way with two of Cook's apprentice chefs. Andy, please inform the Skaldi to cut down some dead hardwood trees for the smokers. Determine if they are aware of the correct tree species to avoid a bitter taste. Have them wait until I arrive to supervise. Oh, and some trees are poisonous. On second thought, they should wait for me to pick the trees I want."

I hadn't realized that burning the wrong tree could cause a bitter taste or even be poisonous to someone. Bill's depth of knowledge continued to amaze me. He arrived with his dogs and his new helpers. He began looking through the building's rooms after getting the Skaldi on the right track for suitable trees for the fires. Bill and his crew started to clean the metal grates and found and organized an outdoor grill of sorts.

"Bill, is this for smoking the fish when the fishermen bring in their first catch?" I asked.

Bill gave me a friendly glare and replied, "No. RJ, this is for lunch." He chuckled with his big-hearted laugh. Waving me inside, he showed me the actual smoker room. "After lunch, we will clean this room to my high standards.

"Then, I will organize one crew to fish and one to operate the smoker. I suggest that Skaldi cut some planks and begin work on the roof of this building. If we are going to provide enough food, we need a dry and sanitary environment, as soon as possible."

"We should build a bunkhouse for those remaining here, fishing and working the smoker," I said.

Andy quickly pointed out, "For safety, a far better solution is staying in the first tower at night. We don't know what animals might live in this area."

"Good point, Andy. We have yet to explore the entire west side of this new city." I was letting my guard down as I began to feel comfortable in this new world.

Jim suggested, "Let's explore the area around this side of the lake. I estimate the lake is approximately forty miles across and easily twice that distance going west."

With no one to tend it, the grass around the lake's edge had grown nearly as tall as a man. In some spots, the grass appeared to have been mowed down. I was walking several yards ahead of Jim when I heard a snort to one side of me. Instinctively, I wished for the sword to be in my hand, but I flicked the trigger guard off my 9mm when it didn't appear.

Before I could pull my weapon, however, something was upon me!

Hot breath on my neck. Hair flying around me. I scrambled to keep my footing, but it was too late. I closed my eyes, waiting for the end to come. Then I felt the slime dripping from some fearsome beast's jaws.

I heard boisterous laughter as Jim said, "Let me pull you to safety!"

My eyes flickered open, but I heard no sounds of a gun's discharge. "You let that thing go? What was it?" I yelled.

Jim continued to laugh while pointing toward the water's edge. The animal stood, all four legs on the ground with its head dipped to the water's edge, drinking. Now, it was my turn to be embarrassed as I saw a massive bull that had led a small herd of cows and calves to the water. These cattle and their ancestors had not seen humans for a thousand years.

Every once in a while, Andy said something profound or spouted off some tidbit of knowledge that made everyone wonder. I'm not saying Andy isn't intelligent; he is. Often, the subject matter was what had us thinking.

This time, it was Jim's turn to be profound. He was a Navy SEAL, not just a team leader, but a chief. A man among men. "Those appear to be 'Heilan Coo.' Well, to be proper, they might be 'Bo Chaidhealach,' but they are undoubtedly Scottish cows," Jim stated.

I looked at Andy, and he stared at me. Neither of us was familiar with Jim's cows. "Boo Coo cows?" I asked.

Jim took a moment to reassess the herd. "These are Highlander cattle. They are an excellent source of meat, blankets, and drinking horns. Their milk isn't good to drink, but it is high in butterfat for making butter and cheese. I believe they come in about seven different colorings as well."

Andy and I looked on in dumbfounded silence as the amount of knowledge spewed forth.

"What? I read!" Jim exclaimed.

Then, it was my turn to point. A growing herd of curious cattle had come to see a rare sight, one not seen for more than a thousand years. Humans. We snapped a few photos to show Bill, then returned for a grilled fish lunch. We pulled Bill aside to show him our selfies when we arrived at the small camp.

"Ah, Heilan Coo!" Bill exclaimed. "Here?"

"Yes, a decent herd of them," Jim replied.

Bill demanded to see the cattle for himself. We agreed to show him when time allowed. Bill wanted to return to the city to oversee the mass feeding later that evening. We decided to return to the lake in a few days to see how the fishery was working and to visit the cows we had discovered.

As we traveled to the tower for the night, I heard Bill mumble about 'glorious cheese' and 'butter for my bread' and 'the cattle on a thousand hills.' He roared in delight, causing the Skaldi to look around and grab their weapons.

"Bill, how did your day go? Did you get everything in order?" I asked.

"A good day, indeed! I return to East Gate, feeling secure that the two men I left in charge know what they are doing." Bill replied.

Before leaving the lake for the day, I instructed the Skaldi to continue work on the building and any other needed repairs. However, I stressed that everyone must shelter inside the west tower well before the sun went down with watch fires for warmth, light, and protection. By everyone, I meant both Skaldi and Quaylin.

We arrived back in the city a few hours before supper. We realized that setting aside old differences between Quaylin and Skaldi might take longer than expected. Kraq had suggested that he and his men find housing in the North Gate Castle, to which SunGru and I agreed. There were only about a hundred Skaldi, but I was sure that Kraq would eventually convince more of his brethren to join us.

It was hard to watch the little Q children scream in terror at the mere sight of the Skaldi warriors, who had sacrificed everything to join us. SunGru and I assured Kraq that we would speak to the Quaylin people the next day to fully explain the Skaldi presence.

The Quaylin capital city, Hu'ang Se City, sounded like a city with hundreds of thousands, perhaps even a million people. It didn't surprise us, as over the next month, nearly 10,000 refugees found new homes and jobs in the city.

Shops began lining the wall between the southern and northern gates. This market growth was a sign of progress. However, the Guild Master informed us that most people had no money to buy items, and only a few could trade for the goods offered. Currency and coinage still needed to be fully considered. SunGru and a small group of merchants had contributed their small chests of coins to the city coffers. While generous on their part, the coffers required much more. Distribution and minting were now an issue. Who should get money, and how much? We started an economic movement in the marketplace with virtually no means for ordinary citizens to participate.

Allen, the closest thing we had to an economist, ran pricing and market values through his computer. I could not wait for him to create a solution; I had to have one. I thought back to the fallen angel, Batariel. What would I have done with my time trapped in a deserted city for a thousand years or more if I were him? Eventually, I would find a beautiful place to relax and store the goods I found while roaming the city. Jim had taken Bill to see the Scottish cattle by the lake, so I grabbed Andy.

What did he think of my theory?

Andy thought a moment. "Do you think a fallen angel would have been comfortable living in a church? Or do you think that would have been a bit too creepy?"

"What church? You found a church?" The prospect of a place of worship delighted me.

"The second tier has a huge cathedral. Maybe Batariel was hiding in there?" It appears that Andy had been quite busy exploring without me.

"All right, let's check out the church."

Andy captured an incredible panorama from the heights of the wall that we all got to see on the "big screen" during our first 'movie night' in the Other Realms. The movie had become so popular that people insisted it played each night. Some of those who had seen it several times began skipping the show, but each night new faces replaced them in the crowd.

Allen was busy creating a visual map that corresponded to an official city map and an electronic version for our phones. As long as we charged our phones at night with Allen's portable solar collector, we could use the application he had downloaded and updated daily from his laptop. Allen had secluded himself in the rooftop tent, buried in his work for many hours a day. This arrangement was fine with me. The results would be worth the effort, and a side benefit was that it kept him out of the way.

Gretchen and Rachel worked with SunGru's field surgeons to staff and supply two of the medical centers. Becky had found several Quaylin teachers and now took over two large warehouses for a daily school. Quaylin artisans provided her with long, wooden tables and benches. The goal was to provide classrooms that would give the children stability and a welcome break for mothers to work in their households or at the local shops.

CHAPTER 22

"Are we heading to the unexplored second tier?" I asked.

Packs on, Andy and I began walking from the first-tier walls where we had set up our temporary camp, three-quarters of a mile to the second-tier city walls. There were four such levels, with some grand buildings and towers at the top. The city was so big that further exploration was not a priority.

"The second-tier gates aren't open. However, no force field or device stops anyone from throwing and securing a grappling hook."

"You threw a grappling hook and secured it at this distance?" I knew Andy was good, but not that good.

"No, I had some help," Andy said with a chuckle.

"Help? Really? Did you bring Kraq out here and ask him to take a try?" I grinned as I was sure even Kraq would have failed in such an attempt.

"I may have borrowed Jim's toy to help in my endeavor," Andy admitted. "I returned it promptly but left my line to reach the second level again."

Sure enough, a large knotted rope dangled from the parapets, far enough away that someone exploring the gates would not have spotted it. For our safety, we did as Andy had on his first trip. We kept to the top of the wall.

We began our trek through the city, and I noticed that this tier was almost precisely a duplication of the first. While the walls contained shops and workspaces with housing above, as on the first level, we began to see more gardens on this level. The houses were an upgrade from those on the first tier of the city, which seemed commonplace compared to these more impressive buildings.

The church that Andy had spoken of was near the North Gate. Should we open the gates for Kraq and his men so they could explore on their own? I decided not to do that as his resources were stretched thin, with only a hundred Skaldi to guard the bridge and tower system that led to the North Pass.

Then I saw it.

No wonder Andy had suggested we check out this building. In the real sense of the word, a grand cathedral, this building reminded me of the style of the Canterbury Cathedral in Kent, England, a fortress unto itself. Later measurements revealed a nearly twenty-three-acre campus, surrounded by a fifteen-foot curtain wall, with two gatehouses. There were many buildings of interest inside.

The main cathedral building was over five hundred feet long and one hundred and fifty feet wide. The two main towers stretched more than two hundred feet into the clear blue sky at the north end of the building. The spire tower on the south end of the building was nearly two hundred feet tall. We could see bells hanging in all three of the main towers. There were monastic quarters, sparse and dusty, with wood-frame cots that had long ago lost their bedding to moths and time.

We found a shrine that should have housed the religious art and relics of the cathedral. It was bare? On the walls, you could see where the sunlight had discolored the stone where each banner had once adorned the hall.

"Well, that was disappointing," Andy said, interrupting my thought.

"No, you were spot on with this building complex. There will likely be something here of use to us. We have to find it," I responded, patting him on the back and grinning. I knew he was bored. Without the ability to hop in his bird and fly, he needed some adventure to restore balance.

We moved down the stairs at the second-tier gates closest to the North Gate Castle and worked our way back towards the cathedral. I wondered if anyone else was still inside the city. If there were more enemies, would anyone sweep in to save us this time?

The cathedral's high doors wouldn't open. We had no great Skaldi warrior with his battle-ax to make a hole for us, nor would we have wanted such beauty destroyed to gain entrance. We walked the entire complex until we found a much smaller single door leading into the basement of an annex building. We were able to pry this door open without damaging it.

Luckily, we had our packs, which included flashlights. The cellars were packed with armor and weapons, human-size, not Skaldi-size. Andy and I made our way through the basement until we found steps leading up into the cathedral's atrium.

We passed through the atrium, a tremendous pillar-lined area where the lower classes might sit on the stone floors. This area was now filled with weapons and armor, leaving a narrow passage through the endless piles of arms to the narthex's steps.

Moving up the series of steps into the Narthex, which separated the atrium from the Nave, we noticed wooden chests of every size and shape stacked in neat rows based on size. The crates in the narthex held bronze, silver, and gold coins, along with gems of every type!

Entering the Nave, its ceiling arched nearly one hundred feet above our heads.

"RJ, this must seat well over five hundred people," Andy said in awe.

That estimated number did not include the side annex seating off to the right and left of the nave. There were piles of treasures, including paintings, tapestries, maps, and items dipped in silver or gold. We now bore witness to the vast horde that the fallen angel Batariel, had acquired over his imprisonment here.

Towards the far end of the Nave seating was an open area, followed by choir chairs and the steps leading to the cathedral's bema. The bema held the altar and the pulpit area. Behind this, it looked like Batariel had made his place of rest. Random stacks of books surrounded an area covered in pillows, furs, and blankets.

I had no idea if angels slept, but being locked up in an abandoned city for a thousand years might require a place to relax. The area looked like someone had used the church as a warehouse for as many grand objects from the city as he could find and carry back.

Perhaps these treasures would have funded a war or his dreams of another throne. We would never know. It would take an army to transport everything to a more secure location. We had an army. Could we trust them with the job? Would infighting occur?

"My friend, we have a decision to make. I don't think we can leave this here. The urgent question is, where do we put the treasure?" I had many answers, but this one was complex.

"Maybe we could secure a storage location. Then, each family will have an income to begin their lives. Then do the same with the business owners?" Andy suggested.

"A logical idea in theory, but I think it'll be challenging to implement." I had grave doubts.

"We could find a cart and get smaller chests to the second-tier gates. We open the gates and push the cart through. Then I'll close the gates behind you and climb down the rope," Andy suggested.

"Then what do we do?" I was confident Andy had a plan, but would it work?

"We find a building further away from the crowds. I will wait with the cart until you bring SunGru and Kraq back to see what we found." Andy had come up with a viable plan.

"What about the giant cathedral full of treasure? When do we break that to them?" I asked.

Maybe Andy had another idea for this problem.

"I don't know. We need to judge the reactions of SunGru and Kraq to the smaller chests we deliver. See if they can come up with a plan. After that, we worry about the treasure that might cause rioting," Andy replied.

I nodded. Now was the time to find a cart to load several small chests. Andy locked the main entrance doors behind me, and went back through the basements. We weren't greedy. We removed any jewellery mixed in with the coins, so all we had was the currency. We took none of the treasure for ourselves. Before we left the area, I used the comms to contact Kraq and tell him where to meet us. Kraq told us he would be there in two hours. I hoped we could make it there in time, pushing the treasure-laden cart.

Not long after we arrived at the rendezvous spot, SunGru and Kraq each came with a small contingent of men. I asked that only the two leaders join us inside for the meeting.

"RJ, what could be of such great importance that we convene in secrecy in an abandoned part of the city?" SunGru asked.

"A burden that has been heavy on my mind of late has been commerce," I began.

"You took me from my work in the north to talk about silks and spices?" Kraq was having a rough day.

"No, my large friend. Not trade goods specifically, but the matter of currency. Money is necessary to pay the soldiers, so they, in turn, can buy in the shops without bartering," I began. "We need to return a sense of civilization to those entrusted to us within the city."

SunGru looked at Kraq, then back at me. "Could we not have spoken with the Quaylin Ministers about this over the evening meal?" Kraq nodded his agreement.

"No, not after I show you what Andy and I discovered," I replied, lifting the cover off the cart to reveal several small chests.

SunGru opened one of the chests to reveal the gold and silver coins. "RJ, this is a small fortune. Where did you find it?"

"I fear the revelation of such details wouldn't be a healthy burden for any of us," I responded. "Can this be properly divided and dispersed to the people, used in a civilized fashion that won't lead to corruption and theft?" I looked at Kraq. I had no idea how a Skaldi's life and commerce worked.

"I request one chest from which I will pay my men; I leave the rest to you. There are not enough of us to worry about. We eat with the Quaylin army while working or hunting for food in the North Pass. We care little for trinkets, but I would like to pay for custom armor and weapons to fit us better. We lead a simple, uncomplicated life," Kraq stated.

This response was both fitting and surprising. It was upsetting that my thoughts had pegged the Skaldi as great greedy brutes. That was not my intent.

SunGru understood what I was saying. Money was a necessary evil. "I have a Minister of Finance, whom I trust would be able to help set up a system for payment of both soldiers and workers. I am confident he could loan money to the shop owners and the trades."

"No. That is not what I am saying. Yes, the soldiers and military workers need to be paid. I want an account set up for each family as well. There will be no loans to business owners and artisans; each will start with seed money in an account."

SunGru looked slightly confused, but I saw Kraq could see where my train of thought was going.

"But RJ, this is not how things are normally run," SunGru protested.

I nodded. "This is not a normal situation. I want no man to wonder about his livelihood or how he will feed his family. There will be fair prices, with everyone working together."

"Capitalism on steroids," Andy stated, although only I knew what he meant.

"Yes. That's right. We will call a meeting with all the shop owners, artisans, and craftsmen. I want them to form guilds based on their goods, crafts, or services. Each guild's leaders will form a guild council to ensure cooperation, fair prices, and reasonable wages. First, we will see if these men and women can help govern people through commerce. If there are problems, we can help them resolve any issues."

Then I turned to Kraq. "Eventually, more of your people will join us. I want your artisans involved. For peace among the races, the Skaldi must also represent themselves in trade and service matters. I won't allow prices to vary due to race. Yes, the Skaldi are larger, so armor may cost him more, but it will be a good price nonetheless."

Once we all seemed to agree, we met with each group, who voted one of their own based on their merits to be their Guild Master. Each guild master was appointed to the guild council. It will be their duty to set fair trade and establish laws to govern commerce.

Thus, we began establishing an eternal city, built by the Old Ones, abandoned for a thousand years, and now gloriously reborn. We christened it with a new name - the City of Hope.

An elite unit now guarded the grounds of the cathedral.

CHAPTER 23

The next issue we faced was the inventory and warehousing of the weapons stored in the cathedral. Armories around the outer wall once more held dazzling displays of weapons and shields. The Quaylin were permitted to exchange their secondary armaments and armor for new pieces from the cathedral stockpile. Several blacksmiths discovered the city's ancient blacksmith forges. Thus began the long and challenging process of melting and reforming human-sized armor and weapons into Skaldi-sized pieces. Kraq should not bear the cost of this undertaking alone. I met with the blacksmiths and brought a small chest of gold and silver coins.

"I have deposited another small chest of gold into your guild's account to cover additional costs for the Skaldi. If you need more gold, let me know. It is a priority that the Skaldi who fight on the Maker's side are better protected and armed than those we meet in battle. Do you understand?"

"Yes, Àrd-Rìgh. We are honored to provide our friends with far superior armor. We will make battle axes to crush the rock if it opposes them," the smithy guild leader pronounced.

These were the assurances I expected from my men, even though I now stood in a strange city on an alien world.

That evening, I found that Jim had taken Bill to see the operational center the fishermen had set up at the lake. Fishing provided an alternative to the wild game.

They returned in time for dinner. As we ate and talked. Bill began with a request. "RJ, I need some of our Skaldi friends to help me."

I nodded, wondering if Bill was considering starting a pro football team, but instead, he pulled out a notebook and placed detailed plans for a ranch on the table. Bill continued while I looked at the notes and drawings.

"I need help building fencing, horse corrals, a barn, and the main house."

"Is this because of the cattle I discovered?" Bill chuckled, and Jim nearly spit his drink on me.

"We took horses with us and went for a longer ride this time," Jim replied, clearing his throat. "We found many more Highland cattle, along with several other cattle breeds, and the perfect location for a ranch."

Bill took it from there. "The Quaylin need a place for their horses. We can provide milk and meat now and even make cheese!"

I could see he had thought this out.

"Once we have the infrastructure in place, we can begin plowing the land and planting seed."

I had to chuckle to myself, "The farmer and the rancher can be friends?"

They had discovered a seemingly endless plain for the cattle and horses to graze. There were several thousand heads of beef and dairy cattle, and large herds of different horse breeds. They all ran wild in the lush meadows around the lake and beyond.

The news spread quickly. Nearly forty Quaylin families, all former farmers, volunteered to help Bill with his new project.

Kraq had very few Skaldi to spare, but Bill and I arrived at North Gate Castle a few days later with a treat for him and his followers.

Bill had prepared his famous BBQ, and after a taste, Kraq and his captains were practically begging to be involved. We left the wagon of cooked meat for the Blue Clan Prince and his group when he agreed that two dozen Skaldi would report to Bill at West Gate Castle the following day.

Bill assured Kraq that fencing would be up in no time with the help of the Skaldi.

The Skaldi split into three groups. The first group went to work with axes, cutting down tall, straight trees of appropriate size. The second group trimmed and moved them to the building site, where the third group used a sawmill to rough-cut timbers for a bunkhouse. Another large tent, provided by SunGru, housed the mess tent, where Bill cooked for the workers. Once housing was complete, the third group switched from making planks to producing split-rail fencing.

Meanwhile, every man and boy who could dig joined Bill in the fields. They split into two groups, one led by Jim and the other following Bill. Jim marked out a mile between himself and Bill with his range finder, and the digging started. They moved forward, with men digging holes and boys driving wagons with split rails to either side. Other men secured the posts and slid the wooden fence rail into place as a Skaldi worker pounded the next fence post into the ground.

At night, fish, meat, and fresh milk were available to all who wished to partake. Bill's dream of a land of milk and honey was beginning to take shape.

The Skaldi made furrows in the ground so the farmers and their families could begin planting crops.

Bill had also planned for housing, and while he lived in one corner of the mess tent, his plan began to take shape. The mill would make fencing for three days and then planks for two days. At first, this didn't make sense to me until a second pattern appeared. For three days, they fenced the land as an area for the horses. Then, in the following two days, they built living quarters. Once the horse and cattle enclosures were completed, they built homes. Now, I say houses, but not in the same manner as you might be picturing. They were not what I had imagined at all.

The Skaldi, alongside the Quaylin, erected a frame structure approximately 60 feet long and 20 feet wide, with 15-foot-high raised ceilings. Stone was used to create the first several feet of the home walls, then finished with wood planks and a thatched roof. There were three entrances to each building, which three families shared.

In a few weeks, three of these structures will be complete. Four structures form a square in a defensive formation to protect the families. They were in a row with a stone wall at the end of each one, creating an easily defended perimeter and a place of safety for the children to play.

An entrance gate broke the stone wall at the end near the stream. Children, chickens, goats, and dogs roamed the open area between each longhouse—outbuildings such as smokehouses, a forge, and a dairy for churning milk into butter and cheese.

It took several months for the farmers' fields to yield crops. Next year, we should have a fully sustainable system to feed everyone in the city if an enemy blocks the passes.

Next year? What was I saying? I hadn't asked any of my friends if they wanted to try to return to our former lives. They all seemed to have their pet projects in the Other Realms.

The discussion about whether or not to return to Earth mostly turned into an analysis of project management and progress reports. The common sentiment was, 'There's no way I can stop in the middle of this and leave them with an incomplete project.'

I left it alone since I had no desire to return to my regularly scheduled programming either. This otherworldly adventure was one of the best vacations in a long time. Exciting tasks filled my days. In the evenings, Rachel and I took long walks exploring the city and visiting new friends.

Bill and Jim had been busy at the ranch. Fresh milk, cheeses, and meats were carted daily into the city markets. On the ranch, wild horses were broken and trained, now serving as substitutes for the cavalry horses, which were put out to pasture.

The fishermen had established a small, thriving community. However, they would most likely return to the city's warmth when winter arrived.

Rachel could see how useful the Quaylin archers were to the military. She focused on the Skaldi and what they could provide. Her goal was to create an army division with a double the height advantage, and four times the draw weight for a bowman.

"Allen, I need your technical assistance, please. The calculations for enlarging the necessary equipment are far from simple!" Rachel said.

"Yes, the magnification plan uses many equations," Allen stated. "But we can equip a Skaldi warrior with a giant bow once calculated. Give me a minute to think."

The first issue Rachel faced was that of materials. Not for the bow, as the Quaylin craftsmen assured her they could make such a weapon. The bowstring, on the other hand, vexed her.

Without looking up from his laptop, Allen said, "Sinew."

Rachel rode to the ranch, where Bill and Jim assured her a constant supply of sinew from any slaughtered cattle or dead cows. For arrow fletching, the hunters received additional coins for a supply of usable bird feathers.

Slowly, the testing began. Once crafted and tested, the giant bow produced incredible results. Even Kraq was amazed at the accuracy, speed of delivery, and distance attained by his new archers - both of them.

Kraq had so doubted Rachel that he had delivered to her two test subjects, not the best or the brightest of his warriors, either. Not only had she achieved the appropriate bow dimensions and arrow lengths, but her two Skaldi archers now carried a second archer's weapon that Kraq had never seen - the crossbow.

These would be useful against enemy Skaldi with heavy armor or against cavalry from a distance. A Skaldi warrior with a crossbow and quiver slung over his back, carrying a bow with an excellent broad sword at his side, was a fearsome sight to behold.

Andy had continued working with the Skaldi warriors on what he called 'team tactics'. The Skaldi primarily fought with little care for themselves or their comrades. Andy trained them to form a defensive ring around a group of Quaylin cavalry. While their Skaldi shields were up, the Q cavalry could fire their arrows at the enemy from a sheltered position.

Andy showed the ground troops the shield wall made famous by the Romans. Protected by the impregnable walls of Skaldi shields, Quaylin could thrust their spears at the enemy through the gaps. As promised, each of the Skaldi warriors had a complete set of new armor crafted from what we had found at the cathedral.

CHAPTER 24

Allen and Becky made slow progress through the thousands of parchments, scrolls, and books in the cathedral. We all wondered how the translation occurred in our brains between the Quaylin, the Skaldi, and ourselves. Becky believed that the ability to understand and be understood was an innate quality found in the very air the planet provided.

Some people could barely grasp their own native tongue, while others could understand multiple tongues easily. That did not explain how we had come to comprehend two new languages. We had never heard the Quaylin or the Skaldi speak their languages, back on Earth.

Bill gathered us like children for a Bible story and told us about the Tower of Babel and the king of the world, Nimrod.

He began, "Nimrod had decided that he should be king of not just earth, but of Heaven itself. He brought three groups together to build a tower. It was not about the tower's actual height."

Like the Lion's Gate, it was a portal from which they would assail the very throne room of God. God was displeased with his creation. Less than one hundred years after destroying the entire world in a massive flood, a man used forbidden knowledge to attempt to kill the Creator.

"In a devastating response, God had one of the groups killed for their crime, and another group turned into elephant-faced and ape-faced creatures. The remaining group separated into seventy tribes, each with a unique language. Each of the seventy tribes, while speaking their tongue, still knew who their leader had been. Each tribe called him by a different name."

Allen called this the 'Babel Dissemination Theory'. I theorized that it was merely the translation of nanoparticles in the air. Allen could neither verify nor refute such an idea, but called it an exciting conclusion.

Q scribes helped translate writings, which Allen and Becky used to translate documents, which were then stored in Allen's mini servers. It was a painstaking and time-consuming process.

Gretchen worked tirelessly on the medical project with the healers and surgeons of SunGru's military. She worked with Quaylin and Skaldi to gather as many medicinal herbs and roots as possible for planting in the Healing Gardens. She also had Bill's farmers growing mass quantities of the herbs and roots for drying and storage. Some of her projects resulted in delicious teas and spices. Gretchen and several Quaylin shopkeepers went into business. They sold tea for home use and ran a small café where shoppers could sample more than a dozen varieties of tea and various baked goods.

On a clear summer day, Rachel and I put aside our work to join a mixed group traveling to the location of the first battle that had taken place on the plains. The struggle there had started our involvement with the inhabitants of the Other Realms. Our group rode out to honor the dead. The two magnificent battle mounds of the Quaylin faced the two impressive battle mounds of the Skaldi. Each stood as a testament to the significant loss of life that had occurred here. SunGru and Kraq placed battle standards for both armies between the tributes.

Both Quaylin and Skaldi participated in the ceremony. Rachel and I reflected on how two enemy races could meaningfully connect shortly after such a battle. That is the power of mutual service to the Maker. We camped on the plains' edge but decided against visiting the nearby Lion's Gate before returning to the City of Hope.

The day after our return from the ceremony at the battle mounds, Rachel was at the North Gate Castle, fitting and training some additional Skaldi archers. Bells in the towers closest to the pass would announce the return of scouts, hunting parties, enemy invaders, or new visitors. What might have occurred had this large group of refugees faced only Skaldi at our gates? As luck would have it, Rachel and her 'Red Brigade,' a group of Quaylin and now Skaldi archers that followed her around, also happened to be there.

SunGru and I were working on the cathedral grounds when a messenger arrived with news of the visitors. We were at the cathedral with a small group of friars to establish a place of higher education and religious studies.

We made our way to North Gate Castle. What a sight to behold. Stretching from the North Gate Castle's very gates to beyond our view deep into the canyon, a strange race had arrived.

SunGru instantly recognized them as the Eridu, a merchant race found in every location that sprouted civilization. They were very secretive about their homeland, but if they were to stop trade, every corner of the Other Realms would feel the effects.

The Eridu are a tall, thin race of people with blue-grey skin, most standing close to seven feet tall. They wore long, very colorful robes. While you saw the occasional dagger, most carried a stave, each tip coated in metal, their weapon of choice. They were very fluid with these staves. Their beasts of burden moved their goods and portable tents.

It was perhaps the strangest sight that I had ever seen. I can only describe their beasts as a giant raccoon form, with great black and grey stripes and a bandit's face. If necessary, the Eridu could ride them into battle. I had already spotted several of the armored animals. There was a moment of hesitation by the Eridu as they approached the final tower bridge before coming to the North Gate Castle. One lone Eridu rode towards the gates. SunGru and I walked out from the gates alone to speak with the Eridu, who now approached us on foot.

The tall, blue-skinned being spoke first. "I am Shal-Dir of the Eridu. We seek commerce and peace."

I had already decided to let SunGru speak on behalf of the rest of the city. "Welcome, Shal-Dir of the Eridu. I am SunGru, General to the Fifth Army of the Quaylin and Ambassador of the City of Hope. You and your people are known to us. They are welcome to rest and sanctuary here as long as they require."

"Are you a hostage that you would welcome mc and offer me safety when the enemy of all nations operates the walls of this place?" Shal-Dir responded.

"I am not a hostage. These Skaldi work peacefully side by side with the Quaylin in the hope of a better world than the one offered by the Fallen Ones," SunGru explained.

"These Skaldi have turned away from the commands of their overlords?" Shal-Dir questioned.

"Yes," SunGru answered.

Shal-Dir had a look of disbelief on his face. "How is this possible?"

It was then that I realized SunGru was pointing at me. I pulled back the hood of my cloak to reveal the slight blue glow from my forehead. I flicked my wrist and spoke my sword into being. Shal-Dir stepped back at the sight of the blue flames. Since he understood, I returned the sword to where it had come.

When I focused again, Shal-Dir and his bodyguards were all on their knees. "Àrd-Rìgh, as you serve the Maker, so shall the Eridu serve you," came the reply from the leader of the Eridu.

"Friend, we welcome you and your people. We strive to create a sanctuary for all people, regardless of their race. There are homes for your people. I know the community will welcome the goods you offer in the markets. Many empty shops are ready to display your wares. Again, welcome to the City of Hope," I declared.

Thus, the Eridu graced us with their colorful canopies in the marketplace and traded goods from every corner of the Other Realms. I appointed the Eridu leader to the council to represent the more than 3,000 Eridu refugees. The Eridu beasts of burden were aptly named the 'Fortis Latro' by Allen, translated in Latin, meaning 'Giant Bandit.' They grazed near the cattle on the ranch and into the groves of trees on the surrounding hills.

Word spread in the Other Realms that the City of Hope offered sanctuary to all races. Work was available from the common to the artisans. Food was also available, which was a rarity for many refugees. Small groups of Quaylin would arrive almost daily. The occasional group of Skaldi, who believed the city was still a rallying point for their kind, was always offered the option to leave unharmed or join us. More often than not, they choose to follow Kraq's leadership rather than face the wrath of their Fallen One overlords. The ranks of the Skaldi had gone from Kraq's original hundred men to nearly a thousand in just a few weeks.

On one such occasion, a Prince of the Red Clan named Bolvi, a leader equal to Kraq in clan status, arrived with five hundred Skaldi warriors. Bolvi wanted a place for the Red Clan to call their own. As Bolvi and his men had entered through the East Gate Pass, I took him back to that spot and spoke about fortifying the end of the corridor.

He liked the idea; it would occupy his men's time while building a series of lasting stone defenses. It was also better for the Skaldi to create defenses scaled to their size, rather than for the smaller races to try to adjust their work to fit the larger Skaldi.

Bolvi's men began a quarry on either side of the pass in the middle, keeping the beginning and end narrow. The Skaldi engineers planned to replicate the fortifications as closely as possible, using the mountain's stone.

Kraq and his Skaldi begin building defenses on the South Gate Pass. As the weakest guarded place in the City of Hope, each tower bridge had retracted its drawbridge, making it virtually unassailable. Outside each pass, a small camp of humans acted as a welcome party, as we feared that anyone seeing the Skaldi presence might run rather than join us.

The primary processing center was just inside the South Gate Pass. The scribes recorded the family's information, assigned housing, issued work orders, and provided coins for food and household goods, all in a nearly seamless transaction. The carpenters working on furniture for the city's residents provided a simple set for each family to start with at no charge. This generosity was made possible by the coffers of the City of Hope by order of the Àrd-Rìgh.

Additional furniture could be purchased as needed to supplement some of the original costs. These people had grown accustomed to a blanket for a bed and a pack or bag for a pillow. So, these new items and living quarters were a luxury, and the latest arrivals truly appreciated it.

CHAPTER 25

Today would be a day to celebrate the arrival of a new race of people into the City of Hope. Standing on the roof of the East Gate Castle's gatehouse, staring across the bridge and tower network, I had to do a double-take.

I grabbed my field binoculars and focused on the most unusual group of refugees who had entered the city since the Eridu crossed our path. SunGru was with Kraq, inspecting the progress the Skaldi were making on the newly required pass defenses, when this small band of two hundred that Kraq referred to as 'Wise Ones', arrived.

They were easily mistaken for children because of their small size. Their heads were disproportionately large in relation to their bodies, thus supporting the belief that they had relatively large brains. On the top of their hairless head was a strange, raised crown of bone. Allen seemed to think this was for communication. They were a thin, pale-skinned race with large teardrop-shaped sky-blue eyes. They wore different colored, tight-fitting uniforms.

Andy also did a double-take when he saw them and whispered to me, "Ancient Aliens."

The oddest thing about this situation was that these little people rode what looked like massive dogs.

I know! Could it get any stranger than it already was?

If you put a toddler on the back of a Great Pyrenees, you would have an accurate visual of what we were seeing. I heard no verbal directives given to the dogs, which brought a small contingent of their leaders toward us. SunGru told me they preferred telepathic communication to actual speech. The enormous dogs were both steeds for, and protectors of, the diminutive beings.

Later that evening, I spoke with Shal-Dir, who, as the Eridu leader, knew a great deal more about the aliens known as the Acrucians. I learned that the Eridu and the Acrucians were both aliens to this world.

The Eridu were not as old as the Acrucians or 'Wise Ones." By that, Shal-Dir meant in the Other Realms and the universe in general. He pointed into the southern night sky to the region where the Crux originated, commonly known on Earth as the Southern

Cross. Dominating the constellation is Alpha Crucis, a massive blue-white star. I asked Shal-Dir if he could tell me what he knew about their story.

Shal-Dir began. "The Maker, not bound by time or space, created the Acrucians. They were knowledgeable and built ships that traveled from their home world across the great expanses of space. They were renowned for their exceptional counsel and their expertise in architecture and technology. The story goes that the Acrucians, along with the race known as the Dvergar, helped create the Other Realms. The Other Realm was a gift to the Five Races. They were being pushed from Earth by the human race, which the Maker had recently seen fit to create. Humans waged war against non-human tribes and among themselves, so the Maker created the Other Realms for peace. The Other Realms' great cities were to be ruled by lesser Angels.

"The Creator chose humans to rule the Earth, not angels. Great jealousy grew in the hearts of the Angels of Heaven. Angels who visited Earth came back with stories of the extraordinary beauty of the Daughters of Eve. Evil crept into the hearts of those who had forgotten what had befallen many of their brethren in the First Great War of Heaven.

"Choosing to sin against the Maker, they took the Daughters of Eve and defiled the human women and themselves in this act of disobedience. The Maker, filled with deep-burning and righteous anger, sent an army led by the Archangel Michael to remove the fallen angels from their thrones in the Other Realms and many who now claimed rule in Earth's kingdoms.

"The Maker also raised his hand in judgment against the unholy offspring of the human females and the fallen angels. Michael and his army slew one-third of the Nephilim firstborn on the first day. The Maker granted five hundred years to the remaining Nephilim.

"Some became the great heroes of old, and some continued to commit evil against heaven. Some set themselves up as great kings and rulers of men with fair intent, and others allowed the thirst for power and the greed that comes with it to overwhelm them. The Maker sent holy men to shame and topple them from their high places, those whom men openly worshiped as gods. Finally, having honored the peace of a thousand and five hundred years, the Maker saw that little left of his creation was good. Finding one righteous man left in all the earth, the Maker spoke to his servant Noah."

I interrupted him. "Wait? How do you know about Noah?"

Shal-Dir raised his right eyebrow and continued. "The Maker spoke to his servant Noah and commanded him to build a great boat. The Ark would be a boat the size of which the world had never known, but it would save the last best hope for humanity from the ensuing floods sent by the Maker to destroy the world of man.

"The Acrucians had the keys to how the Lion's Gate worked and were determined to save as many Nephilim that served the Maker as possible. One of these was a twin to one that served himself rather than the Maker. Not wanting to see his twin drown, the good twin shared the secret of the Lion's Gate with his brother. In turn, the brother shared the same information with Nephilim of evil intent.

"The Maker destroyed Earth and all that dwelt therein. But evil survived in the Other Realms and returned to the world of man. The battle between the servants of the Maker and the Fallen Ones continues today, as evident in your current struggles."

Shal-Dir had not given me any information on the Acrucians. "That was an impressive account of the story of the flood of Noah. How does this link to the story of the Acrucians?" I asked.

Shal-Dir nodded and took a sip from his goblet of wine, the sign of another lengthy dialogue to come.

"The Acrucians had spread through the universe in their great ships that could span the stars. Although they had no malice in their hearts, the Acrucians involved in the Nephilim incident were punished severely for their involvement. They went to work as counsel for great leaders and shared brief insights into forbidden technologies. They were forced to roam the land, never to travel the vastness of space again or set foot in their home world. Blessed with a long life, they are doomed to continue their work until they die."

This conversation provided more information about one of the races than I had learned in my entire time in the Other Realms. I was about to ask another question when a voice beside me spoke.

"So, are there spaceships hidden somewhere around here? I am pretty sure I can fly one." Andy mumbled something about maybe needing Allen's help initially. Yet, Andy was pretty sure he could fly one if we stumbled across it.

I had forgotten how much Andy missed flying, but I had urgent questions that needed to be asked. "Is it possible that some of the Acrucians here now walked these same streets at the conception of this city?"

"It is not only probable, but some of these were also likely involved. That is how the Acrucians knew how to get here," Shal-Dir agreed. "You haven't figured out how to turn on the running water."

I now had a look of complete surprise on my face. What other mysteries did the fabled City of Hope yet hold?

CHAPTER 26

What did Shal-Dir mean by 'running water'? He seemed to know something but had divulged no further information on the subject the evening before. I knew I had to meet with the Acrucians' leadership, to get the answers I needed.

At South Gate Castle, SunGru showed the two hundred Acrucians the legendary hospitality of the Quaylin.

When I arrived at South Gate, I found SunGru immediately. "I need counsel from the Acrucians. How do I go about asking them?"

As a result of my inquiry, Fer and Tuc were 'assigned' to me, being the Àrd-Rìgh.

"The Quaylin emperor had twelve Acrucian advisors in his court," said SunGru. He assured me that, due to my status, more Acrucians would be made available to advise me in the future.

I assured him that more was unnecessary at this time.

I spoke to Fer and Tuc. While they did not respond to me verbally, they telepathically summoned their canine steeds. They followed me to the city's southern gates. I showed them the panel I had touched to open the gates that had initially unleashed the Fallen and the Ator upon us.

"Am I the only one who can open these gates by touch?"

The answer that came back was "no" from within my mind.

"Who can open the gates?"

"Unknown variable," the answer echoed in my head. "Narrow the search parameters of your query."

"Can anyone else in the city open the gates by touch?"

" Two hundred and one beings currently possess the knowledge or the capability to do so."

This whole mental thing was going to get old fast. I should pass these two on to Allen since he would love to communicate this way.

"While we can process at a far superior rate, we are certain you would not survive such a temporal overload. Who is this Allen, whose intellect you contend is greater than your own?" arrived moments after I thought those ideas.

I smiled. Allen is a friend who speaks binary and wants to meet you two. Can the security protocol be downgraded to allow other beings to access?"

"Yes. Or set to unrestricted admittance between intervals."

"Can you set the gates to open between sunrise and sunset with a manual override?" I asked, hoping that was clear enough.

Tuc touched the panel, and a keyboard extended out with strange symbols that I was sure Allen could figure out. He made the delicate changes. "The gates will open as you necessitate. Supplementary personnel may be added to the user interface control panel and ingress."

My following query was, "Does the city have running water and what humans would call bathrooms?"

"Yes, from the control center on the fifth tier."

"Can we go there and turn all facilities back on?"

"Yes, that is an uncomplicated concern to resolve."

I needed to learn the details of the city's tiers as we moved through them. Fer and Tuc seemed to have all the vital information available. The second tier remained virtually unexplored beyond the Cathedral campus area. The circumference was almost sixteen miles around via the walls and five miles across. As with the first tier, it was a mile from the second-tier border to the third-tier border.

The towers on the walls of each level were offset, providing crossfire against any enemy. The layout resembled the first-tier buildings built into the walls and the traditional marketplaces. This second-tier housing was slightly upgraded from the first-tier accommodation, reflecting the caste-based social hierarchy that existed at the city's inception.

The third tier of the city was, in many ways, a more miniature replica of the last two, featuring larger house plots and more expansive villa-like homes. This tier measured nearly 9.5 miles in circumference and 3 miles in diameter. The walls no longer housed shops and work areas, and the marketplaces were smaller but more fashionable.

On the fourth tier, there was a well-stocked armory and many barracks. I saw a series of buildings with a similar design, resembling a college or university. One of the grandest buildings was a library seemingly untouched by the Fallen during the city's plundering. Perhaps the Fallen had not made it this far. Books and scrolls lined the shelves that stretched from floor to ceiling. Alcoves held desks, seating areas, and work tables, covering the main floor.

A great open room had staircases coiled around a majestic globe hung from the ceiling at one end. The globe interested me, as it might have been a map of the world we were on, but Fer and Tuc were on a mission to take me to another area of the fourth tier.

Then we came to a building against the walls of the fifth tier. It had no windows and appeared to have no entrance.

A symbol appeared, and the control panel looked just like the one at the gates. A door appeared in the seamless exterior wall. Inside the room were panels of controls and view screens. I let Fer and Tuc fill Allen in on all the components connected to it.

Fer and Tuc found the control panel they were looking for and powered up the board. They explained that the water must run for several hours to flush out the system. The purification devices would then begin to process water. Once that occurred, the waste disposal systems would come online. The new systems made life so much easier. Before leaving to head back to the first tier, I asked whether there was anything else that could be "turned on" to help city residents at this time.

Tuc went over to another panel and made what appeared to be a few adjustments. "This city will shine as a beacon as it did long ago."

That sounded good until I realized too much light would draw unwelcome and unwanted attention. "If there's a dimmer switch, I would like just enough light not to stub my toe going to the bathroom."

Tuc returned to the panel and made adjustments, "I have engaged the necessary settings."

That evening at dinner, I saw Shal-Dir approaching my table. I motioned for him to join me. "Good evening."

Shal-Dir nodded, "Good evening, Àrd-Rìgh." I still couldn't convince people to stop calling me that.

"How was your day?" I inquired.

Shal-Dir took a sip of whatever it was that the Eridu liked to drink. It wasn't water; from what I could tell, but it had no odor whatsoever.

"I enjoyed my first shower, courtesy of the Acrucians. There are what you humans would call turbines. These great machines, hidden beneath the lake and the waterfalls, produce energy from the water flow at the falls. I heard them turn on early today. Will you keep us guessing each day what new marvel you will reveal to us next?"

"I asked Fer and Tuc if there was anything they could do to pull us out of the medieval lifestyles we have been living. I am sure it won't take long for everyone to get accustomed to all the city offers." I wondered if the city did not hide more than what Fer and Tuc had shown me. "Maybe you can join me on my next trip to the command center and see if we missed anything."

Shal-Dir nodded. "I would be honored."

A moment later, there was a massive crack, as if someone had touched the black and red wires of a car battery charger together. A humming sound pierced the air. The sound disappeared as the sun began to set on the horizon. Then, a strange thing happened. All around the city, a light blue neon glow began to appear. There was a gasp from those around us, and several groups were hooting and clapping, many waving at me. Soon, the sun set, but there was enough light to navigate the streets. I looked at Shal-Dir, who grinned and stretched his hand to the nearest panel. He tapped it three times, and in the glow we could see our plates and each other clearly, continuing our conversation into the night.

"Àrd-Rìgh, you did have another trick up your sleeve. Delightful! I wondered if they would turn the lights on, or leave you in the dark."

I shook my head. "I had no idea the intent when they said the city would be a beacon once more. Although if that glow alerts the enemy to our location, that might not be good."

"I'm unsure, but I hope the mountains help hide us. I am sure they have placed the lighting on the lowest setting possible to keep us from prying eyes."

"If you don't mind me asking, Shal-Dir, how long have your people, the Eridu, been in the Other Realms?" I had no idea if the train of thought I was going down was wise, but I felt I needed to know as much as possible about all races.

"Interesting question. I was born here in the Other Realms and am a little over six hundred years old by your human accounting."

I stared in disbelief as Shal-Dir continued.

"My father and mother were born here in the Other Realms, but their parents were born in space. Their parents came from a planet far across the galaxy, possibly even from a different galaxy altogether. We were a space-faring trade collective with ties to many planets. My grandfather's father commanded a ten-vessel fleet bent on outer-rim exploration and trade expansion. Unfortunately, they ventured too close to what you humans refer to as a wormhole. Only six ships arrived at this galaxy's other end of the wormhole."

He paused to allow a sip from his goblet, and possibly for my mind to catch up.

"The star charts were completely unknown to the navigators. As fate had managed, they were now several hundred light-years from the edge of this galaxy. At some point in the wormhole, the engines failed. The Eridu engineers lacked both the necessary equipment and parts to perform the required repairs. My grandfather once told me they floated for several months, keeping together and moving along with a limited burst of their sub-light engines.

"They had to choose between traveling, or simply having the life support systems to survive. It was nearly another year before a small group of larger ships approached them. That is how the Eridu began our friendship with the Acrucians. After a brief meeting with the commander of what appeared to be a small flotilla, returning to our galaxy was a nearly impossible task. The Acrucians were familiar with the star maps we held. They were a much older race. They had traveled and explored more space than I imagined my people had even considered existed."

I used the moment he came up for air and another sip from his goblet to interject. "How did the Acrucians and your race end up here?"

Shal-Dir looked at me. Do you know that look? The one where the guy's glasses are at the tip of his nose, and he peers over them at you, not through the lenses, with one eyebrow raised? Yes, that was the exact look I was now receiving,

"You humans are not well known for patience, are you?"

I confirmed that with a nod and a grin.

"Where was I? Oh, yes, their ships were quite large and, in some cases, even larger than this city. The Acrucians resumed their journey after our smaller Eridu ships docked within them. It was several years before a command from a higher being would send ten of their vessels on a special mission to this planet."

"The Maker commanded the Acrucians to send ships here?" My mind had stopped processing information.

"Yes, the Maker. He wanted the Acrucians to help a race called the Dvergar. Have you met any of them yet?"

The utterly blank stare on my face was all the answer he needed.

"How many alien races are there in the Other Realms?"

I received the same look as I had earned earlier.

"The Dvergar are not an alien race. They are alien to you, but the term alien itself means not of this world. While they are not from your world, they are from this one. As opposed to the Eridu and the Acrucians, whose origins are not of this world, or your world."

He waited for my brain to catch up, and I nodded, thinking I understood.

"After the Maker created this world, He then created your Earth. Of course, He created the universe and all the worlds before and after the creation of Earth. I am unaware of anything special about this planet or why the Acrucians came to assist the Dvergar. The Acrucian technology and the Dvergar race's engineering and architectural knowledge began building nine great cities.

"The story told to me was that ten great ships landed over several years, one of which our spaceships were inside. Nine of the Acrucian vessels became the nine great cities of the Other Realms. Meanwhile, immense slabs of stone, cut from quarries on a neighboring planet, were used to build the foundations of these great cities.

It was a lot to process. "So, there are eight other cities like this one?" I asked.

"Yes, nine cities in all. However, I do not know how many of them survived. I have only seen one other like this, and it was long ago in my childhood."

"What happened to the tenth vessel? Where did it go if it wasn't dissected and re-purposed for building a city?"

A ship capable of traveling interstellar distances would be an incredible discovery for humanity.

"As I said, the Maker hid the tenth ship from the Acrucians. They do not know its resting place."

Then he paused and gave me that look as if what he was about to say would make all the logic in the world to me. "I think you might know where it is if you put your mind to it."

"Trust me. If I had an idea where such a thing might exist, I would have shared this information!" I stated.

Then I thought I saw Shal-Dir roll his eyes, which would almost have been impossible considering his eyes' thin, oval nature.

"Do you not have a story on Earth of a great ship that the Maker used to save the indigenous flora and fauna species before the great flood and the sin of the Acrucians?"

"Noah's Ark was made of wood!"

Shal-Dir nodded. "Or did it look like wood to the humans who mocked Noah?"

Now, my mind was spinning. What was Shal-Dir saying? "Can you prove even the smallest part of what you are talking about?"

Shal-Dir smiled. "I can try, but I have no idea if the Acrucians will agree to show you. Have Fer and Tuc meet us on the fifth tier later today, and we shall see."

Later that day, as requested, the two Acrucians arrived on their dog-like steeds at the spot where Shal-Dir and I sat. The nearly seven-foot-tall Shal-Dir sat cross-legged with the two small Acrucians barely four feet tall. In a language my brain didn't translate, they began what seemed to be an argument among the three aliens. After about ten minutes of not being included in the conversation, Shal-Dir finally glanced my way. "They refuse to show you what I have asked of them, even when they agree that revealing such a thing is harmless."

"They won't share something harmless. Why?" I felt out of the loop, considering I had only heard Shal-Dir talking in a language I did not know as the two Acrucians stood silently before him.

"They will not," came the reply from Shal-Dir.

The Maker, help me! How was I to do my job when left out? My job? I was Àrd-Rìgh, wasn't I? What is the worst these two could do to me? Say no? It was worth a shot.

"Fer and Tuc, please answer what Shal-Dir was asking you." There were moments of silence, and even what I perceived as an almost mental wall between us. I added, "The Àrd-Rìgh demands compliance in this matter," and put on what I hoped was my most stern face.

A few moments passed as both small aliens stared at each other as if in deep conversation. Then, inside my head, I heard 'as the Àrd-Rìgh directs'.

Fer moved to one of the large wall panels and placed his hands on the plate, forming a triangle with his fingers. He then set his head in the triangle as if speaking directly to the wall section. What happened next utterly surprised me as the entire panel changed. Instead of the seamless, bold white rectangle I had been staring at only a moment before, beautifully grained hardwood planks now appeared. They were gone in a moment, replaced again by the cold white wall.

I turned towards Shal-Dir, who was already walking away. "Are you kidding me?"

Shal-Dir turned and motioned me to follow. "My people are well known for their humor, but in this case, I was not 'kidding you,' Àrd-Rìgh."

The technology existed for an Acrucian ship to have altered its profile and features to resemble an Ark-like wooden boat. The implications were hard to stomach and went against every fiber of my being. Then again, who was I to argue? I was standing on an alien planet, calling a strange city my home, and had aliens calling me the 'high king.'

CHAPTER 27

That evening, I ate dinner with Rachel and all our friends. Shal-Dir was notably missing. I shared my odd conversation and the weird display by my Acrucian advisors with my friends. There were looks of excitement on at least two of their faces. Of course, Allen, to whom the scientific ramifications would be undeniable. I also remarked that I could already see Andy standing on the bridge of this ship, shouting things like 'ready photon torpedoes,' 'battle stations,' and 'engage.' That was payback for the wizard's remarks every time I touched a doorway. There were questions, and I tried to answer them as best I could, recounting the story Shal-Dir had told of his people and the Acrucians.

I have always believed you should have both sides of a story for an accurate comparison, so I consulted Fer and Tuc. These two confirmed the report Shal-Dir had told me, but they used harsher words. They did make some insightful additions. The Eridu were the ethnic name of Shal-Dir's people. Eridanus is an area of space with a sizable blue-white star named Alpha Eridani. The system has 32 stars with planets orbiting them.

Allen later helped me pinpoint the exact location on a star map and pointed out the Eridanus Super Void. A substantial gap in space, a billion light-years, separated the Eridu explored area and the place where the Acrucians had found them floating helplessly in space.

I had not let the general population explore the city's second, third, fourth, and fifth tiers. Allen was busy mapping and inventorying those levels with the help of some Quaylin. When Fer and Tuc saw what he was working on, they took him to the same control room as they had taken me. Over a couple of hours, they imparted to him many of the city's features, including how to track individual community members. The map provided great detail in building sizes and uses, including new armories and a state-of-the-art prison.

Allen informed our group about the prison. "Why hadn't the 'ancient ones' locked Batariel in there?" I wondered aloud. I had to see the prison for myself. "Andy and Jim, would you care to join me?

"Yes. Let's take several large Skaldi in case we need them," Andy quickly replied, always up for exploration.

Allen handed me a small tablet with a prison map and codes to access locked doors, as well as a distress beacon in case of emergency. At the primary gates of the prison, we came upon a scary scene. The Skaldi formed a protective circle around me as I brought my sword to life.

Massive skeletons on the ground around the gates were a testament to a hard-fought battle eons ago. These weren't Skaldi skeletons but something more substantial. The gates were no longer intact. They were bent outwards as if a massive force had buckled them from the inside.

"Andy and Jim, any speculation on what could have done this? If Batariel had done this, why couldn't he escape the city's main gates? What if something much worse than Batariel has been imprisoned here, and is now loose somewhere else in the city?" I continued chewing on this thought like a dog with a new bone.

We came across more skeletons inside. A single large cell stood at the end of the hallway. We found the cell's door melted into the wall on the other side. I couldn't imagine the force it would have taken for any being to have accomplished that feat. I contacted Allen, who, in turn, reached out to Fer and Tuc. They arrived once more on their dog-like steeds. I heard them communicating.

I couldn't hear the words, but a static-like noise with an aggravated tone. Perhaps it was anger, disbelief, or both upon seeing the condition of the prison's main gates. The reaction to the cell inside was even worse. Whatever happened here clearly upset them.

"SunGru, Shal-Dir, and Kraq, would you please recon at my current position?" I called over the comms. If we had to lock down the city and search room by room, building by building, and tier by tier, it would be a task that would need to involve everyone.

Upon arrival, SunGru quickly admitted, "I have no idea what could have caused such destruction."

When I turned toward Shal-Dir for input, he was nowhere near us. He was speaking in earnest with the two Acrucians. Shal-Dir's face looked stoic as he approached us with Kraq, who had just arrived at the meeting.

"Well, I take it that whatever those two saw here was very upsetting. Therefore, I think that we are in trouble." I began.

The blue-skinned Eridu leader nodded, confirming my fears. I didn't know how bad it was until he began.

"My two Acrucian friends believe in this prison, like each of the other eight cities, this city held one of The Nine as a prisoner, awaiting their judgment at the end of days."

"The Nine? Who are you talking about?" Jim asked.

"The Nine refers to the fallen angels that were the lieutenants of Samyaza, the Chief of the Watchers," Shal-Dir began. "Samyaza was too powerful and could not be detained. His accomplices were condemned to live out eternity in the highest security cell of the times, one per city. This tablet names those incarcerated – Arakiel,

Kokabiel, Penemue, Tamiel, Ramiel, Danel, Chazaquiel, Baraquuiel, and Azazel. Fer and Tuc believe that our city once held Ramiel."

Indeed, this was grim news if we were to find a furious angel hidden in some building of the city's final tier. The thought that worried me was that one of these surprises could await us in any of the other cities we might explore later.

"Why was Ramiel in this city?" Andy asked.

"Ramiel was what humans call an Archangel or ruler of Angels. Fer and Tuc loosely translated his name into the 'Thunder of God.' Which might explain the damage caused here once his Nephilim prison keepers had left," Shal-Dir explained.

"Do you think he's still in the city?" I was worried about everyone's safety. I was unsure I had it in me to face an even more powerful being than I had already battled. "Wait! The name of the fallen angel that I killed was Batariel. Is he not one of the nine?"

Shal-Dir seemed deep in thought or possibly in conversation with Tur or Fer. Then he spoke. "The one known as Batariel was a lieutenant of Samyaza and listed within the twenty, but he was not among the nine. Perhaps he was caught along with Ramiel and imprisoned here. It was not Batariel that blew the doors off this prison. Tuc believes that Ramiel left Batariel to rot in his cell when Ramiel broke free of his own. It was Ramiel who killed the Old Ones guarding the prison."

"Do the Acrucians believe that Ramiel is still in the city?"

"They do not believe so, but there is no way to be certain. SunGru and Kraq will begin coordinating with Allen to conduct a comprehensive map search of the city's grid. If the Arch Angel is still in the city, they will await your arrival, Àrd-Rìgh. No one here has a chance against such power except you."

That was not the answer I was looking for. I instinctively flicked my hand, which brought the sword into my hand, dripping in blue flames. While that gesture gave hope to my friends, it did little to calm the butterflies in my stomach.

After searching the entire city, we found no new enemies. Allen informed me that the two Acrucians had run a grid search on the city's computers. The lake's hydroelectric generators were the only source producing the power capable of what had occurred in this prison. Either there was a being of extreme power hiding where the generators' signature would mask his presence, or Ramiel had long since departed the city.

Andy and I went alone into the recently discovered power plant's depths, below the lake's edge. I hoped my sword and powerful automatic weapons could overcome Ramiel. The fate of the City of Hope rested with just the two of us.

With great rejoicing, the people saw Andy and I emerging from the depths several hours later. I explained that we had found no sign of the Archangel.

CHAPTER 28

Day after day, I watched the city and the various races work together harmoniously for the Other Realms' greater good. I sat through countless council meetings.

The council comprises the following leadership: SunGru, Shal-Dir, Kraq, Bolvi, Fer, Tuc, and other team members as needed. No council member worked harder than SunGru, and rightly so, as the Quaylin were the most numerous of our city's citizens. The Quaylin brought in many resources and most often risked their lives for us.

I recently ordered the second-tier opening based on need and community support. The residences were slightly larger and were usually allotted a small parcel of land.

One of the families that had received such a reward was one of our first Quaylin food merchants. JanCee and his family fed all the new arrivals and made housing arrangements for them. No one went hungry. I took him and his wife, along with SunGru, to show him his new home. I pointed out the building we had given him to convert into a permanent restaurant along the way.

I was overwhelmed when he bowed low to thank me and humbly asked to continue his work on the lower tier. He wanted no one to go hungry. I told him his work would continue, but that we needed to create a society with some form of normalcy.

SunGru spoke with him briefly. He and his wife agreed to open the first Café and business on the second tier in the City of Hope.

Today, I had made plans to meet Rachel at the Café. The owner, JanCee, made every effort to save a table for us on the rooftop. I seldom wore ceremonial armor, as blending in with the crowds was easier.

The armor drew much attention, not unwanted attention, but it constantly attracted a crowd. My perceived status required kissing babies, shaking hands, and shouting 'Àrd-Rìgh!'; this often delayed any trip. This morning, I had donned a hoodie and slipped out of my home without either of the giant Skaldi warriors being any the wiser.

I later learned that SunGru and Kraq had expected this behavior, and the Skaldi were my distraction. At the same time, the four Quaylin scouts tracked me from a safe distance. Readily available if trouble presented itself, they made me think I was alone. It seemed even Rachel knew about this arrangement, and if one of the scouts got into my line of sight, she distracted me. I slipped out of the house and managed to borrow a horse from one of the barracks.

On the way to the Café, I passed the cathedral and its twenty-plus-acre campus. There was no hustle and very little activity in the buildings or the church. There were only a handful of holy men. The cathedral guards saluted and attempted to follow me, but I begged them to stay on post. Why wouldn't I be safe in the House of God?

As I approached the high building corner, I saw a horse tied to one of the iron rings of one of the outbuildings. I instantly recognized the horse. It was unmistakable - pure black, with a giant white star on its chest. SunGru. To my knowledge, no religious ceremonies have been held yet. My first thought was, what was the general doing here?

I meant no harm and certainly did not want to appear intrusive. I decided to act as naturally as possible. I quietly entered the nave, or the main seating area of the cathedral, hiding behind one of the massive columns. The general was kneeling on the steps that led to the dais. I looked around in amazement. Someone had cleaned this area, and a large wooden table sat on the platform. A simple gold cross stood on the table alongside a goblet of silver.

Later, I found the letters AO carved on the table. Then I remembered where the decorations had come from; all this had been found in Batariel's treasure horde and restored to its original places within the church.

My location in the church only allowed a partial view of the general. Yet, I could hear him earnestly begging the Maker for an answer to the whereabouts of his family and the rest of his people.

SunGru never mentioned the possibility that his family might have survived with some of the Quaylin, nor had he ever asked men to search for his missing wife and children. Hearing him plead that he was willing to forfeit his own life if the Maker spared his family broke my heart.

He had no idea where his family had gone or if they had survived the past months. SunGru had worked tirelessly and selflessly to create a place of refuge for so many. I had almost forgotten that his own family remained lost to him. I also knew that Q scouting parties worked tirelessly to find displaced people and offer them sanctuary in the City of Hope.

There was no mention of the whereabouts of the general's family during this time. SunGru was the face of courage for his people while carrying such a terrible daily burden since our meeting.

My eyes began to tear up, and in that moment of slight blurriness, I saw a glowing blue figure embrace the general and whisper into his ear. I quickly wiped my eyes and looked back up at the dais where SunGru stood - alone. I had to move swiftly or be caught by the general. I had just mounted my horse when SunGru, walking briskly, arrived back at his horse.

"Àrd-Rìgh, what are you doing here?"

"SunGru, I was on my way to meet Rachel for lunch and saw your horse tied up here. What are you doing here?" I asked, hoping that he had not seen me in the church.

"I was seeking the Maker's face," the general replied.

"Did you see the Maker?"

"No. Àrd-Rìgh, my hands have spilled too much blood. I am unworthy to stand in my God's presence, at least not while I am still drawing breath in this life," SunGru answered.

What I blurted out next revealed that I had been inside the church. "Who was that then, who embraced you and disappeared in a moment?" I asked.

A flare of anger filled the general's eyes, but something else overtook that emotion. Instead, he explained, "You saw the Herald of the Maker bring me a message that makes my heart sing for joy." SunGru's eyes seemed to rejoice, while his body remained the rigid military leader atop his charger.

"A message? What message did the angel bring to you?" I had begun to wonder less and less and take things at face value here in the Other Realms. I chuckled. I enjoyed some good irony.

Here, I stood in a city constructed from an alien spacecraft outside a building built to worship the God of my childhood.

Here I stood before a House of God in a city partially constructed from parts of an alien spaceship.

"The Maker has seen fit to answer my heart's cry. I know you don't see me as an intensely religious person. Sometimes, I am far from my God in the heat of battle. I have killed my rivals, the enemies of my people, and their numbers are without record. Since the day my family fled our homeland for safety, I have prayed every day that we would be reunited. I desired that some scout would bring me word of their arrival at the gates of this city."

I nodded in excitement for my friend. "You have their location? Is it close?"

SunGru nodded. "I have their location, but it is far from here, a month maybe by horse, faster through the Lion's Gate with the correct destination."

"Where are the runes that will lead us to your family?" I could lead an army through the Lion's Gate to the location of this man's family and fight any battle necessary for their freedom.

What happened next made me wonder how this man was still standing on his feet, let alone mounted upon a horse. SunGru rolled back his left arm's sleeve, revealing the raised, puckered skin where runes now appeared.

My hand went to my comm. "Allen, where's Gretchen? A medical team is to meet me at South Gate Castle. The general has suffered a burn."

The comms responded with Gretchen's voice. "Copy that. RJ, I have a team. We will meet you there as quickly as possible."

SunGru told me he needed no healer, but he only desired to go to the Lion's Gate above the vast plain and find his family.

"Don't leave before you get that looked at, and before we can assemble the council to make a plan. A proper plan. Is that understood, General?"

"Yes, Àrd-Rìgh. I will seek medical attention and the council's will in this matter." Some of the light had left his eyes.

"SunGru, you can be assured that the moment the healers release you, we will meet with the council, followed by your family's rescue at any cost. You have my solemn vow to such an end."

The light quickly returned to the elder Quaylin's eyes. We urged our mounts at full gallop toward the guards who hurriedly opened the gates.

I had missed my lunch date in all the excitement. Rachel hurried to meet us at South Gate Castle, hearing my call for a medical team through her comm. When we arrived, the medical team was on-site; a chair and a table were already waiting for SunGru.

Gretchen's eyes widened when she saw the burn, the welts, and the raised runes. "Gentlemen, how often has my husband stressed to you that playing with alien objects may cause serious injury or even death!" When Gretchen looked at the two of us, she glared at me.

"Gretchen, it was not RJ's fault. It was no one's fault." SunGru attempted to curb her anger.

"Really? How do you explain second and third-degree burns all over your forearm and these markings then? Like a branding iron burn?"

How would the general explain this to someone who hadn't seen what I had? "I prayed to the Maker, and He heard my cry. He sent his servant with the location of my family and the remaining survivors of the Quaylin capital," SunGru said as he winced in pain.

Gretchen was spreading salve across the wound. She didn't seem convinced. "He couldn't have written it down on a piece of parchment or etched it into a stone tablet?" Her sarcasm matched her worry for SunGru and his visible pain.

"It is here that I may never forget that the Maker heard my plea. He answered me in my time of need," SunGru answered.

I whispered something in his ear, and he chuckled despite the pain.

Then he continued, "I am a man. If written on paper, it might be lost or misplaced. Stone tablets are from another man's story, not my own." That made Gretchen and Rachel both smile. No man ever spoke more accurate words.

Over the comms, I announced, "I need all council members to make for South Gate Castle with all haste." I had hardly finished my sentence when Shal-Dir and Kraq arrived, followed shortly by Fer, Tuc, and the rest of my team.

The council meeting was brief, as the runes spoke for themselves. It was now just a matter of whom to send and how many. The Skaldi were required to remain behind to ready wagons and supplies in South Gate Pass. If we found anyone, they would need transport, food, and medical care. Two hundred Quaylin scouts under the command of SunGru, Andy, and Jim made for the Lion's Gate above the plains. The journey to the gate took two days.

I received word of SunGru's arrival at the Lion's Gate late the next day. His early appearance meant he and his men pushed their horses and themselves to reach the device as quickly as possible.

I didn't receive good news, as the runes did not match any nearby Lion's Gate addresses. There were three sets of runes that SunGru's arm partially matched, which meant splitting up into three separate groups to search each of them, one at a time. I asked SunGru to wait for Allen to see if one destination matched his arm's runes better. But, he would not allow another two days to go by waiting for Allen.

The first gateway that opened, SunGru, and a hundred scouts passed through. In his opinion, it was the best of the three possible options. With Andy advising him, fifty scouts under Quaylin Captain BenKido's command passed through the second Lion's Gate address. The final party of fifty scouts under Quaylin Captain ShiUle's leadership, with Jim as an advisor, took the third possible destination. These are the stories of each group's hardships, as recorded by my scribes.

CHAPTER 29

The following expedition logs provide details from Quaylin Captain BenKido, Andy, and fifty scouts.

Day Twenty-Six – Command – Second Expeditionary Force – Captain BenKido

Last night, our forces camped in a mighty forest on the border of a vast plain. I had to decide: should I take my party across the prairie in the dead of night and make for the mountains on the far side or continue to use the forest to cover our tracks? Several days of rain have not dampened the troop's spirits. Here, the nights were cold, and the days perfect in the shade of these massive trees. Andy, the human advisor to the Àrd-Rìgh, told me of trees in his home world that grew to four hundred feet tall. Twenty men could circle their base, just touching fingertips. He also informed me that the native redwood trees of his world only grew near coastal areas, so we sent two scouts to search for such a water body. The scouts returned a week later to tell of a magnificent sea coast, four days' ride to our east, but there were no signs of any Quaylin refugees along the way. We stayed in our camp one more night to allow the scouts to rest and continued their journey through the forest the following day.

I was preparing to enter my tent when Andy pointed into the sky above us and handed me his binoculars. Surprisingly, a great bird circled on the high wind current above the plains on the forest's edge. The bird continued on a downward spiral. Then, just as it dipped below us and back into the sky, I saw what appeared to be a human form straddling the bird. I ordered all fires extinguished. We spent the night, alerted to the fact that we were not alone.

Day Thirty-Four – Command – Second Expeditionary Force – Captain BenKido

I have sent six scouts to explore the mountain area across the plains. We have had several additional sightings of magnificent birds ridden by humans. All of them seem to head west. I have decided to continue along the edge of the forest. I want an encounter where we can ask if they have seen our kinfolk.

Day Thirty-nine – Command – Second Expeditionary Force – Captain BenKido

The scouts who went west returned to report a small Skaldi army assaulting what they could only describe as a city in the trees. With Andy by my side, we moved forward to a better vantage point. Skaldi armies with siege weapons had positioned themselves out of bowshot. They were slinging projectiles at a little city built within the trees. Every time the Skaldi scored a direct hit on the town, a faint cry rose from their ranks. Andy advised immediate action. It was nearly dawn, and the Skaldi had placed a limited guard at the front of the siege weapons. The rest returned to their camp, some distance from the siege weapons. I agreed with Andy but wondered how our lesser group might overcome the catapults and the Skaldi army. Andy patted his backpack and asked me to trust him as he slipped into the night. His arrival at my side nearly two hours later startled me at first. He urged me to follow him to a higher position for a better view. Andy produced a small black box when we had achieved the height necessary to see the Skaldi siege weapons. Flipping a switch on the side, he announced, 'Fire in the hole.' The siege weapons exploded one by one. What a fantastic sight. Great pieces of wood and iron filled the night sky.

Chaos followed in the Skaldi camp, and those in the trees took advantage. The sun rose across the plains as archers and spearmen took to the air. Their mission was to harass and kill the Skaldi. I sent several scouts to approach the riders to request a meeting with their leaders, following Andy's advice. The meeting took place soon after it became clear that the remaining Skaldi we rapidly moving north. We learned that their leader was Adoeete, or Chief of the Great Trees. His city was in ruins, and many of his men were dead or missing. Yet he thanked the one he called 'Gitche-Manitou,' the Great Spirit Creator.

We discovered that his people had been numerous at one time, but the Skaldi destroyed their homes and tracked them wherever they went. His people numbered less than five hundred, and only one hundred adult birds had survived the attacks. Yes, they wanted to join us at the City of Hope.

Each scout wagon carried two additional sets of wheels. The men of both races built more carts to transport several dozen eggs and at least as many hatchlings. Andy told Chief Adoeete that our lands had no trees of this size. He sent word to a group of men who climbed in pairs high into the trees with torches. When I inquired about what they were doing, they explained that one man held the flames close to the large pine cone, and the heat released the seeds into a sack carried by the second man.

I was delighted that the origins of the great trees were coming with them. We later found that these kernels were a primary food source for the people and the birds. Every wagon we assembled held the injured, young, and older people of the tribe, extra bags of seeds, and the large eggs on grass beds.

In the end, I led the wagons and my remaining men, along with the Karuk people, to the site of the Lion's Gate. Meanwhile, Andy, Adoeete, and his riders took to the sky on the remaining birds, attempting to journey back to the City of Hope. Sadly, I also note that the Karuk people have not had the chance to meet any of the Quaylin people on their journeys.

Day Forty-Three – Command – Second Expeditionary Force – Captain BenKido

May my journey back to you be quick, and may the Maker keep Andy safe from harm. Andy and Adoeete will attempt to locate the City of Hope using a tracking device provided by the Acrucian advisors.

The following expedition logs provide details from Quaylin Captain ShiUle, Jim, and fifty scouts.

Day Twelve – Command – Third Expeditionary Force – Captain ShiUle

The land we journey through is dry and desolate. Water is scarce, and the winds threaten to cover us in dust and sand. Advanced scouts have reported no signs of humanoid life, except for our own. Jim, a friend of Àrd-Rìgh, says Earth has a comparable landscape called deserts.

Day Sixteen – Command – Third Expeditionary Force – Captain ShiUle

If we continue, we will need more water to return to the Lion's Gate. The advance scouts have reported a series of massive structures. Jim advises that we should at least recon the area from a safe distance and record what we can for Allen to review.

Day Eighteen – Command – Third Expeditionary Force – Captain ShiUle

There are no signs of life here. The tops of three pyramid-shaped buildings rise at a great height before us. Jim and several scouts looked closely and found an engraved stone stating, 'Abezethibou, God, and Provider.' We could not see any doorways into the buildings or pyramid structures. We can find no entrances above the sand line. We can waste no more time in this place or will surely perish.

That was the last report from Captain ShiUle and Jim as they traveled with haste back to the Lion's Gate to return to us. A note from Allen as a supplement to this final report stated, "RJ, the name Abezethibou refers to the name of the angel that hardened the heart of Pharaoh against Moses. He ruled Egypt after the Pharaoh died with all his armies at the Red Sea crossing." That was a concern for another time, but it was a concern.

The following expedition logs provide details from Quaylin General SunGru, one hundred scouts searching for SunGru's family, and as many as ten thousand Quaylin citizens.

Day Sixty-One – Command – First Expeditionary Force – General SunGru

The terrain is significantly more rugged than it was when we first started. The advance scouts report that they have seen signs of a small camp of men a day's ride ahead near a large lake-fed stream.

Day Sixty-Three – Command – First Expeditionary Force – General SunGru

We have observed the small camp for a day now. There are no signs of women or children here, and no sizable group of people nearby. We are advancing to make our camp near the settlement. I am riding ahead to meet the men of the field as they appear to be unarmed and oddly dressed.

Day Sixty-Four – Command – First Expeditionary Force – General SunGru

Our men were allowed to explore, rest, fish, or swim in the lake. As stated in my previous report, the men in this camp wore simple brown robes. No one in the encampment had hair on their heads, but many had beards. It took a bit of talking and introduction before their leaders admitted they were holy men, Monks of the Order of AO.

While there are several orders of religious and educational monks, the AO is the oldest. I pressed them for any information they might have on a large group of Quaylin refugees. They would not yield an answer. Finally, their leader, Father Emmaus, said that perhaps we had a sign to help us with our quest. The only indication I could think of was those burned into my forearm. As I rolled back my sleeve and removed the poultice, Principal Emmaus's eyes grew wide with wonder.

"The Maker be praised!" Father Emmaus exclaimed. He pulled a tablet with marks identical to those on my arm from the leather pouch at his side.

A flurry of activity followed as, without any verbal commands, the monks began to pack up their meager belongings and take down their tents.

"We will take you to the Lion's Gate," Father Emmaus stated.

After a day's march deep into a veiled valley, we reached a stream that poured out from a high waterfall. Under the waterfall, inside a cavern, stood another Lion's Gate, the likes of which I had never seen. It was not made of solid rock but seemed carved from a giant crystal. Upon it were runes. We could read only one side, as the others were in languages unknown to my advisors or myself. I matched the gateway to the runes on my arm, thanking the Maker for his mercies, and took a small group of men to see what lay before us.

My family met me on the path! My joy is too great to describe.

Members of the Quaylin governing body and a great crowd of citizens were followed by even more of the oddly dressed monks. Many thousands had perished in the years following the Quaylin capital's fall to the armies of the Fallen Ones. Our dear emperor was among those who died. These few remained. We moved to the Lion's Gate to bring my family and all my people back to the City of Hope.

On a side note, the same scout who brought the good news from SunGru back to the council asked for a private audience with the Àrd-Rìgh.

I agreed, of course. The scout only disclosed that he and SunGru had been the last two through the Lion's Gate. Moments before the scout had stepped through the gateway, he saw the general with a figure that glowed blue. The character spoke, then embraced SunGru, and was gone. That night, the scout helped the general remove his armor and noticed that his arm was healthy again. No scars or runes remained. I kept all these things in my heart and pondered them on the way to the celebration.

The arrival of Adoeete and the Karuk people a few weeks earlier had caused quite a stir. BenKido and Andy had the job of bringing them through the city to the West Gate Castle.

"RJ, how have things progressed while we have been gone?" Andy asked me as I arrived at the castle by horseback.

"There have been discoveries, and I have a surprise for our new friends, the Karuk." I dismounted to greet my old friend and BenKido.

"What sort of a surprise?" the Quaylin captain asked eagerly.

"A recent discovery has revealed a great cave system behind the waterfalls near the lake. I think this would provide a great place for the birds to nest and a safe place for their eggs," I answered.

Andy gave me a look. "Who discovered the caves?"

I laughed. "I made Bill take a day off and gave him a couple of choices on what we could do. Instead, he told me he had something he thought I should see. Bill took me to the gatehouse of the tower bridge system that led to the West Gate Castle. He directed me to a wall with a shield hanging on it.

When I asked him what we were doing there, he chuckled and spun the shield. The wall behind it moved back, revealing another door. A passage took us to a relatively long, straight, extra-wide tunnel. At the end was a pair of double doors. The first set led us into the power plant. The way Andy and I had gotten in the first time was much more difficult. The second doorway led down a wide, sloping ramp. It circled us down to the caves that eventually opened on the cliff's face near the waterfall."

Andy had a look of amazement on his face. "What do you think we could use them for?"

"It was pretty chilly in the caves that aren't open to the air and are further towards the lake. Bill thought that a good use for them would be dry winter storage for some vegetables, smoked meat storage, and even wine."

I responded. "I don't think that the Dvergar finished their project down there. I wonder what their plans were."

"Not to change the topic entirely, but you are giving the Karuk people the West Gate Castle?"

I nodded yes.

"Adoeete says if we don't get the eggs and young birds into a warmer climate, they may not survive the winter." Andy added, "I think I might have a solution." It was true that Andy had some engineering ability.

"What is your idea?"

Andy shrugged, "I am sure the idea will work, but I am unsure how to pull it off."

I patted him on the back, "You tell me your idea. If it is possible, we will make it happen."

Andy took me to the caves below the turbines and placed a hand on the rock. I did the same, and the stones were warm to the touch. "Remember how hot those rooms were when we were hunting for whatever escaped that prison ward?"

I nodded yes. "If we could vent that heat into the open caves, the Karuk could build nests for the birds, hatchlings, and eggs. They might even survive the winter down here."

"You're a genius! Don't tell anyone else I said that, or I will have to deny it," I said with a laugh. "I think I know a few people who can make your idea a reality."

Adoeete also informed us that several other tribes of riders existed along the hundreds of miles of the coast. The search for them would have to wait until spring.

The high towers of the West Gate Castle were a hard sell to the Karuk people. They instinctively wanted to be with the birds. It was even worse when they saw the Skaldi marching down to carry the precious eggs underground. I assured them that these Skaldi were free men and would fight alongside us to defend the city. Of course, who else was big enough to carry each one of the giant eggs down into the depths of the earth? However, I decided that carts manned by the Karuk people would be better. This way, the Skaldi would not be blamed if an egg broke.

On top of this issue was the imminent arrival of ten thousand or more Quaylin. They may have little besides the clothes on their backs and a sack over their shoulder. We had begun to prepare as soon as Andy had landed with news of the Karuk, which was well ahead of SunGru and the latest refugees.

Many city families were eager to prepare their homes for the latest arrivals. Businesses shut their doors that day at noon, and everyone took on work assignments. Some furniture was already in place, and now was the time to make the homes as comfortable as possible.

Teams placed linens on beds, adding creature comforts to each house. Skaldi, with great carts of firewood, moved through the streets, dropping off bundles at each residence. A number of the bread makers had spent many long hours so that bread, along with cheese and a sampling of smoked meats from the ranch, could be placed on the table of each household as a welcome gift. The guild master and his team were ready to locate families based on trade or skills. Bill had temporary quarters along the western wall for anyone joining him on the ranch.

The hint of winter was already in the morning air. Bolvi had arrived to announce that he and his men had partially finished the South Gate Pass fortifications. I wasn't sure why he had used the word 'partially'; there were walls, a gatehouse, barracks, and horse stables. He claimed the project was incomplete, but I thought he had done an excellent job. Kraq informed me that Bolvi was a perfectionist and an engineer of great renown.

Since Bolvi was around, I asked him about getting the heat from the turbine rooms to the caves. He grabbed a tiny pen and a clipboard from a nearby Quaylin man, who, for a moment, seemed to be more than annoyed at the big Skaldi prince. However, upon turning to see me, he bowed and stood patiently waiting for his instruments. Bolvi scribbled on the paper and made a few crude drawings. He handed me the picture, turned, and thanked the man. As he strode away, I heard him say, "Àrd-Rìgh, if you can find me the things I need, you shall have your hot air regulator for the giant chickens!"

At that moment, the Quaylin man and I watched the Skaldi prince moving briskly down the street. As I turned to the man, I caught him laughing into his hand. I joined the man with an inner chuckle.

Rachel and I had ridden into the city to meet the first arriving Quaylin. We welcomed SunGru. Rachel promised to show his wife and two daughters around the city, especially the shops, as soon as they felt up to it. The general's family was delighted.

Some of the more decorated Q society members crossed the bridges, followed by men dressed in brown robes with shaven heads and no facial hair—monks from the Order of AO. This city will have plenty of work for over three hundred holy men. They were not just religious men but educators, healers, and men of science. In turn, they shared the knowledge they had acquired with their communities. It was their responsibility to teach the next generation of leaders.

Eventually, the monks would fill various roles within the city, including scribes, teachers, healers, and priests. The monks all bedded down in an empty warehouse the first night.

I was delighted to invite Father Emmaus and his second, Brother Mathis, to breakfast with Rachel and I, in the morning. Of course, they tried to say no, that it was too much trouble on their account.

Kraq made a point to make the holy men understand with one simple phrase, "The Àrd-Rìgh gets what he wants. It matters little how big you are or how holy you appear."

I had to keep from laughing out loud. Rachel's elbow in the ribs helped stop my initial reaction to Kraq's words. As we climbed the steps to our rooftop table, I pointed down the street past the market to our next tour destination.

"Is that what I think it is?" Brother Mathis responded joyfully.

"That, my pious friend, is our cathedral, the House of God. It is a twenty-three-acre campus featuring a church, a suitable university facility, and communal living quarters with baths and kitchens. It is your new home if I can persuade you of our need," I explained.

"I must protest. We are but simple men serving the Maker. The luxury of such a place is for holier men than those who now stand before you," Father Emmaus responded.

"Father Emmaus, our people need to have the words of the Maker spoken to them. Our young people need education. I, for one, would like to celebrate many more weddings and births. You can't all be scientists and healers, nor have your heads stuck in the books of the great library. I need normalcy in this city, and you and the Monks of AO are what is required. Have a little faith, my friends."

The two monks looked overwhelmed, but I was sure they would acclimate to their new jobs.

"What will you do about the Fallen Ones?" Brother Mathis asked.

I was sure that the story of the fight between the Fallen and me had been recounted several times by this point. "They will all face justice," was my staunch reply.

After breakfast, we traveled to the gates, where the cathedral guards welcomed the new inhabitants of the campus. The monks toured the campus grounds for several hours, investigating each room with its purpose and simple furniture. The university's offices had taken shape thanks to several skilled Skaldi and Quaylin master woodworkers. The tables, benches, bookshelves, and workstations were of the highest quality.

This project had been underway even before news of the monks' arrival. Books now lined the shelves, and tapestries hung from the walls. Along with the kitchen and pantries, the dining hall was ready to serve its first meal to the monks in their new home.

There were other discoveries, many of which were related to the fourth and fifth tiers of the city. I had avoided going there because I was sure my quarters would be in some lofty tower. Such a situation would add a horrible commute to my daily work in the city.

I was right. Andy had discovered a throne room, council chambers, and a great hall at the base of one of the two great towers.

In the towers above the public areas, a three-story condominium called 'the King's Tower' was being prepared as my living quarters. Rachel told me to shut up and enjoy the ride regarding my constant retreat from my duties as the Àrd-Rìgh.

To further the Àrd-Rìgh legacy, Rachel hatched a plan with Jim to put me on the path to particular Arthurian fame. Jim had brought back a cross-section of a tree from the Karuk forest with one thought: build a round table for the council. They surprised me with it during an emergency session, which turned out to be a birthday party, not a council meeting.

Adoeete, as well as Father Emmaus, had been added to the council. At their first meeting, I remember the old priest muttering louder than he realized. "What devilry is this? What manner of king wouldn't sit at the head of his counsel?"

My response to him was to do what I did best. I told them a story to explain the table, and it was not to be the last time I would share it. I explained to him that there had been a wise ruler from my world named Arthur once upon a time. For his kingdom to enjoy peace and prosperity, he felt all his leadership must have a say in its crucial decisions. To achieve this, he had a massive round table, so no one person sat at the head; all had an equal vote. This story, of course, amazed Father Emmaus.

I took the two men to the kitchen, where Cook promised to fatten them up in no time. They were then shown to quarters below the council rooms, designed to accommodate council members during prolonged meetings, including a bedroom, a sitting room, and an attached office.

A few weeks later, as everyday life seemed to slow to a snail's pace, I stood atop the gatehouse of the fifth tier. As a snowflake drifted past me, my breath was visible in the morning air. The turbine generated energy for the city's heating, but it was still cold outside.

From here, I could see the steam where the heated air escaped from the caves and met the chilly winds around them. All around the city walls, the dying watchfires with their frozen sentries waned in the coming sunrise. The entire world was at peace.

It had taken us a year to bring together all these people, and we would celebrate our first Christmas in the Other Realms. As planned, the Christmas celebration would begin at dusk on the nineteenth day of December in the City of Hope's first year. The most recently acquired friends and those we had met on our arrival joined those we had known for a lifetime. All would celebrate the City of Hope.

Our first Christmas in the Other Realms. Dozens of Christmas trees appeared on each tier of the city. Children made decorations or strung popcorn. 'Santa Claus' Kraq and Rachel, who I will say made an utterly charming elf, passed out treat bags to children. Merchants passed out goodies and warm drinks along the busy streets.

The holiday was not unknown to the city's people, but celebrations are the least of your concerns when you are on the run. As Rachel and I walked hand in hand through the streets of the City of Hope, we could hear the words 'Merry Christmas' uttered in many languages, but in one spirit. I have visited nearly every major city and have experienced Christmas and New Year's Eve in most of them. I saw fireworks from the Golden Gate Bridge to Niagara Falls. Yet, nothing could compare to the happiness and the joy I could see in Rachel's and everyone else's eyes.

The Christmas celebrations lasted the better part of the week, leading to what Andy called the best New Year's Eve ever, which could only mean one thing. Andy was going to make some big explosions. We exchanged gifts among our small group of friends and within the council. Throughout the week-long festivities, I witnessed many exchanges of gifts between members of the various races. Long and bitter rivals were now living together and working towards a greater good.

CHAPTER 30

A.E. Two

After Earth – Year Two, this was the designation that now appeared on all my official memos. It had been a quiet January. February was the same until a messenger arrived, bringing news from Captain BenKido and Kraq with three thousand Quaylin and two hundred Skaldi troops.

They assured the safety of our borders and collected any big game from the hunting parties we sent out a few weeks ago to supplement our stores. A scouting party had ventured further than recommended and had nearly ridden into a large Skaldi encampment southwest of South Gate Pass.

This small army was within twenty miles of our extended – Andy called it the pretended border – the border of my 'kingdom.' We surrounded them in the middle of the night with a much larger force. A closer look was necessary to assess the situation.

Kraq immediately pointed out that members of four different clans comprised the bulk of this army. Banners of the Blue, Green, Black, and Silver Clans could be seen in the breeze as they flew above the night watch fires. In the dawn, the Skaldi camp woke to a hedge of steel at their throats. The 'never surrender' Skaldi reaction was typical and not a rational thought. It was winter, and they had not eaten in several days.

"Kraq, tell them we have food for any that join us. Do not use the word 'surrender' either. Perhaps a warm meal and a full belly will persuade them of the folly of resistance," I directed.

"Yes, Àrd-Rìgh." He bowed slightly, touching his fist to his chest. He seldom did this salute since he knew how I felt about signs of reverence. However, in this case, it revealed to the enemy who was in charge.

This salute had the expected reaction from the Blue Clan, who saw the blue tunic and the large medallion hanging from the gold chain around Kraq's neck. They now recognized the Prince of the Blue Clan, who took commands from me.

As a group, they agreed to lay down their arms. Their leadership looked over a parchment drawn up by Kraq and Bolvi to guarantee sanctuary and individual rights to any Skaldi that renounced the Fallen Ones. They all needed to swear allegiance to the new Skaldi leadership, the will of the council, and pledge loyalty to me as the Àrd-Rìgh.

The Blue and Silver clan leadership admitted that they had been protecting the retreat of a smaller group. This group was transferring dangerous prisoners to a more secure fortress to the east.

The Green and Black Clan leaders seemed unimpressed. They were unwilling to let go of their allegiance to the Fallen Ones. Whether out of fear or a distaste for being ordered around by blue and red clan leadership. The latter is more likely.

As the Blue and Silver Clan leaders pledged loyalty to Kraq, the council, and the 'high king,' they were cursed by their brothers in the Green and Black clans. The Blue and Silver leadership requested the return of their weapons.

Once granted, they fell upon the Green and Black tribe leadership before we understood what was happening. Our archers almost filled them with arrows, but for my sharp command. So was the way of the Skaldi. While brutal at times, they had a high honor system. When the Green and Black clan troops had a choice, many immediately swore allegiance to follow the Blue and Red Clan leadership to whatever end necessary. Those who did not swear allegiance died in the same manner as their masters. It was a bittersweet day. While many lives were lost, nearly seven hundred Skaldi troops joined our ranks.

The smaller group of enemy Skaldi that formed the prisoner transfer was a day behind this main force that had been a thousand strong the night before. At first light, we arrived on a high plateau overlooking the valley below. I secured our position and stationed men waiting to surround the fast-moving force when spotted. It appeared to be a much larger group of Skaldi than had been suggested.

I knew this might happen as a test despite the oaths of sworn allegiance. At the center of the enemy host, hooded and chained, ran at least a hundred captives. The captives appeared shorter, and had a far different look from the Skaldi surrounding them. What was so valuable about these prisoners that moving them in the middle of winter required such a massive force?

Jim and Andy agreed that it was worthwhile to investigate the situation further. These were not simple prisoners, but a group that held such a high value, one that the Fallen Ones seemed unwilling to lose them. Unfortunately, the banners flying with this army were not of the easily swayed Blue and Silver Clans but of the Black and Green, with a few Red banners.

Bolvi could convince any Red Clan to join us, but he was not with us.

I asked Kraq what he thought. "The ratio of ten guards to one prisoner is a rare thing. I initially thought I was certain who these prisoners were. However, I have never seen more than four or five at any given time, so I doubt they are the ones who first came to mind."

"Àrd-Rìgh, if we don't signal the attack, they will be out of range shortly," Kraq reminded me. A voice in my head told me that all deserve freedom from oppression and the safety of the City of Hope.

"Have our cavalry welcome those who serve the Fallen. Split the infantry to either side of the cavalry. Announce our presence!"

Battle horns blared in the crisp morning air. Although it caused some disarray, the enemy did not come to a sudden halt. Instead, the leading battle group continued to move onward. They seemed more confused when they came upon Quaylin cavalry and infantry supplemented by a sizeable Skaldi force. When Captain BenKido moved his horse forward to address the enemy, a group of foes attacked him. Without hesitation, Kraq and his new ally, Aig of the Silver Clan, strode to a position before the Quaylin military leader.

During this confusion, I rallied my forces. We left the ridge and came up behind the second group of Skaldi in tight formation, far behind the soldiers still guarding their prisoners. Aig took a moment to initiate conversation, calling for the immediate surrender of those before him.

A volley of spears greeted him, ending any further discussion. As the two forces clashed, my group moved to take full advantage of the situation. Almost a full mile separated the larger Skaldi group and those guarding the prisoners. I dismounted. The Skaldi at the rear soon turned to face my direction.

I watched his face turn from a sneer to amazement. And then to fear as I went from being an unarmed human to carrying a sword that dripped blue flames. Just like his master's sword! I moved into the midst of the rear troops. Both spear and arrow felled those who didn't die by my sword from those who followed after me.

I rushed to the end of the prisoners' line, where I was met by a massive Skaldi wearing a medallion on a gold chain and a green sash. It was sad that such a mighty warrior would choose death rather than disobey his masters.

I dodged his battle ax and watched the horror in his eyes as my blade cut through him like a hot knife through butter. I approached the rear row of prisoners. There were four chained together in each row.

Coming behind them, I shouted, "Kneel!"

There was no response.

"You must kneel for me to remove your hood and break the chains that bind you." I moved back to the Green Clan leader and pulled the ring of brass keys from his belt, and to my surprise, the last row of prisoners now knelt. I moved to the first prisoner and unlocked the chains. I pulled the hood from the captive's head.

As the hood came off, I stepped back with a gasp, as if coming face to face with something out of one of my deepest nightmares. You would think I would be used to such moments, having spent an entire year on an alien planet with Kraq and Bolvi.

The prisoners had clawed hands and feet. Their faces were the likeness of a lion. As others helped remove hoods and chains, I looked around. The Quaylin cavalry that had joined me now dipped their lances to the ground as a sign of honor. Those on the ground bowed.

Reverent whispers of 'Glav' identified the prisoners for me. The Glav, once freed, grabbed the nearest Skaldi weapon they could find. The last Glav captive was released, and all the Glav burst out of our ranks, running full tilt at the enemy army's rear.

I rallied my troops to follow. It was then that I sensed something, and as I approached, it revealed itself amid the enemy troops.

The Glav formed a half-circle with me at its center as my forces collected behind them. The emerging Angel's troops were cut in half, facing my group with Kraq and Aig and my smaller army with the freed captives. I watched as the Angel moved toward my position.

"You can't hope to stand against me! Even with a hundred Glav, you have no hope!" It declared.

I flicked my wrist in annoyance, and my sword revealed itself. The Angel seemed taken aback for a moment. "What is your name, Angel?"

"What difference does my name make? Another puny human deemed the high-king by the Maker? You will meet Him now!"

I tried a different approach. "By YHWH, you will tell me your name!"

There was now a worried look on his face. Even the mightiest of the Fallen tremble at the name of their Father. "Why must you know my name?"

I could tell he was fighting the command. "I would have it to put on your grave marker, just like I did for Batariel!"

There was some anguish on his face. "Batariel is dead, then?"

"By my hand!"

"What is your name so I may inform the others of your deed?"

"I am the peace bringer, the chain breaker, and the servant of the Maker! I am the Àrd-Rìgh! I will know your name before your end!"

"Goodbye, human. When you see my father, tell him Tamiel sends greetings!"

I shouted for all to attack. Tamiel's face was horrified and confused as my blade parted him from his left arm. I was sure no one in their right mind had faced him and survived. With that look still on his face, I evaded his parry and cut him across the beltline. As he fell, I noticed Kraq, Aig, and all our Skaldi allies making short work of the remaining enemy.

As I turned, I realized the Glav seemed intent on attacking the Skaldi that stood with us. I moved between the two groups as they approached with my sword still blazing.

"It is a new world where Quaylin and Skaldi fight and work together, against the Fallen Ones. You are now free! Free to choose to be part of this new world and join us in the City of Hope. Your other choice is to leave this place, for if you attack those who gave their own lives to free you, then you are no better than the Fallen Ones.

If any harm befalls any of my men, I will turn the sword that took this Fallen One's life against you".

I pointed at Kraq, "This is Kraq of the Blue Clan and Aig of the Silver Clan. They stand with us, together with the Quaylin. If you oppose them, you oppose me. Any attack on them is an attack on me. I invite you to the City of Hope to see the truth I speak of, where all men are free. You will find rest in my halls. Choose now whom you will serve?"

There were tense moments while the Glav communicated with hand signals.

Kraq directed his men to provide cloaks for the remaining Glav, since they were in simple loincloths in the chill of the winter.

CHAPTER 31

As we returned to the City, there was quite a disturbance. It seemed that to catch a glimpse of one Glav in your lifetime was highly unusual, and you spoke about it in hushed tones and quiet reverence. Just over a hundred of them now lined the bridge behind me as we entered the city.

SunGru told me that when a ruler of note was born, several Glav mysteriously appeared to serve as bodyguards. The Quaylin emperor had a bodyguard of twenty Glav. They defended him to their last breath as he attempted to flee the capital. You can only imagine what stories were circulating now about Àrd-Rìgh and the one hundred Glav at his court.

While I had been at hero status, to my chagrin, this pushed me beyond that straight into the legendary realm.

I spoke to Shal-Dir about this, and his response left me feeling both wonder and fear.

"Embrace your destiny, Àrd-Rìgh."

I looked at him over my coffee cup. "I am going to stop asking your advice if you are going to make stuff up about me."

Shal-Dir set his glass of wine down dramatically and grunted. Rising from his seat, he gestured for me to follow him.

The tall tower rose three hundred feet into the air and was the only one with an elevator. The lift moved flawlessly between the twenty-five floors, twenty above ground and five below the base. The top levels housed the royal apartments; the two stories below were used as servants' quarters.

I bring this up because, at some point, someone determined I should live in that apartment above the clouds without consulting me. The flats had been remodeled and redecorated, and furniture filled the hall, waiting to be moved in - all under the watchful eyes of Rachel and SunGru's wife, TeiLin.

A whole year had passed since I had proposed to Rachel on the mountainside overlooking the valley, but there is no official wedding date yet.

TeiLin had spent her entire life at the Quaylin emperor's high court. Long ago, her great-grandfather had been an ambassador to the Kingdom of Midia. TeiLin's knowledge of etiquette and decorum was highly valued in the Quaylin High Court.

The Glav swore allegiance to the Àrd-Rìgh as if fulfilling a prophecy. They now wore the 'King's colors,' and I could go nowhere without my private guard. They positioned themselves along the way and at the location, if I had somewhere to go.

Several mornings following the Glav's arrival, I awakened to a loud commotion. There were so few people in the tower that I seldom saw anyone till I reached ground level. I cracked the door slightly, glancing first right and then left. I found a seven-foot-tall Glav warrior to either side, fully uniformed. I saw an open doorway down the hallway with two more Glav spears crossed to deny entrance. I could see Rachel, red hair blowing in the cross breeze, hands on her hips on the far side of those crossed spears.

I smiled until I realized what was happening, then I threw on my slippers and pants. I caught a few words she was spewing at my new guardians. She talked fast when upset.

"No, I am not the Queen, but I expect that to change any day now."

She had spotted me, and the last part of her comment was for me. Before I could speak, she reached out and grabbed the mane or beard of the Glav guard. What to call it at this point? The Glav is cat-like in its facial appearance. Rachel pulled the startled Glav closer to her face. "You can move it or lose it, big guy. Your choice!"

I made it down the hall and rushed toward the 'catfight' about to ensue. The fight stopped as the first syllables came out of my mouth. She was dangling about three feet off the floor, screaming. "Put me down, kitty!"

I motioned to lower her to the ground and put my index finger to my lips. I escorted her to my chambers. I returned briefly to let my guardians know that Rachel had unrestricted access to my home regardless of whether she was armed. Returning to my quarters, I returned her bow, which she tossed on the bed, still a little angry.

"I am so sorry! I am sure that SunGru had mentioned your status to the Glav." I had never seen anyone lay hands on Rachel without leaving bruises to prove it.

She looked mad, but a grin slowly spread over her face. "Holy crap! You have lion-men guarding your bedroom!"

"So, you're not mad?" I asked.

"Hey, if they let some girl waltz in without asking questions, especially an armed one, I would have to question their reputation." The grin was still there. "So they're your bodyguards?"

Then, the questions and remarks began to fly. "Did you know they can communicate with your dogs?"

Lion-men talking to my dogs on an alien planet? Now, why would that surprise me?

Rachel still lived in the villa on the second tier of the city. "You are up very early. What is the occasion?"

The glimmer in Rachel's eyes usually meant a surprise, even though she knew I was not fond of them. "SunGru, TeiLin, and I have someone for you to meet. Well, a couple for you to meet."

We exited the elevator and went down six stories to the first floor of my 'area' of the tower. This area had been the servants' quarters.

When we arrived, I saw SunGru and his wife. Behind them stood a Quaylin couple wearing what was now called the 'King's colors.'

CHAPTER 32

SunGru stepped forward. "Good morning, Àrd-Rìgh. May I introduce Leo and Lynn to you?" The two Quaylin, each taking one of my hands, bowed low and then moved back from me.

I was as uncomfortable as a kid in the principal's office. "It is very nice to meet the two of you."

SunGru waved the couple and his wife through the apartment's door and led me to a couch on the balcony overlooking the city, where Rachel joined us.

SunGru began. "RJ," and he called me in private, "Leo and Lynn have been chosen as former members of the Quaylin court to serve as the stewards of your household."

Rachel could see the protest welling up from my heart and rushing towards my lips. "RJ, this is not a big deal. They will ensure your laundry gets washed, your rooms are clean, and you have food when needed."

SunGru saw his moment and added, "Leo is a master scribe famed for his flair with words. Lynn will try to keep everything tidy and can help cater to any needs from the market and later with the birth of your heirs."

Rachel could still see there was the potential for protest. "RJ, they are here to help you in any way. They will live here below you and are not servants. They are of noble birth and volunteered their services. It is a great honor for them. Please accept and don't make a big deal out of this."

I knew that look, which meant if I made a fuss, I would regret it. "All right, I'm not going to make a big deal out of this, but you two keep ambushing me." It was my turn to give my signature look; "Some warning would be fair."

Rachel turned to offer another expression of a pushed-up lip, raising an eyebrow. I was about to protest when SunGru opened the door for an informal get-together with my newly appointed steward and his wife.

In time, Leo and Lynn became valued assets and family members. SunGru had not been lying about Leo's skill with the written word or its placement on the paper. Lynn met with Rachel to discuss my likes and dislikes, ranging from food and drinks to clothing and décor. The two Quaylin stewards insisted that they were to be 'bothered', my words, not theirs, at any hour, day or night, for the needs of the Àrd-Rìgh. In private, I insisted on them calling me RJ, but they insisted on my formal title even when only the Glav guards were nearby.

I will tell you more about the City's fifth tier, where my residence was situated. I will start at the top and work my way down. Above the four floors that contained my apartment was the highest point in the city.

As the elevator floor rose level with the tower's roof, you could see across the city's vastness; out over the great lake and ranchlands, even to the three passes. There was a very ornate chair, which I doubted I would use, as I suspected the last inhabitant had placed it here. However, I sat down anyway.

What an incredible place this was. What more could God show me that would amaze me more than I already was?

A transparent dome covered the roof of this tower. I wasn't sure if the Acrucians had done this for the first ruler or for me. It did keep me from being blown off the chair and rushing to meet my doom three hundred feet below, so I was grateful for it. I believe I had only sat down for a moment and closed my eyes, thankful for some alone time, when I heard a popping sound and a quarter portion of the dome opened.

I was sure I could make it to the elevator if I tried, but something more than fear had me gripping my chair. Slowly, the head and wings of a great bird appeared, along with a rider. It landed inside the clear dome. At almost that exact moment, the elevator platform arrived with SunGru and Leo.

As the rider dismounted, I instantly recognized the chief of the Karuk people, Adoeete. I was then subjected to a quick mount-and-dismount lesson, followed by learning the verbal commands for the great bird. It was then that I realized what was happening. One of the Karuk birds and it's rider were standing nearby. For me to reach any place in the City, outlying fortifications, or travel even further still, my personal Air Force One was just moments away.

I now felt uneasy that all these instructions were only a prelude to an actual ride. I was right.

The first flight was personally overseen by Adoeete, accompanying me. The second time was a solo flight. I told SunGru and Adoeete that it needed to be a short trip. Ultimately, I spent nearly half an hour with my great winged friend. I circled each of the four castles and flew out over the waterfalls and the lake to the west before returning to the transparent dome atop my tower.

Suddenly, there seemed to be some incredible benefits to being the Àrd-Rìgh. On a side note, I wondered if Andy would be jealous of my sudden ability to fly.

The top floor of my apartment is nearly empty, at this point. The next level down holds my private chambers and bath. The story below features an entertaining area, two additional suites for guests, and a small kitchen. The first level houses a small barracks for the Glav, an armory, a supply pantry for dry goods and wine, and my office, which includes a small library.

There is also a foyer for those awaiting the courts' audience, Leo's office, and the War room.

To get to me, you had to go through him. Leo was quite confident in that boast as well. I would be, too, if I had six Glav guards at the doors of the first level. The two levels below this were my steward and his wife's private apartments, which required an access code held by only five people.

I wanted Leo and Lynn to have as much privacy as their titles would allow. According to SunGru and Shal-Dir, the rooms on the floors below were offices filled with people whose sole purpose was to carry out the kingdom's everyday administration.

At ground level, many other buildings covered the fifth tier of the City. It was hard to believe its size, as the fifth tier was three miles across and nearly nine and a half miles around. Villas with acreage started at the outer walls and worked inwards to the center. Smaller estates with less land but grander homes ended where the government buildings and my tower began. The Great Hall is a sizable building, divided into a throne room that accommodated several hundred people, a banquet hall, and kitchens.

The king's library is a majestic domed building. Allen has practically claimed it as his headquarters. Several hundred of the Monks of A.O. and an above-average number of Acrucians are now working on restoring this building to its former glory. The Room of Maps is just off the main hall, aptly named, as nearly every square inch of its walls is covered with maps of every shape and size. However, what caught your eye was towards the rear wall. A globe hung from the ceiling, and four grand wrought iron staircases twisted around, allowing a closer look at the large sphere.

From the ceiling, the hanging world model was a wonder, and a panel at the base could control its movement, standing four stories tall. The globe appeared incomplete, lacking both a map and geographical features. There were many other notable buildings, but I will not bore you with such details.

Are you wondering about the five floors below the ground floor of the King's Tower?

DEFCON One, aptly named by Andy, is where all the Acrucians live, so I never see more than a handful of them together at any given time or place. They built the City from their ships, and it only made sense that their living quarters should be private and secure.

The level below, you guessed it, DEFCON Two, is where the Acrucians worked. This area contains a series of labs and workshops. I have no idea what their use is. A long tunnel with its high-speed shuttle leads to the control room on Tier four of the city. Besides the Acrucians and the council, no one else knows about the levels below the King's Tower.

DEFCON Three is a vast warehouse of leftover parts from the deconstructed space-faring vessel used to build the city. The Acrucians are doing an inventory of the warehouse.

DEFCON Four appears to be a giant greenhouse - unused for thousands of years.

No natural plants had survived, but two trees glowed at its center, surrounded by a stasis field. On my first trip down to this level, Shal-Dir motioned me to follow him. We left my Glav guards at the elevator and walked down a hall to the greenhouse entrance.

"RJ, there is something you must see but tell no one about."

I nodded in agreement and followed him to the base of the stasis fields surrounding the glowing trees. He stopped me again at some distance and pointed at the foot of the two massive trees.

There stood a figure brandishing a sword wreathed in flame. Three more giant beings, each holding a sword, appeared as we moved closer to the trees.

I looked at Shal-Dir. What did this guy know about all of this?

"Àrd-Rìgh, I can go no further with you. If you choose to approach the trees, I have no idea what will happen, but I thought you should see it yourself. Perhaps the Acrucians can reveal information about the trees and the beings guarding them."

I nodded and motioned him to return to where my Glav bodyguards waited at the elevator. Once the Eridu leader had disappeared, I began my approach. I had a flaming sword, too, after all.

CHAPTER 33

The closer I got to the trees, the bigger the being appeared. I realized just how large the greenhouse chamber was and how small I was. I estimate that the being before me was at least thirty feet tall. It had four faces and four sets of wings. The body was nearly indiscernible. The sword it held was real and quite a bit taller than I was. It appeared to hover off the ground rather than stand and seemed to awaken upon my approach.

By this point, I had sweated through my shirt. I was considering my words and also my actions. The being before me had four wings and four faces of a man, a lion, an eagle, and an ox. The brightness of the being's glory was so that I had to shield my eyes with one hand. In his hand, it held a sword eternally wreathed in flames.

As I got closer, the face of the eagle screamed out a warning. The head began to rotate until the human face was before me.

Then the large human-like eyes blinked open, "Son of Adam, why do you trouble my slumber? I will grant you four questions, then you will go, and I will again sleep."

Four questions? Then it hit me. Four questions, and then this giant would fall back to sleep. Now I wish Allen were here to provide some great questions. "Who ... what are you?"

The being made a grunting noise as if I should know who he was, "I am Zophiel, of the First Sphere, Guardian of Eden."

Eden, as in the Garden of Eden? Now, the two giant trees made more sense.

"Ask me your second question, Son of Adam."

How do I wrap my mind around all this? I was suddenly wondering if I could save my other three questions for a later date and walk away now. I risked it all, turned, and began a quick retreat. Behind me, there was a noise that sounded like thunder-like laughter. But I could not risk turning back around.

"Son of Adam, wisdom is a path few dare to walk upon."

I kept walking. I planned to return with the best three questions that my team could come up with at some point soon. My neck hairs were still at attention when I arrived at the elevator.

Shal-Dir met me some ways out from my Glav guards. "What did you learn, Àrd-Rìgh?"

I cleared my throat. "One is named Zophiel of the First Sphere, Guardian of Eden."

I had never seen Shal-Dir's face change in such a way, but it seemed less blue and more of a grey tone for a moment.

"An angel of the First Sphere is one of the Ophanim. Only eight of them are known. If four guard the trees, then the trees are of great importance."

In the elevator, I thought, "You have no idea." After all, I had just seen what could be on the final level.

"This last level is a bit of a disappointment to me," Shal-Dir remarked.

As we entered the room, there was a stone stand and a substantial red ruby-like gem. No markings and no runes? What was the purpose of this room?

Shal-Dir replied as if he had read my mind, "I do not know this room or its use. Perhaps it is unfinished. Maybe it is a dead-end." Shal-Dir had a puzzled look.

"Dead end. What do you mean by that?" I asked.

Shal-Dir seemed to think momentarily, "What if this is an exit and not an entrance? You arrive here from somewhere else but can't go anywhere from this point."

"Copy that" was all I could get out. After a full year and several months in the city, we were still discovering the unexplained. For all I knew, the Acrucians and Shal-Dir himself could have been hiding all these things from me for months.

"How long have you known about these levels below the King's Tower?"

Shal-Dir looked at me as if to make some grand excuse, but decided against it. "To be honest, RJ, I knew the Acrucians were working on the first two levels because they all seemed to disappear into the night. SunGru conducted some scouting, which led us to determine where they had gone. Which led to some blackmail."

I rolled my eyes, "Blackmail? Really! Who did you have to blackmail?"

"Your best buddies, Fer and Tuc. I told them to show and tell, or I would bring you down to make them do so. The panel in the elevator stops at the ground floor unless you or one of the council members enters their code. Oh, there is one other thing I thought I would show you that held my interest."

The elevator took us back to DEFCON 3 and the warehouse of leftover parts that the Acrucians were inventorying. The Glav moved out in front of us, but the doors shut before I could step out, leaving several very upset guardians on the other side.

Shal-Dir pulled me around until we were facing the back of the elevator. He waved his hand over a marked panel, and a digital palm scanner appeared. He grabbed my hand and placed it on the scanner. The elevator's rear opened to reveal a long, curving hallway. "This is the only level I found that has this," Shal-Dir stated as if he already knew what I was thinking.

"What's down here?"

"Nothing exciting unless you realize you are now almost seven hundred meters below the King's Tower. Come, I will show you."

My mind began to spin. We couldn't see the land below us from the tower bridges. We knew there was water below because of the waterfalls. Clouds and mist obscured our view. After over a year, we still had no idea what lay in the abyss. If this tunnel took us to the ground floor, a new world might be ripe for exploration.

Shal-Dir looked back at where I had stopped, "Stop worrying!"

"I was just..."

"I know what you were doing. Math. If we are in the center of the plateau and the first tier of the city is nine miles across, then we have a very long walk ahead of us?"

"Yes, but..."

Shal-Dir waved for me to follow. "You don't think I am walking seven miles, do you? Come, this will take but a moment."

Around the bend sat another of the Acrucian bullet trains. Shal-Dir was very accurate; it took about sixty seconds. We were now standing, looking out from a window carved into the very rock of the cliff itself. I felt a bit of vertigo as if I were once more standing by the window of some magnificent skyscraper. The floor of the canyon itself was still several hundred feet below us.

"What good is a great window plastered to the side of a cliff? I asked.

"RJ, through that door." I followed with my eyes in the direction he was pointing. "There are stairs that lead down to another room identical to this one but much larger. Instead of only viewing access like this window, the window below us opens and provides access to the valley."

Why was he showing me all this?

"What advantage does this offer? What can we do with this place? What was the purpose of this place?" I asked, partly to myself and partly out loud.

Shal-Dir shook his head. "RJ, I am a humble merchant here for counsel and to impart every advantage I can offer you."

I was beginning to wonder how a simple merchant knew everything he did.

"I know you are wondering how I know all these things. I will share this story with you. It was long ago. My grandfather had saved a Dvergar family from a Skaldi raiding party and their Fenri hunting pack. The Dvergar father had been an architect of the Bridge of Eternity. Please don't ask me what the Bridge of Eternity is; I have no idea. You will have to ask one of the Acrucians or a Dvergar. That is if we can ever find one. May I continue?"

I nodded. I hadn't realized I had interrupted.

"Where was I? The Dvergar gave my grandfather a map, which he passed to my father. No, I do not have the map. It was never passed to me by my father. I only remember the few glances I caught when he had it out over the years. The map showed a great tower five levels below it, which I can only assume is what we found here. As the story goes, there is a great treasure on the map, along with my people's sign, a great river. We have seen every square inch of this mountain, but I see no sign of my people or treasure."

"What about the trees guarded by the Cherubim?" I asked.

The prominent Eridu leader shook his head almost in disgust. "My people pondered the stars and saw things that no human, living or dead, has seen. Our hearts do not yearn for the things humans do. Those trees were not our undoing but yours. They are a curse, not a treasure."

Well, at least I knew where he stood concerning the virtual Garden of Eden, a floor below us. In my mind, there are only two possible answers left. Something was in the abyss, or the ruby held some power we could not yet access.

CHAPTER 34

I desired a few days to gather my wits. I set out early to spend the day with Bill on the ranch, seeing how they prepared for spring planting. On the second day, I made it no further back to the city than the long pier, where I spent the day in a boat with several unsuspecting Quaylin fishermen. We brought in quite a haul, to the delight of my Glav guardians.

On the third day after my little tour with Shal-Dir, I sat down for breakfast with Rachel. Leo and Lynn joined us, as was our new weekly habit on Wednesdays. The usual banter around the table ensued.

"RJ, what does today entail for the two of you?" Rachel asked, which was her way of asking if we had any intention of getting into trouble today.

Leo had the uncanny ability to turn tedious governmental paperwork into less of a task and more of a fun, objective-filled assignment. A job by any other name is still a job. I needed to pick a subject and hope the rest of the day won't end with Leo explaining each document.

I would then sign the form – repeat this process until lunch, and then repeat it until supper. Fearing what today might hold for me, I announced the first thing that came to my tongue, as I had not taken even a moment to think about it before speaking. "I promised

Father Emmaus that I would gather as much information about the Monks of AO as possible and write a report of my findings."

"How is it that Father Emmaus is not writing you the report? Isn't he better suited for such a task than you?" Rachel stated. I could see she thought I was up to something.

"No, Rachel, you misunderstood. It is more of a personal research endeavor by RJ to learn more about his people than an actual report," Leo added, saving my proverbial butt.

"I agree with Rachel. I can't see you two spending any more time than necessary locked away in that office," Lynn added.

Both women were suspicious of the true nature of our day, but they had a day at the market planned, so our fishing plans or paperwork did not matter to them. Leo packed us a sack with cheese, bread, and freshly smoked fish. As we walked out the door, he grabbed two flasks of wine and looked at me for approval.

"Bring them, my friend." I said, "It may be a long day."

We went to the ground floor, avoiding the great hall, where some council members finished breakfast. You would think sneaking around with two Glav guards would cause some commotion, but they make no sounds, becoming one with any shadow that avails itself for their size.

We didn't need to be sneaky. I was the Àrd-Rìgh, and eventually, the word would spread about my location. Once we arrived at the Great Library, Leo arranged for a large private room. Allen was there with his usual troop of twenty monks and an equal number of Acrucians. Allen was busy with his projects, nearly day and night, but he sent two monks my way to help with our project.

The two Glav remained outside the door. I heard Leo tell them, "No one in without my say. The Àrd-Rìgh requires peace."

The responding grunt meant a firm agreement.

Once we were alone, Leo was slightly less formal. "RJ, what are we doing here?"

I had grown quite fond of Leo and considered him a friend. "Leo, no one knows what I am about to tell you, not even Andy or Rachel."

He nodded his head. As Steward of the Àrd-Rìgh's house, Leo knew almost every secret, state-related or otherwise. Pouring each of us a goblet of wine, he spoke. "Out with it. Spill the beans and let the cat out of the bag."

This slang brought a grin and a chuckle to my lips. Leo had been working on two American language barriers: sarcasm and sayings.

"Well done. My friend Andy has been helping you with that, hasn't he?"

Leo nodded.

"All right, I will be blunt. Several days ago, I was with Shal-Dir. I touched an object that did nothing to our Eridu friend but seared a single word into my memory. I don't know what the word or name means on Earth, and I have no idea how it involves the Other Realms."

The two assigned monks joined us for their duties.

"I want to gather and record the history of the Monks of AO and anything involving the name or word Hanokh." I had to start somewhere. "Scrolls, books, tablets, maps, anything we can find. If Allen has it, take it from him. If there is resistance, tell him, 'The Àrd-Rìgh requires it.' Let's get started."

What did I know about Hanokh? About an hour into our research, the door opened, and a giant paw passed a small scroll with a wax seal — the seal of the Duke of Abacus. I grinned, mostly to myself. It was sometimes hard to read Allen, but this was humor on another level.

I waved the note at Leo, who carefully opened it. "Allen says Hanokh is the biblical Enoch."

Enoch? Did Allen mean Enoch, the great-grandfather of Noah? I had something to go on. Allen had stopped by with a book he needed back as soon as we finished it. Hearing our discussion about Enoch, he then threw a wrench into the works by adding, as he left, "Cain's first son was also named Enoch. He was pure evil."

Enoch, 'the good,' was so favored that he was taken to heaven by God without knowing death. Adam himself had named him the first in the line of high priests. Enoch lived three hundred and sixty-five years on Earth. He wrote a first-hand experience describing two hundred angels known as the 'Watchers' and their subsequent fall from grace. He chronicled the acts of the Fallen, including the human women they took as wives. Their children are the giant Nephilim and the half-breed Elioud.

What did we know about Evil Enoch, the son of Cain? Deep into the night, we talked. The deeper we went, the more names piled up. Thoth and Hermes are from both Egyptian and Greek mythology. Mercury from the Romans and Idrus from the ancient Hebrews. He was also known to the Arabs as Edris and to the Phoenicians as Thaut. Of all the names, those of Hermes and Thoth were the most numerous.

Evil Enoch utilized the secret symbols and understanding provided to him by the Fallen Angels to begin writing down all the knowledge of the seven sacred sciences, the highest wisdom of heaven, which had been imparted to only a few angels.

The Fallen took this knowledge upon their exile from heaven. Once Evil Enoch had written everything down, he built nine underground vaults to house the hundreds and perhaps thousands of volumes. Over the information storage vaults, he constructed the Great Pyramids of Egypt. Thus, ensuring they would survive the coming flood.

Evil Enoch is not a known historical figure; however, the pyramids were built around 2500 BC. He also created two great pillars. One was made of marble and would not burn. On it, he inscribed the fundamental truths of the seven sacred sciences. The second pillar is made of a brick-like material called Laterus and would not sink in water. Inscribed upon it are the directions to the hidden vaults' locations.

Then came the flood, which I have dated around 2288 BC. Since Evil Enoch reappeared after the flood as Hermes and later as Mercury, one can only speculate that he managed to survive either in the vaults or within the pyramids during the flood.

In 2198 BC, Evil Enoch, now known as Hermes, can be found with his nephew, Nimrod, to the sixth power. Nimrod now ruled the known world at the age of ninety-eight. Nimrod and Hermes devised a plan to build the Tower of Babel, a portal they would create using the seven sacred sciences. Evil Enoch and Nimrod aimed to open a gateway to heaven and attack God, taking heaven for themselves

Noah's wife Naamah was of 'like spirit' with Noah. She served God. Noah and Naamah's sons married Naamah's cousin's daughters, the daughters of the sons of Mehujael, grandson of Evil Enoch.

I had no idea when Leo and I drifted off to sleep, each with an ancient book as a pillow.

Sometime in the small wee hours of the night, a knock came. Leo woke me and then answered the door to find two Glav guards towering over Fer and Tuc's figures. Accompanying the two Acrucians was a floating disc filled with more books, scrolls, and maps.

Once the monks had unloaded the tray, the Acrucians and their empty floating library cart prepared to leave. I was about to say something out loud when I decided to think about my question.

"Why not tell me what you know rather than me wasting days searching through thousands of manuscripts to find the answers I need?"

The response echoed in my mind. "Is this not how hominids acquire erudition?"

"So, staring at all these pages is the only way to gain knowledge?" I thought.

Their response was, "Enoch is known to us. Enoch lived here in the Other Realms for a time. Enoch used the Bridge to Eternity to traverse the universe. Enoch continues his journey even now."

"That is a large amount of data based on my simple question. Why are you telling me this?"

"The Monks of AO hold the key." Then, almost as an afterthought, I heard a 'get to work' filter through the flurry of thoughts that now overtook me.

I was tired of riddles. Do the monks hold the key? There weren't that many monks in the City. What was the key? Good Enoch lived in the Other Realms after he departed Earth? Enoch left Earth? At some point, Enoch goes to the Other Realms and continues his journey five thousand years later. We all took copious notes on the first day. By the second day, I realized I might have to call on Father Emmaus and Brother Mathis for help.

When the Father heard about my project, he arrived early that morning, leaving Brother Mathis to continue the work at the cathedral. The Father shared a brief account of the Monks of AO with us, passed down through oral and written tradition. An older man in gleaming robes had arrived through a Lion's Gate and founded the Monks of AO. The people who followed Enoch in the Other Realms called him Hanokh.

Well, finally, a piece of the puzzle that made sense. It didn't take a genius to determine that Hanokh appeared to be Enoch. The followers of Good Enoch in the Other Realms built places of learning and worship. They became one of the most revered religious groups, which made sense as Enoch was the first high priest anointed by Adam. It began to spread so much that Nephilim and Elioud, who had escaped Earth, started persecuting the religion.

In some areas, the monks were hunted and put to death, but the movement stayed alive underground. Great leaders in other regions who opposed the Nephilim and Elioud protected the monks from harm. There were new groups that sought out the far reaches of the Other Realms. They rebuilt their places of worship and learning, which the armies of the Nephilim and Elioud would find more challenging to reach.

Amid all the chaos, Enoch or Hanokh disappeared. Fearing that Enoch had been captured or assassinated, the monks' leadership put all their effort into building a fortification that would stave off capture and safeguard the movement's greatest treasures.

According to AO tradition, the Tower of Erudition was chief among such places. A magnificent fortress was aptly named to counter the Tower of Babel, filled with church resources and warrior monks. With great regret, Father Emmaus informed me that no monk within the City's confines had ever been there or known its location.

Andy showed up with a scroll to display what appeared to be a map, but it was written in a language no one could read, not even Shal-Dir or the Acrucians. By then, it must have been breakfast time. I told Leo to get me Allen and breakfast, but not necessarily in that order.

I had no idea that Allen and Gretchen had left the second tier of the city and moved into one of the fifth-tier villas. Gretchen had turned the land there into her medical gardens. It got Allen closer to the Great Library and the Acrucian workshops below.

Allen had wasted no time returning with the monk we had sent after him. "I hear that no one in the city, perhaps even all the Other Realms, could answer this question you have."

Ego. The bigger the brain, the less you can control it.

"Yes, I need to see if you can identify this writing for me." He nodded as I pointed at the scroll. I wanted him to see. "Even the Eridu and Acrucians could not help me."

Allen scanned the document briefly. "This is Geez, and no one has spoken this language for over a thousand years."

"Can you translate it for me?" I was sure Allen could.

"I could take a stab at it, but this is early work. I would probably butcher the translation," Allen replied.

He told me the truth. I had never heard him claim to be anything but the best in any language or computer-related field. The look of utter devastation on my face must have given him a clue to the importance of my finding. He sat down and stole a piece of bacon off my plate.

"I have a friend who is an expert."

"Let me guess. Is this going to require a trip back to Earth?"

CHAPTER 35

Allen's friend, Wilson, did not live in the Other Realms or Colorado, not even in the United States, for that matter. Wilson Cunnington III was a somewhat eccentric British archaeologist and expert in ancient languages. His family had amassed their vast wealth between his grandfather and his father, both world-renowned archeologists.

The family estate, located on the coast of Wales, between two small villages on the western edge of the Isle of Anglesey, was about a four-hour trip by car from Liverpool's International Airport. Getting this expert to join the team would require us to leave the Other Realms and figure out how to travel from Colorado (USA) to Liverpool (UK), more than 4,000 miles away. I would also have to convince the council to let me go on this adventure, which seemed nearly futile. Rachel's advice made it clear that I would have to assert myself as Àrd-Rìgh.

It was a wet and mist-filled March morning when I had worked up what I thought was a considerable amount of nerve. I burst into the great hall, disturbing everyone's breakfast, and sat at the head of the main table. However, before making my announcement, Cook brought me a steaming plate of pancakes and a side of bacon. I ate, then paused as if I was about to speak, causing everyone to turn from their meal and look at me, and then I ate some more.

SunGru and Shal-Dir continued to look at each other.

Finally, SunGru spoke. "Àrd-Rìgh, do you have something you wish to say?"

By this point, I had only finished half my meal. I wanted to play this out as long as I could and build on the atmosphere of thick, knife-cutting tension. I raised one finger for silence, then continued eating. When I finished my last bite, everyone at the table exhaled in unison. I grabbed hold of that moment.

"Am I not the Àrd-Rìgh?" I asked.

There was nodding around the table, but no one put a voice to answer my question.

"Am I not the Àrd-Rìgh?" I asked again.

This time, there was more than nodding agreement as many simple 'yes' responses came from around the table.

But it was not enough. Jumping to my feet, I pushed my chair back and climbed onto the table, an act that no one had seen coming.

"Am I not the Àrd-Rìgh?" I shouted so loud that I heard pots and pans falling to the floor in the kitchens behind us.

Suddenly, there were plenty of answers. "Yes."

"Yes, sire. You are the Àrd-Rìgh."

"I am going then!"

I immediately realized my grave error when I heard SunGru somewhat awkwardly ask, "Going where, Sire?"

In my mind, it had played out differently than that. Then, as I turned around, Shal-Dir, who was the voice of reason, should I appear mentally unstable, and who had guessed my intentions, spoke.

"Sire, there is no way we can protect you beyond the Lion's Gate. Neither the Skaldi nor Glav can accompany you to Earth."

"I neither require nor ask of the council's approval. If I am indeed the Àrd-Rìgh chosen by the Maker, then His hand will protect His servant."

"Yes, but who will protect you on your journey?"

"Jim and Andy will accompany me. I have an old friend whom I will call upon for aid. If, for some reason, I do not return in a timely fashion, then in my stead, SunGru will lead the city."

One of the last things Shal-Dir said to me was, "Proceed with caution. The Fallen Ones have eyes and ears everywhere. You now pose a threat to them."

A few days later, I stood overlooking the plains where we had first seen a Quaylin army about to be overrun by Skaldi forces. It seemed like a lifetime ago. I wanted Allen to come with us, but he merely handed me a list of required items and placed his head back between the pages of some ancient book. Everyone else seemed to have their agenda as well. Bill's list said, 'Raid a ranch supply for all Heirloom seeds.' Gretchen wanted medical supplies, Rachel requested some archery equipment, Becky wanted school supplies, and Jim wanted to return unharmed.

We spent the night under the same trees we had lain under on that first night in the Other Realms.

The smell of food on the open fire, the cool mountain breeze, and the distant sound of wildlife settling in for the night brought many fond memories rushing back. We made our way to the Lion's Gate in the morning, which brought us out at the cavern and the stream that we followed down to the meadow. Andy had planned to return to winterize or store the chopper at the lodge, but there had always been more pressing matters for him in the city.

Jim and I were worried that sitting this long could have damaged Andy's toy. It was no surprise to him when the bird's blades began to turn in the Colorado dawn, with a bit of coaxing and some added fluids.

The lodge was not the same without the dogs welcoming us; there were no smells from the kitchen and no sounds of laughter from the great room. There was nothing fresh to eat in the house, but we had some food left from our journey, thanks to Cook. There was running water, electricity, and the internet. Payments were still being deducted from my account like clockwork. Andy made the mistake of opening the fridge, and an overwhelming smell forced us to clean it out thoroughly.

I sent Wilson an email about our intended visit, and the airline tickets we're procuring. In addition to the plane tickets to Liverpool, I placed online orders for the items to bring back from Earth. Everything, from seeds and ammunition to technology and spices, would arrive at the lodge in a few days. The local delivery driver knew what to do. An old red toolbox that held a key was sitting beside the garage. The delivery driver would stack all the boxes in the empty bay. I always left him a note and several 'Ben Franklins', as a token of appreciation for his troubles.

The letter informed him that I had been out of the country and would likely not be here when the orders arrived. I suggested the driver take his wife out for a nice dinner with the tip I left him.

That day, we took my SUV into town, grabbed breakfast at one of the local restaurants, and made sure to be seen by the Chief of Police and several of the nosier townsfolk. They all knew I traveled extensively, and this would lend a hand with the cover story. We left town around 9 AM and arrived at Denver International Airport just before noon.

While we all had the proper identification and papers to carry a firearm, we could obtain what was needed from my friend in Liverpool, once we arrived. We had only packed a small bag for the trip and made a quick stop at an ATM to withdraw travel funds as we headed to the airport. The papers we carried allowed us to get through security and onto our flight to JFK quickly at the airport. When they looked at their tickets, a surprised look crossed Jim and Andy's faces. First-class!

"I thought we deserved a little pampering," I said, patting them both on the back.

The only real scare we had was when we landed at JFK and saw a black SUV racing across the tarmac, its blue and red lights flashing. More worry set in as a uniformed man, followed by two military police officers, boarded the plane. Then, they paged a passenger over the intercom, and a young man in fatigues arrived at the front.

As he left with his escort, he turned to grin from ear to ear and shouted, "I'm going to be a dad!" His wife was waiting in a local hospital, and he was getting a grand escort.

The layover was about an hour, and we talked while we waited for the announced takeoff time and the roar of the engines. About an hour into the flight, our hot meals arrived. We each settled in for the in-flight movie.

Once we arrived at John Lennon International Airport, security personnel met us and detained us. It wasn't odd. However, they wanted to know what three Americans with top-secret clearance were doing together in their facility. I had called an old friend who assured me he would meet us and get us through any difficulties. His arrival caused quite a scene, and his guarantee that we were 'with him' seemed more than enough for those holding us.

Two electric golf carts bullied their way to our location. We quickly weaved our way through the bustling airport in comfort. Waiting for us between two black Range Rovers, was a 1964 Rolls-Royce Silver Ghost. The 'Earl' was, without a doubt, the classiest man I had ever known. We were in for a treat. He spent about three minutes assuring us that our hotel reservations, and his table at a local restaurant, were available.

Finally, he hung up the car's phone and spoke to us. "Majoor, afti scran, we tinnie discuss yer needs. Ay tinnie provid mun and wepons. Nah questions asked. Yous tinnie enjoy de hospitality o' me 'otel as blimp as yous wanna."

The earl's accent was so thick you needed a steak knife to cut through it.

I translated. "My friend says we can discuss our needs after dinner. He can provide men with weapons. We will enjoy his hospitality here, for as long as we need."

The earl nodded, laughed, and continued. "As yous tinnie see me secity firm is do'n quite bright. Ay trust yous enjoyed de ride in me Rolls-Royce limosine. Ler rus kun wa' else ay tinnie ellp yous wi'. Let's eat."

I chuckled. "His security firm is making hefty profits, which paid for his Rolls-Royce. He hoped you enjoyed the ride. If there's anything else we may desire, please ask. Let's eat!" As I finished translating, the chef and a small army of staff brought out large platters of food and filled our wine glasses.

"Ter loife!" the earl said as he raised his wine glass.

"To life!" We all responded. The food was magnificent, and the bed sheets were smooth as silk.

True to his word, the earl had a table set aside for our breakfast the following morning. A small notecard on my chair said, "RJ, see ye in a week fur tea 'ere, or ah wull come keekin fur ye myself."

At the stroke of eight AM, six casually dressed men arrived to sit at the table with us. After brief introductions, we all ordered breakfast. I briefly overviewed an estate between Aberffraw and Rhosneigr on the Isle of Anglesey in Wales.

Shal-Dir's final words resounded in my mind. Was I being too careful? These were Fallen Angels and their minions that we were up against, after all. What if they knew we were going to England to get this scroll translated? Was I really that big a threat? How would they know I was back on Earth? I had so many unanswered questions.

Was Allen's friend in danger just for his knowledge? We didn't need the real expertise of the earl's men. These men had been with the earl since his fighting days in the Middle East and Africa. I did not doubt their ability to follow commands under fire.

CHAPTER 36

After breakfast, we all returned to our suite to change into our tactical outfits. We got into a pair of black Land Rovers. It was a four-hour drive from the hotel to the estate; the exact location I kept secret until we got closer to our intended destination.

We exchanged war stories with the six men. Most had SAS backgrounds; one was a former ARW and GAC. In short, there were four English, one Irish, and one Welsh special forces personnel. We stopped at a pub for lunch. I showed them a hastily sketched map Allen had sent with me. The main estate house was on a slight hill. Below and to the back were garages and a barn-like structure. Trees lined the road to the main house.

Additionally, there were trees on the slope around the home. A low stone wall, likely where farmers had stacked rocks from their fields, could be used as a pull-back position if we needed cover. Allen recalled that the garage was a two-story building with eight, possibly ten bays, and that the second story housed all of Wilson's research labs.

Wilson came from a family steeped in archeology and conspiracy theories. Family members had been granted dig site privileges on every primary continent of the world, and discoveries gave them both land and title as English citizens. Wilson's father, who had disappeared some twenty years ago, had been knighted by the Queen for his work. The estate was not large, but the family's finances were substantial.

Wilson's father had made some canny investments. If your discovery is worth a million pounds, then that is what England pays you for. Allen mentioned that the family owned a Gulfstream G550 and had a hangar at the local airport. Whether the jet was purchased new, a patronage gift, or partial payment for services rendered, the Gulfstream was a forty-million-dollar plane.

The drive to the estate was nearly ending, and I shared more specifics with our lead driver. The estate seemed void of life in the daylight, but that had been an illusion as night crept in.

I needed to let these men know what we might encounter. "I hate to alarm any of you, but you may see some things tonight that will make you question your mental health."

Almost in a queue, we rounded a bend, and in the distance, I could see larger-than-human figures on the hill ahead. "Andy, are those Ators moving about on the hill?" We had not seen one of the giant reptilian beings since our first day in the city.

"Wha's a At'r?" Brock, one of the former SAS agents, asked from his sniper position.

"Oh, just your typical bug-eyed alien reptile man, standing about two feet taller than you, Brock," Jim replied.

"Theur guys av getten ta be jokin wi' wee. Aliens dooant exist," Brock stated in his thick Yorkshire accent.

"Wait until you meet one face to face. Let's move out! Jim's group flanks left, Andy's group flanks to the right, and I am going straight up the middle."

Two of the men I had left at the remains of the rock wall with sniper rifles in case we needed cover fire to return to the vehicles. "I don't see any Skaldi, so that is a good sign," Jim added over the comms.

"Wha' t' blazes ar' Skaldi?" Quinn asked, following Andy up the right side of the hill.

Andy responded. "Think ten-foot-tall gorilla, with the head of a bull dressed in armor, carrying a battle ax."

Jameson, the Irishman in the first vehicle, commented, "When dis is o'a, ah want eur taste o' whateva drugs theur av bin usin."

There was some nervous laughter over the comms. "You have been warned. Fire at will. Secure the perimeter and find Wilson," was my final order before all hell broke loose.

The snipers began picking off the Ator patrolling alongside the home. Then, each took one armored car and slowly drove it toward the house, using the headlights to blind and disorient those defending inside. The face-to-face fighting was the worst.

The man with me went down at the sight of his first Ator and froze. He saw the blade that cut him in two, in slow motion. The man following Jim lasted about twice that long. I had been warned, after all. This was the moment I realized that the opposition would do whatever they could to entangle my purpose.

In my mind, I could hear my dad's voice quoting Ephesians. "For we battle not against flesh and blood, but against the spiritual forces of evil in the heavenly realms." It didn't seem to matter whether I was on Earth or in the Other Realms; I was firmly in someone's crosshairs.

The most disturbing part of our fight on that hill was that humans were fighting against us on the side of the Ator. When I say humans, I don't mean they brought some over from the Other Realms. These were local humans, not just hired thugs, but contracted security. I did not recognize the logo as any group I had ever worked with. Evil knew no boundaries, and enough money bought weapons and men – it was a universal law, not just an Earthly one.

The human contractors and the Ators outnumbered us three to one. If God is with you, who then can stand against you? Those are brave words until a giant lizard is trying to kill you.

My team handled itself well, and we took the upper hand. Using the two vehicles as cover, we followed them to about thirty yards of the main doors. Just as we arrived, the massive carved wooden doors at the front of the house burst open. A half dozen Ator led by a strange-looking human now faced us, all armed with swords. There was something decidedly off about this man, and since he had chosen me for a little one-on-one time, I intended to find out what made him different. All around me, I could hear the crack of small arms fire, and as I moved to engage my target, the sword in my hand erupted in blue flame.

The unexpected sight of my sword dripping with blue flames brought doubt to the reptilian's shrouded face. Its blade was lovely but not angelic. As we fought, it appeared to know how to handle itself in a duel.

I had spent an hour a day with the finest swordsmen the Quaylin empire had to offer. About a full minute into our exchange, my sword missed its mark. Instead of piercing his heart, it took a chunk out of his shoulder. He gasped in pain, and his sword hand moved to cover his shoulder. At that moment, I saw that the gloved hand clutching his shoulder contained not five but six fingers.

An Elioud!

The Fallen Angels had two types of children: Nephilim and Elioud. The children with more human DNA were Nephilim, giants that ranged from the famed Goliath to the 'Greek Titans of Old,' who were as tall as the Cedars of Lebanon. The Elioud were of standard human height and had six fingers and toes. The power they gained from their supernatural fathers was magic all of their own. In the Other Realms, they were considered to be sorcerers.

The vast majority of Elioud and Old Ones were beings of evil, just as their fathers had been. It was not always a fair assumption, but often, they were just malicious creatures. During my fight with the first Elioud, who was moving back towards the house, I noticed a second Elioud.

This one was carrying something or someone out to the barn. Pursuing the one heading towards the barn structure would be prudent.

"Just saw someone heading into the barn carrying what looked like a person, perhaps Wilson," I added over the comms.

"Copy that, Major," came the reply from several positions.

As I approached the barn doors, a great light shone between the barn planks' cracks, filling the walls and doors. As the fire grew more intense, the barn doors began to shake. Then, the barn doors shattered, sending pieces of wood fragments all around me.

What stood before me was something from wherever nightmares come from. It stood nearly twenty feet tall. Its midnight-black fur bristled in the moon's cold light. It dripped saliva from its fangs. While one set of claws raked the air, the other clutched the unmoving body of Allen's friend Wilson. Behind the beast, I could see the wounded Elioud kneeling over a large duffel bag, stuffing items into it. These two would attempt to escape with Wilson and his knowledge.

The beast snarled at me and began a slow lope in my direction. "Move, human. I will not ask a second time."

I summoned up the reserve of courage I kept for just such an occasion – sarcasm noted – and flicked my wrist and moved to meet it as my sword rekindled in the near-dawn light. The sword appearing out of nowhere caused a brief pause in the enemy's forward movement.

Turning its head back to the Elioud, the creature bellowed, "Is this the one who cut you?"

I saw the figure behind him nod, and a bellow erupted from the beast. "That's a pretty sword you have. I will be sure they bury you with it."

I had never fought anyone of this size. When I swung and missed my first attempt, the hand-carrying Wilson knocked me to the ground, pinning me down with its clawed foot. Several of the men arrived, including Jim and Andy. They could not risk firing upon the creature for fear of hitting Wilson's limp body in the beast's grip. Off to my team's left, I could see a shimmering blue orb forming and growing larger by the moment.

When the horror gripping Wilson saw it, he bellowed out a scream that echoed across the estate. It wasn't so much a noise from a place of fear but one of recognition – as if a hyena had spotted a lion coming for him.

Another roar came from the hairy beast as the orb pulsed, and a figure stepped out. "This is not your fight, old man!"

"Did you think you could desecrate the land under my protection without an answer?" The grey-haired man, dressed in a simple blue cloak, addressed the creature like a schoolteacher scolding a child. "SanSan, there is no place on Earth where I hold greater power than here. The Maker appointed me guardian over Albion long before the first human set foot here." The blue-cloaked man continued to move toward the creature. "You should have died five thousand years ago, but I will rectify that now."

The creature snarled, and a hint of desperation was now becoming apparent. "I will crush the human in my hands and the one under my heel if you don't move away. If you allow me to leave, I will allow the human at my feet to go unharmed," it bellowed.

"You have no honor in words or deed. Your time is at hand; prepare to report to your master in person," the old man stated, never wavering.

In a puff of smoke, the man disappeared. In that instant, I felt the weight of the beast's foot lift enough weight off my body to roll free. Then I heard the Elioud scream, "behind you," but it was too late for the Nephilim beast, as a blade wreathed in blue flames split SanSan from breast to belly. I barely had enough reaction time as the giant roared its final breath. It also propelled Wilson's body into the air toward me. Somehow, the body seemed to slow and then, to my surprise, dropped into my waiting arms as Jim and Andy arrived to assist.

I turned and saw the old man was hot on the trail of the Elioud, who was attempting to escape.

"Your authority as it concerns me is somewhat limited. You can't murder me!"

"No, I can't murder you or execute you," the elderly man agreed, as he returned the sword to his sheath.

The Elioud breathed out, and as his eyes closed in a moment of thanksgiving, the older man's staff united with his temple, knocking the six-fingered out like a prizefighter in the ninth round.

"Captured, imprisoned, and awaiting execution, it is then. You have everything under control now, Robert John Armstrong, yes?"

He touched Wilson's forehead, winked, and disappeared into another, still forming blue orb, with the dazed Elioud in tow.

"Who was that?" Andy and Jim asked almost in unison.

"I have no idea. The Elioud called him 'The Master of Albion' or something," I answered, pulling a med kit from my pack. Seeing the confused looks, I said, "I will explain once we have revived Wilson. Secure the house."

In the breaking dawn, we moved Wilson back into the house and onto the dining room table to examine his wounds. Wilson was breathing, which Andy felt was a good sign. Removing tattered clothing, we were astonished to see that the many wounds were healing or already healed – the doing, no doubt, of our friend from the blue orb. Now, all that remained was dried blood and grime from his days of captivity.

I had Brock contact the earl. We needed him to send a clean-up crew to remove the humans and Ator bodies strewn about the compound. When he regained consciousness, Wilson told us he had been attempting to answer the email we had sent him from Colorado.

The estate had gone silent and dark. Three days before, the staff, a cook, a driver, and his three-person security detail had all died in the first hour of the attack. Wilson had artifacts and manuscripts that he believed pre-dated Noah's great flood. His work on the Geez language had nearly fallen into enemy hands.

I spent part of the morning explaining why we had contacted him, and all the fantastic things we had seen. He seemed unsurprised by many things I spoke of, which I assumed was due to his recent torture. He agreed that he was now a target. It took little to persuade him that his best chance for survival was coming with us.

Wilson was about to call his pilot when Jameson suggested leaving the flight to him, and keeping the pilot in the dark. Andy and Jim suggested that we spend as little time here as possible.

"Wilson, can we help you gather as much of your work as possible that might help us? Then we need to get to that plane!" I stated.

"Yes, there are military-grade cases in the barn. We should pack as much as possible. I will give Jameson the airport contact number. He can order the plane fueled and a flight plan," Wilson responded. "If you are wondering about my accent or lack of one,

I spent most of my youth in American boarding schools. I hold a Ph.D. from MIT, a Ph.D. from Harvard, and a double Master's degree from the University of Oxford. I spent far more time in the US than in the UK." It made sense as Allen had met him at MIT, and they remained friends.

Jameson walked back into the garage carrying another case for us to fill. "Okay, t' plane is bein fueled 'n ah gev 'em eur fleight plan ta wee destination i' Coloradoa. Brock' n ahl start loadin t' lan' rovers for transpoarts."

I acknowledged Jameson and helped him carry a fully packed case to one of the waiting vehicles. "I know that the earl never hires men with families. Perhaps you and Brock might want to tag along with us? I could use a few more men who can handle themselves in battle."

Jameson grunted. Was it in response to my invitation or because we had just lifted the case into the rear of the Land Rover? The vehicles were loaded, including a container packed with Wilson's clothing and another filled with electronic equipment, and we prepared to wait for the earl and his "clean team" at the end of the road.

The wait didn't take nearly as long as I expected. The earl explained that all his men wore unique watches, and when those watches sent out three "loss of life" signals, he decided to send backup to our location. I explained that we had run into trouble and suggested they burn all the bodies. A two-person team would remain on site to monitor and report any further suspicious activity.

A wink from the earl and I was back in my vehicle.

I heard the earl call out at me before he drove off. "If any o' des tre lads wanna join yous dee' uv me approval. I also left yous a present in de' anger at de airport."

I waved goodbye. I hoped to see the earl again someday.

There were six military-grade cases beside the Gulfstream in the hangar when we arrived, containing weapons, ammo, and other toys. A seventh case was a bit larger and had a note taped to it that said, "Andy-Lad, do not open this until you are home!"

Wilson made another call to a company that restocked the Gulfstream with food and beverages for our flight to Colorado. Soon after, we were all buckled in and heading for an open runway.

A voice came over the loudspeaker, "Wellcom abord. Thes es Capt'n Jameson. Plees remean seaated till ay tirn oaff de seatbealt lights. We wul be fly'n at therrty-thousend webs. De flight wul take opproxematly forteun ors. Thenks ageen fe fly'n Wilson erlines."

Then we heard Brock. "Whun did yous get promoated tah capt'n?"

Everyone had a good laugh. The earl had convinced the four men to see us to our destination. He had issued them open-ended one-way tickets back to England should they desire to return to him.

The first portion of the trip took about seven hours to New York. I had not intended to stop, but the East Coast offered Wilson an opportunity to purchase additional scientific equipment. A city with so many shopping opportunities gave Andy, Jim, and I a chance to fill nearly every wish from our many lists.

CHAPTER 37

The four surviving men from the earl's team, who were sent to help with Wilson's extraction, had asked to join us: Brock, Jameson, Tobbin, and Quinn. As military men, they knew that evil needed to be stopped. Most of the Other Realms' problems had their foundations on Earth. However, if I could secure the help of great military men, perhaps we could combine a unique vision in strategy and warfare.

I spent most of the plane ride from New York City to Buena Vista, Colorado, showing pictures and explaining to our recruits all the odd beings they would soon encounter. I recall all that talking going to waste when Quinn met his first Skaldi. When I stepped between him and his intended target, he had his weapon clear of his holster. "Quinn, holster your weapon. That is one of the good guys. You want this one to have your back in a fight." I didn't even have to raise my voice.

I arranged for the local airport to house the Gulfstream, and Wilson paid several years of rent in advance. To make the matter as official as possible, I showed the man my credentials and the typical 'that's classified' rhetoric. While I had not lied about this, I hoped he would not push me past the line I had drawn in the sand regarding how far I would go to protect said rhetoric.

Another matter was getting all the cases and gear from the airport to my property. Only seven of us moved everything by hand. Once on-site, it was much easier. Andy rigged up the cargo net for the

Blackhawk. We made drops right onto the island outside the cave leading to the Lion's Gate. A quick pass through the Lion's Gate to let our people on the other side know we had arrived. Then, an army of Skaldi and Quaylin muscle came to load and deliver the goods to the city.

The most important part of this cargo was Wilson. Allen met his friend at the fortifications of South Gate Pass. Was Allen here on his own accord, or had Gretchen insisted he meet us this far out from the city?

Wilson now saw the Skaldi and their engineering and understood the massive workforce required to make the pass fortification a reality. Allen also informed Wilson that while this was a marvel, it was not the fabled City of Hope.

We did not spend the night at South Gate Pass, but we pushed on to the city. As the sun rose over the eastern mountains, we broke from the cover of the pass to a glorious dawn.

Wilson stood up on the wagon when he saw the city. "Merciful God!" was all he could manage.

We all knew what he meant.

What was in all these cases?

Bill had requested spices, seeds, and several additional pairs of boots. Gretchen had asked for some medicinal plant seeds and a few personal items. Becky's list was more for the children than for herself. A case containing books, crayons, pencils, and a vast quantity of paper now sat in her office at the school.

Allen wanted more solar panels and other technical items. However, he could have asked the Acrucians what he desired. Wilson, of course, had brought as much of his work as possible. There were several cases of weapons, ammunition, and toys that the earl thought might be useful. But the oddest case was the one with the earl's note to Andy. Andy secreted that case away in the chaos of our return. I loved a good surprise, but I would have to wait until Andy was ready to reveal his gift.

To say that Allen and Wilson got to work immediately on the Geez Project would be an understatement. They worked nearly day and night translating the small book Andy had discovered. I began receiving daily reports on their progress. About two weeks into this process, they announced to the council and I that they had decoded or translated most of the books and maps.

This process could have taken years if we had not had Wilson's subject-matter expertise. I started by asking Chief Adoeete if he could have his riders do high-altitude searches with Andy. At the same time, Allen coordinated the grid mapping from West Gate Castle. Adoeete had become a valued member of the council. Although initially reluctant, he soon realized what a valuable addition his people made to the city.

While time-consuming, grid mapping was both practical and necessary. It was made possible by an apparatus that provided GPS coordinates and a live video feed of what the birds and riders saw. Allen was confident that the Acrucians had enough spare parts to create and launch a small communications satellite. However, it sounded like fuel was the main issue on the project.

For the moment, Andy's role was to locate ruins, villages, enemy movements, fortifications, and other cities. He also was to discover the highest points in an outward spiral where Allen could find communications towers. One was already working on the second-tallest building in the city. Its counterpart for test purposes is at the western valley's far end, past the green meadows and lake, to the surrounding range's mountains. It gave us communication capability over 20 channels and four frequencies. This new ability allowed several military channels, a couple for Bill at the ranch, and dedicated channels for me to each council member.

In the middle of the night, I heard noises from the tower floors above my sleeping chambers. Then Leo burst into the room with the two Glav hot on his tail.

"Àrd-Rìgh, so sorry to disturb your rest, but Andy is landing above us right now with news that can't wait for the dawn!"

I nodded my head as Leo helped me into a robe. We headed to the elevator and down to the war room, a few stories below.

Kraq was already there, having slept over after a meeting ran late earlier in the day. "Àrd-Rìgh, SunGru should be here at any moment. Shal-Dir is inside, as is Father Emmaus, Adoeete, Jim, Allcn, and Wilson."

I nodded at the large Skaldi and then turned to Leo. "Leo, my friend, this could go long. Can you see if Lynn or Cook can dig up some snacks and coffee for us?"

Now Kraq nodded. "Yes, pancakes!"

"Kraq, you know pancakes are a meal, not a snack, right?" I teased.

My large furry friend then mumbled something about how puny human snacks were.

"Leo, please see if Lynn can start coffee and maybe some pastry. Have Cook start a very early breakfast of pancakes and sausage."

Kraq's face lit up like it was Christmas morning. "Little brother, you are the best Àrd-Rìgh ever!"

"I thought I was the only Àrd-Rìgh?" I asked, feigning concern and pushing my lips into a pout.

"You are the first; all others will have to measure up to you," Kraq replied.

"Well, that is all the more reason to keep everyone happy," I said, sitting down to my cup of coffee as the remaining council members arrived.

Just as I was sitting down, Andy burst through the door, supported by a Q scout on either side. An arrow was stuck through his left shoulder. Moments later, Gretchen arrived with Rachel to tend to his injury.

"Please now, don't be alarmed. 'Tis but a flesh wound."

Gretchen pushed him back into his chair and forced a leather-bound notebook into his mouth, "Bite down! This is going to hurt!" She broke the end of the arrow with the head on it off and slowly pulled the wooden shaft back through his wounds, opening. Alcohol was applied to Andy and the stitches and wound coverings. It was only then that Gretchen said he could speak.

"Let me say what I need to, and then I will rest," Andy said. Clearly, he was in pain, but surely this could have waited for morning.

As if he had read my mind, Shal-Dir said, "Andy, you are hurt. Can this wait until you have medical attention and rest?"

"No, I can wait, RJ. Priorities first – report now, then stitches after."

"Okay, Andy, how did you get wounded?"

"If it pleases the council. While many riders have been grid mapping, I have been finding Wilson's mapped clues. He is working on the Geez Project."

Everyone had met Wilson and knew the importance I placed on his work. "To summarize the story, I have been following a series of clues hidden on the map. If I had been on foot, the journey might have taken years. The first clue took me far east to the sea coast, where I found a great castle and a city overrun by enemy Skaldi." He saw the look on the council members' faces and continued. "Its location is on the grid. I am sure Allen just forgot to inform everyone about it."

All the looks then turned towards Allen.

Shal-Dir broke into the conversation. "Everyone, please calm down. Andy, please continue."

"Of course, it was not what we were looking for because, upon my return, Wilson had discovered a second clue, which takes us southwest many miles to a large bay on a vast sea to the south and the northern tip of the vast forest where Adoeete and his people lived. At first, I spiraled lower toward the ground. Yet, I could not see any structures or anything unusual. When I gave up, I spurred my feathered friend towards the sky and took one last look below me. I saw something odd on the highest peak overlooking the bay. The higher I went, the more pronounced the clue became. On the mountain top was a jagged, almost crown-like feature, and inside it was a grove of Fire Ash."

The Fire Ash tree was rare, according to everyone at the table. Few had seen one.

Wilson broke into the conversation. "This is how we knew we were on the right track. The first part of the clue was vague, but then it mentioned another Fire Crown." Wilson waved for Andy to continue.

"The third clue took us far to the west. Find the Land of Redana."

"I have never heard of such a kingdom," SunGru remarked.

"It is not a kingdom. It is simply the best translation to the most modern verbiage I could manage," Wilson added. "Redana is old Germanic for the word 'riddle'.

"Again, this clue stumped me. When I reached a great height, I saw a peninsula shaped like a backward question mark. The final clue was a distance and a nearly specific nautical direction to where X marked the spot."

"What did you find?" SunGru demanded.

"It was cloudy, so I had my bird take me below the clouds, which took me much lower than expected. As I flew over forested hills and an open field, I missed the Skaldi camped in the hills, which led to my wound. As the bird began to gain altitude to get us out of range, I spotted a massive semicircle carved from the cliff we were facing. Inside that stood a large stone tower. My haste is due to a Skaldi army of some size currently besieging the tower and its small town."

All eyes now turned in my direction. "Thank you, Andy, Allen, and Wilson, for working diligently on the Geez Project. Besides sounding like a fortress of worth that we might consider retaking, what is the find's significance?"

"I am glad you asked because inset into the grey stone of the tower are two massive letters in a curious blue stone. The two letters are A and O!"

There was a gasp from Father Emmaus, who shot out of his chair, spilling his wine. "That place is a myth!" The head of the church seemed quite flustered.

"What do you think we have found, Emmaus?" SunGru asked, taking the wine from the cleric.

The holy man cleared his throat. In the most respectful of tones, he said, "If what Andy says is true, he has discovered the location of the fabled Tower of Erudition."

The Tower of Erudition was one of the greatest, if not the most significant, bastions of the church's wisdom, knowledge, and artifacts. According to Wilson, those 'myths' Emmaus had heard were part of a secret oral tradition passed down through leadership. If a Skaldi army now advanced against it, the chances of this being a mere coincidence were slim.

Luckily for us, Andy had been keeping track of his location. We would not have to retrace his entire trip through the clues. The journey with an army overland would take the better part of three weeks, which, according to Andy's story, was not a commodity we had in abundance. Chief Adoeete pointed out that we had over two hundred adult birds. While that would not provide us with the necessary numbers, it might enable us to deploy enough personnel to change the tide.

So, in the wee hours of the morning, we hatched a plan, fingers sticky with syrup and veins coursing with caffeine. Andy was off to the hospital. I got several very stern looks from Gretchen as she escorted him away.

The fastest way to the Tower of Erudition was by air, which limited the number of warriors that could be deployed. Then, Rachel suggested a rescue mission followed by a later attempt to retake the tower. With some modifications from SunGru and Kraq, we all agreed on the immediate and long-range attack plan. At dawn, the City of Hope's armies would form and leave through South Gate Pass. Reaching the Tower of Erudition might take up to a month. Meanwhile, the goal was to save as many lives and relics as possible with the smaller, faster group of airborne fighters and support teams.

Andy and Adoeete were appointed to lead the air expedition, along with Quaylin archers and the Glav. With Gretchen and a team of healers, Jim and Becky were tasked with setting up the camp atop the nearby cliffs. The plan had half the birds attacking the ground troops. Simultaneously, the other half will shuttle survivors and relics to the safety of the clifftop camp. Andy worked on several projects with Adoeete's birds, including a quick-release cargo net and a system that could deploy Glav or Skaldi soldiers. The first goal was to secure the survivors and relics. Then, wait for the large ground army to capture the structure.

The first details I received from the war front came from Becky. After she tested the communications array, they informed Allen that the camp was being set up, including medical, food, and sleeping tents. Andy's group dropped the fifty Glav onto the plain. They engaged the enemy even as Adoeete and his group harassed the Skaldi and Ator from above.

Becky informed Allen that Jim had already landed and secured the top five stories of the tower. The survivors, carrying relics and other prized possessions, were ferried to the cliffs for medical attention, food, and rest from the siege. "RJ, I have a monk here who wishes to speak to our leader."

"Copy that. Put the monk on comms. Father Emmaus is with me as well." I hoped it was good news, but we had no idea how long the attacks and siege had been going on before Andy had spotted the tower.

"Àrd-Rìgh, Father Emmaus, I am Brother Eliezer. I come to you with grim tidings." There was a sob, and I could hear Becky telling him it would be all right. "I am sorry to inform you that my master, Thaddeus, the Patriarch of the Basilica, and the Arch-Fathers' Damion and Altus, while offering a peace treaty to the Fallen Ones, have been murdered."

Ill news indeed: unarmed holy men slain without provocation. Standing beside me, Father Emmaus was pounding his right fist on the table while his left hand held my arm in a vice grip. My two Glav guardians had almost removed him, but I waved them off. If the older man needed to pound the table and squeeze my arm, perhaps the pain I felt would help me focus.

"What else can you tell us, Brother Eliezer?"

"A Skaldi and Ator army led by two Fallen Ones arrived a week ago. They attacked the village, but we had gathered all the townsfolk inside the outer wall. A unit of warrior monks stood on the walls, but they were too few, only holding the wall for a day and a night. All the villagers were given refuge inside the basilica.

"When the Patriarch and two Arch-Fathers went out to negotiate for peace, they were beheaded. We barricaded the gates and moved everyone to the tower's top floors. We nailed doors shut and piled furniture in front of them on the first five floors. This morning, they broke through to the sixth floor of the tower. The village men had been defending against them until we saw the great birds. A horn sounded, causing the tower's enemy to retreat and reform ranks against some unknown assailant. Much gratitude to you and your people for arriving just in time."

Becky spoke on the comm, "RJ, he needs to rest. Jim just dropped off another load of women and children. I have to go. I will radio back in one hour."

"Thank you, Becky!"

Father Emmaus looked like death warmed over. Leo was trying to get some wine into him when he sputtered, "They will pay! By the Maker, they will rue this day!" He went running out of the war room in the direction of the stables. I sent orders that he must not be permitted to leave the city by horse, wagon, or any other means. Not for any reason.

Shal-Dir had then graced us with his presence. "There were several murders perpetrated by the Fallen against the church?"

"How do you know of this, already?" I asked.

"I heard about it, as did anyone within earshot of Father Emmaus. He seemed to be in a hurry. He swears he is going to gather men for a holy crusade."

"The news was horrific. I can see why the Father is upset. I assure you there will be justice."

"Our aid arrived in the nick of time, it seems. The destruction of such a place would be paramount to the sacking of your world's great cathedrals. Shal-Dir continued, "I have come up with a fitting punishment for the Fallen Ones if you happen to capture them alive."

"What are you thinking?"

"Why have more blood on your hands?" Shal-Dir began, "You have the perfect executioners hiding in the basement."

"Do you think the Cherubim will kill their own?"

"If I were guarding the Tree of Life and someone told me that two of the Fallen were within striking distance, I would do whatever I could to stop them."

"You are cunning, my friend. Remind me not to get into a battle of wits with you."

Shal-Dir nodded. "Remember, I have been around for a few more years than you. How did Andy's quick-release GCC work?"

"GCC? What are you talking about?" I asked.

"The Glav Combat Carriers," Shal-Dir stated while maintaining a serious expression.

"Oh, I had no idea they had an official name. They seem to have worked well. No injuries to the Glav."

"You know Andy once called them the SCC, but Kraq said there was no way he was testing that out," Shal-Dir added as a deep chuckle echoed in the war room.

"Perhaps we can get a Skaldi volunteer now that they seem to work?" I asked.

"I doubt it. Andy's math was a little off, considering the Skaldi weighs more than three times what a Glav weighs." Shal-Dir was right. The birds couldn't handle that kind of weight.

"Wilson is still working on a translation of that book Andy found. We hope he will uncover more answers to our questions."

"Did you hear where he found the book?" Shal-Dir asked with a twinkle in his eyes.

I wondered what would happen to my tall, blue-skinned friend if he were not the first in the City with all the best rumors and gossip. "I didn't think to ask."

"Well, that seems odd." It wasn't often that you caught a look of surprise on the Eridu leader's face. "Behind the throne, there is a great hanging tapestry."

I nodded. The throne room was a place I avoided, but I had been there often enough to know which one he meant.

A group of Quaylin ladies was tasked with cleaning the small tapestries and discovered what appeared to be a door indent behind the large tapestry. They called out for help, and Andy was near enough to hear them. When he brought a light, he noticed the door-like indent had a built-in shelf. The shelf held that book.

"Has anyone taken a closer look at that area? There may be more to it than just the book?"

Why hadn't I been told about this earlier? "Leo, remind me to look where they found the book."

Leo wrote something in the leather-bound notebook I had brought back to him with one of his new pens. What had previously been acceptable had now become more comfortable with our recent trip to Earth. I had brought Shal-Dir a gift selection of fragrant tea bags from England. He had seemed quite delighted.

"Do you think the Acrucians would part with some of those wall panels we saw downstairs?"

Shal-Dir usually had little trouble keeping up with my mental wanderings. "It is your City, Àrd-Rìgh, and they could and would part with whatever you desired from their junk pile. I assume you think that the basilica could use some upgrading?"

"The outer wall could be a good place to start. Three hundred-plus miles away is quite a distance for an outpost."

Shal-Dir nodded. "My best guess is this will not be the only outpost you discover or retake. While I am unfamiliar with this area of the Other Realms, I know plenty of places I have traveled to that would welcome you without hesitation. The Fallen Ones are not the only tyrants in this world, but they are the greatest threat to you."

I was about to ask whom Shal-Dir was talking about when suddenly the comms sparked to life again. "RJ, are you still there?"

"Yes, and Shal-Die and I are here. What is the problem?"

"Too many of the enemy for us to continue attacking them on the ground is the concern. Andy and Adoeete are pulling the Glav back. It looks like we lost several in the fight. They will try to hold off any attack from within the tower itself. Also, on a side note, we have villagers and monks, but there is a small group of about twenty-five that I can't identify," Becky announced.

"What are you talking about?"

"They are all less than five feet tall, rugged looking, but super smart engineers. They already made some adjustments to the communications array!"

Short, rugged, super-smart builders and engineers? I didn't want to say the word out loud. Dvergar?

CHAPTER 38

The City of Hope's armies wasted little time covering the distance; all they had to do was follow Andy and his wingmen. SunGru and Kraq pushed their men, covering nearly twenty-five miles a day. A supply train had always been the primary option for transporting food and medical supplies to the troops.

Adoeete and his wingmen began moving the camp and supplies 20 miles ahead of the army each day. In just over two weeks, the army arrived at the lush forest bordering the plains leading to the basilica. Andy and the Karuk riders staged the final base camp ten miles southeast of the tower.

This location gave access to an ancient road that ran east to west from the basilica's position. The roadway was surprisingly well-maintained despite its apparent age.

Following and crossing this ancient road would be much easier than navigating the surrounding terrain. SunGru led the main army, consisting of a brigade of Quaylin cavalry, followed by a brigade of Quaylin infantry. On the left and right flanks of the Quaylin stood a battalion of Skaldi, led by Kraq and Aig of the Silver Clan. Andy, Jim, and the Karuk riders would deploy the Glav atop the tower as soon as the army advanced within range of the tower.

Scouts reported that any remaining monks or townspeople were now being held as prisoners and forced to perform menial tasks.

They also reported large numbers of Skaldi and Ator, and a group of tall, human-like, robed beings that sounded strangely familiar – Elioud.

The army's movements at this point were almost impossible to conceal. Nearly eight thousand men were stirring up dust. SunGru took his men up the front toward the main gates. Kraq and Aig each took their battalion to the right and left of the tower's gates. There was an immediate flurry of activity within the walls. The enemy had burnt the outer village, and a makeshift blockade stood before the nearly repaired gates.

We had no idea what the twenty Glav would face once they landed on the tower's upper floor. We now had them outnumbered ten to one.

Getting over the gate or going through it would be the most significant issue, with minimal loss of life. Aig had sent several groups carrying ladders to test the wall. Several Elioud arrived on that wall, using explosives, and drove them back. Despite our overwhelming advantage in sheer numbers, this siege might take us longer than I had imagined. Had someone identified who I was? There were two possible answers. Either someone was providing explosives from Earth or manufacturing them locally. Either way, it was a problem for us.

On day three of the siege, the army remained outside the wall. Andy and the Karuk riders occasionally dropped grenade-like missiles on the enemy. The enemy stopped us by using monks and civilians as human shields.

Karuk scouts reported unknown troop movement from the Southwest. Heavily armed short humans under the banner of a blue griffin on a white field moved towards our position. Shal-Dir confirmed that this could only be one of the Dvergar clans. All

Dvergar clans could be known based on the color of the Griffin on their banner.

A Griffin? It's like some fantastic tale from Greek Mythology. The Griffin had the head and front legs of a great eagle, and the rest of its body was like that of a lion. Their battles in Earth's ancient past had nearly put the two races on the endangered species list.

Upon their arrival, SunGru spent a whole day convincing Adalwin, the Dvergar Chief, that our Skaldi warriors chose sides *against* the Fallen Ones. Adalwin finally agreed, somewhat reluctantly, to a truce between his five-hundred battle-hardened Dvergar warriors and our Skaldi forces.

The actual reason for Adalwin's timely arrival had nothing to do with our appearance. He thought Blue Gryphon Clan members remained captive within the tower. The number of his people at the basilica during the attack was unknown, but he was aware of their presence. SunGru disclosed that we had rescued around 25 of his kinfolk nearly three weeks earlier.

SunGru also offered to let Adalwin speak with the group leader they had saved, who was recovering at the City of Hope, in the court of the Àrd-Rìgh. His suspicion disappeared when his relative came on the comms singing the praises of the City of Hope, its ruler, and council members. Adalwin was grateful that we had saved many of his clan members from the Fallen Ones, even though not everyone from the Dvergar party visiting the tower survived.

When asked what Adalwin's reason was for bringing such a large armed force to the tower, his answer was simple. Any prisoners of the tower were now on their way to the Mines of Verlaq.

Neither SunGru nor Shal-Dir knew of such a place. Kraq had heard the name before, but only whispered in the darkness. As much a prison as a mine, it is where rebels went to die. According to

Adalwin, this is where the Fallen Ones sent prisoners to extract minerals from the ground to fuel their war weapons. Shal-Dir and I were worried that properly mined minerals could explain the explosives the Elioud had used against us.

SunGru asked, "Adalwin, what is your plan for attacking the outer wall and tower?"

The Dvergar chief explained his battle strategy. "We shall harass those on the tower's wall during the day while digging multiple tunnels under the fortress at night. I assure you that this is the only way we can win this fight."

However, after several hours of strategy discussion, Adalwin was convinced of SunGru and Kraq's new plan. The Dvergar required cover to begin their tunnels near the walls. Otherwise, they were targets of the Elioud. Panels from the Acrucian warehouse at the City of Hope had begun their arrival even before this plot hatched. Skaldi carried the boards for wall repair to a spot near the tower walls, erecting a sizeable open-ended hatch cover where the Dvergar engineers began their work. Skaldi were sent into the nearby forest to cut beams to support the tunnels as the Dvergar moved further underground.

Andy saw the two Fallen Ones who had confined themselves to the tower. He estimated a dozen Elioud, along with several hundred Skaldi and Ator. The tunnels were progressing well ahead of schedule, and the goal was to ultimately bring down sections of the walls, allowing our army to pour in through the breaches.

It was just like life to throw a wrench into the works. Soon, we found ourselves facing a new problem. Karuk riders reported a small, fast-moving army, about two days' march from our position – Skaldi and Ator. Adalwin knew that these were reinforcements from the Mines of Verlaq. The Dvergar chief also pointed out that this left the mines vulnerable, and possibly the only time we could free prisoners and hurt the Fallen's war efforts.

The Dvergar were working through the night to finish their tunnels. Once the tunnels were complete, Jim rigged our explosives. The walls would crumble at the time we desired. In the meantime, a few of the Dvergar would keep up appearances around the tunnel entrances. Simultaneously, the main body began a march with several hundred Skaldi and Quaylin troops on a mercy mission to free the prisoners of Verlaq.

Half our forces continued facing the tower walls on the fields before the Tower of Erudition. At the same time, the remaining warriors moved toward the small enemy army approaching from Verlaq. Adoeete's riders would split into three groups. The first were to help create chaos around the tower once we were ready to storm the breaches. The second planned to wait for the appropriate moment to ambush the incoming enemy from Verlaq. Finally, the third group of riders would help remove any prisoners too weak to flee the mines on foot.

Then it dawned on me. Who would deal with the two Fallen Angels and the group of Elioud that followed them if I were not there? I sent word to SunGru, who led our army that encircled the tower to recover the basilica, but not to engage the Fallen Ones or Elioud. They were to be allowed to leave. SunGru, of course, was not happy with this order. His troops could not openly engage the powerful enemy agents on their own.

Andy's camera work, combined with Allen and Wilson's week of research, was fruitful. Our two Fallen Ones trapped in the tower were Zaqiel and Gadreel. These discoveries led to great concern and a flurry of activity. Zaqiel, whose name means 'Purity of God,' one of the Fallen, taught man the science of explosives. The next name filled us all with apprehension. Gadreel's name means 'Wall of God,' and he was an archangel. The same archangel that God tasked with Eden's defense. He failed the task when the Serpent led Eve astray. Some of the discovered texts suggest Gadreel was searching for a way to redeem himself for his failures. I needed the counsel of the heavenly kind, but who would answer my cry?

The Mines of Verlaq were a place of dread, a death sentence to those sent there to work. Prisoners mined coal, sulfur, gems, and minerals from the mine's depths. It was not just men working in the mines; women and children were there as well.

The Dvergar had been working on a tunnel that they planned to use to free as many prisoners as possible. The Skaldi and Quaylin troops would attempt to remove resistance at the top of the mine pit. I had ordered that any products from the mine be secured for our use. I wanted the mine destroyed and the Fallen Angels' military machine crashed, but I could not allow their materials to go to waste.

The even more critical thought running through my mind was how I could stop or contain Zaqiel and Gadreel. Was that even possible? I had to visit the only heavenly being currently in the Other Realms. Zophiel! I took my Glav guards as far as the elevator.

"Please remain here. No one is to follow me under any conditions," I told the Glav.

As I entered the greenhouse, the immensity of the place and the daunting nature of my task overtook me as I approached the two trees and the four guardians.

"Son of Adam, why have you disturbed my sleep once again?" came a great rumbling from the being Zophiel as its head turned full circle, revealing each face in turn, blinking at me in reaction. "I will grant you three questions, then you will go, and I will sleep."

It was true that I had wasted a question finding out who this angel was when I approached what seemed an age ago. The man's head now faced me. "I don't have a question. I need counsel," I responded. The human eyes blinked at me, so I continued. "We have discovered the Tower of Erudition. Two fallen angels and their armies defend it."

The eyes flashed again. At least Zophiel seemed to be listening to me. "We believe the angels to be Zaqiel and Gadreel."

At the mention of the two names, it was as if the being was now fully awake. Simultaneously, there was a snort from the ox's head, a scream from the eagle's head, a roar from the lion's head, and the human shouted with rage, the likes of which I had never heard. The screams echoed through the great chamber.

"I am thc only one in the Other Realms with a sword that can kill an angel, and I am three days' hard travel from the battle. Zaqiel and Gadreel will slaughter my men. Will you assist me?"

At that moment, I saw a bluish light that encircling Zophiel and the other three beings, almost as if it linked them.

Then Zophiel spoke. "I have petitioned your cause before the Mercy Seat, and the leader of my order has granted leave to address this issue. Àrd-Rìgh, I am at your disposal."

I do not remember the walk to the hallway leading to the elevator, the Glav groveling on the floor, or the journey to DEFCON five. Instantly, I was standing before the great Ruby Jewel on the pedestal.

"Take my hand, Son of Adam," and one of the wings unfurled to show an outstretched hand. "Then touch the gem and speak the name of the place or person we are to travel to."

I had to think for a moment. I couldn't say the Tower of Erudition, as that would land us in the occupied tower. So, I spoke the name of my friend, the general of the Quaylin armies. "SunGru." I felt a burning sensation fill my body. The Cherubim's wings folded around me. The journey itself may have lasted seconds, mere moments, but I saw many things I will recount later in my mind's eye.

It was as if the sun had arrived in the night of the large command tent where SunGru sat poring over battlefield reports. I had not counted on the bewildering arrival or the near-death encounter my friend would have. Shading his eyes, the Quaylin General stuttered, "By the Maker! Àrd-Rìgh, is that you?"

"I am sorry, friend, to arrive in such a manner. My companion is Zophiel, Cherubim of the First Sphere. He is here to help me stop Zaqiel and Gadreel."

SunGru nodded. "It is near enough to dawn that we can look over the battlefield." The old general quickly threw on robes and moved out of the tent. His guards later said something unseen and terrible followed the Àrd-Rìgh and their general.

"Zophiel, can the Fallen sense you? I only ask because of the brightness of your vestige." I was worried that I had used up one of my questions, but I did not want to announce our arrival early.

"No, Son of Adam, they will sense me when it is time and not before," came the reply from the twenty-foot-tall ball of light. As we reached the leftmost portion of the wall, the lion and eagle heads made a slight movement and noise. "Elioud. They are here as well."

I had forgotten to mention them. "I am sorry, Zophiel. Are they a problem?"

"I could smell them the moment we arrived."

"Smell them?"

"Souls all bear a certain smell. Angels, humans, plants, and animals all have souls. God did not create Nephilim and Elioud; their souls are not from the 'Breath of God,' and are corrupt."

Just then, one of the Dvergar arrived. "Àrd-Rìgh, we plan to blow the tunnels and the gates simultaneously. We will leave the far-left tunnel unprotected, allowing certain members inside the tower to have a route of escape. I suggest you take up positions and ready yourselves for battle."

I nodded in agreement. "We'd better start..." I never completed the sentence. Zophiel had gathered me once more in his wings. The two of us now stood on a small hill facing the wall.

"Prepare yourself, Son of Adam. I will take Gadreel, for he is the more dangerous of the two." Zophiel's four sets of wings unfolded. He held a flaming sword in each of his four hands.

CHAPTER 39

From inside the tower, Gadreel and Zaqiel felt the blasts from the tunnels and gates. Dirt and rock showered the air like hard rain. Chaos ensued as Skaldi and Ator raced to face the free forces of the City of Hope and the Dvergar troops. As predicted, the dozen Elioud sprinted their masters towards the small, undefended tunnel.

"This must be a trap," Zaqiel shouted at Gadreel through the scrambling Elioud, eager to make their escape.

"Yes, it is a trap, but a single Son of Adam poses no threat to me."

"A Son of Adam? You have seen this?" A flash of doubt entered Zaqiel's eyes.

"I am a chief among the Grigori. Do you think I fear a Son of Adam? There are two of us and a dozen Elioud at our disposal. Take courage! Soon, we will stand over the dead body of this feeble Maker's pawn. We will come back with troops from the mines to finish destroying this holy site and its relics."

Zaqiel nodded in agreement, his sword pulsing to life, casting a red light visible through the smoke and debris. They walked towards the sunlight when another blast from the shaft covered them in smoke and debris. Adalwin's engineers had rigged an explosive to seal the tunnel behind the enemy after they had entered.

Meanwhile, at the Mines of Verlaq, a smaller-scale battle was unfolding. Adalwin attacked from beneath the ground, and the

Dvergar sought out the prisoners. Several thousand captives arrived at our secure camp, for medical attention and food.

On the surface, the Skaldi and Quaylin troops systematically removed the remaining mine guards. They removed the barrels of gunpowder stockpiled by the Fallen Ones. Once the barrels arrived at a safe distance, Andy and Adoeete dropped enough C4 into the mouth of the open pit to make it useless as a mine or a prison.

Zaqiel and Gadreel, along with their small company of Elioud, emerged from the tunnel's rubble about a hundred yards from my position. I heard Gadreel yell, "Come, Son of Adam, you can personally give an account of this battle to the Maker."

My 'David and Goliath moment' was about to take place. The Elioud stood about seven feet tall, but Zaqiel and Gadreel were over nine feet tall. With great strides, the Fallen Archangel brandished a sword ringed in red flames. He began to shorten the distance to the hill I stood on. He looked delighted as he approached far ahead of Zaqiel and the Elioud. At about twenty feet from me, there was a blinding flash of light as Zophiel, his lion face forward, smashed Gadreel from the side to move them far to my left.

For a moment, I thought I was alone. Any left tackle in football would have been proud of Zophiel's move. Always protect the quarterback! Then it dawned on me. Only Zaqiel and a dozen Elioud remained for me.

Then I heard the still, small voice in my mind. "I have given you the authority to tread on serpents and scorpions. I have given you victory over all the power of the enemy. Nothing shall stand against you." The paraphrased words from Luke gave me courage as I moved toward the enemy gathering before me.

Several blurred figures walked past me, and I heard the word 'Àrd-Rìgh' as they passed. I felt the thunder of a thousand horses.

Quickly looking behind me, I saw Kraq and several hundred Skaldi racing at breakneck speed toward me. Kraq must have finished off the reinforcements sent from the mines and returned to help in the battle. Turning, I ran towards Zaqiel, and the four Glav with me engaged the Elioud. To my left, Zophiel was unleashing the Maker's wrath on Gadreel.

Zaqiel and I now stood a few feet from one another.

He loomed over me with an evil sneer. "Come, Son of Adam. I will send you to meet your god."

Thus, the battle began, counter and parry. The Glav, though outnumbered, were soon aided by Kraq and several of the fastest of the Skaldi.

I tricked Zaqiel and pressed my advantage, yielding a cut across his right forearm. "You are not the first angel to feel my blade."

A look of pain crossed the angel's face, followed by a moment of concern and distrust. I took full benefit. "Yes. I think the angel's name was Batariel. His death sentence was for crimes against Creation and the Maker." I did fail to mention that I had a couple of angels to help carry out that punishment. Zaqiel's face now went ashen. I continued. "Then there was Tamiel, who failed to imprison the Glav. Those same Glav are now attacking your Elioud."

Zaqiel knew both names, Batariel and Tamiel, who were Samyaza's lieutenants. Samyaza is the leader of the two hundred Watchers, those who defiled creation and lain with human women.

I saw his hope snuffed out in a split second between my announcement and my sword's upward motion, cutting across his torso.

His sword fell to the ground, no longer ringed in flames. As his body crumpled to the ground, there was a flash of light as his spirit left his body. After the flash of light, all that remained was a soul burn in the field and the sword. I reached down to retrieve the blade in my left hand, and blue flames now danced on its edges. Another to add to my collection. The remaining Elioud were now either dead or captured.

A tremendous flash of light led me to believe that Gadreel had met a fate similar to his friend's.

Zophiel arrived shortly after. Bending down, he took a handful of Zaqiel's ashes and placed them in a bag tied to his belt next to another wallet that hung there. Zophiel turned to me and spoke, "Son of Adam, well done. I trust you no longer require me and can find your way home."

I nodded, and in a flash, he was gone.

Our losses were not small, but having two Fallen Ones perish in the fight made things more palatable. Several Elioud were now captives. We had thwarted the attempt to arm the Ator and Skaldi with modern weapons.

We had gained a new ally in the Dvergar Prince Adalwin, who agreed to visit the City of Hope. The Tower of Erudition was back in the hands of the faithful.

Before returning to the City of Hope, I devised a plan to repair the tower. Skaldi quarrymen began to produce large stone blocks for a new wall being built half a mile from the existing walls, which enabled the development of a new town and later expansion. Set upon by Dvergar and Quaylin craftsmen, repair of the tower's interior began.

Father Emmaus had hoped to return the basilica to its former grandeur. The tower was too far from the city. It would serve as a temporary border defense. I informed him that all the tower's treasures would now find a home with him at the cathedral campus. We could not allow such precious items to be so far from the city's solid defense. He agreed. Brother Mathis was sent back with a small group of monks to continue the basilica's traditions, which would now serve as a physical stronghold rather than a spiritual one.

The panels sent by the Acrucians would form the gatehouse and gates of the basilica. Aig, Skaldi Prince of the Silver Clan, and a Quaylin captain named DanWin would share duties as the permanent military attachés to the basilica. I was lending more than eight hundred warriors to the rebuilding and defense of the tower and its town.

I was lucky to have survived the latest battle with only a few flesh wounds and bruises! My thoughts turned toward my responsibilities to a specific redhead. She waited for my return to the City of Hope.

CHAPTER 40

I had my Karuk rider drop me off at South Gate Castle, where I needed a quick chat with SunGru, who had just landed. Looking up at the massive gatehouse, I spotted four faces I had nearly forgotten. Brock, Quinn, Tobbin, and Jameson. SunGru had them training a group of his scouts to use some of the small firearms brought with us from our last trip to Earth. I had a new job for them now and went to greet them. They got used to all the alien races in the city, but this would be an actual test of their abilities, an opportunity to explore beyond the second tier.

"Major, where are we going now?" Jameson was the most talkative of the three and a born leader.

"Grab your gear. You are heading to new bunks and a new project," I explained while calling for two more Karuk riders.

"Copy that," came the response from all three, rushing back to South Gate Castle for their packs.

Upon their return, I sat with my bird.

"Sir, you don't expect us to ride those, do you?"

"Saddle up, boys. It's time for a tour!"

They were helped by several of the Quaylin who wished them 'luck' and 'Godspeed,' a bit of sarcasm for the trip, I was sure. Jim and Andy had also arrived, and I invited them to join us.

"Major, where will we live now? I was beginning to understand the lay of the land down here." Brock asked just moments before take-off.

Andy seemed to know the answer, and he pointed to the city's top tiers.

"Up in those towers?" Quinn asked.

Before I could answer, Andy was already responding, "Yes, Quinn, those towers, the one with the blue banners. That is where his majesty lives."

Oh boy, thanks, Andy. I knew he was going to have some fun at my expense.

"The king? When do we get to meet him?" Jameson asked.

Once more, before I could think of a delicate response, Jim said, "You have met him."

There were odd looks on the faces of the three men. "He is sitting right there," Andy said, pointing directly at me.

It took them a few moments to process the situation. "You mean RJ is the king! You live way up in that tower?" Jameson asked.

Andy chuckled. Now was the time for my delicate answer. "Look. It is not king. I am known as Àrd-Rìgh."

Andy could not resist, "Yes, he is not just the king. Àrd-Rìgh means high-king."

I gave Andy a stern look, "Yes, it does mean High King, but I didn't ask for any title."

"Well, you are the most down-to-earth monarch I have ever had the good fortune to meet," Quinn responded. "And I mean that in the most reverent way."

"If you want us to rough this one up for his irreverent ways, you just give us the word," Brock added, pointing at Andy and flexing his biceps.

"What? Wait! I am not being irreverent," Andy stammered.

They all flexed their impressive biceps at him.

I chuckled. "All right, gentlemen, we are about to taxi and get airborne. Prepare yourselves."

Our group winged eastward, flying over the East and North Gate Castles. We were flying high over West Gate Castle and diving like rockets for a closer view of the caves and waterfalls. Then, back up over the lake and the ranch.

Finally, we swung back over the city, circling the high towers and coming to a landing at the base of the building. Dismounting, the Englishmen commented on what fun that had been. Andy pointed out where they could acquire a bird and rider if they wanted to take another ride.

We walked around the corner of a building, moving towards the Glav barracks and training facilities.

The men stepped back as they met with more than a dozen Glav warriors in full battle gear. The captain of this group, Rab-Rosh, announced the arrival of the Àrd-Rìgh, and the twelve warriors sank to a single knee in unison.

"These are the Glav, the eternal guardians of God-fearing rulers," I announced, asking the Glav to return to an at-ease position.

"Pardon my asking, sire, but if they are eternal, what do you need us for?" Quinn asked.

Andy immediately understood the man's question and answered. "Quinn, they are not immortal. When RJ said 'eternal,' he means that for thousands of years, the Glav have been guardians to rulers of both Earth and the Other Realms."

"I have never heard of any lion-men being the bodyguards of any king I ever heard of," Jameson replied, scratching his head.

"Historically, the last time they were named was in the Bible. The ruler they were bodyguards for, was King David," I answered.

Brock mumbled, "The Lion-men of Moab?"

I turned toward Brock. "You have remembered the Bible story about the ancestors of these guys."

"Well, I remember in the book of Chronicles that a group of warriors, experts with shields and spears, with faces like lions and the speed of a gazelle, joined David at his stronghold in the wilderness," Brock replied. "Do you mean to tell me these are the descendants of those same Lion-men of Moab?"

I nodded. "Yes, they disappeared after serving King David and spent many years hiding in the Other Realms. These Glav have renewed their vows of guardianship to me, the Àrd-Rìgh."

"Well, this bunch seems fierce enough. I don't see how we can help," Quinn answered.

"That is the problem. There aren't just a dozen of these Lion-men. The major rescued more than a hundred of them," Jim answered.

"I certainly wouldn't mind having a bunch of these guys beholden to me," Jameson said as he began to walk among the seven-foot-tall warriors.

"The Glav can leap over lower walls, but I want them trained in scaling walls. I would like you to educate them on military strategies and battle formations. They are prone to getting caught up in the fight. Please teach them to use small arms in combat, so their personal beings' risk is minimal. Can you boys get that done for me?" I asked, already knowing the answer as they snapped to attention.

"Sire? Their hands are so big. What do we have to train them with?"

I called forward two Glav carrying a large lockable military case. "With these. We will need more of them, but this will do for your first dozen trainees." I popped open the case, revealing a dozen Dessert Eagle 50 Caliber hand cannons with holster belts.

"Oh, those should work nicely!"

"Very well. Please submit weekly progress reports. Dismissed!"

The new home for the Earl's men was much more beautiful than the one at South Gate Castle. They now live in a small villa near the Glav compound with a view and a small pool. I had Jim round up a case with some rappelling gear and grappling hooks to help with the training.

I desperately needed a hot bath and food in whatever order I could find them. I was sure Leo and Lynn had some mind-reading ability, or someone had phoned ahead to let me know I had arrived.

The bathwater was steaming, and I felt the weight and worry of the past days begin to lift. A lunch tray filled with fresh bread, cheeses, fruit, and a fluted pitcher of wine was on my table. Alongside the food were a pen and a stack of papers that required signatures. Would the paperwork ever be done? After drying off and putting on a fresh pair of clothes, I sat down and began to nibble, taking a drink of the wine, and started to read the top report on the stack.

I was startled slightly by the hands that grasped my shoulders, but I kept reading, "Leo, please let me know when we run out of paper to write on. I plan on banning paperwork shortly."

Then, to my surprise, a voice like silk addressed me. "Leo? I hope I do not look like a Leo!" It was Rachel, the love of my life. Kissing her, I realized how long it had been since we had sat with our friends on that first evening and committed ourselves to each other.

We talked for several hours. Rachel told me about the progress she had made with the Red Brigade. While I was gone, she and the girls visited Bill at the ranch. She detailed several outfits she admired from an Eridu merchant. After I napped and finished this paperwork, I promised her we would have dinner at our favorite Quaylin restaurant. I also promised to buy her whatever outfits she wanted. As she left, she met Lynn, who was there to collect the lunch tray. They went off, talking and laughing. I knew I had to do something. There was a great deal of planning, but not nearly enough time. There was only one person with the power to pull it all together. Leo.

It was eerie, as no sooner had I thought I needed Leo desperately than he showed up.

"Anything I can assist you with, RJ?"

CHAPTER 41

There was a wedding and a coronation to manage. Months of planning fancy dinner parties, elaborate gift exchanges, and wedding celebrations were not my 'cup of tea.' A couple of weeks of normalcy were indeed in order. I wrote that on a parchment piece, signed it, and added my seal.

Leo just laughed and tossed it into the nearby wastebasket. Of course, I muttered something under my breath; I was unaware that the steward had veto privileges.

"The Àrd-Rìgh may certainly run off to satisfy his whims whenever he likes. He needs to know that the same stack of papers will await his eventual return," Leo responded by placing another stack of reports next to me.

I looked over the first several. "Leo, these are military reports. May I pawn these off onto SunGru's pile?"

There was a disapproving look from across the table, where SunGru was also working on reports. "RJ, those are the reports I wrote for your approval. I can't sign the reports I wrote."

I nodded at my lead general and returned to Leo, who politely placed the reports on my stack.

"Would the Àrd-Rìgh and his generals like me to find our dinner then so that we may finish all this paperwork tonight, leaving tomorrow, meeting free?"

We both nodded in agreement. It's better to get it all over with and have a full stomach. Leo wrote a quick note and passed it to one of the Quaylin couriers. The letter said, "Find Cook. Dinner for three in the war room."

I never knew what Cook would come up with when I didn't specify what I wanted, but he usually prepared something delicious.

"What else is on the schedule?" SunGru asked as we could no longer avoid the subject.

Before I could speak, Leo broke in. "I am very excited for the wedding in just a few weeks!"

SunGru would play along, knowing that it was not my favorite subject to talk about – not that I didn't love Rachel. "Oh yes, I did hear about that. The food should be amazing. I hear they will give out presents, too!"

"Oh my, presents for everyone?" Leo feigned surprise.

"Yes, of particular wonder, I imagine, when considering the occasion with a coronation to follow!"

I saw a light bulb go on in Leo's head. He hurriedly wrote himself a note.

They might persist with the ribbing they seemed so bent on giving me when the food arrived. A tray of fruits, cheese, bread, stew, and wine is simple enough for two old military men and the steward.

I had survived meetings about formal wear and fittings by Eridu tailors. I had attended a cake tasting and testing event. Cook and Bill had spent hours refining the process of cake building and decorating. I sat through budget sessions where Leo would finally throw up his hands and say, "Spend whatever you like."

Who was going to say no to Rachel?

I had been honest about what would be attractive for the gentlemen and gave my list of groomsmen. I kept getting these stares from Rachel. The look asked, 'Who are you? What have you done with my RJ?' It would all be non-traditional. There was no way I could send Kraq in to be measured for a tuxedo. I tried to imagine Kraq standing for his tuxedo fitting.

Regardless of how I worked it in my mind, that outcome wasn't good. While working on this project, I assured the ladies that the boys and I would shine our armor. That went over like a lead balloon.

My mind returned in time for the whole 'honeymoon question.' Andy had explored the large bay on the ocean several hundred miles south of us on his scouting missions. Magnificent beaches of white sand stood below the peak where the Flaming Grove stood. Andy felt we could happily be ourselves with a limited number of guards and servants.

Andy and Jim took the liberty of flying some Quaylin workers to the beach. They constructed a 'honeymoon hut,' a small barracks, and a place where a select few would live while attending to any needs. These projects had been in the works for the better part of the last two months. Before the conversation got out of hand, I blurted out that I had already planned the honeymoon's location and pointed to the levels above our heads.

"There is no way I am spending my honeymoon locked away in your tower," Rachel announced.

"The beach sounds like a winner to me."

Gretchen and Becky looked somewhat shocked, but I knew the looks were fake. They had both heard about the beach and approved. They had helped with the decorations and provided the necessary staff for the week of bliss. Once I had adequate time invested in the celebratory plans, I excused myself and headed for bed.

Rachel and I, along with members of the council, had been invited to another 'grand opening' of an Eridu-and-Q fusion restaurant. Every shop was hoping for favor and eagerly awaited the upcoming nuptials and coronation. We had finished our meals and were about to start the dessert course. This reminded me a lot of Tanghulu, a skewer of various fruits coated in sugar syrup.

The two owners had come out of the kitchen to ask for our blessing when a rider on horseback arrived, asking that the council members and I make haste to the East Gate Castle. I could not leave Rachel behind, so I pulled her up behind me on my horse, and we galloped away as if a whip snapped at our very heels. SunGru and Shal-Dir had taken to the air, beating us by a slight margin. On foot, Kraq was only moments behind us.

The sight we beheld before the castle gates nearly brought me to tears. The woman holding my hand allowed her tears to flow like a river. These were not the tears of a sobbing, hysterical woman but a warrior maiden staring at a host of broken warriors.

A great company of knights on horseback lined the bridge before us. Weary, bloodied, and bruised, their eyes begging for the help that their heraldry would not allow. The knight at the forefront held something he highly valued, wrapped in a blanket. I saw a child's face peer from beneath the blanket and cloak.

"I am Cedric, a captain of the Knights of Midia. If you cannot offer us shelter, I ask that you at least take the child and protect him." There were rumblings from the knights behind him, protesting the decision to send the child away.

Rachel squeezed my hand, and SunGru moved to stand beside me. He whispered something in my ear, "Long ago, they were allies of the Quaylin. You must find out what has happened."

"Cedric, what has befallen the mighty kingdom of Midia that you stand before us in such dire need?" I asked.

"Many months ago, the Fallen Ones came to offer a peace treaty with our king. The king sent for the nobles to debate the treaty, and they were to arrive the next day. Instead, in the darkness of the night, the Fallen's agents inside the walls opened the gates to the lower city. Their armies of Skaldi and Ator burned their way to the king's castle. The king trusted me with his only son. A thousand knights fought their way back out of the city; less than half of those stand here with me."

"Open the gates and find these men food and lodging. Wake the kitchen staff. I will not have them starving on our doorstep. Have the healers attend to the wounded," I commanded. "Cedric, if you will, please follow me."

The East Gate Castle was Shal-Dir's and the Eridu people's. It now stood nearly abandoned. Most of the Eridu people lived near the marketplaces where they worked. Shal-Dir and his family spent very little time at East Gate Castle. He had an ambassadorial villa on the city's fifth tier. Some troops were stationed there for practical matters, but the castle itself was empty for the most part. Our stable hands took the knight's horses.

Cedric and the captains of Midia drew their swords at the appearance of Kraq, but Shal-Dir and SunGru both assured them that he was a trusted ally. We moved into the castle's main hall and took seats as the staff reheated stew and that day's leftover bread for the knights. The knights ate with great dignity, which amazed me, considering how long it appeared since they had a proper meal. Rachel was holding the boy with whom Cedric had been unwilling to part.

"Cedric, how did you know where to find us?"

Finishing his last mouthful before answering, Cedric began the story of their travels from Midia to the City of Hope. In the end, it had been many weeks of dodging the Skaldi army sent to finish them. A scout had spotted, he claimed, a man on a bird moving Southwest. Andy. Soon, Skaldi raiding parties became smaller and ceased to exist. A small village to the east, situated beside a lake, provided them with bread and water and described a great king and an ancient city, which led them to this spot.

These core leadership groups for the knights were very uneasy with Kraq standing behind me, even though I had informed them that these Skaldi united with me against the Fallen. I recounted several occasions when Kraq had saved my life. The child, Josia, the boy king, was terrified of Kraq.

Cedric picked the boy up and brought him to stand before the Skaldi Prince and I. "Now is the time for courage, little one. Those who oppose us will pay dearly for what they have done, and we must show respect to those who stand with us."

Then, moving Rachel from tears to laughter, Kraq pulled his great battle ax from his back and, kneeling, presented it to the child. "I, Kraq, Prince of the Blue Clan, swear to protect my friend, Josia, from all harm."

I saw every knight with a hand on his sword. Then something happened that turned the hearts of even the most stalwart warriors in the room to mush. The little boy reached out, pulled on Kraq's beard until they were eye to eye, and whispered, "Do you give rides?"

Rachel and I laughed as Kraq handed me his battle ax.

"I will be back for that." Turning to the boy, he hoisted him onto his shoulders, saying, "Indeed. I give the best rides!"

They went off, making great circles around the table. I could see hands that had remained on swords trembling as the knights watched Kraq dancing around the courtyard with Josia shouting and squealing. Exhausted from their journey, these men faced the prospect of their people's extinction.

However, they were now safe in the City of Hope.

Cedric planned to keep the child, but the boy needed both the love of these battle-hardened men and a woman's touch. Rachel pointed out that he needed schooling, manners, and all the other things a young king would need to know. The knights would never be far from him, and Cedric could oversee all matters regarding the boy.

I decided something official needed to transpire, so I called Cedric to the front of the room. I asked him for his sword. "Kneel." There was a moment of hesitation. I repeated my command, this time softly, and nodded. "Kneel." Cedric responded, and I continued, "A noble man without a king or country has come to me this day! I believe it is acceptable in recognition of bravery in the face of certain death to offer my hand, title, and land."

I took the sword and gently laid the blade first on his right shoulder and then on his left. "Rise, Cedric, Lord Marshal of the Knights of Midia, King's Regent, Member of the Council of Hope, and friend of the Àrd-Rìgh. Rise!"

Nothing brings warriors together quicker than moments like these.

While kneeling, Cedric spoke, "Let all that love Midia take notice that I have not turned my back on Midia. Rather, I have gained us a great ally. Until Josia sits upon his father's throne or my final breath, I serve the Àrd-Rìgh."

In turn, each knight knelt, sword outstretched in my direction. Kraq took Josia off his shoulders and back to the floor. Josia hugged Cedric and then ran willingly over to Rachel's side, placing his small hand in hers. That night, Lynn stayed at Rachel's villa to help her with the boy while we figured out how to care for him.

In the morning, I met with Shal-Dir about East Gate Castle. He was delighted to relinquish his holdings there for his villa on the fifth tier. "The Eridu do not need castles," he said.

SunGru was also happy to see the knights of Midia occupy East Gate Castle. It would allow his troops to focus on South Gate. Meanwhile, all the knights enjoyed a hearty breakfast, and each man was issued new clothes. Over the coming weeks, the knight's armor would be repaired and polished, and many of their horses would be turned out to pasture at the ranch for a much-needed rest.

Cedric arrived in my office shortly after breakfast. He could not stop thanking me.

"Lord Marshal, please have a seat. Things here in this office are not as formal as the throne room. Call me RJ or Major when you are here. Now, on to the business before us. The Knights of Midia, under the Lord Marshal's command," I pointed at Cedric, "have been granted divisional garrison headquarters at the East Gate Castle. Defense of said garrison is to be carried out by the current and future members. Patrols by the members shall include, but are not limited to, East Gate Castle, the bridge and Tower system, and the defense of the East Gate Pass."

As I spoke, two Glav entered, carrying a small chest, followed by Kraq. "This chest is for you to pay your troops and anyone tasked with supporting the East Gate Castle, a fair wage. I suggest that your first payment be generous."

Cedric seemed overwhelmed by our immediate gestures of friendship and trust. "My lords, there is no way to repay your kindness to my men."

I moved to put him at ease, "Cedric, I have done the same for every man in this room and every man and family that goes to sleep under this city's protection. I suggest you ask Andy for a tour of the city, as he is best suited for the quicker and more comprehensive flying tour."

Lifting the top of the chest revealed varied coin types and some gems.

"My lords, what am I to do with such treasure?"

Kraq then spoke. "Men need different things, blankets, pillows, candles, food when not on duty, better weapons. Rather than having them walk around desiring an item, they can make the purchase."

Turning to the big Skaldi, Cedric bowed. "Thank you for showing friendship to Josia. I have not heard him laugh for a long time."

Kraq responded, "It was my pleasure. I do give the best rides. The Glav rides are faster, but I think my rides are better!"

"You have Glav here?"

"Yes. Did the King of Midia have any Glav?

"Four," he said, deeply saddened, "I do not know what happened to them. I am sure they fell protecting the king from the Fallen ones."

Cedric then asked, "If I may, Lord Kraq, what do you and your soldiers do with your pay? What creature comforts do the fierce Skaldi warriors require?"

For a moment, I thought Kraq might take offense at mentioning 'creature', but I saw a grin on his hairy face. In almost a whisper, he said, "I buy cookies."

Visions of a blue monster puppet with spinning eyes devouring cookies flashed through my childhood memories.

I almost laughed.

"Kraq and a few of his captains indeed keep one of the local Quaylin bakeries open almost single-handedly," I said.

Shal-Dir then added a piece of his wisdom. "One of the lessons paying the men has taught us is that a man who can acquire what he desires, is a happier man."

CHAPTER 42

I always enjoyed reading Bill's reports from the ranch and often read them aloud to Rachel or a gathering of our friends for a meal. He seemed most content with his simple life. It didn't seem to matter what world he was in.

Allen had gotten power to the ranch and the fishing village and was working on a project that might allow power from the city to reach the defenses at the end of each pass.

Andy spent much of his time leading scouting expeditions, tracking enemy troop movements, and enjoying his time with the Karuk people.

Wilson worked on translating and historical matters.

Becky had her hands full with the several thousand children she worked with five days a week. A select group of mothers and grandparents helped with verbal and written language, and each race's historical stories. In addition to the children's families, nearly three dozen monks shared teaching duties and administrative work. Becky and her team managed a working school system in the city and the small village at the East Gate Pass.

This year was the first graduating class of seniors. Like on Earth, seniors would choose their next step in society. The top five percent would be offered scholarships to Regis College or King's

College to further their education with the cathedral campus monks.

Those remaining graduates had options, including apprenticeships with craftsmen, internships with the merchant class, joining the military, or learning about plants and animals on the ranch. With the help of the restaurant and bakery owners, Cook taught courses after graduating from Bill's culinary school. I chuckled, remembering that first day with the Quaylin and Cook's terrible food.

Gretchen offered work in the healing words and teachings on becoming herbalists and healers. It was Gretchen's area that bothered me the most. The level of care could only go so far without more modern implements for civilian and military medical needs. These changes may require returning to Earth to assemble supplies and equipment. Gretchen's other point was valid; she was not a doctor.

While Andy spent much time in the air, Jim was the opposite, choosing the ground and forming an elite group of scouts that combined all the races' talents. He used his skills to ambush enemy units, raid their supply convoys, and gather intelligence.

During one of our meetings, Jim revealed his desire to verify the scouting description of a large group of Fenri in the North Gate Pass and the Vale that led to the base of Mount Djuprot. Mount Djuprot was the tallest peak in the mountain range known as 'The Line.'

Kraq himself had moved from the North Gate Castle to a villa on the fifth tier of the city. He claimed that the giant wolves' howling kept him awake at night. Something should be done before winter, which leaves little time. These big wolves had hunted and fought alongside the Skaldi before. The Fenri had a mind of their own, and they were not suitable inside a city or around unarmed civilians.

However, unlike the Skaldi, the Fenri had no problem eating any form of life. While Kraq informed me that Skaldi and Fenri could communicate, they were not to be trusted. They are brilliant killing machines. He also told me that in high numbers, they posed a danger even to the Skaldi.

"Kraq, how would you hunt a large number of Fenri properly? I asked.

"We need three things. Fire, spears, and arrows." Kraq replied.

The plan was to drop large amounts of brush at the city side of the North Gate Pass, wait for a stiff breeze from the south, light the bush on fire, and remain at the other end with spearmen and archers. I decided that the Red Brigade would draw the final line of defense on this venture.

Quaylin cavalry would also be necessary for rescue or escape from the jaws of these beasts. This eradication of the giant wolves became more than a passing fancy or small project as it had begun, becoming a full-scale military undertaking.

Andy oversaw the Karuk riders dropping the large bundles of brush covering the pass's breadth and filling it several hundred feet deep and twenty feet high. This giant bonfire had gone far beyond the marshmallow or hot dog roast I had initially thought was required.

Quaylin light cavalry gathered with Skaldi spearmen at the East Gate Pass, ready to march into position. Joining them were Rachel and five hundred of the Red Brigade and wagons full of supplies.

A stiff breeze from the south started in the early morning about a week later.

It was more than a fifty-mile journey from the base of Mt. Djuprot that began near the East Gate Pass around the massive geological feature to where the bottom of the mountain formed the beginning of the North Gate Pass.

Smaller groups of men on foot might have traversed the terrain more quickly along a different route. However, the infantry and archers followed the horseback riders across the plains' natural topography for safety.

One last message went out that morning when a somewhat out-of-breath Adalwin arrived. He announced that if any white Fenri were spotted, they should not be harmed. Instead, they were to be allowed to flee or be captured alive. According to Dvergar legend, the white Fenri were, in fact, allies of the Dvergar clan under the banner of the white wolf.

The white wolf banner. It was the only non-Gryphon banner, and the clan that carried it had passed into myth and legend.

"I have never seen a Fenri with white fur," Kraq claimed.

Bolvi nodded in agreement.

Adalwin said, "I had only recognized the wolf clan members in my childhood when my father took me to a clan leader's meeting. These only occur every twenty years."

The chances of seeing a white wolf were about the same as seeing a Dvergar under the white wolf banner. That had been more than fifty years.

"If all are ready, let's begin," I said.

Karuk riders dropped torches into the giant brush piles. You could see the great billows of smoke from the plains where we waited. Skaldi warriors, with their sizeable long spears, began to walk into the pass, followed by the Red Brigade leading groups of Quaylin archers.

Andy initially sent me reports detailing a large pack of Fenri moving away from the smoke. But when the breeze turned to gusts, smoke quickly filled the pass, and the wolves were invisible to the riders in the sky.

Adalwin and I, along with several Glav bodyguards, were already in the pass, now filled with smoke. I took us closer to the left side of the pass, where the smoke seemed less dense, but suddenly, it was only Adalwin by my side.

Then, that sixth sense that I had developed tingled. Was this the danger tingle or the 'pay attention' tingle? I was still working them out.

The apparition appeared to Adalwin and me simultaneously, and it was a white wolf. The female wolf crept along the base of the pass walls, occasionally looking back to see if we were still in pursuit.

Then I could see the entrance to the Vale of Djuprot, barely visible through the smoke and nearly impossible to discern in broad daylight, deep within the very roots of the mountain itself. I wasn't the biggest guy, but I was sure that no Skaldi or Glav would be able to pass through. The Dvergar seemed best suited for this tight, short space.

An overpowering stench filled the tightness of the Vale. Around the corner, the two of us came to a place where the Vale opened. The reek of death remained heavy in the air here. Then, we saw the cause of the stench: hundreds of rotting Fenri corpses. Some were only bones, and others were half-eaten, gnawed on by something bigger.

Further on, we came to a place that widened even further. I could see why Jim had spotted the Vale from the air, but we had completely missed it in our scouting on foot.

Then the 'tingle' happened, piercing my mind like a dagger. It was confusing as the danger tingle and the pay attention tingle intertwined in my mind. A female white wolf now stood between the Dvergar and me. I am unsure why I allowed my hand to linger near her snout. You do this to let a dog smell you, but it is not advisable for a wolf.

Instead of Àrd-Rìgh, perhaps my new nickname would have something to do with my missing digits. Instead, I felt a nibble and then the warm sensation of my hand being licked. I reached back to place my hand on her head. The tingle was back when my fingers brushed through the silky fur. In my mind, the wolf warned me of the danger ahead, then added Fagr, whom I assumed was her name.

At that exact moment, I saw her pack running together in a green field. A feeling of profound loss nearly overwhelmed my human senses. The she-wolf continued to follow us as we moved forward. Before us, in the distance, I saw wide steps carved into the living rock, leading to a flat area that, in turn, gave way to a sheer cliff wall. More Fenri bodies lay in piles, bones, and rotting flesh on the massive stone steps.

What could be doing this? I found out quickly enough. There, lounging at the top of the steps, were two massive Fenri-like monsters. More wolf than man, they walked upright. The two beasts crouched here and there to rip into the body of a dead or dying Fenri.

The white wolf telepathically spoke to me again, "Fenrir!"

I sensed that 'Fenrir' must be the word for whatever these monstrosities were. I now brought my sword to life. I saw Adalwin, battle ax in hand. One of the creatures saw us nearing and spoke. Well, Adalwin seemed to understand it. All I heard were wolfish growls and guttural sounds.

"It says you must wait for their master, Àrd-Rìgh," Adalwin translated.

"Who is their master?" I asked.

There were more growls and what sounded like a whine as the first beast communicated with Adalwin.

"They serve a dark winged nightmare. You are to turn over the white wolf to them, or risk their master's wrath."

"I'm not in the waiting mood. Tell them the white wolf is under my protection."

More whining and grunts.

"They say you have no authority here. They say you may be a great warrior, but you still can't defeat their master."

Then, the two monsters faced us. Crouching at the top of the steps, they charged us. There was a moment of hesitation when my blade sprang to life. Blue flames always had that effect on the enemy.

The white wolf was about the size of a normal Fenrir. She immediately sprang at the beast, headed to attack Adalwin. I assumed she thought the blue flames were a sure sign that I could handle myself.

I will say that the teeth and claws of the thing before me seemed to be of an almost steel-like quality. Yet flesh is flesh. I soon made the fierce beast bleed and then howl in pain. I turned to see how Adalwin and the she-wolf were faring. The she-wolf lunged towards the beast's throat, and Adalwin hacked a chunk of flesh from the arm as the thing head-butted him to the ground.

At the same time, I suffered a blow to the chest, knocking me several yards from where I had been standing a moment before. Standing up, I saw my attacker crouching for another attack. Looking down at my breastplate, I saw the deep ridges left by the monster's claws. Well, so much for the Acrucians telling me nothing could make a dent in my new armor. Then, with cat-like reflexes, it was upon me once more. I hacked the limb closest to me and then at the other as it knocked me over again.

343

As my sword hit the Fenrir, it uttered a sickening sound and lost its balance. As the beast's suffocating weight hit me, I moved my sword between us. The light left my eyes, and the world went dark. The next thing I recall was distant voices getting closer.

I heard Adalwin's voice say, "Push. You have to push."

The she-wolf, Fagr, inside my mind, answered, "I can pull or tug, but I can't push."

As they pulled the beast's body off of me, I could hear the voice of Adalwin again. "That thing should have crushed him like a bug. He is still breathing. Praise the Maker!"

I felt a wet sensation as the wolf licked my face. Then I heard what a laugh would be if a wolf could laugh. I heard what I heard. After a few minutes resting with the two of them fussing over me, I opened my eyes, "I am okay." There was some sign of relief in the wolf's deep blue eyes.

"But are you unharmed?" Adalwin asked.

I grinned through the pain as I took a knee. "I think I have a cracked rib, and the cut over my eye will require stitches. Other than that, I seem to have fared better than the two of you."

The she-wolf had several deep gashes on her side, and her fur was now more pink than white. The Dvergar leader was bloodied and bruised. His armor, too, showed signs of deep gouges, and blood dripped from a shoulder wound. I didn't bother to ask how they had overcome their attacker as we gingerly made our way up the stone stairs.

CHAPTER 43

As we reached the landing at the top of the stairs, I could see an impressive set of iron doors set into a cleft in the rock. They were battered and nearly unhinged. I heard what could only be a sound of awe come from Adalwin's mouth as he ran his calloused hands over the outline of a griffin etched into the iron of the door. When both doors were closed, two griffins with outstretched paws faced one another.

As we entered through the gap between the doors, we walked into a massive hall filled with cobwebs and the dust of a thousand years. The dust on the floor showed large paw prints. The Fenri had used this place to keep from the winter cold and the summer heat.

A grand staircase led to a landing and an open archway. From there, a massive hall with a dozen staircases carved into the rock led to what I could only imagine were many passages through the mountain.

It was just instinct to follow the Fenrir paw prints on the dust-covered stone steps. Whatever their master was, it must have been too large to use the staircase or the many tunnels branching off from it. Every landing revealed more doorways and halls. Not wanting to lose our way, we stopped looking down hallways and continued up the steps.

After what seemed like an eternity, the steps ended in a great carved hall. At mid-point, a great dais was carved into the rock, and at the end of the hall, a grand opening in the mountain itself. With the proper pilot, you could land a plane in the hall. A great stench came from the dais, where a giant bed of ancient wall hangings and banners. If this was where their master usually took refuge, we were lucky he was not present.

Beyond that, a series of steps led down to a hall with its doors barricaded. At the top of the stairs, the she-wolf let out a fierce howl, which I thought would undoubtedly alert any other enemies nearby of our arrival. But the only answer was a single, lone howl in response coming from one of the barricaded doors.

The three of us limped towards the sounds as the she-wolf spoke to me. "My kin are prisoners sacrificed to the Fenri's god. Some seem to be still alive."

"Adalwin, help me break down these barriers so we can open the doors." I nodded to the one with the most activity behind it.

"Àrd-Rìgh, what if Fenrir is behind this door?" the Dvergar leader questioned. "We might not survive another battle."

I looked at the she-wolf. "Fagr says her pack of white wolves is behind this door."

The Dvergar looked shocked, as if seeing more than one white wolf this decade might cause him to faint. Adalwin began hacking at the boards covering the door with his battle ax.

Once opened, the first door revealed three adult males and two adult females in need of medical attention. At the same time as Adalwin worked on his door, I started prying open another door, from which we heard faint whines coming. The door I was working on disclosed a dozen pups of varying ages in even worse shape.

I reached for my throat, hoping the comm would work after the fighting, but all I got was static. Static meant no damage, but my signal couldn't get through the mountain's sheer thickness.

"Adalwin, see if you can find water. I think that dais back there may have held a well. Let me try to get a hold of Andy or Jim." I raced for the rock overhang, ignoring the searing pains in my chest and head. When I reached the large opening, I tried to reach out to Andy and Jim again. "Overwatch, do you copy?"

There were a few moments of static when a response came back, "RJ, where in the world did you disappear to?"

"Jim, you won't believe me, so you must come to see for yourself. We uncovered a Dvergar fortress. Anyway, what I need you to do is fly over Mount Djuprot. When you are over the northeast side, let me know. I will fire a flare. You can't see it from above, but there is a sizeable cavern on the side of the mountain open to the air. Please bring your wife and several healers, water, firewood, and medical supplies."

"Copy that. RJ Good to hear your voice!"

I sat down a few feet from the edge and leaned against the rock wall when the she-wolf walked towards me with a tiny pup in her mouth. She gently placed the wolf pup in my lap. It was alive.

"From my litter of three, this one survived." Her voice trembled with the overwhelming grief that only a mother could feel. "You must ensure his survival."

"I am sorry for your loss. The Fenri will pay for their crimes if any have survived the fires and arrows that my men have already visited upon them."

I reached to my side for the small pack I wore, which held my canteen, and poured a little into the cup for the pup to drink. Weak though the wolf pup was, he eagerly lapped up the water. I poured more.

The she-wolf left the animal in my care while she went to assist Adalwin, who was doing his best to care for the other wolves. I reached into the pack, hoping that I had not eaten all the beef jerky from the stash Bill had brought on his last visit. My fingers curled around the small pouch. I broke off a small amount for the pup to nibble. As the tiny animal finished the piece of jerky, he licked my fingers.

Again, a thought sparked in my mind. "Smar is the runt of my litter."

I turned as I saw the she-wolf coming towards me once more. Smar had now climbed my chest to lick my neck below my chin. I laughed as the roughness of his tongue tickled my skin.

A moment later, the comm went off. "RJ, shoot that flare! We are on approach."

"Copy that." I set the pup down, moved to the edge, and fired the flare gun into the air.

"We see you. Be there in five."

"Copy that, clearing the runway," I turned.

The she-wolf already had her pup by the scruff of his neck. She moved towards the back of the cavern where Adalwin waited. I quickly explained to Jim what had happened and told Gretchen that she and the healers need not fear the white wolves. A group of healers began treating the adults, while Gretchen and another group treated the younger wolves and pups.

At first, we thought about rigging the birds and flying the wolves to the city. However, Gretchen suggested that we send Jim back for milk and meat. Jim left and arrived about an hour later with Rachel. They brought furs to keep all of us warm, firewood, and food. Rachel was delighted when I introduced Smar to her. After a large portion of milk, he curled up in her lap for a long nap.

I sat nearby and conversed with the she-wolf and her mate, who had survived as prisoners. If captured, the white wolves were often ritually sacrificed to Nidhug. As best as I could, I explained how the City of Hope was a beacon to those fighting against the evil that had taken the Other Realms. I told them how some Skaldi and other races now stood with us as allies.

The two leaders of the wolves, Fagr and her mate, Vigr, told me they yearned for the old ways, where the white wolves fought and lived alongside the Dvergar and their allies. They also shared the meanings of their names with me. Vigr was the male's name and, loosely translated, meant 'able fighter.' The she-wolf's name, Fagr, meant 'beautiful one.'

We spent several nights and days caring for the wolves and their pups, helping them recover. I had wagons brought from the East Gate Pass to carry the wolves and horses for those of us who stayed with them. The wagons took them to the fifth tier of the city, where we set up an empty villa to care for those still needing medical attention.

Gretchen did what she could and often reminded us she was not a veterinarian. Adalwin and several dozen Dvergar had returned to the Vale to begin exploration. I approved, as no remaining signs of Fenri had survived the fire and arrows that pierced the Vale. Allen and a small contingent of Glav for protection joined the Dvergar to map the ancient Dvergar stronghold. This fortress could predate the city.

CHAPTER 44

Hasty meetings and spirited kisses filled the following week. Cedric and the Knights of Midia were now in residence at East Gate Castle. Our new friend, Josia, spent his days between Rachel and Lynn, and of course, he got plenty of rides from Uncle Kraq. Uncle Kraq had become UK, as it was hard for the child to say his name.

There was no end to the well-wishers and merrymaking, building into a crescendo on May 1st, AE2. The cathedral was ready for the most incredible celebration the city has witnessed since its founding. Andy, Jim, and Kraq stood to my side, dressed in regal blue robes. Gretchen, Becky, and TeiLin, beautiful in gowns, were to our right. Shal-Dir and SunGru were in the front row with their families. Above us at the podium stood Father Emmaus and Brother Mathis, ready for both vow and ring exchange.

We had no flower girl, but Josia came down the aisle, followed closely, to my amazement, by the wolf pup Smar. Josia took his time waving to people he knew and bowing to each guard who nodded to him. He hugged Cedric, who stood on the aisle side in the second row with several other dignitaries, then ran to Kraq and sat on the steps playing with Smar. The little boy made many people smile.

Then the music began, and my smile grew as I watched Rachel in a stunning, white pearl-beaded, fur-lined dress. Beside her, arm-in-arm, strode Bill in his version of Other Realms meets Wild

West, including his hat and boots. He hugged us as he passed the beautiful bride off to my care. The Erudian artisans had transformed the dress into a work of art befitting a queen, with delicate Dvergar stone work adorning her neck. I was awestruck.

There was no doubt I had put this off for far too long, but in this place, at this time, everything seemed to have come together. Brother Mathis delivered a lengthy sermon on the seriousness of the vows we were about to exchange and the duties of a husband to his wife and of a wife to her husband. Then came the lighting of the three candles, and the significance of each one was explained.

The next part of the ceremony faded. I could only look into those eyes and marvel at the fiery red hair that cascaded to her shoulders beneath the white veil. We had each written vows. I had barely memorized my own in the time allotted, but I managed somehow. Rachel's vows brought tears to my eyes. I glanced down as Rachel and I exchanged rings.

What I really wanted to do was grab her hand and run, but a different ceremony was about to begin. Two of the Glav brought chairs for Rachel and me to sit on. Then, a long line of dignitaries gave their blessing to both our marriage and titles.

My pledge of service to the kingdom and Rachel's to serve the people ended with my kneeling before Father Emmaus, who placed a crown on my head.

I then put a crown of a more petite design on Rachel's head – minus the veil. Then came the long line of military and cultural dignitaries, pledging their allegiance to the Àrd-Rìgh and their queen. That portion of the reception line seemed to take forever.

Josia and Smar arrived with what looked like grease from some meat on both the silk shirt and the muzzle.

Josia pulled on my arm, and I knelt. He whispered, "Cook is mad!"

I nodded, trying not to laugh. "Kraq, take these two and feed them. Give my apologies to Cook as well."

The big Skaldi liked that idea and, taking Josia under one arm and Smar in the other, he sniffed the air. Josia announced, "That way, UK."

They headed for one of the outer buildings from which the smell of cooked meat was coming. If Kraq were with them, they might get into less trouble or more.

Finally, it was time to eat, and the whole city had arrived to celebrate with us. The preparations and cooking of the feast had started days before. Thousands had come to celebrate not just the wedding but also the first coronation in perhaps several thousand years. I will not take the time to describe all the incredible foods available.

Table after table, a remarkable feast awaited us. The cake was a quality blend. Only one man could have pulled off such a feat. Bill stood before the cake with a team of Quaylin bakers, beaming from ear to ear, eager for us to participate in the cutting ceremony. Rachel gave me a 'behave yourself' look as we fed each other a bite of cake. We stayed with our friends for a while longer.

We were staying in the tower tonight and leave for Regis Bay in the morning due to the two-hundred-mile flight. Josia and Smar followed us as far as Leo and Lynn's apartment, where we hugged them all and explained that he would have to stay with them for just the night, while Rachel and I went away.

Leo mentioned the storybook that Andy had found in the library, and the young boy was happy to comply. That and more cake, of course!

What happened after that is – well, private!

The next day, we all got dressed for travel. We ate a quick bite before heading up the steps with Leo, Lynn, Josia, and Smar to the waiting riders. Smar was now the constant companion of the young Midian Prince. He was welcome to come on our adventure. We attempted to explain to Josia that Smar was not a pet, and we got a serious look and a nod, but the tiny prince did not explain himself. Rachel figured Josia thought he was not a pet because Smar was family.

Along with a select group of troops and servants, Cook had left last night after the party's end and was already on location awaiting our arrival. We were all bundled up against the morning chill as we flew out over the still-sleeping city. Andy had assured me that the temperature on the coast would be much warmer, and the water would be perfect for swimming.

A small group arrived as we landed. Lunch was the first thing on my mind. We ate on the beach with Josia and Smar chasing each other across the sandy inlet. Rachel soon had a large pile of shells beside her as Josia and Smar found better and better ones. It looked like a tropical resort on an island somewhere on Earth. After a long day of entertaining in the sun, swimming, and splashing, it was all I could do to carry Rachel into the honeymoon hut.

It wasn't long after we snuggled into our bed when I heard a giggle and bark. As we both peered over the side of the bed, Josia and Smar stood there. "I come up," was all it took, and I pulled the boy and his white fur ball onto the bed. The two unceremoniously made their way to the middle of the bed and were fast asleep in a few moments.

I crawled out of bed to get a message to Leo and Lynn about where their young charges had run off, too, and then crawled back into bed.

The week went by far too quickly. We didn't get nearly enough alone time, but by the end of the week, Rachel had convinced me that I should begin plans to build a town on the bay that we could visit.

Shouldn't every good Àrd-Rìgh have a few boats for trade and, of course, a Navy? Remembering that the kingdom of Midia needed to be rescued constantly weighed on my mind. The Karuk Forests and the massive redwood-like trees were off to the Southwest. You might even find that one tree could make a ship or two. I would need to appoint someone to oversee such a project over the winter and hope to have good progress by spring.

The morning before our return trip to the city, I was sitting high on the heights above the beaches, just below the Fire Grove. I had been sketching ideas for terracing the hills to my right to accommodate buildings and fields. I was far from an artist, but the military had at least given me the skills to sketch targets and maps. I looked up, and Jim landed near me, waving. I waved him over.

"Becky and I can't get enough of this place. It reminds me of the Caribbean. What have you been sketching?" Jim, despite his SEAL background, held a Master's degree in Architecture. He often helped Bolvi with defensive fortifications; the big Skaldi oversaw most of the projects.

"What about building a permanent settlement here?" That was all I needed to say as I handed over the sketch pad.

Jim looked over my basic sketch and flipped the page. He made some hand motions as if measuring some distances without a line or a level. Then, he began sketching and talking. "You will, of course, need a royal villa."

I nodded in immediate agreement.

"I see you have added fields for growing food. Adding some fruit trees would also boost the town's self-sufficiency. Walls and larger barracks are also needed. You can build at least fifty homes within the walls along with the usual businesses."

He sketched a few moments more and returned the pad to me. I flipped back to look at my pathetic sketch on the front – and Jim turned to the previous page. "RJ, I was always better at this, but you gave me the basics. I improved your idea."

Indeed, I now have a clear vision and a comprehensive plan.

"Okay, my old friend, how long do you think this might take you to accomplish it?"

Jim looked at me. "Me?" he laughed. "Becky is going to love you for this!"

I made the hand signal to get his attention. "What do you think for a time frame, and how many workers?"

I recognized the 'Are you serious?' look Jim gave.

When he realized I wasn't joking, he responded, "With the loss of the bridge tower system at the North Gate Pass, Bolvi has nothing to do over the winter or this coming spring. We could have his crew head to the north end of the Karuk Forest and cut several trees to get them started. They would winter here. It would almost be a vacation after the work they have accomplished this past year. I could help oversee, and Becky would love to spend time with me, here."

I nodded, happy to oblige. "What would be your first project?"

I could see the wheels turning, and I half-expected to see smoke billow from his nose or ears.

"The riders are great for the small amount of travel we require. However, if we make a permanent settlement here, we must hew a road from the South Gate Pass to this location."

"I agree. Make some markings for the road from South Gate Pass until you hit moderate brush, and then carve a clear road to the bay."

Jim nodded. "When would you like Bolvi and I to get started?"

"It's about five hundred miles from the city to the bay, but half of that is plains until you hit the hills. We should put up some mile markers so that no one gets lost. Later, we can add way stations. You and Bolvi figure out what you need to make this happen. I expect you, Becky, and Bolvi for Christmas, but this will give you six to seven months to make progress. It will also give you time to move from bikini weather to a slight chill from the ocean."

Jim slapped me on the back. "I had no idea why I flew up here just now, but I sure am glad I did."

I laughed. "Yeah, well, send a rider to pick me up so I don't miss supper."

"Copy that!"

When I returned to the beach, everyone gathered for our final night. With Jim's help, Cook had prepared several seafood dishes, and there was even a table covered in large leaves with local fruits. What I wouldn't do for a rum and Coke, instead, wine would have to do. Rachel sat beside me, and we looked over the bay at the sunset.

A four-year-old and his wolf pup chased each other up and down the sandy beach before us. Before the sun faded from view, I pulled a folded-up paper from my shirt pocket and handed it to Rachel.

"What is this? Oh, RJ, are you serious?"

"Yes, my love. Jim and Bolvi will begin work on a permanent settlement above the beach, including a villa for us to holiday at." It took about ten seconds for her to realize I had taken her advice seriously before I lay on my back, smothered in kisses.

When we returned for air, we were face-to-face with Josia and Smar. Josia reached out and touched Rachel's lips with one chubby finger. She grabbed the boy and Smar and gave them kisses, too. There was sand flying, tickling, giggling, and barking, enough to bring a Glav out of a nearby hut to ensure something hadn't crept out of the jungle to attack the Àrd-Rìgh and his queen.

All I had to do was say 'cake,' the little guy took Rachel by the hand and led us to where Cook was handing out the evening's dessert. Leo and Lynn arrived to take Josia and Smar to their tent, but a look from Rachel told me it was okay. I told them the boy was welcome to stay with us again.

The trip back was exciting. It started with Becky's big hug and kiss, who now knew of our plan to build on the bay. Everyone was in high spirits, and our welcome upon our return to the City of Hope was overwhelming. Shal-Dir announced that he had a surprise for me.

Shal-Dir had resolved the issues with my living space. Rachel had left some basic guidelines for color and décor, and even Leo and Lynn had their say. It started with a comfortable bed for a man who had slept half his career on the ground. I also remembered a small writing desk with a view facing the lake and West Gate Castle.

I used two small wardrobes: one for clothing and the other for my pack and several weapons. A small table and two chairs – that was all the furniture I needed. Things had changed while we were on our honeymoon.

At the top of the King's Tower, the Karuk had stabled birds and messengers for my personal use. The next floor down housed a barracks for riders and messengers. The following two levels had remained empty until now. Then I had my tiny apartment, followed by Leo and Lynn's two-story apartment, and the War room level.

What I saw now blew my mind. Shal-Dir and the Acrucians had made some adjustments to the Tower. Just off the elevator was a large landing where the Glav stood constant watch. I was then faced with great wooden doors leading to private offices for Rachel and me, as well as a play area for Josia. There was a restroom on the floor and a private elevator to access the three levels above. There was a small barracks and break area for the constant presence of Glav.

We had a kitchen and pantry in the main living quarters, as well as a dining area that could easily accommodate twenty people around the table. My favorite change was a large room with comfortable seating and a fireplace. The entire outer wall of the Tower was now transparent from floor to ceiling, offering spectacular views of the city and the South Gate Pass. In addition, on the outer ring of the Tower, there were five complete guest suites.

On the final living level was a room similar to the one below, with the same floor-to-ceiling windows and seating around a cozy fireplace. A large main suite with a king-sized bed now stood in the room, covered with soft, warm fur blankets and great fluffy pillows. In the empty room down the hall was another bed and a play area.

Rachel had insisted on it for Josia, who would undoubtedly share it with Smar. Far enough around the corner to give us fair warning of his arrival, but not so far that he felt alone. I was sure that not many years from now, he would ask for a room, far from ours. Why were there five additional bedrooms on this level? Rachel and I had not discussed how many children we wanted.

The final room was large, with a wooden table, perhaps for games or homework, and several empty bookshelves that I was sure I was meant to fill.

New furniture was everywhere, and marks were on the walls where paintings and wallcoverings were due to be hung: a proper home for a lord and his lady. I was a man blessed beyond measure.

CHAPTER 45

Several weeks had passed since the honeymoon trip, and we had all settled into a routine. Upon waking, I decided to partake of breakfast in the main hall.

I don't know why my best ideas now came to me in Josia and Smar's presence. They had become inseparable since meeting each other at Rachel's villa. At this very moment, they ran through the hall before me.

I walked out to see Josia stop in front of one of the Glav guards. He cleared his throat and saluted the warrior. "Josia and Smar, reporting for duty!"

The Glav nodded and opened the door leading from this back hall into the kitchen. The boy and his wolf marched through. When the Glav realized I was watching, he moved to reopen the door, but I waved him away. I took the front entrance and saw what those two rascals were up to. I snuck around the outside wall of the great hall and peered into the kitchen.

I heard them long before I spotted them. Cook was making cookies; well, he was trying to.

Josia was full of baking questions. "Sir Cook, I like corn. Why can't we put corn in cookies?"

Cook nodded, making a humming sound. "Well, I make corn muffins, but I don't think corn in cookies would be that tasty," he responded. He pulled out a tray of already fresh cookies for Josia to sample.

"What about Smar? He needs a treat, too!" Josia remarked, which got a bark from Smar when he said the word 'treat.'

Again, Cook covered all his bases and made Smar sit to receive a beef piece he had saved for just such an occasion.

"What about pancakes? Can you put them into our cookies? Me and Smar love pancakes."

Cook chuckled, "Well, I don't think that would work, but we could put maple syrup and nuts in the cookies just like you do when you eat pancakes."

Vigorous head nodding occurred, and an agreement was reached regarding the next day's batch of goodies.

"We can try those tomorrow. I have another meeting to go to," Josia announced. Cook helped him down from his seat at the counter. They saluted each other, and Josia and Smar headed in my direction. I went back around and slipped behind a pile of chairs. If Smar smelled or spotted me, it was all over.

I watched from a distance. Josia saluted every guard in the hall on his way out of the building. The pair had my full attention at this point. I followed and watched until the two ducked into a structure. I couldn't recall entering that particular building and had no idea what its purpose was.

I looked through the front window to see the boy and wolf exit the rear door. Josia sat down at a table with someone I couldn't see. I saw Josia pull a paper from his jacket and place it on the table. I walked around the side of the building and made my way to the end to hear the ongoing conversation.

Missing the first part of the discussion, I could now hear Josias's high-pitched voice. "But you said to make a picture, and you would build it."

The other voice answered was gruff and easily recognized as Skaldi, but not anyone I could identify. "But my Prince, how will you pay for this?"

I then heard a few coins hit the table. "Here. I have saved all my candy money to pay you."

There was a brief moment as the other person counted the few coins.

"Prince Josia, I am sorry, there is no way I can make this exactly as you have drawn it without much more candy money."

There was an outburst of tears. "But UK said you were the best at armor."

"I am, but this isn't enough money to pay for these jewels in your drawing. Maybe Rachel or Kraq can loan you the money for this, but until then, you will have to change your drawing and put only one or two gems."

"Pinky swear and don't tell anyone about this!"

"All right, I will wait. But remember, if we wait too long, it will be too late to build."

"Okay," came Josia's reply.

I heard his feet hit the ground. They did not see me in the side alley, so I waited for them to leave and move down the street before heading into the shop.

As the door closed behind me, a deep Skaldi voice stated, "I am not open for business today. I had a special meeting, but I would be happy to see you later." The big Skaldi turned to face the counter. His demeanor changed, "Àrd-Rìgh, I am so sorry. I had no idea it was you!"

"It is okay. What is it that you do here?"

"I am heraldic armorer for the Blue Clan, my liege. My forge is on the first tier, and this is my design shop".

"My son was just in here with a white wolf. Can you tell me why a four-year-old might need someone like you?"

"I am not sure I should discuss the needs of my clients with other people." The big Skaldi chuckled. "It might be considered a breach of confidence."

I smiled and chuckled. "He is a child, and I heard you tell him he did not have enough money for what he desired. I was wondering how much money he was short. I want to help him if I can."

"I will not pretend to know what lies in the royal coffers, but I am not sure even the Àrd-Rìgh has the resources necessary to fulfill the prince's drawing."

"Can I see this drawing? I understand if you do not want to show me, but if anyone can help, it would be me."

The Skaldi chuckled again, "All right, I will show you. If you procure the necessary jewels, I would happily make what he wants."

"Jewels? What could he possibly want with jewels?"

From under the counter, the Skaldi armorer produced a crudely drawn picture. I could discern the word 'King' in crayon across the top. There appeared to be ceremonial armor covered in gems and a generously decorated helm.

"Now I see why he didn't have enough money to cover your fees."

The big Skaldi choked back another laugh. "I was having trouble making him understand my plight."

It was my turn to chuckle. "Well, my friend, if he comes again, let him drop off any money he has gotten from Rachel or Uncle Kraq and assure him he is getting closer, but you still need more. In the meantime, I will do my best to get you a couple of gems. Enough gems to make the armor in his size, at least."

There was a look of confusion on the armorer's face, "Àrd-Rìgh, that is a problem. The armor isn't for Josia."

Then, the same puzzled look took my face. "Well, who is Josia making this for?"

"Sire, I hate to ruin this surprise, but we are halfway there anyway."

Then it hit me. Josia had been lying between Rachel and me a few mornings when she asked me what I wanted for my birthday. "It's for me, isn't it?"

The big Skaldi nodded, yes.

I placed my hand on his forearm. "Worry not, my friend. This secret is safe. I will get some gems for Josia, even though I have no idea how."

The armorer thought for a moment. "Sire, have you asked anyone in charge of the quarries if they have found anything in their digging? Perhaps they have something we could use for this project. They do not have to be expensive, just nice and big like in the picture."

It had been a few months since I had last spoken to the quarry managers. "Good idea, my friend. I will check and then secretly get the gems to Josia."

CHAPTER 46

I left the shop, wondering at the child's resourcefulness. It was nearing lunchtime. I decided to wander to the first tier of the city and eat at a place I had not been to in many months. Bill had personally trained the man to cook at the ranch.

After getting my fill at the Eridu restaurant specializing in barbecue, I barely pushed myself away from the table.

The crowd of citizens slowed my progress by shaking hands or saying hello as I walked from the eating establishment to the quarry managers' headquarters. The crowds were tolerable, as I needed to show my community that I was accessible.

The door I approached had a Skaldi guard on either side, but even dressed as I was, they recognized me, saluted, and let me through the heavy oak-and-iron doors. Inside were several offices on either side of a long hall from which a Dvergar and Skaldi head popped out when I rang the bell on the counter.

"Àrd-Rìgh, what brings you to our offices?" The Dvergar master miner, named Rulk, took my hand in his.

"Exactly. Perhaps twenty minutes ago, we sent a message requesting an audience meeting with you at your earliest convenience. I beg your pardon, but we never expected you to have to come to us," Jihl, who was the Skaldi counterpart of Rulk, announced.

"Gentlemen, I did not get your message. The poor messenger will arrive only to find that I am here and not there. My business here can wait. Please tell me about your concerns or needs." I had no idea what their sense of urgency could mean. They helped provide essential building supplies for fortifications, repairs, and even roadwork. "My apologies, please. What can I help you with?"

The two took me back to the end of the hall, where we passed through one doorway into a relatively small room with nothing in it. Pressing on the bracings on the right side of the room, I heard a click, and the whole wall swung on a pivot, revealing a secret room that the two men had designed. Inside were several chests of varying sizes.

"What do we have here?" I was curious to see what was so important that it had to be hidden behind a secret wall, but it had not made it to the official city vault.

"Well, Sire, we had no idea what to do with these," Rulk admitted as Jihl helped him open one of the larger chests. What he revealed amazed me: uncut gems, bags of gold nuggets, and silver ore.

"Where did this all come from?"

The two men exchanged looks. I saw what must have been going through their minds with that question.

Before I could retract, Jihl answered me. "Sire, from the ground, of course."

I laughed to break the awkward silence. "I should have asked that question differently. Of course, from the ground. What I mean is, did this all come from the quarries?" They both nodded vigorously. "Why hasn't all this been brought to the vault?"

They looked at each other again, almost as if revealing this might be wrong somehow. "Àrd-Rìgh, we hid this with no ill intent.

Every king must have his treasure store," Rulk stated, his face slightly red.

I took a moment to consider my words carefully so as not to embarrass the two further. "Is this the best of what you have found?"

They both nodded yes.

"What happens to the smaller gems and nuggets?" The two looked at each other again, as if this would reveal some crime committed without their knowledge.

This time, Jihl spoke. "For what I am about to say, please only hold the two of us accountable if it displeases you, Àrd-Rìgh." Then he waited for my response.

"I would never punish someone for an offense they had no idea they had made. Of course, I agree. Speak, man."

"Sire, we used lesser gems and melted down the smaller gold and silver metals to pay wages to the men of the quarries to buy carts, tools, and food from the ranch. If this were wrong, we will make it right immediately."

My status made it harder for those who worked for me to see that they worked alongside me. Like so many others, I had to put their minds at ease.

"No, my friends, you were innovative in taking care of the needs of your workers and their families. Your help in providing for our defenses is equal to that of those who stand guard on them. You have done well. Continue storing what you find here and using what you need. When you have goods you deem worthy of the royal vault, we will transport them to the fourth tier. I will use it for the good of all the people, not hoard it for a rainy day."

Again, the two men looked at me curiously. I sense that once more, an Earth saying had impeded my meaning.

"On Earth, saving something for a rainy day means holding on to it for some matter of significance. I will use the treasure as necessary to continue helping all our people to prosper. On a side note, I do have a matter that you can help me with. It is personal."

I explained my current dilemma with Josia. The two men's eyes lit up.

Jihl reached over a stack of larger chests to pull a smaller one from the back. "We have just the thing for the young prince's project."

Rulk explained as he dug for a small pouch inside the chest. "We discovered this when we created this room." He motioned for me to hold my hand, then poured the contents into it. Gems of every color cascaded into my palms.

It was enough to ransom a king!

"Are you sure about this?" I didn't want the word to spread about the designs I had for the treasure, even though I had just specified that it was for the people's use.

The two smiled. Jihl took my full hands and folded them inwards. "I like Josia. He asks many interesting questions. Àrd-Rìgh, this particular bag of gems, is pretty to look at but has little measurable value."

I looked at the two of them as Rulk had given Jihl a look as if he had just given away a 'pinky swear.'

"Your secret is safe with me. I trust that a Glav was shadowing the boy and his bundle of fur?"

Both men nodded yes in agreement, and I smiled. "All right, as we agreed, send word when you have anything left after you take care of your men and their families. We will transport them to the royal treasury. Also, a month from today, present yourselves with a plan for smelting and coining the silver and gold ore."

"Will you be putting your face to currency, sire?"

I winked and bid them farewell. It was then that I wondered if we could put a queen's face on the coin instead of my ugly mug. I chuckled to myself.

I had work to do of a secretive and stealthy nature. It wasn't hard to get away with things with Josia. He was only five, after all. After he was all tucked in by Rachel, I waited about an hour before leaving.

"Where are you going?" Rachel asked, placing her book on her chest and waiting for a reasonable response.

"Do you want the long story or the short one?" I said with a chuckle.

She thought for a moment, "Does this involve a little guy and a white ball of fluff?"

"Why, yes, it does!" I chuckled.

"The long story then, I suppose."

I told her about Josia's drawing, his bartering with the old Skaldi armorer, and his need for gems.

"What will you do for gems for his project?"

I pulled the small bag from my side table drawer and poured the contents into her hands.

"Oh my! You're going to entrust this small treasure to a four-year-old?"

"I have been assured that these are far more decorative and much less valuable than anyone would guess. It is for a good cause."

"Your birthday is now a good cause?" She laughed. "What is your plan?"

I poured the gems back into the pouch. "I am going to tie this to the neck of Josia's teddy bear and hope he discovers them when he wakes up."

I got up to leave, and she stopped me. "Have you forgotten the ball of fur? He will bark, and your plan will end in ruin." She reached into her nightstand and pulled a small piece of Cook's beef jerky. "This will keep the furry one quiet while you tie the goods to the bear."

I kissed her on the forehead and began to tiptoe down the hall to where Josia slept. Rachel's part of the plan worked like a charm. Didn't that wolf ever sleep? Now, I will have to wait until morning for the outcome.

CHAPTER 47

The following morning, Shal-Dir and SunGru joined me in the great hall for breakfast. Nearby, Wilson and Allen debated something they had discovered. Kraq was eating with several of the Glav. When he finished his meal, I waved for him to join us. He headed our way while signaling to Cook that he needed a second plate.

We began discussing the plans for the day when Bolvi rushed through the doors, carrying a large chest. Adalwin followed closely behind. Setting the strongbox on a nearby table, the Red Clan leader sat down, and Cook brought him a plate of food. Adalwin waved Cook away, stressing that he would eat after he had 'shown the Àrd-Rìgh a rare and valuable treasure.' Silk padding covered the inside of the chest. Bolvi smacked my hand when I attempted to reach inside.

I looked down at the Dvergar, and the look I received made me sit back in my seat. It was all Kraq could do to contain his laughter when he saw the pout on my face – real or imagined.

Before me, Adalwin placed a silk package. Wrapped and cradled in the silk was a very solid-looking blue gem.

I looked at it briefly, "Could you cut this into smaller jewels for my crown?" I received another rather stern look, and then the Dvergar prince announced that this was an 'egg.'

Before I could stop him, Kraq took the gem. It looked small in the Skaldi's giant hand and began moving toward cracking it against the side of his plate. The yell that left Adalwin's throat brought Quaylin and Glav guards into the room at double time.

Adalwin threw himself across the table to stop the downward swing of the big Skaldi's hand. Kraq gave me a wink, so I knew he would not have harmed the 'egg' or whatever it was.

"I am sorry, Adalwin. Did you not just say that this was an egg?" Kraq innocently asked.

Adalwin placed the egg back on the silk wrap in front of me. "Yes, I did, but not the eating kind, you big clumsy ball of fur!"

I decided not to upset the Dvergar even more and politely asked, "What sort of egg makes it so wondrous?"

"May it please the Àrd-Rìgh to know that we found six such eggs hidden within the fortress under Mount Djuprot. If our Acrucian friends can incubate them, we may once more have griffins serving this kingdom as in the days yore."

It was as if I had not seen so many amazing things already! My life was sometimes more like a fairy tale than reality. I broke up the argument that Wilson and Allen were having and insisted that they focus on the task at hand. What temperature and how long did a griffin egg need to be heated for the eggs to hatch?

Bolvi had finished his plate and said his farewells. Lifting the chest and its eggs once more, Bolvi followed Wilson, Allen, and the Dvergar out of the hall in search of the Acrucians.

I looked at SunGru, who shrugged his shoulders.

"No one has seen any Griffons since before my great-great-grandfather. SunGru said that Griffins attended the Quaylin emperor of his time."

I made my way to the council chambers for a series of meetings. One of the reports I read was Father Emmaus's note regarding holy relics and writings sent to the cathedral for safekeeping. It was all to be kept in a different building to ensure they remained separate collections. A note in Brother Mathis's handwriting was at the end of the report. It requested that specific scrolls from the library be brought to Wilson for review.

I signed off on this report and decided to check in on our friend from Wales and his current work. Several hours before I needed to prepare for the evening, I headed to the great library. Allen had taken over an unprecedented amount of space. Wilson chose to work in a smaller wing now named after and in honor of Wilson's family name, The Cunnington Pavilion. I spotted Wilson surrounded by an unusual number of Acrucians.

"Wilson, not to interrupt, but I have a paper that requires your signature. It should provide some resources that you might find interesting."

"You mean from the basilica?" Wilson hadn't even bothered to look up, which was very Allen-like. "I just received them this morning, and you are correct. We have found some items of interest."

Some of the items in the silk-lined crates pre-dated the Flood itself. "There is mention of something known as the Path of the Winds. I am good with riddles, even ones five thousand years old," Wilson added.

I was quite the opposite. I did not enjoy riddles, but I was happy with straightforward answers.

On the Day Adam's Seed Enthroned

Cast, not the Crow's blood or the Bones

When Second Born Blood doth Atone

The Orb shall Breathe a Light Pursue

While Dragon's Fire Furnace Spew

The Paths of the Wind will be Renewed.

"What does that mean?" I asked, dumbfounded.

"That isn't all of it. Parts are missing by design. We found pieces like this written on the back of different scrolls. They might not even be from the same prophecy, so we have a lot of work ahead. The first line indicates that you were crowned as High King, we surmise. Do we also find a reference to what is perhaps a satanic ritual? I have no idea who the Second Born refers to," Wilson stated.

"Well, it can't mean angels. Angels do not experience birth in the same way humans do. Humans were the First Born. I wonder if Second Born is the Nephilim or Elioud?" The Acrucians became visibly agitated when I said the word Elioud.

"I will make a note of that, thank you."

CHAPTER 48

Almost six weeks to the day of the wedding and coronation, the same armies that had crushed the kingdom of Midia in a single night came knocking on our doorstep. While others on the council believed we were invincible, I disagreed.

The great Skaldi Red Clan leader Bolvi had been busy before he started on the great south road. He had foreseen the days when fortifications would come in handy at the entrances to the three passes. Bolvi began with the East Gate Pass, his Skaldi army carving stones from the pass's center. Large squares of stone now formed a thirty-foot-tall defensive wall, equal in thickness. The fortification's top level had parapets for hiding archers. A watchtower sat to either side of the gatehouse. The two-foot-thick gates, made of tall planks from the Karuk Forest, would stop most armies.

The Acrucians provided a solution to seal the gates. When applied to wood, this liquid resembled a clear coat, but gave the wood steel-like qualities. The gates were nearly impervious to fire and would withstand a prolonged siege. Achieving the main gates' surrender, you might think you had accomplished something, when in fact, before you lay thirty feet of space at the end of which you would have another gate to breach. Worse than that, behind you would drop a portcullis of immense strength, cutting you off from escape or rescue.

Enemies trapped in the narrow twenty-foot-wide gatehouse tunnel were now vulnerable to what came from the slots in both the walls and ceiling. Projectiles from the sides and hot oil from above would rain down on the enemy. If you made it through that, you would hit the second set of gates thirty feet further. It was a brilliantly rugged design. A nearly identical fortress was in the planning stages at the South Gate Pass's entrance.

The East Gate was no longer lightly manned as Cedric and the Knights of Midia had made it their place to defend. Banners flew unfurled from the two watchtowers. Footmen and archers patrolled the walls day and night. Mounted knights now rode from those gates on daily patrols.

I will tell you now, that matters of state care little for your hunger pains. If you plan a breakfast meeting, especially if you are looking forward to that meal, someone or something is bound to interrupt. It happened the day we were to plant the seeds from the giant trees of the Karuk Forest to celebrate our Karuk friends.

The ranch, which sat between the two lakes, was the new resting place of the seedlings of the giant trees. For those who embrace the circle of life, it is a never-ending series of interruptions or opportunities. This morning, such was the case. With meetings planned and a fantastic breakfast about to be devoured, I was excited!

One of the Midian captains arrived out of breath, bearing an urgent message from the East Gate Pass fortifications. My fork was near my lip, a cut of three layers of pancakes dripping with raspberry-like syrup and a chunk of sausage. Then I realized that if I didn't stuff the contents of my fork into my mouth that instant, I might not get the chance to enjoy my meal, so I proceeded.

I waved to him to speak as I ate. It seemed that a lone figure had advanced to the newly fortified East Gate Pass gates and collapsed.

Then, the knights brought him through the gates and gave the man water when he announced that an army of some size would soon reach his village. This town had told Cedric and his men about the City of Hope.

The man's name was Gelfan. Gelfan was the son of the village's leader, known for his tremendous stamina and running ability. He had come to warn us and ask for assistance in defending his home.

Further attempts at bites of my breakfast were far from thought as the council went from a typical day to war room status. Thanks to Bolvi, the fortifications at the East Gate Pass could hold back an invading army.

It would be several months before the defensive construction at the Southgate Pass was complete. The entire Quaylin army would pour out of it to crush anyone who attempted to breach it.

The North Gate Pass was another story altogether. Mt. Djuprot was still being mapped out, but a force of several hundred Dvergar now claimed it as home. While there were no fancy fortifications at the mouth of the pass, the tower bridge system had not been repaired from the devastating collapse caused by the Nidhug.

The mountain range surrounding the city and our hidden valley was known as The Line – it was the best natural defense of our lands.

I watched as the outer halls filled with the sounds of messengers arriving and departing, carrying out the will of the Àrd-Rìgh to every corner of our small kingdom. Our friends had asked for aid, and we would answer.

There were always little arguments between the aged Quaylin general and the prince of the Blue Clans, as expected when two great warriors have different opinions. Still, you could now hear a pin drop as I rose to my feet.

When I did that, I wondered what would happen if I said something like 'just getting a refill on my wine' or 'going to take a nap, be back later.' Such times seldom allowed for light humor.

"I gather from all this talk that we have no idea of enemy numbers. Yet they are within several days' march of the Eastgate Pass?"

SunGru and Kraq turned their heads in my direction, having been nearly eye to eye, fingers jabbing at the map on the table, stating the obvious. "Yes."

Adoeete's Karuk riders were now the fastest means of scouting. Their messengers were already winging their way to the village as our meeting progressed. Adoeete spoke, "Àrd-Rìgh, by tonight, you will know more about the enemy than they know about you."

I nodded. I was thankful that the Karuk people had become part of our close-knit community. Andy called them 'the Àrd-Rìgh Air Force.'

"Thank you, Adoeete. Your riders are key to us having as much information as possible." Turning back towards SunGru and Kraq. "You two can argue and point all you want, but I will not move to march until we know what we are facing. If the numbers are too great, we will engage them at the East Gate Pass defenses and harass them with Skaldi from the north and cavalry from the south. Until the riders return, I will not put this city or her people at risk. Raise the bridges. Only messengers and soldiers will cross them."

There was some grumbling from the end of the table, which I expected.

News of the enemy's location and numbers would take the riders several hours to acquire. Dividing our armies into three equal groups, the city's defense was complete. Kraq had pointed out that he already had the tower bridge system closed down at North Gate Castle. "I will leave a few men on the walls, and the rest of my men will help defend the South Gate Pass."

"What if the enemy occupies the North Gate Pass?" SunGru asked.

"I need a whip to make my men patrol that place. It is a dark place. If the enemy wants it, they can have it! If they were to make such a mistake, we could easily drive them back up the pass where they would fall off the edge of a cliff just within reach of the city." Kraq and his Skaldi army were appointed to reinforce SunGru and the Quaylin army at the South Gate Pass. Bolvi and his men were already at the East Gate Pass with the Knights of Midia.

Riders flew to the basilica to warn Brother Mathis and Aig of our situation. The repairs at the Tower of Erudition were well underway but far from finished. I would leave it up to Father Emmaus and his Skaldi general to determine whether they planned to defend their current position or retreat to the City of Hope's safety. Adalwin and his people were assigned to guard the Vale and Mount Djuprot.

From my vantage point atop the King's Tower, I could see many Skaldi moving across the bridge tower system towards the South Gate Pass. I saw men pouring from South Gate Castle as SunGru rallied his enormous army.

With Cedric's help, Rachel could get as many defensive units to the battle mounds as possible. Her deadly group of skilled archers, known as The Red Brigade, could be carried to the front by the Knights of Midia. The Red Brigade was the top one percent of the kingdom's archers, led by Rachel. These bowmen employed all the tricks that Rachel and Jim could devise. In addition to their stealth and deadly accuracy, they were also quite explosive. Thanks to Andy, they now had explosive-tipped arrows.

The Quaylin infantry will arrive several hours behind Cedric and Rachel. For now, five hundred knights and five hundred archers stood ready at the Battle Mounds. Leo, Lynn, and the excited toddler Josia showed up to see me off. Leo and Shal-Dir were charged to lead the city in my stead if things went badly for us. I flew to the East Gate Pass defenses and lead the Infantry onto the field. Always present were my Glav bodyguards.

The remaining Glav paced the walls of the city, ever vigilant. Facilitated by the gunpowder Adalwin and his Dvergar had saved from the Mines of Verlaq, Adoeete, and Andy prepared for their initial bombing run.

The same video technology Andy had used to help us map and measure the city would also help us identify the enemy leaders. The answer was unsettling. The Acrucians identified Abezethibou and Dumah as the leaders of the opposing army. Abezethibou was a name I had already come across, written on the walls of a pyramid discovered by one of the parties searching for SunGru's family.

The fallen angel gave Pharaoh's wise men the power to match Moses when he went to face Pharaoh and reveal God's power. This same angel led Pharaoh's army to a watery grave at the Red Sea.

The second angel, Abezethibou, had once been well-favored by God. He belonged to the Order of Thrones. These two would be powerful on their own, even more so together. Andy estimated that as many as 10,000 enemy troops were marching to our location.

Our adversaries included Skaldi and Ator warriors, but more than half were human. The discussion on my virtues, trying to sway any enemies to my side, went sideways when some of our knights seemed to recognize a unit of Skaldi. Time to get our war on!

Andy took a right and Adoeete took the left as the Karuk riders took to the sky. The bombardment will first serve as a devastating smokescreen, allowing Kraq and SunGru to move their troops. Explosions always have the desired effect.

The units on the outside move away from them, causing the main groups to bunch up and become less effective in combat. Most of the Skaldi clan flags were green or black, indicating that no diplomatic help would be forthcoming from Kraq or Bolvi.

The Ator unit flags made no sense to me. I once saw a banner that bore a field of blue and a yellow sun. Inside the yellow sun was the black outline of an eye. These were the humans who followed their God, Abezethibou. The remaining humans also carried flags with a field of blue, but at its center was a red sphere with golden wings of the God, Dumah. It was shortly after the second bombing run by the Karuk riders that I noticed clouds of dust. Kraq and SunGru will soon be within striking distance.

Enemy archers took their positions, and I called for a shield wall that proved unnecessary since the enemy found us out of range for their shorter weapons. I turned to see our red-headed queen stand, raise her bow above her head, and motion for all the knights to make ready. The few Eridu were all in the Red Brigade. The Red Brigade now stood, and the battle horns sounded. As Rachel brought her bow from her head to her side, the sound of the Skaldi and Eridu's longbows release along the line was my sign to begin my charge.

Before I had the word 'charge' shouted from my lips, the longbows had sent another deadly hail of arrows into the enemy's ranks. As the third wave of projectiles let loose, I motioned for the Knights of Midia to form ranks behind me.

The job of a heavy cavalry charge is to split the enemy right down the middle. As the initial mounted attack drove into the belly of the enemy, I glanced to either side. The enemy was breaking ranks to face the great battle axes of Kraq's men and the Quaylin light cavalry charge from the south. In our first attack, the heavy cavalry used their javelins. These great spears could skewer three men at once if appropriately used. We turned to our swords as we fought against both mounted and ground troops.

A group of about fifty knights had swept past me in the melee. There was no worry for my safety as several Glav fought around my position. I stood in my saddle for a better vantage point. I saw several knights seemingly mowed down as they charged a group of better-armed enemy soldiers who formed a defensive line. Still, more enemy troops began to rally to this group. I sent word to sound a signal to reform the massive cavalry formation and moved those with me in seeming retreat through my com.

As we reformed, I noticed we were missing a few knights. We would miss their stories around the campfires and their swords in the next charge. The group forming against us revealed their leadership as the two fallen angels stepped from their troops' ranks. They were like the noonday sun on the field, mighty and resilient in their armor, holding their flaming swords.

Behind them, I could see a group of at least twelve Elioud. Then, as if hidden from our eyes by magic, the figures of three massive Nephilim began to form. I could almost see a sneer forming on the lips of the two angels. The Nephilim were at least thirty feet in height! Giants!

In the chaos of my mind, I could hear another voice fighting against the fear that would take me. As I took several deep breaths, it broke free. "Fear not! If the Maker stands with you, who can stand against you?"

I stammered the word 'Lailoken'?

The figure sitting on the horse next to me was not Lailoken. To my right, astride a warhorse, was Brock with a .50 caliber sniper rifle across his legs. "Yeah. Now would be a good time for Lailoken to show up! If your majesty doesn't mind, I am going to get you the head of one of those things", Brock said, pointing at the approaching Nephilim.

I nodded as I raised my sword to announce the second charge.

I looked back to my right, and the figure staring at me was not anyone I recognized.

"Robert John Armstrong, I am the Archangel Saraqael. I am the judge of those who violate divine law. I am sent in your hour of need to bring hope where there is none. No weapon brandished against you this day will prevail. Go and fight without fear!"

Then, the horse and figure blurred in an impossible push toward the enemy. I was already nearly at a full gallop. Just ahead, I could see a giant Nephilim fall to one knee as Brock emptied a ten-round magazine into its shoulder, which now hung limp. The giant's sword also dropped from its hand and embedded itself in the ground.

Even as this happened, Brock had already slapped another clip into the weapon and fired a volley directly at the giant's head, protected by its large helmet. The giant responded, removing its helm and tossing it in Brock's direction. With the giant's helmet rushing through the air at him, Brock fired another burst, tearing apart the giant's left cheek and blinding the giant in one eye.

Within a second, I saw the helmet smash Brock and his horse while the thirty-foot titan took its last breath, bleeding out on the battlefield. There was a sudden change in the morale of the humans who had witnessed this. A single human on a horse had killed one of their great warriors.

The effect on our side was a roar as new hope and vigor overtook our men. Abezethibou moved against us while Dumah turned away as Saraqael revealed his identity. I could see the rage that filled Abezethibou, and the words on the stone tablets resounded in my ears.

I am the Lord your God. I brought you from Egypt out of slavery's house. No other gods shall be served before me. Do not make for yourself an idol, whether in the form of anything in heaven, the

Earth beneath, or the underground waters. You shall not bow down or worship them. As the Lord your God, I am jealous, punishing children for parents' iniquity to the third and fourth generation of those who reject me. Yet, there is my steadfast love for the thousandth generation of those who love me and keep my commandments. You shall not wrongfully use the name of the Lord your God, for the Lord will not acquit anyone who misuses his name.

At that moment, I saw not through my human sight but the glimpses I would get from time to time as the Àrd-Rìgh. For a moment, time stood still. Saraqael stood before Abezethibou. I could see the angel in all his glory, including the single crimson wing he now sported.

"Brother, your crimes against creation and the Maker are beyond measure, but I will list a few. In the First War in Heaven, you sided with Beelzebub and were thrown from Heaven's Gates even as Archangel Michael cleaved a wing from your back. After that, you took up residence in the land of Egypt and ruled as a deity, breaking the laws of the Maker. You stood against the Maker and opposed his chosen people. You escaped imprisonment and continued in your evil ways. Let justice now be served. As you have lived by the sword, so shall you die by the same."

There was a flash as Saraqael moved towards the one-winged fallen angel. Even as Abezethibou raised his shattering sword, a blue flame split his head from his body. The next moment, I saw Saraqael standing over the now kneeling Dumah.

"Brother, your crimes against the Maker are grievous as well, but for your great deeds in the First War of Heaven, your sentence this day would be death. You stand on the knife's edge. You can choose to do the one thing you hate most, which serves man, or I can judge you and find you wanting. Which shall it be? I will remind you that should you fail the Àrd-Rìgh in any way, I will not hesitate to return and deal out a terrible and swift punishment."

Dumah nodded and presented his sword to Saraqael, who waved me forward to accept the sword. In the next moment, the battle rushed over us. We stood back to back; blue flames now wreathed both blades.

While Dumah moved to attack the last remaining Nephilim titan, Saraqael, and I began with the six Elioud standing before us. Looking back, I could see the remaining Elioud joining Dumah. As I continued the battle, I saw the second of the Nephilim titans brought to the ground. Its body looked like a giant pincushion laced with the long spears of the Quaylin cavalry. The Skaldi were busy trying to remove its head from its torso. From an engineering standpoint, I almost regretted seeing a being of that size lost. Think of the work Bolvi could have accomplished.

That night, we withdrew to the battle mounds and moved our wounded towards the East Gate Pass and its defenses. We could hear the howls of the Fenri deep into the night as packs of giant wolves roamed the battlefield and fed on the dead and dying.

In the morning, they were gone, but carrion birds now took their place. The captured Skaldi and Ator prisoners dug two great ditches as we sorted our dead from the enemy and scavenged the battlefield for armor and weapons. Most enemy soldiers had been cut down in battle or had refused to surrender. I had hoped to secure most of Dumah's human troops, but as soon as he chose my service over death, his followers no longer saw him as a god, a fitting tribute and humiliating, to be sure.

The battle mounds had become monolithic tributes to the battles fought to sustain the City of Hope. Between the two sets of burial mounds were the now earth-covered trenches filled with the bodies of those who had made the ultimate sacrifices. Dumah had helped drive two of the titan's swords into the ground at either end of those trenches, leaving the hilt and a portion of the sword blade sticking above the ground. Then, a giant's helmet was placed over each sword, sheltering it from the weather. I stared down at the .50 caliber rifle that now hung across my saddle. I will miss Brock, and we buried him with full military honors inside the grounds of the cathedral.

I wondered what future generations would believe happened here. The enemy had destroyed the empty village, but the inhabitants had fled into the forest. When we discovered them, Bolvi insisted on plans for a town at the East gate and convinced the surviving villagers to relocate to the safety of the fortifications.

CHAPTER 49

I was happy to return to the tower and see Josia and Smar. When Rachel and I arrived in our bedroom, I started a small fire in the fireplace. "You look tired. I didn't see you eat that much at dinner. I thought you liked the mulled cider and cake?"

Rachel nodded, "I haven't had much appetite the last couple of days. Possibly the flu or something."

"Make sure you see Gretchen and have her give you something for it."

With a kiss, I tugged back my share of the blankets. Rachel responded by yanking all the blankets from my side. I countered with tickling and another tug to get some general coverage.

The battle, I assumed, was over. Neither party had gained any ground until I felt a very cold foot wrap around my calf and the sound of giggling coming from beneath the covers.

Revenge! I was too tired to care. I was the happiest man in this realm, or any other.

I was not alone in the morning. I meant to say that Rachel was already gone, and Josia and Smar were asleep in her place. I felt someone trying to open my eyes. There, as close to me as he could get, was Josia staring at me.

"Are you awake yet?"

"No."

"You look awake."

"No, I am not."

"You're talking."

"I am sleep-talking."

"What is sleep-talking?"

"Never mind."

"So awake?"

"Yes, I suppose I am."

"Smar and I is hungry."

"Smar and I are hungry," I corrected.

"Yes, and me too!" Josia giggled with Smar, voicing his own excitement.

I laughed. Correcting a four-year-old was impossible. "Okay, get dressed, and we will find some food."

The prince looked me eye to eye. "I dressed," he declared.

He was wearing his nightshirt and cowboy boots. For a four-year-old, that was appropriate breakfast attire. I climbed out of bed.

"Put clothes on?"

I shrugged and put on my crown. I had that and my underwear on.

"I am ready!"

"Please no." Josia giggled.

"Why not?"

"Mommy will be mad!"

"Right." I decided on a shirt, trousers, a fur-lined bathrobe, and slippers.

With Josia and Smar under each arm, we headed down to the great hall for breakfast. Rachel was not there, but we decided to eat the pancakes, or they would get cold. A few more council members and their families arrived, but there was no sign of Rachel.

Finally, Rachel, Gretchen, Becki, Allen, and Jim came to sit at our table.

"RJ, Rachel has some news to share," Gretchen said.

"She has the flu," I added between bites, wiping the syrup off my beard.

"Oh, she has more than the flu, RJ," Jim chuckled.

Andy and Bill arrived to join in on the fun.

"Oh yes, she is not contagious, just antenatal," Allen added.

I had no idea what antenatal meant.

"RJ, I have been throwing up every morning for a week," Rachel said.

I nodded, feeding Josia a bite of pancakes and passing a piece under the table for Smar. "You have the flu."

Becky laughed. "You shouldn't be so negative. Be like Rachel. She's positive."

Kraq reached over and set what appeared to be a crude wooden manger in front of me, which he had hastily carved. I took little note of the clear statement he was attempting to make. It was almost Christmas after all. Looking back on this, I must have been the most oblivious man ever.

Bill walked over to my end of the table and whispered in my ear. "I feel like I am going to be a grandfather, and it's about time!"

Okay, things in my brain started calculating. Perhaps it was some algorithm or neutrons slamming into protons. I had no idea what was going on. Rachel leaned over and whispered something into Josia's ear. He stood up on his chair and pulled my head over. He whispered in my ear.

"Who's my Daddy?" I asked out loud. I was a little confused now.

Rachel whispered in Josia's ear again.

The little boy said, "Oh, you are the daddy!" he announced to me, and the whole table laughed.

Then, all that stuff in my brain came together – the loss of appetite, the throwing up, a positive, not an adverse reaction. Was I going to be a dad? I got up, gave Rachel a huge hug, and a kiss.

Josia wormed between us. "Hey, what is going on here?"

Smar was there barking in excitement. Rachel leaned down and whispered something else in his ear.

Josia's eyes got big, and he blurted out, "I'm going to get a brother?"

Well, this would have happened eventually, so we took a walk together and found the quiet of the throne room for a talk. Josia knew that we weren't his biological parents. He was young, and there were some complex issues he would not understand until later in his life. So, he had figured that since he lived with Rachel to start, they had both moved in here when Rachel married me, which made us a family. Josia agreed that we would be a family, with the understanding that Smar would be included.

I am unsure how the word got out that Rachel was pregnant, although my spies point to Andy and Shal-Dir as two of the primary spreaders of the joyous news. Jubilation and celebration swept through the city. I had better enjoy the peace while I could. In nine months, I would undoubtedly be a delighted sleep-deprived man.

CHAPTER 50

We had defeated a significant threat to the City of Hope only a few months ago. It felt strange to see the once-fallen Dumah working with Allen and Wilson in the library, or to see him hovering over a project the Acrucians were working on in their workshops. He had not attempted to leave the city. Stranger yet were the actions of the six Elioud who had chosen to remain loyal to him.

I had just finished my morning briefing and was about to take the elevator down to the city to discuss the recent events with Cherubim Zophiel. One of the Glav guarding the King's Tower's open doorway beckoned me to his side. I found it unusual for one of my guardians to act in such a manner until I realized his reason for the silent come-hither treatment. There stood Dumah, who looked like a quarterback in a football huddle with his six Elioud. There was no clapping of the hands or a shout of blue forty-two, just a dismissive look.

The angel walked away, reading one of the library's manuscripts. He didn't look in my direction. I had no idea whether he could sense I was hiding in the nearby doorway. I pulled the Glav who had alerted me further into the shadows and said nothing. I merely pointed two fingers at my eyes, then out towards the Elioud, walking towards the gatehouse that would take them from the fifth tier of the city. I could not even guess where they were going or what they would do when they arrived. Yet, I had to know. A simple nod from the Glav, and I knew the Elioud would pick up a tail. Shortly, I would know what they had planned.

Beyond a doubt, I had to see the report in person to verify its claims. I returned to the room and excused myself from the meeting. Then, I wrote my speedy response on the back of the report and informed the Glav captain of my plans. I then hurried to the rooftop to find a rider waiting to take me wherever I needed to go.

My first stop was the South Gate Pass, where Bolvi had nearly finished putting the final touches on the defenses. Andy had heard I was in the air and joined me once I told him over the comms what was happening. Together, we landed where Bolvi and SunGru now stood, looking skyward. We were just inside the mountain pass, several hundred yards from the gates.

"RJ, what is going on?" SunGru asked.

"I was going to ask you two the same thing. I have no idea. Two of the Elioud were on the move after they met with Dumah. I put them under Glav surveillance and was informed of their locations while I ate."

Bolvi pointed to his newly built twin towers above and on either side of the gatehouse. It was getting dark, although inside the pass, it was hard to see beyond the torchlights of a growing number of Quaylin and Skaldi warriors. They now gathered, staring up to the spot where Bolvi pointed.

I broke the awkward silence. "I don't see anything. What am I looking for?"

"My Skaldi eyes are a bit keener in the dark. Give the darkness a moment to settle in," Bolvi announced in an almost whisper.

We stood there momentarily as dusk set in, and a few stars came alive in the night sky. Then, I could see a slight glow in the towers.

Just before the brightness hid them completely, I saw the outline of a single Elioud. Sword raised before their chests, standing in the highest window of the towers facing onto the plains.

Like a pair of lone lighthouses on a ragged seacoast – a beacon. A beacon? I did not want to jump to any conclusion, but were they signaling our enemies?

Cedric announced a similar situation over the comms, affecting the two towers of the East Gate Pass. Jim was with Cedric and asked if he had a kill shot. Should he attempt it?

I told him to wait. Then, there were signs of action at the gates, shouting from the Skaldi and Quaylin guarding the gates. As we watched, the gates swung open. Many refugees stumbled through the opening, led by one of the Quaylin captains, ShiUle, and several scouts.

ShiUle staggered towards SunGru and me. I saw several crude arrows protruding from his left leg and side in the torchlight. SunGru rushed forward as Bolvi caught the Quaylin captain as he collapsed from his saddle.

ShiUle passed out in the Skaldi's arms. The next moment, Bolvi ran at full speed toward one of the medical tents. As the gates closed, I could see archers tensing on the parapets above and releasing a hailstorm of death at a foe beyond the walls that I could not see from the ground.

One of the scouts, who seemed less injured, bowed low before his general and king. "Àrd-Rìgh. General. We were out on a simple recon mission and came across this group.

They claimed that Fenri and Skaldi had been attacking them for nearly a week. Their numbers were twice this when we met them, but the attacks over the last three nights dampened our resolve. We had all but given up on reaching the pass when the light of the beacons blazed to life as if in answer to our despair. It seemed to repulse those chasing us, but it did not keep us completely safe. Thank you for lighting the beacons. We lost our way in the darkness like some power blurred the night sky, hiding the stars from us."

SunGru sent the scout off to the tent, where they served the group water and day-old bread with cheese. I called over the comms, "Jim?"

"Yes, RJ?"

"Leave the Elioud be, but have the men on the walls shoot some flaming arrows up to be sure there are no enemies at your gates."

"Copy that."

Then it hit me. There were no defenses on the North Gate Pass. "Andy, let's fly. I have a feeling that Kraq may need our help."

The North Gate Pass was a lonely place I had passed over and looked out at but never desired to enter. Even on a clear day, the surrounding mountains made it dark. Where the Skaldi has no desire to go is a place better left alone. The pass was far steeper, taller, and narrower than the other two. Nearby stood the highest peak in "The Line," the name we had given to the protective mountain range surrounding the city and the land beyond the lake.

As we landed at the North Gate Castle, Kraq greeted us in the courtyard. To my surprise, beside him strode Adalwin. Seeing my surprise, Kraq looked down at the Dvergar.

"Oh, we had an issue with one of the bridge tower systems. Adalwin was more than happy to take a look. What is happening?"

Once we had climbed to the gatehouse, I pointed out a faint blue glow in the distance at the pass. Kraq picked up the Dvergar clan chief and set him on the parapet's top for a better look. Kraq and Adalwin both looked at each other, nearly eye to eye. "That wasn't here last night," Kraq stated, and Adalwin nodded in agreement. I explained what had begun earlier in the day.

"We don't go out there anymore," Kraq pointed at the pass. "With the meat Bill sends us, I don't even have men positioned in the bridge tower system. I raised every bridge and pulled my men back to the castle. If we need the bridges down, we send a company to re-establish the connections and go from there. I am sorry, RJ, I have no idea what that glow is."

I put a hand on my friend's arm. I recounted the story of Dumah and the Elioud, who now operated the towers in the outer defenses. "Something about that place makes the hair on my neck stand on end. I would have pulled back as well, but I need to get a closer look. I wouldn't mind a group of heavily armed Skaldi following me while I did."

Kraq nodded and gathered some of his men, with Adalwin following. When they returned, I counted about fifty Skaldi and many Dvergar fully armed and ready for combat. In the meantime, several Glav had also arrived. They sensed danger and were prone to stand between it and me.

With Andy circling above, a hundred of us began to move across the bridges. We left two men at each tower, who pulled the bridge behind us and lowered it as needed. I saw that Jim had joined Andy in the air about halfway across the chasm. To my relief, they each had a .50 caliber rifle slung across their shoulders.

Crossing the final gap between the last tower and where the bridge met the jagged edge of the pass, Kraq and Adalwin moved slowly towards the glow of the two Elioud. Just beyond the blue luminosity given off by the two Elioud's swords was a wall of black, more profound than the night swirling just out of reach.

Adalwin sniffed the air and then moved forward, waving for us to stay put. Behind us, Kraq and the combined Skaldi and Dvergar battalion tensed and waited. The Dvergar Prince stood between the Elioud and, removing his helm, pushed his large nose into the air. I will swear that his ears wiggled along with his nose.

I almost yelled aloud when he took several steps beyond the Elioud and their outstretched swords, whose light grew even more intense. Again, with the nose and ears, Adalwin, Prince of the blue griffin clan, turned and marched back to whisper something in Kraq's ear, and then he took off running back towards the castle.

I don't know which I noticed first: Kraq's eyes bulging behind the monstrous eyebrows, or Adalwin, now running towards the bridge system at full speed. I heard some decidedly Skaldi oaths coming from Kraq. As I turned to ask him what was going on, he breathed a word in a roar caught somewhere between sheer terror and total disbelief.

He managed to say one word, "Nidhug."

There was no direct translation, which occasionally happened. Kraq grabbed me and tucked me under one arm. He did the same to Adalwin as we approached the running Dvergar. I looked into his eyes as I saw his mind trying to grasp a word from my language that would equal his terror. Finally, one word escaped his lips - dragon.

Sensing something was amiss, Andy and Jim reacted with two grenades dropped into the darkness. Several shots rang out. I heard the explosions, then felt them. As Kraq ran with me under one arm, I turned my head just long enough to see the two Elioud with swords that had merely given out a powerful blue light only a moment before. Now, they seemed to battle with the black mist itself.

The grenades had hit their mark, and the two Elioud seemed to be taking a toll against whatever was within the darkness. Screeches that made the hairs on my neck stand on end emanated from the darkness behind us.

Suddenly, I saw a third being appear between the struggling Elioud. Dumah! He seemed to wait for everyone to cross the first set of bridges toward safety. When all were safely moving towards the second bridge, he grabbed both Elioud. In an instant, he had gone from the edge of the swirling darkness to the three of them standing behind us on the parapets of the Skaldi stronghold.

Andy and Jim had landed nearby and were already firing shots across the quarter-mile span. The .50 caliber shells kept whatever was within the darkness at bay until we had all reached the safety of the castle. Then, a massive swirl of darkness rose and hovered on the first tower. Inside the swirling night, we could see occasional bursts of red flame.

Kraq, the Dvergar prince, and I started up the winding steps to the parapets. I heard the not-so-calm voice of Shal-Dir yelling for everyone to get out of his way. I saw the Eridu leader carrying a sizeable metallic object towards the steps of the gatehouse. Kraq and I arrived just in time to see Shal-Dir shoulder what appeared to be some Acrucian weapon, yelling for everyone to get clear of him.

He aimed and fired at the swirling blackness on the peak of the closest tower to the pass. The weapon pulsed, the recoil nearly knocking the Eridu leader off his feet. A projectile moved across the void at a rapid rate and hit something. We could feel the impact as the whole system of bridges and towers shook.

Did I see a wing in the swirling smoke? Shal-Dir balanced himself against the rock wall and fired a second shot. The second shot hit center mass. There was no question this time. We saw a tremendous dark bulk fall upon the tower it perched on. As it toppled forward, it hit the bridge connecting the first two towers.

The bridge buckled and twisted. We watched as the total weight of the Nidhug pulled both buildings and the bridge between them into the gorge. I wondered what sort of being the Nidhug was, as it never fully revealed itself to us.

If the brave Skaldi had not been able to raise the bridge at the third tower, the entire bridge system for the North Gate Pass might have fallen into the abyss. Many people shook hands and patted Shal-Dir on the back, when I approached. "First, let me say I appreciate you coming to our rescue! Then I have to ask what that thing is?" as I thrust my hand into his.

"The Àrd-Rìgh is most welcome. I suspected it was a weapon and brought it when I heard about the situation here," Shal-Dir replied.

"Well, then it was lucky they had something like that to give us," I said graciously.

"Luck had nothing to do with this at all," Shal-Dir said, looking rather grim-faced.

"What do you mean?" Kraq asked.

The response was unnerving. "The Acrucians told me I had one shot, and then it would no longer have the energy for a second blast. I fired the weapon a second time, but did not expect any result. The Acrucians no longer possess the technology to repair it," Shal-Dir said.

Andy then muscled his way into the conversation. "You're telling me that the first shot, which had an effect but failed to kill that thing, was the only shot left in the weapon's energy reserves?"

Shal-Dir nodded yes.

"Then luck indeed had nothing to do with this. Far more providence was involved in this case," I responded. "Post guards! I will stay here tonight, though if it returns, I do not doubt my sword but the arm that wields it. We will take riders to see what we can find tomorrow. I also want it known that anyone who doubts the loyalty of Dumah or the six Elioud with him need no longer have any doubts. Without them, this night, many lives may have been lost."

We ventured onto the bridge system in the morning to examine the damage. The first two towers, including their bridges, were gone. You could see the remains of the base pinnacles were still there, a hundred feet below. Adalwin informed me that he could repair the tower bridge system, but it would be a lengthy process. Even the plans to fortify the far end of North Gate Pass seemed senseless. We had no way to cross, and neither could an enemy. However, the Dvergar leader pointed up at the tower behind us. To my surprise, two Elioud stood with their swords outstretched.

When I questioned Dumah why they needed to be in the tower, he merely stated, "Something is still out there," and continued browsing the scroll he had picked up to read.

Is something still out there? Did he mean in the mountain pass or the world in general? I was grateful that his pride had given way to reason when choosing between serving me and death.

"Dumah," I waited for his gaze to move from the scroll to lock eyes with me, "thank you, you saved many lives."

He nodded. His eyes and face seemed slightly more relaxed now.

CHAPTER 51

I had often thought about flying to the bottom of the gorge. I recalled the day that Shal-Dir had shown me from underneath the city. Finding the spot where the nightmare from the evening before had landed was not difficult. I use the word landed loosely, as it had more or less crashed a thousand feet to the canopy below. The Nidhug had smashed fully grown trees and several acres of brush beneath its weight.

The ruins of the two towers and both bridge systems were nearby. Adalwin was charged with overseeing a team to recover the mechanics of the tower-bridge systems. The creature itself sent a chill through everyone in our group. It was massive. I could see why Adalwin had thought 'dragon' at that moment.

To be fair to the Dvergar prince, the meaning of the word Nidhug might not have been anything like the image that entered Kraq's mind. Kraq's idea of a dragon might not have been my idea of a dragon. Perhaps the translation was measured by the intensity of Adalwin's fear, standing toe-to-toe with my worst nightmare.

Ultimately, the body that lay before us in no way changed the fear we felt or the horror that we had survived. It was clear that the .50-caliber rounds had taken their toll on the monster, but how many more snipers would we have needed to stop the beast, rather than just making it angrier?

Now a 'dragon,' at least one from Earth, looks lizard-like with almost serpent-like wings. This gruesome specimen was as much a wolf as a serpent. It had two legs, and its arm-like wings were more bird than bat-like. Not an Earthly dragon by any means, and the legs ended in paw-like appendages with great razor-sharp claws.

We could see a silver disc that had nearly ripped through the connecting tissue between the ribs and the wings located behind the front shoulder on the left side. This wound might account for the initial loss of balance that occurred before the second shot took it down. The second disc was lodged in the front of the beast's neck, piercing a major artery and causing the monster to topple from the first tower to its final resting place.

Adalwin and his men were cutting the claws from the beast's paws. Some were working on cutting out the teeth from the massive, crushed head. I wasn't sure why and didn't bother asking the purpose.

Later, I reflected on what would have occurred had Abezethibou used this monster from the abyss against us. Together, they might now hold the city. I needed some answers, so I asked Dumah to join Shal-Dir and I for supper in my war room.

Dumah seemed more laid-back after I thanked him for his help. He briefly commented on the impressive job of bringing the people together and mentioned several accomplishments he had noticed during our guest's visit.

I will also state that he could have read all those things in the same library reports that any citizen could browse. "Let me cut to the chase here. Where did you and Abezethibou come from with that army?"

He first looked at Shal-Dir and then back to me. "From the east."

Shal-Dir stood up and seemed to loom over the former Babylonian God of agriculture. "You will answer the Àrd-Rìgh. When you do, remember the oath you swore to serve him."

Dumah nodded, "I am sorry, Àrd-Rìgh. I will provide more details in my answers. Yes, from the east to the seacoast and the capital city of the Kingdom of Midia."

Capital would refer to other cities that Cedric and I had yet to discuss. Perhaps the Lord Marshal thought the same fate had befallen all his fellow citizens. "Then there are other cities that your army attacked?"

"No." There was a stern look from Shal-Dir. "I mean, yes, but we only helped in the attack at the capital, and then we were sent off to capture the remaining knights and the boy."

"Other angels led attacks against the other cities. Meanwhile, you and Abezethibou needed ten thousand men and three giants to track down a couple of hundred warriors guarding a little boy?"

"Yes, we needed the boy to use as leverage against the leaders of the other Midian cities."

"What other cities, and who controls them?"

"There are two larger cities, smaller than the capital. One is inland, and the other is on the coast to the north. Then, several smaller towns and villages are controlled by the Fallen One known as Oliver, and the others are unknown."

"How many enemies are in Midia?" I asked.

"Somewhat less than we brought to the fight with you," replied Dumah.

"Are there more titans? Giant Nephilim?"

"I do not know. Abezethibou summoned the giants from the north. They were brothers."

"What else can you tell me about Midia?" I continued to question.

"I will be blunt. You will need more men and should use a two-pronged approach to attack. Oliver will prepare himself for a counter-attack when there is no word of the success or failure of our search for the boy or the battle that ensued. I suggest that you attack by both land and sea." Dumah said.

I nodded. It was a solid plan. There was only one small problem. I had no ships!

CHAPTER 52

The push towards Regis Bay was not as easy as everyone had hoped. Building a highway was a monumental task, even with a thousand Skaldi. I had checked with Wilson, and he informed me that the Romans had erected mile markers, often pillars standing 20 feet tall. Also carved on the base was the number of miles. A crossroads mile marker might be more detailed depending on how many destinations were on the road. For now, I just had Bolvi pile a few large stones as they went. A stone road would have to wait until spring or summer next year.

They began their push into the second half of the journey, which would involve some hill country, followed by trees and thicker brush, until they reached the ocean. In the summer, the plan was to build the road itself and small, easily defended outposts every twenty-five miles. A few men and horses will man the boundary.

The design consisted of a lookout tower, a corral, and barracks, all surrounded by a wall. Although we had come to rely on the Karuk riders for most messenger duties, this will be a protected trade route. At the one-hundred-mile markers, I intended to have a fortress built around which a town could spring up, adding to the importance of the road itself. Bolvi and Jim were blazing a trail, marking it as they moved forward. Cut trees were moved to sites where an outpost or town location would be built.

Bolvi had big plans even before I asked him to work on the settlement at Regis Bay. His first thought was that we needed a better road to the basilica, and his quarry was cutting stone slabs. He went to Wilson, who provided details on how the Romans created their thoroughfares, which had survived for more than two thousand years. Was a five-hundred-mile paved trail beyond our capabilities?

Not according to Wilson, who referenced the twenty thousand miles of Roman roads built in Gaul. The Roman legions had built four thousand miles of roads in Britannia. I reminded Wilson and Bolvi that the process had taken hundreds of years. Bolvi pointed out they had only had puny humans to do the work, not the Skaldi.

Bolvi had taken me to the East and South Gate Passes to show me his stockpile of stone slabs, enough to pave a roadway in the two passes, replacing their current dirt road. Who was I to stand in the way of progress? At least the stone slabs for the streets of the two passes would be there when Bolvi returned.

As the time for our Christmas celebration grew closer, old friends began to arrive. First, Bill and Dumah arrived, and we had a long discussion about recent events. They were getting along quite well. They suggested that Dumah attend the preparation and plantings at the settlement at Regis Bay in the spring. The once-fallen angel had nearly singlehandedly doubled our crop productivity, including nurturing a grove of trees from the seeds the Karuk had brought with them. He admitted the saplings might not quite reach the size of the Karuk Forest due to the climate. Yet, he hoped for something at least half their original height. A large grove of two-hundred-foot trees would eventually help us. Rachel insisted Bill stay at least until the baby was born in early January AE3.

 Father Emmaus flew in from the basilica. He would have better survived the winter working at the cathedral and performing his duties at our celebration. About a week before our festivities commenced, Bolvi, Jim, and Becky also arrived. Even after I offered that anyone could take a brief break from the action, their team kept working.

No one had volunteered to make the return trip, which left me to believe Bolvi had ordered the work to continue. Everyone was so excited about this project that they opted to work on it regardless. More likely was the thought of leaving the sixty-plus-degree weather for the cooler temperatures and occasional snow.

Here in the city, it had already snowed several times briefly.

With the help of Bill and Cook, I arranged for a unique delivery for those working in the town by the sea. They would get a taste of what the city would eat during our days of celebration.

Adalwin took most of his people into the sanctuary beneath Mount Djuprot. They discovered a library there filled with a vast treasure of books and parchments.

The writings there were more than ten thousand years old. They included historical references and occasional mentions of where the Dvergar may have lived on Earth. These documents were far older than those at the basilica or the cathedral's libraries.

Throughout the city, the Skaldi were raising 'Christmas' trees. These were not cut trees; they were potted and replanted after the celebration in areas near the lakes. Mainly in the marketplace, on the cathedral campus, and a smaller tree in the great hall beside Regis Tower. Andy had assured me that he and Allen had found a way to light the trees. Quaylin artisans fashioned stars to sit atop the trees. Everyone seemed to be getting into the spirit, even though it wasn't exactly a holiday ever celebrated in the Other Realms before.

I will not take us too far, of course. Yet you must realize that a considerable part of my memories is Christmas-related, filled with happy times of food, family, and friends. I had experienced Christmas as a child and youth, of course. I have also celebrated it in its many forms all over the world. I couldn't just make up a holiday. Then it dawned on me, and I thought, "I am the Àrd-Rìgh. Why can't I make up a holiday if I want to?"

I spoke privately with Father Emmaus about establishing new traditions. Thanksgiving was, for the most part, their traditional harvest celebration. I then wondered, had God's Son been sent to cover the sins only on Earth? Or had His sacrifice spilled over to the Other Realms? It was a question that bore further research.

However, when I questioned Father Emmaus, he replied, "RJ, that is nonsense. We, the Monks of A.O., the Alpha and Omega, celebrate the birth of our Lord and Savior. We normally have a celebration, more for the monks than for others. Ages ago, before wars swept the Other Realms, we even had a feast." The elderly monk said, "I think a celebration is an excellent idea. Along with pulling some of the old ones back out of time's closet and dusting them off."

He then said something that blew my mind. "RJ, you do know that Jesus was born in the mid to late spring and not during winter, right?"

"Father, can we speak more about this later?"

The older man winked and went off whistling.

I had his blessing. He seemed to think that just because the Maker's son came to one planet and died there, what would be the sense in sending him to the Other Realms only to die again? I could see his point, though I wasn't sure how the great theologians of Earth would feel. A savior had been sent to Earth, not the Other Realms, but we would celebrate regardless.

Food stores poured in. Bill lent his hand to cookies, baked goods, and candies. Cook had teams preparing meals as we moved towards the apex of Christmas Eve and Christmas Day. Children had the day off from school. They eagerly awaited this new holiday after learning about the celebration. All the soldiers received a bonus payment from the treasury. I wanted them to enjoy this time with their families. The markets were teeming with trade goods from the surrounding area. Oh, how the city smelled of fresh-baked goods and brimmed with good spirit.

Rachel and I woke up late a few days before Christmas to find Josia and Smar missing. As Rachel dressed, I asked if the Glav had seen the two little guys. One of the guards blinked at me and then, closing his fist, stuck out only his pinky finger.

Then I whispered in Rachel's ear, 'Pinky swears.' Josia had made the Glav guards pinky swear not to tell on him. The idea of a 'Pinky swear' was something that Andy had taught Josia. I now wish he had not!

When we rounded the corner, I suggested that this meant that the little guy and his ball of fur were waiting for us at Leo and Lynn's apartment. They got tired of waiting for us to get up and went to see if Lynn had some food.

"Don't you find it odd that a four-year-old with no true sense of direction or the importance of telling an adult where you are going can boss our bodyguards around?" Rachel asked with a bit of a glare.

It was a fun glare with a smile at the end, but I understood her point. I shrugged, but became more worried when we got to Leo and Lynn's apartment below ours, only to discover they had not seen Josia either.

Rachel and I continued down to the great hall to see if anyone had caught a glimpse of the missing boy. I came around the corner to see Josia sitting in the lap of the elderly Father Emmaus. I was just in time to keep Rachel from walking in. With a finger to my lips, I pointed ahead. The church's leader in the Other Realms was sitting there, explaining to Josia what he was eating and how he had chosen those items. Smar was curled up on the floor using the great furry robe of the father as a bed.

To every answer the old man gave, the little boy loudly exclaimed, "Why?" This line of questioning must have been ongoing for quite some time. I could see Cook peeking out of the kitchen with a big grin. The look on the old churchman's face was entirely different. Finally, I allowed Rachel to rescue the holy man as she swept in to pull the now giggling child from the older man's lap.

Rachel found them a seat further down the table, where Cook brought them a bowl of fruit and a stack of pancakes. It wasn't long before council members began to arrive for breakfast. Josia was off to bother them, asking essential questions. "Which of Cook's soups do you like best?" he asked childishly.

Not waiting for an answer, Josia then proudly announced, "Mine is the cheesy soup!" There was no end to the laughter at our table. Sometimes, serious discussions would degenerate into banter with the young prince, who would laugh at his own antics. There was no end to the joy that washed over the city.

CHAPTER 53

Before I knew it, Christmas Eve had arrived. The city was bustling with monks singing and playing music. People crowded the city markets, greeting each other and buying last-minute food or gifts. That evening, I looked at Rachel and found her staring back at me. She had an odd glimmer in her eyes. That night, everyone from the fourth and fifth tiers of the city gathered in the great hall. Cook set up stations along the sides that served hot mulled apple cider and finger food. The crowd quieted to listen as Jim read from the Bible the first and most famous Christmas story ever told.

The story of the Maker's Son's birth on Earth was a gift and a sign that He had not forgotten humanity. Father Emmaus prayed over the city and our growing kingdom. The children drank their hot cocoa and ate their cookies. When I returned, the children gathered to listen to my story about the most famous toymaker of all – Santa Claus. I told them only the best-behaved children would receive gifts from Santa at Christmas time. Everyone raised their hands when I asked how many good children were in the room.

Not all the children believed that everyone had been good. Siblings disagreed, and laughter from pointing fathers and mothers disrupted my story. Then I revealed that if everyone promised to try harder this year to behave, I had a surprise waiting for them as they left. All the children promised to be good, and their parents reminded them of their promise to the High King, a binding agreement with the monarch. As the families left, the children received a small package containing a wooden toy and several candy pieces that Bill had shown Cook how to make. Happiness descended on the City of Hope.

Rachel and I invited a select group of friends to continue the celebration high in the royal apartment. There was a fire in the fireplace, and a Christmas tree in the big living room, and everyone took their seats. We sang a few Christmas carols and continued to share recent memories and stories. Laughter filled the room until there was a quiet knocking on the door. The laughter ceased, and there it was again. Knock, knock, and knock!

"Who could that be?" Rachel asked Josia, who had no idea himself.

"Josia, go answer the door and see who that is." I pushed him towards the door.

Timidly, he opened the door, starting with the shiny black cowboy boots, his eyes working up to the great white beard, then slammed the door back shut.

"Who is it?" SunGru asked.

Breathless, the prince announced, "Ho Ho is here!" Everyone chuckled, and then there was another knock on the door.

"Are you going to let him in?" Rachel asked.

Josia nodded vigorously, then timidly opened the door again. "Come in, please," he said, tugging on the belt holding the red pants up.

Santa found the perfect spot in a big chair by the fire and began passing out gifts to our adult guests, who said they were from Santa but, of course, were from Rachel and me. Hoping that Santa might call his name, Josia was overly helpful. Passing out present after present revealed that they were for other people.

Finally, he could bear it no longer. Josia whispered in Santa's ear, "Presents are for kids?"

Santa looked at him thoughtfully, then announced out loud, "Ho-Ho-Ho. Silly me. I must have left my other bag in the hall."

Josia was pulling on Santa's arm, trying to help him out of that chair. Indeed, Santa reappeared with another bag of wrapped presents.

Santa pretended to mumble, but he pronounced his finding loudly enough to make Josia jump. "Hum, these all have one person's name on them. That can't be right!" He cleared his throat. "Does anyone know of a Josia?"

Josia was wildly waving his hands in the air. Santa continued to gaze around the room with his hand just over his eyebrows. "Maybe I brought the wrong bag with me."

Josia's dancing began so much that Smar got involved, his little excited barks combining with Josia's attempts to get attention. When Santa finally sat down, he covered his face with his hands. Slowly, Josia pulled each finger away until he looked right into Santa's eyes. "I am Josia," he whispered.

Santa clapped his hands, "Here, I thought I was in the wrong house. Well, let's see what is in my bag!"

Josia thanked Santa for each gift.

The boy opened each gift and showed it to each person in the room. There was a tiny sword, and a shield from SunGru and his family — some cute outfits from Rachel and me. Shal-Dir had commissioned a mini-tent complete with Midian flags for playtime. From Cedric and the other Knights of Midia, there was a rocking chair horse to go with the tent and the toy weapons.

When the evening was over, a sleepy Josia said goodnight to everyone and went off with Leo and Lynn for bedtime. Leo picked him up and turned. I saw Josia holding on to a gift I had not noticed earlier: a very odd-looking teddy bear. Very Skaldi-looking. I looked at Kraq, who had an odd grin, for this toy was the only one that had been carried off to bed.

Rachel whispered in my ear, remarking that the toy was perhaps the ugliest stuffed animal she had ever seen.

I whispered into her ear that I believed Kraq had made it. I also noted that if they came across the particular teddy bear that had been lost in a corridor, they were to bring it back with them.

Rachel and I thanked our guests; many had their own homes in the city. Leo showed our out-of-town guests to their suites.

After Bill had changed out of his 'Santa' outfit, we sat down for a chat. Bill caught me up on all the news about the ranch, then announced he was turning in for the night.

As I lay down next to my very pregnant wife, my mind drifted. We had encountered several of the fallen angels, but their whole purpose had not been revealed to me. What was the connection between these angels and those on Earth? Why so much destruction and death? What was their endgame? Were they set on the complete domination of the Other Realms? How much dominion did they hold on Earth? Who was giving the orders to the Fallen in the Other Realms? So many questions remained unanswered.

CHAPTER 54

I couldn't get to sleep with all the questions on my mind, which is when I remembered a book I had started reading months ago was still sitting on my desk in the war room. I noticed that Rachel was up reading, so I took the side hall and hoped I could acquire the book and return without her seeing how long I had been gone. I would blame negotiations with Smar! I saluted the Glav guarding the room and walked in to grab my book.

Out of the corner of my eye, I saw a bluish light turning the corner to the back stairway to the throne room.

I motioned to the four nearby Glav, "Did you see someone or something enter the throne room?"

There was vigorous head shaking. The answer was a resounding 'no.' Nothing usually gets by the Glav. Their eyesight was impressive, but their hearing was nothing short of miraculous. Maybe I had overdone it today. Perhaps I hadn't eaten enough or slept enough.

There was quite a list of reasons to blame. It was unusual for me to see things that weren't there, so this gave me pause.

However, their 'sixth sense' triggered the next moment, and they formed a defensive ring around me as we moved towards the throne room. Leo had heard the commotion. He had been making some mint tea for himself, so naturally, he forced me to sit on the throne and hydrated me against my will. After drinking it all, I thanked Leo and waved my worried guards back to their posts. They quietly stepped from view, never really leaving me alone. Warmed by the tea from the inside out, I sat beside Leo on the dais steps.

I closed my eyes as visions of the past year flooded my mind. It was almost a new year with many possibilities. When I opened my eyes again, I looked down at Leo, who now leaned against the throne. My Glav guards had taken up a defensive perimeter. They were now kneeling, with their spears upright rather than thrusting forward. A blue orb large enough to encompass a man moved down the aisle towards me.

Leo gasped as the blue ball dispersed, "Bless my soul!" I heard him stammer as he passed out.

On this final day of the year, the archangel Lailoken appeared before me in the City of Hope's throne room, as if out of thin air. There was a certain twinkle in the old man's eye.

"Did you miss me, Àrd-Rìgh?"

ABOUT THE AUTHOR

Jonathan was born in Pennsylvania in 1970. He was adopted into a loving family, and both parents were educators. At age 4, he was diagnosed with Leukemia, and he spent the next 8 years battling the disease. This same struggle during his formative years has shaped Jonathan into the man he is today, one who values family, friends, and God. After High School, he attended Penn State University and earned his degree in Food & Hospitality Management.

Jonathan spent 20+ years devoted to the hospitality industry as well as working for the Department of Defense and private security contractors. In 2006, Jonathan met his wife Beth, a Colorado native, and moved to Colorado in early 2007, where they were married in late 2007. In 2009, on a 2,300-mile trip to move his sister across the country, Jonathan began writing down ideas for a book. Nearly 16 years later, after countless rewrites and edits, with a final nod of approval, here are the results – Bon appetite!